I AM NOT MAD...

What I did, what I have done for the last six decades, was not the result of insanity, neither is what I now put down on the page. There are things that happened that I would rather forget. Things that changed me, things that changed the world. The world should know what happened to me, know why I did the things I did, why I am not mad.

All this time, and I still can't clear the memory of those awful days from my mind's eye. Sixty-two years, and I can still remember it as if was only a few days ago...

the PEASLEE PAPERS
A Lovecraftian Chronicle

by
Peter Rawlik

Lovecraft ezine press

Copyright Peter Rawlik 2017

Front Cover by Raven Daemorgan

Graphic Design by Kenneth W. Cain

Published by Lovecraft eZine Press

Formatting by Kenneth W. Cain

All rights reserved.

This book is licensed for your personal use only. No part of this book may be re-sold, given away, lent or reproduced to other parties by any means. Reviewers may quote small excerpts for their purposes without expressed permission by the author. If you would like to share this book with others, please consider purchasing or gifting additional copies. If you're reading this book and did not obtain it by legal means, please consider supporting the author by purchasing a copy for yourself. The author appreciates your effort to support their endeavors.

Table of Contents

The Crucifixion of Yig 1
Tempus Edax Rerum 9
The Lost Treasure of Cobbler Keezar 21
Professor Peaslee Plays Paris 27
Professor Peaslee's Pandemonium 39
Pr. Peaslee's Price 63
Letter Found On a Dead Sailor 75
The Temporary Chronologist 81
The Time Travelers' Ex-Wife 127
Hannah and Her Mother Take a Very Long Lunch 135
The Statement of Lincoln Robinson 143
Operation Switch 159
Operation Starfish 177
Cold War, Yellow Fever 195
Operation Alice 215
The Watchmaker's Lament 229
The Prognosis of Pandora Peaslee 239
The Pestilence of Pandora Peaslee 247
The Setting of the Sine 259
In the Hall of the Yellow King 271
A Sense of Time 279
Seki 287

Before Recorded History
The Crucifixion of Yig

It was on the Plain of N'Bir that the contingent of Yithians led by the Primus Ys watched the tableau unfold. The Q'Hrell had their servants— fat, rolling metashoggoths that humped and crawled across the grounds ahead of the Q'Hrell, their great chains creaking and straining behind them as they pulled their burden forward—drag the prisoner out to where the gathered crowd could witness his punishment. As the massive dais with its prisoner appeared a terrible wailing came up out of the thousands of Valusians that had been summoned to bear witness. Their cries were silenced by a wave of the gauntleted hand of their Secundus, Set. Infectious laughter spread throughout the Hydran Sisterhood until their own patriarch ordered them silent. The Deep Ones were a servitor race, and while they might have been a favorite of their masters it was dangerous to mock a species that had been created to be free, even if they had refused that gift and were to be punished for it. Ys glanced across the assorted dignitaries who had gathered from across the galaxy. It was an unpleasant association, and he turned away when the Yellow King cast a gauze covered gaze in his direction.

Something small and furry caught the attention of Ys. It was Pezal, a euprimtae, a kind of pet-slave, or *Na*, that the Yith had trained to be extra hands and eyes. The invertebrate bodies that the Yith had stolen were strong and durable, but they were primitive as well. They moved slowly on a single, great muscular foot that formed the base of their conical bodies. Their brains were housed within the cones themselves, but their eyes and mouth were located on the end of a single great tentacle that rose out of the vertex of the cone. Another tentacle bore a complex organ that was a rigid flower-like thing that served to both hear and speak. Two other tentacles bore primitive clawed manipulators that were fine for the brutish work the species had been designed for, but not the fine work that needed to be done, by smaller more nimble hands. That is where Pezal and his kind came in.

The Q'Hrell had not been happy when the Yith domesticated the euprimates and in a generation or so had taught them a simple language. There had been threats, embargoes, even small skirmishes, but in the end the Q'Hrell had acquiesced. It was inevitable really. The Q'Hrell had waged war on the Yith when they had first arrived. The ancient progenitors had not taken kindly to the Yith supplanting the slow and docile minds that had originally been created for the conical beings. The war had gone poorly for the Q'Hrell and within a decade the Yith had not only cemented their hold on the conical beings but had established their own cities and controlled more than a third of the surface of the planet.

Pezal was gesturing at the struggling figure that was bound on the dais. It was a saurian thing, a theropod, the epitome of the reptilian ideal. It rippled with muscles beneath an armor of thick scales, its tail strained beneath the bond that held it to the ebony cross, as did the four great limbs and the talons that occupied their ends. Even the creature's muzzle was bound shut, insurance that the thing known as Yig would remain compliant during the ritual.

Ys nuzzled the little mammal with his facial tentacle in an effort to calm the poor thing. A second later he was hoping that someone would do the same for him. Coming on to the plain was not only a cohort of Q'Hrell, but in their wake came four ultrashoggoths, titanic creatures created to spawn life onto the planet itself. Abhoth, Ubbo, Sathla and Yithra were roiling masses of protoplasmic flesh with eyes and ears and a whole array of sensory apparatus. The Q'Hrell claimed that these were the only four such creatures on the planet, but the Yith suspected the number was more likely triple that. For all their intelligence and precautions, the Q'Hrell had a blind spot when it came to shoggoths. The beasts had a history of rebelling but despite the fact that entire worlds had been lost to ascended shoggoths like Thaqqualah, their masters seemed to forget all that and rely on their slaves for even the most menial of tasks.

It was a mistake the Yith had made themselves, once, and they were still haunted by it. That another species could continuously make the same mistake and refuse to learn from the resulting disasters made Ys shudder.

A quintet of Q'Hrell broke ranks from the others, dancing across the plain on their lower tentacles, their wings folded safely inside their barrel shaped bodies. They walked upright, graceful and majestic, commanding respect and awe. It was the least threatening of their methods of locomotion. If they had come in a horizontal posture, on both upper and lower tentacles, rotating as they strutted forward, their wings flexing in and out, then all gathered would have recognized them as the predators they truly were, and fear, not awe, would have swept through the crowd.

The five primes moved to a point in front of their prisoner. The massive saurian beast tried to roar in defiance, but the muzzle turned it into little more than a whimper. In the audience, the cowed Valusians were silently weeping as the avatar of their collective unconscious was subjugated to the yoke of their masters. The bonds that held the demi-god Yig were more than just physical, but from this distance Ys could not see the incantations that had been inscribed on the chains. Nor was his vision enhanced enough to see into the spectrum where an entire other set of psychic restraints could be seen.

Even without such a sensory range Ys could see the thing that the five elder things carried with them. It was small, crystalline; composed neither of matter nor energy but rather of the strange plasmic forces found in orbit around the devouring nuclear heart of the galaxy. A fragment of Azathoth ejected eons ago, used by the Q'Hrell to propel entire species into the next level of evolution. It was a task they had undertaken innumerable times, on innumerable species, and refusal was rare. It had to be dealt with harshly, swiftly, and with finality.

They offered the crystalline shard to Yig one more time, and one more time he refused. For whatever reason, the demi-god had no desire to ascend. He refused, despite the fact that his entire species had been engineered for just such a purpose. The Q'Hrell were a cautious race. They had seen hundreds of other species ascend, and had come to understand that such an event was the natural order of things. Species evolved, ascended, beyond the bounds of ordinary matter, or they went extinct. The Q'Hrell wanted to control that process, essentially manage the god they would become through the ascendency process. To help them understand, to learn, to attempt to control things, they created species to experiment on. The Valusians were merely the latest of such subjects. Ys knew of at least three others that had been raised up on this world: there was the arachnid Atlach-Nacha who had been cast into the null-space on the edge of reality; the unnamed thing that had been spawned by the civilization of the Gugs, which upon its godhood had chosen to dissolve into the ether rather than persist; and finally, the Deep One Matriarch who was known as Y'ha-dra, who had on her ascendency been driven mad and divided in two. One half had returned to the depths and become something titanic and sedentary. The other had changed its gender and become a leviathan of the seas. Given these results it was no wonder that Yig refused to yield to such an experiment.

Indeed, he seemed unwilling even to accept his punishment for refusal. He was straining against his bonds. You could see the muscles ripple beneath the skin as he sought for a weakness. He flailed and stretched, but the muzzle and the straps on his arms and legs held. Only the length of binding that held his tail showed any sign of weakness, for as he struggled it stretched and slipped down. He pulled his tail up and out of the restraint, the bonds falling from the tip of his tail. Ys realized that Yig could have done this at any time; he had waited until now so that he could carry out one last act of defiance, here before gathered dignitaries, to embarrass his captors.

The tail whipped out and tore through the air. The crowd gasped, and the Valusians cheered as the tip crashed through the quintet of the master race. They scattered, one dodged, and two were just grazed, but two others caught the brunt of the blow and flew backwards, their bodies shattered and broken.

The shard of Azathoth flew through the sky, tumbling like a child's toy, instead of an invaluable artifact of cosmic power. All around them the gathered dignitaries were panicking, retreating, fleeing but Ys and his fellows stood their ground. The Yithians had a purpose in being here, a mission to complete, and standing their ground was in their best interest. The shard hit the earth breaking into two large pieces and a single small sliver, but no one other than Ys seemed to notice. They were after all too busy with the suddenly rampaging Yig. With a flick of one of his facial tentacles Ys ordered Pezal to fetch.

Yards away a horde of Q'Hrell had descended upon their rebellious construct. Tentacles tipped with razors and hungry, rasping mouths carved into reptilian flesh. They cut him, dissected him, devoured him and then rebuilt him for their own purposes. It was a strange and horrid thing, to watch a swarm of monsters reconstruct a god for their own purposes. Ys wanted to turn away, but he knew that watching would teach him something, grant him knowledge that he and his kind might need someday.

They cut off his limbs. They removed his organs of generation. They sculpted his flesh and muscles and brain and turned him into something less than he was before. He was still a demi-god, but he had been neutered, cut low. His thoughts were no longer swift and decisive, he was slow, torpid and cold and what was done to him had been done to the species he had embodied. The Valusians, the serpent men who had been meant to rule the world, were no longer the favored ones. They might live forever, but most of the world would be too cold for them, and they would have no more children. They were a dying species that could no longer even serve those that had created them. They watched in sorrow as all they had ever been, and all they could have been, was reduced to a limbless thing that crawled in the dirt.

As Ys observed the horrific spectacle of Yig's remaking, Pezal returned with the two larger fragments held against his chest, and the third minuscule fragment clutched in his primitive hand. They were dark things, blacker than black, and they seemed to writhe and crawl with some terrible internal life. It hurt his eyes to look at them, and he reached into the satchel he wore around his cone and brought out a small container. In appearance, it was a simple box, but the sigils and symbols carved into its surface cast a powerful spell. Anything inside it was hidden from the sensors of both the Q'Hrell and their slaves. As quickly as possible the small shard, a grain really, was transferred from Pezal's hand and into the ornate box, and then sequestered away.

Once more Ys's facial tentacles commanded the euprimate, and the small creature bounded down from his cone and off across the plain, the two larger fragments of the crystal still clutched to his chest. This was dangerous for the little mammal. He was not a sentient creature, not recognized as important by the Q'Hrell. If he wasn't careful, demure, and subservient Pezal would be destroyed in an instant, and Ys could do nothing about it, but watch. As he entered the reach of the nearest Q'Hrell Pezal ceased leaping and instead began to crawl, slowly, noisily, and with purpose. Just as he had been trained. He squealed and cried trying to catch the attention of the Q'Hrell, kicking up dirt and grass as he did so.

The ruckus worked and one of the masters turned and examined the tiny ball of fur. It trained all five of its eyes on the annoying mammal and then raised one of its tentacles up into the air. It meant to strike, but at the last moment noticed the two pieces of crystal that were clutched in Pezal's hands. The euprimate was pushing them forward, almost begging the Q'Hrell to take them from him. The master roared and the tentacle that had been poised to kill swept through the air and instead tore away the nebulous things. It didn't even bother to chastise the tiny Pezal. It just collected its prize and stalked away.

Pezal darted back, a tuft of brown lightning against the green plain. It streaked back toward its owner and then up its cone, finally coming to rest between the four tentacles. Ys could feel the heat of the thing, its heart beating, pounding in fear. He reached down and with the side of his tentacle tried to comfort his pet.

"Calm down little one," he said in the language that they had been taught. It was a barking speech, better suited to the vocal chords of mammals, than the rasping clicks of an invertebrate, though some of the Valusians could imitate it. "Rest, your work is done, at least for now." His claw slid inside his satchel and he felt the box that lay hidden there as he considered the thing that sat inside. He looked at the wounded Yig as it crawled amidst the dirt. They had meant to use the

Valusians, but that path was lost to them now. A new race would have to be brought in to the game. They would be a young species, a decided disadvantage for sure, but perhaps the crystal could be used to nudge them along the path.

He felt Pezal's heart rate calm and tried to imagine what such creatures might be like when exposed to the shining trapezohedron shard that hid in his satchel. They might be what we are looking for he thought: Terrible, monstrous things for the Yith to displace and use.

They would have to be nurtured, bred, and nudged.
Multiple paths would have to be explored.
But they might do.
They just might do.
Only time would tell.

75 AD

Tempus Edax Rerum

It was raining when Vulpinius and his prisoner entered Rome. Two centurions stopped him at the Porta Latina, but a quick flash of his medallion—the one that bore the stylized X symbolizing the Decemviri—made sure that the guards knew who he was. The Decemviri Sacris Faciundis had been officially known as the Quindecemviri for more than 400 years, but they still used the old symbol and name. The history and tradition behind the name carried weight, age, and respect. Enough respect to not only grant Vulpinius entrance to the city, it also warranted a boy to guide them down the Via Latina and through the city. It had been four years since Vulpinius had been in the great metropolis, and much had changed. Emperor Vespasian had embarked on an unprecedented series of public works projects, and the city was littered with construction equipment. Not that it had ever been easy to get around Rome. The city was a conglomeration of roads and alleyways and bridges, and while the great via helped, moving from one via to the other was notoriously difficult. In all truth it was easier to either pass through the center or leave the city entirely, than to move from via to via. Not that such connections didn't exist; they were just too small and too crowded to make them viable as travel routes. In a city the size and complexity of Rome, roads themselves were valuable commodities.

If they had been able to take a direct route through the city, the trip from a main gate to the Temple of Apollo Patronus on the Palatine might have taken little more than an hour. This was Rome though and such a trip took twice as long and meant moving through secret alleyways and byways and private gardens that the centurions had, through wit or favor obtained the right to pass through. It was a labyrinth and on more than one occasion Vulpinius knew that they had crossed back onto a previous path to access an uncrowded section of road, or to avoid construction. Even in the torrential rain the commerce of Rome and her citizens failed to cease its constant chatter, whether that was in Latin, Greek or Hebrew. Vulpinius, which was not his real name—in fact, it was not even good Latin—knew a smattering of all these languages but was most fluent in the growling Germanic tongue his Batavian mother had taught him. His father was a retired centurion who had never married his mother. The lack of nuptials effectively denied him a proper Roman surname, and so he went by the Romanized family name his mother had used. Neither was proper—and he would never rise high in the ranks of his profession because of it—but in some circles the name Vulpinius Pistorius was respected, in others it was feared, and as far as he was concerned one was as good as the other.

When they finally made it to the temple, Vulpinius dismissed their guide. He and his captive continued to the base of the bridge that linked the Temple of Apollo to the Bibliotheca Apollonis. There was a fresco there, an idyllic scene of an arched bridge beneath which children and women lounged in the shadows. Few patrons of the temple or library paid it much attention and fewer noticed that one of the archways was real, as was the armed and watchful man who lounged in the shadows beneath it. As Vulpinius and his charge approached he again flashed the seal of the Decemviri and the guard opened a well-concealed door.

As they passed the guard nodded and whispered "Welcome home Vulpinius, you have been . . . missed." Whether this was a greeting or a warning the tired agent wasn't sure.

The way down was old and constructed from stones salvaged from the original headquarters of the Decemviri that had been in the Temple of Jupiter before it had burned a hundred and fifty years prior. That was when Sulla had expanded the collegium from ten to fifteen men, and began the quest to replace the treasure that the flames had devoured—a quest that still continued, giving Vulpinius and the rest of the order purpose in life. He served the Empire, he served Rome, but before all else he served the Decemviri, and the mission they had set for him. Once, they had been guardians and interpreters of the *Sibylline Books*, three volumes of prophecies that Tarquinius Superbus had purchased from the Cumaean Sibyll. There had been nine books once, but six had been consigned to the fire before Tarquinius had agreed to the oracle's price. These past four centuries the *Sibylline Books* had helped guide the rulers of Rome, and the Decemviri had controlled their reading and interpretation.

Until they were lost.

Most believed that the Temple of Jupiter had been just another victim of the civil war that had placed Sulla on the throne—that the temple and the original Bibliotheca X with it had been destroyed in battle between one faction and another. The Decemviri believed otherwise.

Whispered histories claim that there was a man, a Quaestor by the name of Titus Sempronius Blaesus, who had one day collapsed as he did his work and suffered through a delirious fever for the next day or so. When his strange spell finally broke his family had found that he had undergone a radical change. Of his friends and family he had no memory. Nor did he have any recollection of his own life, his occupation or his own desires and habits. Cases of amnesia were not uncommon, particularly amongst soldiers, and little was thought of the man and his affliction. Doctors and philosophers came to see him, and some commented on his strange manner of speaking and his own odd questioning manner concerning subjects ranging from philosophy to science to religion and even politics and war. He was suddenly a voracious reader, and devoured not only the news of the day, but the histories of Rome and its predecessors, and he became a common sight amongst the crowds that gathered to hear the orators of the Senate speak. Given his previous position, and his frequent association with Senators and proconsuls, no one gave a second thought when he sought shelter with the other dignitaries within the center of Rome. It came as quite a surprise when he forced his way into the offices of the Decemviri and proceeded to spread oil over the archives that had come to be known as Bibliotheca X. The fire burned the original *Sibylline Books*, their copies and translations, supporting documents and three archivists. Titus Sempronius Blaesus was never seen again, and it was assumed that he too was lost in the flames, or perhaps killed by soldiers when they breached the defenses.

More than one-hundred and fifty years later, the Decemviri had finally rebuilt the archives and was once more able to help the support the Empire through the interpretation of prophecies. The *Sibylline Books* were still lost but there were other prophets and other prophecies, and the world was full of wonders just waiting for Rome and her agents to grab them. Most of the citizenry, and even the patricians, had thought the scouring of the empire for prophets and prophecies had long been completed. The words of the Tiburtine Sibyl and the Brothers Marcius were the primary texts, but they paled in comparison to what had once been, and so the law concerning oracles still stood. Over the decades the Senate had simply forgotten to repeal their decree, and therefore the private possession of books of prophecy was forbidden. Even those with the gift itself were compelled into the service of Rome and the Decemviri.

This was why Vulpinius had gone to Sicilia and returned with the man who may have been a prophet himself.

The man had arrived in Syracuse from Aegypt with no papers, no money and chattering in a tongue no one could understand. The only thing that held any clue to his origin was a scroll found in his belongings. It was tied by an odd chain of rods and crystals and written in a language that—like the words the stranger spoke—local officials did not recognize. It took weeks for the local constabulary to discover that the man was speaking a dialect from an area far to the East in Parthia. Even once they found someone who could speak his barbaric language, the man still could not provide any information about himself. He had it seemed suffered some kind of amnesia. He claimed to be named Beazlae and been a simple scribe from the city of Susa. How he had come to be on board the vessel, or how he had accumulated certain scars and tattoos he could not say. He was confused for when he looked at himself he was older than he remembered, leaner and more muscular as well. It was as if he had aged years and had no memory of it.

All of this would not have been enough to arouse the interest of the Decemviri, but then there were the pages. Pages that Beazlae claimed were written in his own hand, and in his native tongue. Pages and words he had never read before, but somehow he knew were from the *Summa Ysgl*, a legendary book of prophecy that was old before even the Akkadians had walked the Earth and one which some claimed to translate as the "The Prophecies of the Monsters of the Earth." It was a book so rare that even these few pages had attracted the attention of the Decemviri and forced the dispatch of Vulpinius aboard *The Latro* to bring Beazlae and his pages to Rome and Bibliotheca X. There, he and his writings were to be interrogated and investigated by the Decemviri, perhaps even all fifteen members.

All this ran through Vulpinius' head as he and Beazlae descended the torch lit steps that led down from the surface and into the vaults beneath the temple that served as the headquarters of the library of prophecies and the men who ran it. Who those men were was a well-guarded secret; for while the Emperor ruled Rome, the Decemviri made sure that he knew what he needed to insure the continued prosperity of the empire. These fifteen shadowy men guided and influenced the future of the world through the power of prophecy. Of their identities, Vulpinius had his suspicions. One of these men might have been General Aulus Caecina Alienus who had been charged with suppressing Vespasian's attempted coup, but then had suddenly switched sides. Another Vulpinius thought might have been Titus Clodius Eprius Marcellus, the current Roman Consul, the leader of the Imperial Senate and Vespasian's closest advisor. Vulpinius had no proof of this of course, but he had heard these men speak in the Senate, and recognized their voices when he was given his orders in the Shadow Chamber.

The Shadow Chamber was always cold and dark. The only light came from the lamps that silhouetted the members of the Decemviri who deemed it appropriate to be present. Today was no different. He and Beazlae were seated in the dark, the scroll removed from their care and passed to the men beyond the curtain. He could count six men seated back there, six men whose faces he could not see. But he could see their shadows and hear their breathing, and beyond that he could hear the wheezing, labored lungs of a seventh man, an old man, tired and phlegmy. A man Vulpinius had never heard before, and whose voice didn't belong in the chamber. A man who smelled of hemp smoke.

"Your report, Vulpinius." The voice was cultured and tired, and definitely that of Eprius Marcellus.

"I present to you Beazlae of Susa. A man who cannot recall how he left Parthia, or when, or why, or even how he came to be in Sicilia. He recognizes that his intrusion is an insult and begs our pardon. He wishes nothing more than to return home."

"And what of this scroll?" There was a rustling of papers and the thin chain of rods and crystal chimed as it was unraveled. "How does he know it to be from the *Summa Ysgl*?"

"When I and the translator questioned him about this he was very clear that while he had never seen a copy of that book, or could read what he himself had apparently written, he somehow knew beyond all doubt that these words had come from that accursed work."

"You are sure he has no memory of any of this?"

Vulpinius nodded. "I am sure. Whatever task the Gods used this man for they seem finished with him. He can be of no use to us."

Alienus spoke next, or at least so Vulpinius thought. "He cannot be returned to Parthia. We offer him a choice, he can travel to Britannia and live out his life there, or we can execute him here."

"No!" The old man who could barely breathe cried out. "He has no choice. He must go to Britannia. We will have need of him there, someday." He coughed and gasped for air. Two guards emerged from the darkness, grabbed Beazlae by his shoulders and dragged him away.

After the poor man was gone, the old man spoke again. "Bring me the scroll."

"We must translate it first; our best linguists will be set upon the task." Alienus again, imperial but rough, a man of action.

"I have no need for your clumsy translators," coughed the old man, "I can read whatever is written on the page well enough for our purposes." He took a deep gasping breath. "Bring Vulpinius Pistorius as well, he might as well see what he has brought to Rome."

The veil was parted and a new lamp lit, General Alienus

and Consul Marcellus rose from their seats but the shadowy forms of the other members of the Decemviri remained seated. It was all that they could do for they were nothing more than crude statues, busts of the great men that were meant to be sitting in the great collegium that was the Decemviri Sacris Faciundis.

Out of respect for the general, Vulpinius went to one knee and was immediately chastised by General Alienus. "On your feet. You are no Centurion, and I am not your commander. Here in this place we are equals," he looked about the room at the missing members of his order that chose to be represented by silent uncaring stones, "though some are more equal than others."

Through the door in the back of the room the three members of the Decemviri moved. They continued up small steps and along a winding passage to a balcony that overlooked the Shadow Chamber. There in a bed draped with curtains and covered in pale white linens lay a man of such age, such antiquity that most would have mistaken him for one of the dead, or perhaps a victim of some horrific wasting disease. It was only when he moved and spoke that Vulpinius realized that the poor creature was still alive and still capable of rational thought.

He waved weakly with a single decrepit finger. "*Na* Marcellus, my pipe." The smell of hemp, and something more—an extraction of the black lotus that was known to induce bizarre hallucinations that Vulpinius hadn't smelled since his time in the East—filled the air as the ruined figure took the lit pipe and inhaled deeply.

Alienus took Vulpinius' arm and led the imperial agent to the side of the bed. "Vulpinius Pistorius, may I introduce Titus Sempronius Blaesus." The old man waved his pipe in a casual gesture of acknowledgment.

Vulpinius was stunned. "It's not possible, Titus Sempronius Blaesus burned Bibliotheca X more than a hundred and fifty years ago. He would have to be almost two hundred years old, how is that possible?"

The old man hacked and coughed out thick grey smoke. "One hundred and seventy-six years old *Na*, and as for how? Well that is a secret that even your controllers do not know, though I admit that even my secrets are beginning to reach their limit." Vulpinius didn't know what the word *Na* meant, but it was clearly some sort of title.

"The Decemviri captured Blaesus as he ran from the archive. We've kept him all this time and used him as needed." Announced Alienus.

Vulpinius felt a sense of outrage boiling up within him. "What does 'as needed' mean?"

It was Marcellus that responded. "It means that Bibliotheca X is a lie. It is certainly true that the Tiburtine prophecies and those of the Brothers Marcius have some value, but it is Blaesus that provides us with most of our foreknowledge. It is through our interrogation of him that we have been able to guide Rome for this last century. It was because of him that we put Vespasian on the throne."

Vulpinius shook his head. "Vespasian rose to power because the armies lost faith in Vitellius, their commanders came to believe in a Judean prophecy in which an Oracle had divined that Vespasian would be 'Governor of the habitable world'."

Alienus chuckled. "A prophecy seeded and promoted by our agents. Men, not unlike you Vulpinius, but simply with a very different task."

The agent was stunned. "Why, for what purpose?"

"Power, Vulpinius! We control Blaesus, and through him we control the Emperor, Rome, and the Empire."

"Then why was I sent for Beazlae and for the *Summa Ysgl*?"

The old man blew more smoke. "Enough of this chatter, give me the scroll." His shaking hand reached out for the roll of paper and the dangling chain of rods and crystals. He unwrapped the thing and fumbled with the chain, losing grip of the roll and handing it back to Marcellus. "Hold this where I can see it *Na*. As for your questions *Na* Vulpinius, it seems you are slightly more perceptive than your handlers. The *Summa Ysgl* was intended for the only being who knew what to do with it."

Marcellus suddenly ripped the scroll away. "We aren't fools Blaesus and you cannot manipulate us. After all this time, we may not know what you are, where you come from, or how you took over Blaesus' body, but we know that you aren't a man, or a god, and you will do what we tell you to."

The old man was fiddling with the chain and two pieces snapped together. "I will never understand how your kind made it so far without help *Na*." Another piece clicked into place. "You are easily manipulated, unobservant and shortsighted. You have no penchant for planning, patience or the complexity of histories and cultures. In words you won't understand, you simply don't see the big picture. *Ward am Na Tak*." Several pieces clicked together and a geometric form seemed to be taking shape in his hands.

Alienus took a step forward and put his hand on his gladius. Vulpinius put a hand on his better's shoulder, "He's just an old man."

The thing in the bed took his pipe and blew out instead of in spraying the three men with the smoke and ash of hemp and lotus. The effect hit Vulpinius and the others almost instantaneously, and they all fell to the floor at the foot of the bed.

"There you see, a perfect example. A hundred years I've been smoking this stuff, slowly increasing the strength as I've grown accustomed to it. It seemed innocent enough, a habit that kept me calm and compliant. It never occurred to you that I might use it as a weapon. *Na* Vulpinius I am much more than an old man."

He rose out of the bed, stronger, more stable, and more sure-footed than Vulpinius thought he had a right to be. Ringlets of ash and vapor swirled around his ancient and feeble form and seemed to shroud him in wisps of incense and fog. "A smoking man?" Vulpinius managed to whisper as the drug began to overwhelm his senses.

The ancient monster clicked another piece of the chain and crystal into place and the strange geometric formation began to hum, filling the air with weird harmonics and vibrations. "The long game my *Na*, is played not over days, or weeks, or even years. The game is played with moves that last centuries, and consequences that won't be felt yet for eons. Even now you probably don't know what has happened here, what was most important. Was it the placing of Vespasian on the throne? Was it the slow and secret dismantling of the

Decemviri? Was it the strengthening of the Empire, or its undermining? What have I done here that was so important?" He spun his ancient and skeletal form around. "I will tell you this much you fools, the burning of the *Sibylline Books* was only a catalyst, one that I myself set in motion when I wrote and then sold them to you fools in the first place."

With supreme effort Vulpinius spoke once more, "Beazlae!"

The thing stopped and stared at the prone form of the drugged agent. "Well well, color me surprised. One of the *Na* has pierced the veil, and seen one facet of the truth. Is that enough I wonder? What shall you do about it? Do you think that killing him might change things, or is that exactly what I want you to do?" He smiled evilly down at the struggling agent. "Goodbye *Na* Vulpinius, your name suits you. You are as crafty as a fox. I wish you luck, and good health. I shall be watching you and hoping you find a way to impress me, but I leave you all with these words, they may help you understand someday. *Ward am Na Tak*." Then he began to laugh, and Vulpinius passed into madness and heard no more.

It took a week for Vulpinius, Alienus and Marcellus to recover from their exposure to the black lotus. The body of Titus Sempronius Blaesus was found lifeless in a nearly forgotten antechamber, the odd device of crystals and rods was nowhere to be found. There was an inquiry, and in this matter the entirety of the Decemviri, all fifteen members, was convened. The three were questioned, interrogated, even lightly tortured over the loss of something of such great value, but in the end, they were released. Alienus and Marcellus were demoted, they were still members of the collegium, but now were tasked with reviewing the existing prophecies and performing minor interpretations. Once a part of the Decemviri you could not be removed, or resign, but that did not guarantee your rank.

Vulpinius was relieved of his duties, but after a while found work amongst the guards of the Senate. On occasion, he made inquiries concerning Beazlae, but never could bring himself to interfere with the man, his wife or their children. He spent most of his time studying, not in Bibliotheca X, but in several of the other libraries around the city. It took four years, longer than he cared to admit, but eventually he learned enough Akkadian to understand the words that Blaesus had said before the drug took his mind. Four words, "*Ward am Na Tak*", four years, but he finally knew what those words meant.

The scroll that Beazlae had carried with him, the excerpt from the *Summa Ysgl*, was never translated, and in the opinion of the great linguists and cryptographers of the Empire never could be. The symbols on the page looked like language, but weren't. It was all nonsense, a clever hoax, and nothing more.

Not long after, a messenger came from Reate, Emperor Vespasian was dead. The new Emperor Titus acted quickly. General Aulus Caecina Alienus and Proconsul Titus Clodius Eprius Marcellus were arrested and the Senate quickly found them guilty of conspiracy.

Marcellus slit his own throat.

Aulus Caecina Alienus waited for the executioner. As Vulpinius Pistorius formerly of the Decemviri Sacris Faciundis, stood over his former employer a mad smile came across his face. He knelt down and whispered the same words that the thing that had pretended to be Blaesus had said years earlier, "*Ward am Na Tak.*" But this time the words were followed by a translation, "A slave should know his place."
Vulpinius' gladius took General Alienus' head off in a single stroke.

1875

THE LOST TREASURE
OF COBBLER KEEZAR

It was in the summer of 1875 that old Martin Keezar first took his granddaughter Alice to the river. It was her first trip, but for the elder Martin the number could no longer be counted on a single hand, or two, or even ten. For a score of years, he had come to the Merrimac and wandered amongst the fishermen and lovers and ramblers populating the riverbank while he searched through the rocks there. He came mostly after storms, when the river ran wild and muddy and the bank had been churned over. None of his fellows knew why he came or for what he was looking, for Martin was a private man and fearful of two things: that if they knew the truth of what he sought, they might think him mad, or worse, think him wise, and that others might begin searching themselves.

He told none of his fellows what he was searching for, but he told his granddaughter as she searched with him in the cold and wild waters one spring morning. The sun was warm and the sky a brilliant blue, the grass held a clean and still bright green, that crisp green that comes after a good rain. It was on a spring day like any other that Martin Keezar whispered in his granddaughter's ear and told her the family secret. He told her about the treasure that their ancestor had once possessed and had lost. He explained to her what it was and where it came from. "It was in Germany, in a black tower in the forests of Nettesheim that the alchemist Heinrich Cornelius Agrippa first took out a piece of moonstone of no particular value, but rather large in size and rectangular in shape, and bathed it in the light and chemical baths of his trade. He followed the method laid out in Eibon's grimoire, a process they say he stole from a cult who served an obscure rank of ethereal angels. When the treatment was done, the moonstone was instilled with the power to see through time. One still had to know the ways of a cunning man—the use of herbs and metals, and the secrets of the woods—to make it work. When it worked, it opened wide a window into the future or the past."

"The stone was too large for Agrippa's purposes, and so it languished in his workshop until one day he gave it to a cobbler, who also had been a minnesinger, in lieu of payment for services rendered. The cobbler was a most excellent cobbler but he wasn't a cunning man and knew little of herbs or the forest. For him Agrippa's stone was just a lapstone, good for shaping and softening leather, but nothing else. When he died, it and everything else of value went to his apprentice, who carried it with him across the sea."

"That man, that cobbler's apprentice was our ancestor little Alice, and the founder of the American branch of the Keezar family. He was a clever man, and a cunning one, and he knew how to use the lapstone. He knew other things as well, and the puritans who had come to populate the lands around the Merrimac often cast a foul eye in his direction. Some went so far as to accuse him of using witchcraft, but nothing ever came of it. Old Keezar was too smart for those old stern-faced priests and their gossiping wives, and they never could find any freemen willing to stand against him."

"He lived to a ripe old age and in his dotage climbed a hill, and while using the lapstone it slipped and tumbled down the slope and finally plunged into the river. He searched for it of course, but as the years went by he grew older—and weaker—and finally passed away. Not before passing along the secret of the stone to his children, though! Since then, the legend has been passed down through the generations and all the Keezar men have searched for the lost lapstone. They say the scrying stone made by the alchemist Agrippa—the one lost by our ancestor was rivaled only the black stone of Doctor Dee and the Interpreters of Joseph Smith. It's essential that we one day locate it."

"How do you know it's still here?" Little Alice asked as she worked her way along the edge of the riverbank, her eyes searching for the legendary artifact. "It could have been washed down river, or out to sea decades ago."

"Eh, oh. There are stories Alice, of milkmaids and farmhands and mill workers and even fishermen who have fallen asleep on the banks of the river and had prophetic dreams; dreams of love lost and found, dreams of children and family, even dreams of nations and the men who shape them. These dreams have come true. It's the lapstone reaching out from the river and telling the special dreamers the future. It's here Alice, I know it is. It is buried somewhere out there—in the mud, lodged in a nook, caught in the roots of a tree—and we are going to find it."

Alice reached out with her spade and flipped a few rocks as Martin Keezar continued walking down the winding Merrimac River. "What would you do if you found it? Would you make the world a better place?"

"I would Alice, I would make the world a better place for me, and for your mother and father, and for you and all the Keezars."

She dug in the mud a little. "How?"

"If you know the future, if you know what's going to happen, then you can take advantage of it. You can know who to be friends with and what things to buy and sell. You'll know when and where disasters will occur and you'll know of the shortages and surpluses that come with such disasters. We can use all that information, take advantage of it and grow the family fortune."

He wandered round a copse of trees just as Alice's spade hit something hard and oblong in the mud. She slid the blade under it and leveraged it up. It popped out with a satisfying burp of air and mud. Alice knew almost instantly that she had found the lapstone. It was the right shape and size, and even scattered the light in an almost mystical manner. These were clues surely, but what confirmed it was the vision that suddenly formed before her eyes. The lapstone was like a window and the curtains slowly rolled back before her and showed her the future, or at least one possible future.

In the vision, her grandfather was old, older than he was now, older than he had a right to be, and he was rich. With the lapstone in his possession, he had grown rich off of the European war. The whole family was wealthy, she was wealthy, her younger brothers were wealthy, even her children were wealthy. Only death stopped Martin Keezar, and then— knowing the secret— Alice Keezar took over. When the second war in Europe came she used the lapstone and the family grew even wealthier. Then there were wars in Asia, and in Central America, and then the Levant. The Twentieth Century was a century of warfare, and through it all the Keezar family prospered, profiting off of war as if it were simply another business. When she finally grew old Alice Keezar was older than her grandfather had been, and when she almost died the machines helped bring her back. They replaced her heart and liver and multi-folded things like books took up residency where her lungs once were. When they took her stomach, she was forced to stop eating solid food and instead could only drink a carefully cultured nutritional fluid. When her memory began to go, they transferred portions of her brain onto crystals of quartz and lodged these in the empty areas of her skull. Her eyes were made of glass and aluminum and pure light.

There were lawyers employed by her family, her children and her grandchildren, but they were useless against the battalion of solicitors that worked for her. She out-thought them, out-spent them and outlived them all. In time, the great family of the Keezars was gone, the reputation they had gained ensured no one who would even consider marrying them, let alone bearing their children, and only she was left. On the occasion of her three hundredth birthday she was the Keezar family: rich, powerful and utterly alone. She wandered her great house, automatons on wheels and treads following about fulfilling her every need. They weren't really automatons, they were slave-clones, little bits of her own mind copied and edited down to become perfect little servants. Extensions of herself in a way and therefore not a security risk. She had been a target for assassination once; Martian separatists had planted a bomb in her car. They blamed her for something, some perceived slight that did not matter in the slightest. What mattered to her was that they were all dead; she had made sure of that. It didn't matter what happened, Alice Keezar was all. Her wealth and knowledge would allow her to live beyond the lives of her friends, her enemies, and in time, she would even watch both the nations that rose up to oppose her, and those she created to defend her, turn to dust or burn to ash. She would become a goddess and all would bow down to her forever.

All this Alice Keezar saw through Agrippa's lapstone, the treasure of the Keezar family. All this Alice knew was because of the power the lapstone granted. It was a great power; one that she could see corrupt first her grandfather and then herself in this potentiality. There was another way of course, another path through time. The stone showed her this as well: she saw herself raise up the shovel and bring it crashing down on her grandfather's head. She saw herself becoming a teacher, an advisor to leaders, and then a leader as well. She saw the future and how the lapstone could be used to guide, and inform and change the world. She saw others reject her wisdom, her advice, her guidance, and she saw the world plunged into chaos. She saw herself becoming ruthless, tyrannical, and even monstrous. She passed edicts like a petty dictator, without explaining anything. She saw herself addicted to the moonstone, consulting it day and night, fretting over it, growing old and weak and frail as she forgot to eat or drink or sleep. She saw herself as a slave to the future, and to trying to change it. She saw the gaunt, reptilian sibyl she would have no choice but to become. If she was to save the world, she must rule it and herself with an iron gauntlet.

There were other futures, she could see them all, lining up waiting to be played out, all waiting to be chosen, and to be reviewed. She felt sick. She was after all just a little girl, not nearly as smart as her grandfather, but she was wise, perhaps wiser than her grandfather. A moment later she demonstrated just how much wisdom she possessed as she lifted up her shovel and brought it down as fast and as hard as she could. The crunching, shattering sound was still ringing in her ears as she ran to catch up with old Martin Keezar.

For many years after she often joined him in his walks along the bank of the Merrimac River, and when he died he made her promise that she would continue to look for the stone. It was a promise that she made easily, for she had no intention to keep it. She had wisdom enough to lie to the old man, even on his deathbed. In time, the young folk of the village stopped sleeping on the banks of the river and without the dreams on the riverbank to remind them, the legend of

Cobbler Keezar's lapstone faded into obscurity.

Occasionally, some historian or writer or fool would come to talk to the Keezar family about the old stories, but no one knew a thing about it. Both the legend and the lapstone ended there, shattered and washed away into the deep waters of the Merrimac. Alice hadn't chosen the best or brightest future, for her, the family, or the world, but it was the one that she knew the least about, and therefore it was the only future she found she could truly enjoy.

1910-1911

Professor Peaslee Plays Paris

Near the Podkamennaya Tunguska River, 6 March 1910

Even in March, the wind that whipped out of the north across the plains and down the river chilled other men to the bone, but the two who stood on the hill ignored it. Not too long ago this had been a vast and ancient forest, now for miles around them the trees lay scattered like matchsticks, the victims of an explosion that—less than two years earlier—cracked open the sky and set fire to the world. The inferno had burned for weeks, the light of which could be seen for thousands of miles. No one had dared to investigate the disaster, and for that the two men who stood on the hill overseeing the excavation were grateful. It was not the first time that they and their minions had worked to salvage fragments of meteorites, and it wouldn't be the last, though their prior operations had not always met with success.

Below the hill in a pit was being excavated, the men—the eunuchs—suddenly grew loud and excited. An object, a stone about the size of a man's fist and dripping with mud was raised up into the air. A cry of achievement moved through the crowd as the stone was passed from the center of the pit out, and then up the hill. The last man wrenched himself out of the mud and scrambled up the slope, wiping the stone clean with his shirt. He knelt before the well-dressed man with the fur lined coat.

"Count Ferenczy," the mud-covered man spoke meekly, almost apologetically. "Master, we have found it, the stone, the chondrite, it is ours!"

The aristocrat reached for the stone, but then cautiously withdrew. The mud-covered servant was confused for a moment, and then shifted his offering to the second of the two men. He was taller, thinner with glasses beneath his wind whipped hair.

"Professor Peaslee, would you please take this from me?" The man was practically begging. Peaslee took the stone. Even through the mud, he could see the crystalline structure of the treasure they had unearthed. He wiped the last of the muck off and rolled the gem about letting it catch the sun. The servant inched back down the hill and rejoined his brothers in the pit.

The man called Ferenczy spoke for the first time in hours: "You will do what must be done?"

Peaslee wrapped the jewel in a cloth and tucked it into the pocket of his coat. "I will do what you failed to do in 1795. Because of you, we must now deal with men who are more than they should be, who think like we do, who are developing technologies they shouldn't even have thought of. If you had done what was needed of you, I would not have to have come to this time, and live amongst these filth." There was no malice in his voice, no emotion at all as he turned and stared at the dozens of men who struggled below. "These men, you have made sure that they are all castrati?"

Count Ferenczy nodded. "I have. They are unable to procreate, whatever the stone has done to them here, it will not enter the gene line of humanity."

"The risk is too great. We cannot allow another Holmes, or Nemo." Peaslee turned and walked toward the river and the waiting boat. "Liquidate them all."

Paris, 22 August 1911

The painter Louis Beroud struggled up the stairs of the Louvre, his case of brushes and paints banging against every stray object that happened to get in his way. He wasn't normally clumsy, but last night's revelry had left him hung over and stiff. Neither were ideal conditions for working, but he was a creature of habit and the sketches for his own piece, Mona Lisa au Louvre, were nearly complete.

As he came through the entrance, a young man with blonde hair and a forelock curl held the door for him. He smiled at Beroud as they passed, and, for a brief moment. Beroud thought that the boy might make a decent model; he was tempted to stop him and ask him to come round his studio. But that thought was fleeting, and, as he made his way into the galleries, all other thoughts except one left his mind.

The gallery was empty, as it usually was at this hour. The richly colored walls and gilt molding accented the ornate frames that, themselves, served to complement the masterpieces that decorated the walls. For weeks now, Beroud had come to this museum, to this gallery, to this very spot, and sketched. He had come for the light; it was only right for a few minutes every day, when the sun hit the window through the tree and cast itself through the halls, and about the wall in a just so manner. He had grown to love the light, and the shadows, how they played out across the gallery, making the gold and copper hues rich and deeply luxurious.

It had taken him weeks to prepare the right mixture of paints to reproduce that color, weeks and scouring the shops of Paris for the right ingredients. But it had all been worth it. Just a few more days, a few more sketches, and he would have everything he needed to complete his own painting, his study of the Mona Lisa in its place in the gallery at the Louvre.

As he settled into place, he set his case in its usual spot, unpacked a handful of pencils, and settled back onto the bench that he had come to think of as his own. The pages of his notebook fluttered in the light and cast wistful shadows splaying against the wall where his beloved subject hung. Except—the wall was bare! Where Leonardo da Vinci's masterpiece had once rested, there were instead four iron pegs that held nothing but empty space.

The master's masterpiece was gone!

23 August 1911

The statuesque Gascon, who went by the name of Flambeau, stared at the little American who was sitting across from him. All around them the other patrons of the Moulin Rouge were lost in the wild debauchery of absinthe, song and the wiles of beautiful and willing women. Flambeau did not like the American; the little man had a dead face, slack, his eyes were empty and soulless. The women of the Moulin Rouge did not like the look of the man either. He made the girls uneasy, which made Flambeau uneasy. If anyone knew how to judge a man, it was surely these women.

Flambeau took a sip from his brandy. "It is an interesting proposition Professor Peaslee. Is there a reason you bring it to Flambeau?"

The little man with the dead face did not smile. He should have, but he did not. When his mouth moved to compliment Flambeau, there was no hint of any emotion at all. "You are Flambeau. Your physical stature and prowess is unmatched. Your flair for the dramatic, the ingenious, the bloodless, is legendary. It was you who created the Tyrolean Dairy Company, with no cows or carts, yet served thousands in the city of London. Your trick of a fake portable pillar-box was ingenious. The renumbering of an entire street so that you could divert a courier and intercept a single package was sublime. The theft of a shipment of precious metals by sinking them in the harbor channel was simply inspired. I plan on tricking the *Habits Noirs*, one of the most notorious and dangerous criminal organizations in all of human history. You ask why I come to you, why I wish to engage your services? I ask you, who else can I possibly turn to?"

Flambeau nodded. "This incident at the Louvre, it has stirred up the police. This will make things more difficult, though not impossible. We will need some help. I know a girl, she is very good at what she does; she does not like to take risks. It may be necessary to pay them more than what is usual."

"I have told you, Monsieur, money is not an issue." The strange little man with dead eyes paused. "You have a plan then?"

The master thief smiled broadly. "I have an idea Professor Peaslee, I have an idea."

24 August 1911

Inspector Romaine found what he was about to do distasteful but he felt he had little choice. The Louvre was in a shamble, Paris was in chaos, all the roads out of the city had been closed, but to no avail. His colleagues had found nothing, and were now grasping at straws. They had arrested the poet Guillaume Apollinaire, who had once called for Louvre to be set afire. There was talk that Apollinaire had implicated the artist Pablo Picasso. Romaine found the whole affair ridiculous, and was sure that, if he were still in charge, Aristide Valentin would have better organized and directed the investigation and manhunt.

But Chief Valentin was dead, a victim of his own hand. His successor was no detective, but merely an administrator, a counter of pennies and a fanatic for forms and procedures. Crime had suddenly exploded in Paris. The best and the brightest investigators—Broquet, Guichard, Maigret and the like—were doing what they could, but under the current leadership there was to be no chance at recovering the lost painting. Which is why Romaine had taken his own initiative, and come to this place, this temple to crime.

The nervous inspector did not have to wait long before he was ushered from the entry hall and into a dimly lit study. His escort was a young woman, dressed in a provocative leather corset and carrying a matching riding crop, both ends of which were tipped with silver studs. She motioned to a simple wooden chair and Romaine took a seat. She continued to walk and took up a position behind an imposing figure that sat in an ornately carved black mahogany throne.

He was not overly large or muscular but his broad shoulders and confident posture suggested a man who considered the world and all it contained to be his. Who he was, Romaine would never know, for his face and head were covered with a heavy iron mask. Five slits accommodated his eyes, nose and mouth, and Romaine saw what seemed to be grates where his ears should be. In an ironic touch, a crown of short iron spikes lined the brow in mockery of the crowns worn by true monarchs. Etched into the metal was the symbol of the man who had founded the criminal syndicate so many years earlier.

He motioned with his hand and the woman in black leather spoke for him. "You took a great risk coming here Inspector Romaine. We normally kill policemen who come to our house."

"I'm honored," Romaine stammered out.

She smiled. "The night is still young. What do you want?"

He fumbled his hands, and his words. "It was suggested that I come here about the theft of the Mona Lisa. We wish to recover it, undamaged."

She shook her and gestured with her hands. "We do not have it, nor do we know where it is."

"I know; it is not your style." He paused and caught his breath. "I am not here to accuse you; I am here to ask for your help."

The man in the iron mask stood up and crossed the space between them in majestic steps befitting the monarch he pretended to be. He knelt down beside the nervous policeman. Romaine could hear him breathing, a heavy, thick, animalistic sound. "You want us, the *Habits Noirs*, to help you find the men who committed the most audacious crime to occur in Paris in the last twenty years?"

Romaine nodded.

The room filled with deep, cackling laughter from both the iron king and his assistant. The king stood up and spun round, his silken robe catching the air. "Imagine it Josephine, us working with the police! If he weren't already dead, the Colonel would have keeled over by now." He came back at Romaine like a cat ready to pounce. "What do we get in return?"

25 August 1911

Professor Peaslee sat in the cafe sipping his coffee and watching as the little girl ate her pastry. She was a child, but it was with this creature that Flambeau had arranged for him to meet. Though she was but six, the girl called Nardi, with flowing black curls, carried herself with a pride rarely seen in women of any age. She finished her pastry and met his eyes confidently, a stern look on her face. "You have the money?"

He nodded. "Half now, half when you deliver the package outside of the city." He paused and then leaned forward to whisper the lines that Flambeau had made him memorize. "You understand, this stone, the Tear of Azathoth, is more valuable than the Heart of the Ocean, more beautiful than the Pink Panther, more sought after than the infamous Maltese Falcon. That if you fail, my agents will find you, they will kill you and all those you hold dear."

Nardi took the small bundle of bills and made it vanish into her dress. "I understand. I will see you tomorrow at the agreed upon place." She looked up at the sky. "There is a storm brewing."

As she left, she caught the eye of Flambeau who indicated his satisfaction with her performance. Neither Nardi nor Peaslee noticed the statuesque woman with the riding crop rise up from her table, daintily dab at her lips with a napkin, and then rush out of the cafe. Nardi and Peaslee did not see this happen, but Flambeau had, and he smiled as another piece of his plan fell into place.

Vincenzo Peruggia hurried through the streets of Paris as the rain came down in sheets. He had hoped for the storm to cool things off, but instead it just made the heat wet and the streets steam. It didn't help that the driving rain had found its way between the seams of his coat and beneath the brim of his slouch hat. Despite the fact that the storm had cleared the streets, it had also slowed his pace. He kept his head down and his eyes on the wet ground before him, moving as fast as he could while dodging puddles and swollen ditches full of dingy, grey water rushing toward swirling drains. One wrong step and he would be soaked; five more minutes and it wouldn't matter either way. Through it all he clutched the painting, the poplar panel and its frame close to his chest.

Peruggia never saw the man with the umbrella until he plowed into him. He was impeccably dressed, with thick black hair sculpted with pomade, dark olive skin and a hawkish nose. He cursed in Italian as he brushed the rain from his coat. Peruggia recognized the Sicilian dialect and apologized in kind, though he felt somewhat ashamed of his own northern accent.

The man with the umbrella looked him up and down. "You are Vincenzo Peruggia are you not?"

Peruggia was startled. "Yes, do I know you?"

The dapper man smiled slyly. "My name is Stromboli, Baron Cesare Stromboli. I am a dealer in unusual merchandise.

I have a proposition for you. I have clients who would be interested in acquiring what you have hidden within your coat. They would pay you quite nicely."

Vincenzo Peruggia laughed at the suggestion. "I am sorry, Signore, but I have little interest in money. I have done what you think out of national pride, for my countrymen."

As he moved to walk away, Stromboli stopped him. "We will pay you, Vincenzo. We will pay you handsomely."

The Italian janitor turned to face the Sicilian, there was a gun in his hand. "I think not Baron Stromboli." And with that Vincenzo Peruggia faded into the storm.

★

"What do you mean he refused our offer?" The Iron King was furious, and he stalked about the room circling Stromboli like a rabid dog. In the shadows, the High Council of the Masters of the Habits Noirs sat watching in silence, but the Iron King could sense their displeasure. In his mind, he could already hear the things they would say to each other when he was gone. "Did you tell him how much we were offering?" the King asked.

Stromboli flailed about. "He is mad, mad with nationalism and pride. No amount would have swayed him. I cannot tell you how afflicted he was. I have never seen anything like it."

The Iron King roared and started after Stromboli, but a hand reached out and touched his shoulder. Josephine's touch was all that it took to restrain him. "My Lord, the Mona Lisa may have escaped us, but there are other treasures that move through the streets of Paris, and other ways to prove your worth to us."

She leaned in close and whispered through his mask. In the shadows, the High Council withdrew and whispered amongst themselves.

26 August, 1911

The little girl named Nardi moved through the sewers as if she owned them. She was six, and had been running the tunnels since she could walk. She was a courier, a very specialized courier, transporting things that other people didn't want to have seen in the light of day. Today it was a box, small, heavy, wooden, wrapped in paper so she couldn't even see what she was carrying. It was the only thing in her bag. Her client had paid extra for exclusivity. She had one job, move the package through the tunnels that led outside the city and beyond the roadblocks.

The tunnels ran for miles, and in the smaller ones, she had to worry about the buildup of poisonous and explosive gasses, but in the main galleries, with their towering ceilings, she had no such fears, and lit her torch with impunity. The flickering flame cast weird shadows across the pillars and arches, and only served to make the strange sounds that echoed through the tunnels even stranger. But Nardi had no fear of the haunting music that leaked through the underground, nor of the dark shapes that slithered in the black waters. There were places she would not go, culverts that led deeper and radiated a wicked green light that arced like lightning between misty clouds. She would not go down those tunnels, not because she was afraid, but because she knew better.

As she moved from the city center, the tunnels grew smaller; it was the way of things. At some points, the sewer was so tight that only someone of her size could have fit through. It meant that she was safe, that no one could get at her while she moved through the pipes, but it also put her at risk. When the pipes connected to the larger central galleries, they did so in a manner that left her blind. It was the one place she was vulnerable, where anyone was vulnerable, she knew it and so did the men who were waiting for her.

They grabbed her by the collar of her coat as she came out of the pipe.

"Look what I've caught," said the one as he held the kicking child up into the light.

The other looked her up and down. "Rats are getting bigger it seems. Regular Sumatra down here." He grabbed her bag, the one with the box inside and ripped it open. "What do we have here?"

Nardi twisted and slipped the short blade she kept at her wrist into her hand. She slashed at the man who held her, slicing his coat and causing him to dodge backwards. His grip broken Nardi twisted free, hit the hard rock of the floor and rolled back into the pipe. The man lunged a hand in after her, but it was to no avail. He pulled back empty handed and cursed.

His partner whistled. "Jean-Marc would you look at this?"

He had torn the paper away and revealed a dark mahogany box, polished smooth save for a symbol burned into the lid. A symbol the two thugs knew very well. A symbol that they had never expected to find on a box in a sewer beneath the streets of Paris, the symbol of the *Habits Noirs*!

★

The Iron King turned the box in his hands over and over again while Josephine went through the catalog. She slammed the thing shut and sneered.

"The catalog number on the box doesn't match anything in our books. But the mark, and the style of the numbers, the orientation, these are consistent with other cases commissioned from 1876 through 1892."

"Well, let's open it up, shall we?"

The lid slid off and revealed the treasure inside. It was a lump of crystal, larger than a man's fist. It caught the light and radiated it back in an eerie, abnormal spectrum that was at once beautiful and terrifying.

The King stared into it. It was not diamond, not a ruby, or an emerald. There was some resemblance to an opal, but only in its ability to catch the fire. In shape, it was not unlike an egg, but with irregular facets and protruding shards. There was a glow about it, that in itself made it unusual, but many of the treasures in the vault were radiant, it was nothing special.

Josephine slammed the lid back down, and the King winced and grabbed at it, but only for a second.

From the shadows, a figure stepped forward. "That," said the figure, "is quite enough."

A gasp of awe escaped the Iron King as he recognized the voice and visage of Colonel Bozzo-Corona.

"Josephine, my dove, enter the stone into the catalog.

Place it in the vault with the rest of the treasure. There may come a day when we want to figure this little thing out, but that is not today. We have other things to attend to."

"You are supposed to be dead!" mumbled the Iron King.

Another shadow emerged and grabbed the Iron King by the arm. The fallen monarch tried to pull away, but the man's grip tightened.

"It's not possible, you're supposed to be dead!" he whimpered.

As the Iron King was marched out, the Colonel picked up his cane, assumed his rightful place and smiled at the High Council, who once more paid fealty to the true leader of the Black Coats.

27 August 1911

Flambeau sat in the café in the shadow of the Louvre, sipping coffee and watching his niece, Nardi, hungrily devour a plate full of madeleines. Across from them sat Professor Peaslee, drinking tea and adding up the expenses Flambeau had incurred.

The tall Frenchman put down his cup and leaned in to talk to Peaslee. "What was it? The thing in the box what was it? What was so valuable that you needed to get it into the vault, a vault surrounded by some of the most dangerous people in the world?"

Peaslee stared blankly back.

"Why not tell me? It is not as if I am foolish enough to try and steal it back."

Professor Peaslee stood up, and placed an envelope full of bills on the table. "Three years ago, in the wilds of Siberia, a stone fell from the sky, a stone with the power to make men more than what they are. I have done my best to keep it contained, but my time is running short, and I need a more permanent solution. The *Habits Noirs* are fanatics. You, Flambeau, you steal for the art, to show that it can be done. Nardi, for the thrill. But they steal for simple greed. The insane desire to simply take what others have, and what they steal, they keep, forever. It is the only motivation that they and their

Colonel have."

"The Colonel is dead," commented Flambeau, "killed by his own many years ago."

Peaslee put on his hat and shook his head. "The *Habits Noirs* have always been led by the Colonel, and they always will be. There must always be a Colonel."

And as the strange little man with the dead face walked away, Flambeau saw Inspector Romaine find a seat at a table across away. He wasn't alone, and Flambeau did not recognize the regal old man with the cane that he sat with. But the more he watched, the more he realized that if there were men like that in the world, men who could make even police inspectors look ill, then perhaps it was time to find a new line of work, for him and for his Nardi.

1913

PROFESSOR PEASLEE'S PANDEMONIUM

They nailed Al Capone on tax evasion. The cops finally got me on three counts of homicide.

If you are reading this then I am dead, lawfully executed for my crimes. I killed those women, and pleaded guilty against the advice of counsel. Those shysters wanted me to plead insanity. I suppose after they heard what I had to tell them, about all the other things I had done, they thought I was mad.

I am not mad.

They called my brother mad; shut him away in an asylum up in Springwood, Ohio back in 1939. I saw what that place did to him, what it made him and all the others do to that nun. I didn't want to go that way. What I did, what I have done for the last six decades, was not the result of insanity, neither is what I now put down on the page. There are things that happened that I would rather forget. Things that changed me, things that changed the world. The world should know what happened to me, know why I did the things I did, why I am not mad. All this time, and I still can't clear the memory of those awful days from my mind's eye. Sixty-two years and I can still remember it as if was only a few days ago.

It was March 1913, and I was just a few weeks past my thirteenth birthday. I was something of a tough kid back then, an arrogant bastard with no need for school or a job. I lived by my wits, doing odd jobs for whoever would pay me. Mostly I did errands for the bookies in the Sportsmen's Quarter, running bets and cash back and forth through the town. Most of my work was done at the train yard, where the ticket master doubled as a bookmaker. Consequently, I had cause to be lounging around the platform when the stranger came into town. It was Monday, not much after nine in the morning, when the small black rail car came out of the plains and into the city. It wasn't like any other car I had ever seen, it was completely encased, like a fancy carriage car, lacquered black with silver trim. There was no engine, or evidence of any mechanism of locomotion whatsoever. The rail workers all stared as it rolled silently through the yard, and as it slid into the station it did not lumber or hiss as it pulled up to platform and discharged its passenger. He was tall and thin, and he had a tired haggard look. His black suit and black bowler hat were crisp and clean, and when he stepped onto the platform he paused to look around and checked his pocket watch against the station clock. He nodded slightly, and the car behind him gave a strange little whistle causing several horses and cows in the holding pens to start. Then, as quietly as it had arrived, the rail car slid away and sped through the yard. In minutes, it was lost amongst the sea of rolling grasslands.

As I said, I was a tough kid and back then Omaha was a rough town, so as the man moved from the station into the streets, I followed—not knowing exactly why, but certain that it was for more than just idle curiosity. The man walked with a strange gait. There was a rhythm to his step, a beat and pace that was so different, so fast, that it seemed as if he was not walking but rather gliding or sliding across the ground. He was a stranger in town that much was clear, but he moved through the streets as if he knew them. On more than one occasion, I attempted to slip past him by cutting through back alleys or yards, but to no avail. No matter how fast I ran, no matter what short cut I used, he always remained a good twenty paces ahead of me.

He talked to no one, made no note of street signs or landmarks, consulted no maps, but twenty minutes after arriving he was in the city offices and waiting to see the county clerk. From across the road I watched through the large plate window as he waited patiently, while the clerk and his assistants processed the forms and other administrivia of the modern bureaucracy. While he waited, he read the newspaper. He did so mechanically from front to back, read every article, every advertisement, every obituary and notice. He was on the last page of the paper when the secretary waved him forward. In response, he raised a finger, acknowledging his presence but at the same time forcing the stern little woman to wait a moment while he finished reading. He folded the paper neatly and placed it back on the table and nodded politely as he passed through the office door and into the clerk's office.

As soon as the door shut I bolted across the street and into the alleyway where I knew the window to the clerk's office often stood open. The clerk, a short, wiry man with thinning hair and wire-rimmed glasses named Reed greeted the stranger cordially, but the man declined to be as cordial.

"I am Nathaniel Wingate Peaslee, owner and operator of Professor Peaslee's Pandemonium and Circus. I have come to Omaha to secure a permit for the use of a field on the southwest side of town, an area locally known as the Southwest Pasture."

Mr. Reed responded with a lilt in his voice. "An advance man, well I'll say that you are certainly better dressed and well ahead of your competition. We normally don't see people trying to arrange for a summer carnival until May. Will you want the site for a whole week or just a long weekend?"

The man who had called himself Professor Peaslee was forced to correct the clerk, "You misunderstand me sir, I would like a permit to occupy the site forthwith, with the festivities to begin on Friday and run through Sunday."

From what I could hear Reed was flabbergasted, "Surely you're joking. The field is still wet, and even if it wasn't, this weekend, sir the 23rd, it's Easter Sunday. Half the town will be in services, you won't make any money."

Suddenly there were sounds I knew well, the sound of leather sliding against wool, of money being removed from a wallet, of crisp bills being laid on a desk. "The condition of the field is of no consequence. Your concern over our ability to turn a profit is admirable, but not our primary purpose for being here."

I heard the money vanish into a desk drawer, and the drawer close with a slight click. "The permit for the week will be ten dollars. You will be expected to be off the property by nightfall on the 24th, otherwise it will be another two dollars a day. Mr. William Dennison is the local boss; you'll have a visit from his men after you've set up. If you are running women or gambling he'll want a cut, he'll keep the sheriff off your back as well." Reed paused and I heard more money change hands. "Any problems you have with the locals are your own. As long as you don't go too far, the deputies will stay clear. Become too aggressive and they'll drag you and yours in front of Judge Russ faster than grits through a duck." A stamp thumped once, twice, thrice and then without any other words I heard the strange pace cross the floor and the door open and then close. I slunk toward the mouth of the alley and when Professor Peaslee passed, I once more fell in behind him.

In mere moments, he was in front of the home of one of the local newspapers, *The Omaha Bee*. Without pause he went inside, and I—knowing I was not welcome in that bastion of law and order journalism—waited outside for my prey to return. In those days, the streets of Omaha were no place for regular folk to hang about. Things were usually just fine during the day, and the cops, corrupt as they were, did a good job of keeping the women and genteel folk safe. But when the sun dipped low on the horizon, and the wind shifted, it brought more with it than just the cold and the damp in off the river, and good folk scurried to get to their homes before the night wrapped the streets in a cloak of darkness that hid more than just the occasional crime or act of depravity. Even a street tough like me was not entirely safe, but I had become so intrigued by this man, that I resolved to wait for him as long as I could. While all the others in the street quickened their pace and headed for the safety of their homes, I found a small place out of the wind and window lights, and quietly hid there.

It was well after dark and I had long since pulled my coat in tight to try and keep the cold out, when I noticed a subtle change in the atmosphere, the air seemed electric and carried with it a sweet smell like that of burnt caramel. There was a sound, a whistling hum that permeated the streets and buildings. The moonlight, abruptly tinted to a sepia tone, washed the color out of the world and turn most of what I could see into an unfocused blur, others though, like the two figures moving down the street, were brought into sharp relief. Looking anywhere else started to give me a headache, so I focused my attention and curiosity on the two men steadily approaching my vantage point. The first man was tall and well proportioned, with a black top hat and matching tails. His hair was raven black and merged with a neatly trimmed mustache and beard. A pair of black gloves covered his hands, but in the spaces around his neck and at his wrists, traces of color peeked out and seemed to dance in the strange light. The second man was small, only slightly larger than I and dressed in the simple blue tunic, pants and skull cap that were traditional amongst his Chinese ancestors and he habitually stroked the long, grey, wispy beard that hung down to the middle of his chest. Every few seconds he took an animated puff from a long, thin, ivory pipe while peering interestedly at his surroundings through wire-rimmed glasses perched on a funny nose beneath two snowy eyebrows. The two seemed an odd pairing to be wandering along the streets at night, and as they came closer I hunkered down inside my hidey hole and tried to pretend I wasn't there.

It was about then that the door of the *Bee* creaked open and Professor Peaslee came wandering out. In his arms, he carried four bundles of hand bills, and the scent of freshly printed ink and warm paper wafted across the street. The two men converged on Peaslee, who greeted each by handing them a bundle of bills. To the man in the top hat he said, "Go north Mr. D'Arc," I swear I could hear the punctuation mark, and to the small Chinese he ordered "south Doctor Low." Without a word of response Peaslee's compatriots strolled away while Professor Peaslee simply stood there bathed in the strange moonlight, casting long shadows against the cold winds. I sat there waiting for him to leave, to move, to do something, but he just stood there waiting, staring into the night, and this more than anything made me suddenly afraid. For in the darkness, I realized that he was staring exactly at where I had secreted myself.

He crossed the street, moving in that strange gait that was so oddly inhuman, coming closer and closer to the place where I was hiding. Step by step he came at me; until he was so close I could reach out and touch him. He dropped a bundle of bills on the ground, and they bounced with a deep thud that sent me cowering backwards. "I know you are here boy!" His voice bellowed, "There's no sense in hiding, Thomas

Taylor!"

At the sound of my name I shrieked in fear and bolted out of the hole and tried to slip past his feet. His hand shot out and grabbed me by the collar; I twisted as he lifted me off the ground but to no avail. "Let me go!" I screeched in protest.

I was not a small boy, but Professor Peaslee manhandled me as if I was a mere whimpering babe. "You dare to stalk me? I have come here for you boy and others like you. Did you think I would not notice you skulking about?" He twisted me around and looked me in the eye and I was momentarily frozen. He had strange, cold, lifeless eyes, I felt him fumble with my coat. "You want to run, by the time I'm through you all will want to run, but someday you shall thank me. Someday you will realize what I have done here . . . "

I kicked him, kicked him hard. My foot connected with his chest just below the throat and knocked the wind out of him. His grasp weakened and I used the momentum from the kick to twist away. I hit the ground running, stumbling to my feet while Peaslee fell to his knees. I ran down the street, into the cold night, leaving the terrifying man behind. My footsteps pounding the ground echoed the sound of my heart in my head. I ran like the devil himself was behind me, heading for the one place I knew would keep me safe, the church just north of the Sportsmen's Quarter. The main doors were well past being locked, but I slipped in through a side entrance which the priests used to move between the chapel and the home. I slipped through the pews and into the confessional where I prayed to the Virgin Mary until I fell asleep.

The next day I tried to put the whole thing out of my mind, but there was no chance of that. The streets had been plastered with hand bills, gaudy three colored things announcing Professor's Peaslee's Pandemonium and Circus to be performing in the Southwest Pasture, for three days, Thursday through Saturday, with an invitation only extravaganza on Sunday. There was an odd beetle motif to the bills, a repeating pattern that reminded me of the scarabs of ancient Egypt. The whole idea had set the town abuzz, and as I wandered through the morning streets, it was the only thing people were talking about. Even at the street kitchen where I snuck in for a biscuit, it was the only topic of discussion. That the town had been infected with the idea of the carnival, and only I seemed to possess any knowledge that the people in charge were less than wholesome, made me nervous, for I knew it made me a target. I shivered and shoved my hands into my coat, only to find a strange piece of paper. It was stiff, not quite cardboard, but not thin paper either. It was a rectangle, done in three colors and bearing the name and logo of Professor Peaslee's Pandemonium and Circus. It was an invitation, a ticket to the extravaganza on Sunday, starting at nine in the morning. It was inscribed, printed with two words that set my mind reeling. I dropped the ticket from my hand and let it flutter to the ground, those two words flashing as the paper spun down. Two words, two familiar words - words I heard almost every day of my life, words I'd heard most recently as the professor had bellowed them last night - words that now struck terror in my heart. I grabbed the ticket from the floor and hid it back in my pocket, terrified that someone else might see those words, see the thing Peaslee had printed on the invitation to Sunday's extravaganza. Two words, printed in ink, in bold black letters: THOMAS TAYLOR, my own name!

 I spent the rest of that day wandering the streets, fretting over the thing in my pocket. On more than one occasion I stood beside a rubbish bin and tried to find the will to toss it in, but try as I might I couldn't bring myself to part with the thing. Instead I found myself on unfamiliar streets, which turned into dirt roads, and then grassy trails. I don't know how it happened, but by late afternoon I was standing on the grassy knoll overlooking the great field known as the Southwest Pasture. I stood there looking down over the area; it was here that Peaslee's circus was to entertain the people of Omaha. Here is where the circus was to erect its tents, its midway, its rides and animal shows. On Thursday, just two days away, this place was to be filled with hundreds of people, and dozens of temporary structures. But on that day, as I stood there, the place was empty and quiet, still but for the wind moving and whispering through the grass-covered plains.

 It took most of the evening for me to make it back to my familiar haunts. I needed to talk to someone, someone I trusted, tell them what had happened, what I suspected. But when I sat down and thought about it, what was there to say? Here were the facts: A stranger, who knew my name and who consorted with circus people, had arrived in town; his name was the very same featured on the flyer as the owner and he took offense to being followed, and he had yet to set up his circus. It was nothing, nothing to be frightened off, and yet, I could not shake the feeling that something sinister was about to happen. I wandered home, or what passed for my home at that time. The man who said he was my father was passed out drunk in bed, my stepmother curled up beside him. In the bedroom down the shabby, unpainted hall I peeked in on my younger brother. He was fast asleep, a new bruise on his cheek. He moaned a little as I crawled into the bed beside him, but after I hummed the tune to a lullaby our mother use to sing us he settled down back into sleep.

It was just before dawn when my brother woke me up. He was shaking me, rocking me back and forth in the bed and gently calling my name. I struggled against consciousness, but the dreams of a thirteen-year-old boy are no match for incessant cries of a ten-year-old, and I finally succumbed to his pleas to get up. He had something he wanted to show me, something important, and as the sun rose we were stumbling at quick pace through the dim streets dodging horse drawn carts and weaving around the myriad of delivery men carrying all manner of things to various markets, restaurants, butchers, bakers, and such. The crowded streets were nothing compared to the fleet legs of two young boys. At first, I didn't know where he was taking me but we soon rounded the street that led to the train yard. Following my brother's lead, we soon climbed over a wooden gate, headed up some winding metal stairs, and then made our way onto the thin bridge that the work men used to get above trains.

He pointed out into the distance. I was still panting, out of breath from the journey, but I strained to see what he was going on about. "Do you see it Thomas? Out there in the fields, the black train?"

I didn't. I saw nothing. There was no train out there, there possibly couldn't be. No train could be out that way, because there were no tracks that ran in that direction, never had, never would, the ground was too soft. I shook my head.

"No Robert, I don't. There's nothing out there."

Robert whined, like he always did when he couldn't get someone to understand him. "It's there Thomas! It must be a hundred cars long, all black with silver trim. A circus train. You sure you don't see it? It's just there to the right of the observation wheel, and left of the big tent. There's a sign, the lettering is so big! I bet you could see that from the other side of town!" He paused and I could see his lips moving, as he tried to sound something out.

I cupped my hand around my eyes and tried desperately to see what my brother could see, but there was nothing there. I turned him around about to chastise him for such a cruel joke but then he opened his mouth and asked, "What's a pandemonium?"

I ran. I left him there on the bridge and I ran. Robert followed. Robert followed me through the streets and out into the roads and paths and to the grassy knoll that overlooked the Southwest Pasture. As I crawled up that low hill, I closed my eyes fearful of what they might see. I stood up there, the wind blowing around me, the sound of Robert's boots running up behind me, his breath ragged in the air. He stood beside me, not knowing that I had yet to take sight of whatever it was before us. He whistled softly in exclamation, "That's incredible!" and then his boots were running down the hill leaving me behind.

I opened my eyes slowly. At first, they remained unfocused and showed only the blurry light of the world in blue and green tones with shapes moving through it. I blinked, and blinked again, then I rubbed my hand across them, trying to clear whatever was blurring my vision. Something moved something large and dark with streaks of silver. It crawled across the landscape like a titanic snake or worm, or at least so I thought. Whatever the horrible shape was, it never came into focus, and when I blinked again it was gone. In its place was the thing I dreaded most. The Southwest Pasture had been occupied; a small army had taken it over. Tents and other temporary structures had been laid out in a spiral formation, like a gigantic snail's shell from the vast circular opening of the Ferris wheel to the great tower-like tent composed of dozens of colors, which spiraled into a point. The whole thing was about a mile away, but even from that distance I could see the performers, clowns, acrobats, roustabouts and the like, all going about their business. A line of elephants marched down the main thoroughfare, and I could hear lions roar as the crack of a whip urged them into some unseen routine. The scent of food, rich with sweetness and fat reached me, and I longed for a taste of whatever was the source. The sound of a carousel—or at least the music I associated with such a ride—abruptly started and then painfully ground to a slow, discordant stop. My brother was right, it was incredible. A wonder of engineering and a true a sight to behold, but I also knew that the day before there had been nothing here, and feared what dark forces had been used to create such a place, and why. If I had been alone I would have fled that place, left it far behind and never returned, but Robert had already covered half the distance between me and the circus. I tore down the hill in pursuit, desperate to save my younger brother from the horrors I was certain were contained within those tents.

I caught up with Robert at the edge of a tent where he was hiding and watching the carnies carry out various tasks. A few acrobats were tumbling, some clowns, their faces only partially painted, were juggling, and a horse whose rider was a small monkey trotted past. It all seemed very innocent, normal, but I knew that something malevolent lurked beneath the surface. A familiar voice rang out, and I pulled my brother down as I saw Professor Peaslee and the man he called Mister D'Arc appear in front of the tent we were hiding next to. They seemed to be arguing about something, though what exactly I couldn't tell. As they pulled back the flap and went inside, I saw a sign that said CAROUSEL and another above it that said OUT OF ORDER. I pulled at my brother, tried to get him to leave, but he slipped away and ducked under the edge of the tent, leaving me no choice but to follow.

Robert was hiding behind a stack of hay bales. I scooted across the ground—careful to stay out of view of Peaslee and D'Arc—to join him. Besides a scattering of bales, the only other object in the tent was a large carousel, ornately decorated with an outrageously painted menagerie of creatures both real and imagined. Each beast practically dripped with incredibly vibrant colors and to this day, I can still remember the lively green and yellow stripes of the zebra, and the purple plumage of a giant cockerel. Peaslee and D'Arc were standing in the center, hovering over an open panel in the control hub. The interior compartment was filled with a mad conglomeration of mirrors, rods and levers the exact purpose of which I could not discern.

Apparently, I was not the only one confounded by the apparatus, for Mr. D'Arc was none too happy either. "We had a deal Peaslee!" The man barked. "We provide cover for you here in Omaha, and you give us a working temporal engine. You said that you knew how to do that. 'Easy as pie' were your exact words. Our deal ends on Sunday, four days to go, and where exactly is my engine? I am not a fool sir. We aren't your servants either. We had a deal, and if you fail to honor it, I assure you, you and yours will rue the day."

Professor Peaslee remained strangely calm, almost emotionless during this verbal assault, and afterwards responded curtly. "The deal Mr. D'Arc was that by the time we parted ways on Sunday, you would have a working engine. I have already explained to you that a critical component is en route, carried by my personal assistant Mr. Cougar who will arrive on tomorrow's train. Once this part arrives, the engine will be fully functional. Your concerns are irrational. My plan depends on the engine being fully operational. Without it, I cannot power the tesseract, and without that none of us are safe from the forces that will come to bear on Sunday. As for our relationship, I am well aware that you are not one of my servants. If you were, I assure you that your insolent behavior would be appropriately punished."

I pulled at Robert's sleeve, desperate to get him out of this place, but he pulled back, and shrugged me off. "Robert!" I whispered in desperation, "We shouldn't be here!"

A strange voice in broken English suddenly whispered behind me, "Thomas is right, Robert. You not supposed to be here. Funny guys. At least not yet. Get in big trouble with circus boss man."

Robert and I both screamed as the china man that Peaslee had called Doctor Low started to laugh in a strange tittering manner that reminded me of crickets. We both jumped to our feet, exposing ourselves to Peaslee and D'Arc.

The two men ceased their arguing and just stared at us for a moment, then still using that horrid monotone voice Peaslee said, "The Taylor boys, Robert and Thomas." He looked at his watch, "I wasn't expecting you so soon. Doctor Low, would you be so kind as to detain them for me? There is no harm in putting the plan in motion early."

Thomas and I both dove under the tent wall and scrambled through the dusty ground, finally getting to our feet and sprinting away from the circus as fast as we could. I made a beeline for cover, and I could hear Thomas urging me to run faster, as we left the pasture and entered the tall grass that marked the beginning of a marshy area. We crashed through, ignoring bugs and bees, or any threat of snakes, the vegetation whipped at our faces, stinging our cheeks and necks. Rabbits and marsh hens fled as we cut through game trails, something large and gray, maybe a coyote dove out of our way. In the tall grass, I lost track of where I was. I could hear Robert panting behind me like a pony at a full run but I was too terrified to look back.

The marsh turned into a small stream, and I barreled through the shallow trickle, following it toward town, where I knew that it began at a storm drain just south of the train yard. The water was cold, and it seeped through my boots and cut into my feet like daggers. I stumbled over a rock, tumbled head first into the brook, and felt Robert tumble over me, before landing just a few feet beyond. I looked behind me for any trace of our pursuers, but saw nothing. I grabbed Robert by the shirt and pulled him to my side. The mass of cloth had little weight to it, and sprung out of the creek empty, save for the torrent of water that dripped out. I dropped the empty shirt and shot forward to where my brother had fallen, searching for his young body in the inches deep water, but to no avail.

I sat back, ignoring the cold, desperately fighting the need to scream out in anguish. A tittering laughing melody reached my ears, and I turned to see Doctor Low standing on the bank of the brook holding a large round fish bowl in his hands. In it was a large fish with golden scales and red flowing fins, thrashing about in a panic. Low looked me in the eye. There was no malevolence there. Whatever drove Peaslee and

D'Arc had not been passed to the Chinese doctor. He took the fish bowl in one hand, balancing it like a ball, and the slipped it inside of his robes. When his hand came back out, there was no more bowl, no more fish, and no evidence that either had ever existed. Low raised a finger to his mouth and whispered "Shhh. Robert, he is sleeping now. You come back for him later. You come back on Sunday. We need you back on Sunday."

"For what?" I shouted as the Chinese magician slipped into the tall grass.

The grass swallowed him whole, but the wind whispering through it spoke with his voice, "Sunday, Thomas, Sunday."

How or when I returned to town I do not remember, but that evening the priest chased me out of the church and into the street. I tried to tell him what had happened, but he would have no part of it. I tried waking my parents, but they lounged about in a drunken stupor and threatened me with a beating if I didn't go away. When I tried to be more forceful my father rolled over and swatted at me. I spent the rest of the night curled up in my brother's bed, the smell of him filling my senses, while I cried myself to sleep.

On Thursday, my stepmother chased me out of bed, screaming about Robert being missing. I wanted to explain, tried to tell her about Peaslee and D'Arc and Low, but the look in her eyes— that deadly combination of hangover and blind rage—told me it was better to run. So, I ran. I ran to where I knew I would be safe or at least left alone. The train yard was a bee hive of activity. The cars were being unloaded and reloaded with all manner of things; pigs, cattle, sheep, seed, rock, even people. The platform was full of passengers, some getting off, some getting on, others wishing loved ones goodbye, some picking up new arrivals, but amongst them all was a lone figure that stood out, exactly because he could not stand up.

The man had once been large, perhaps a farm hand or a butcher, he had that kind of look about him, but age had taken its toll, and while there was still broadness in his shoulders and thickness about his neck, the rest seemed atrophied. He was confined to a wooden wheel chair, and as the porter rolled him across the platform I could see that his withered hands—trembling with some sort of palsy—clutched a small wooden box. He had a fair complexion dotted with spots and stains, like a mold had taken hold and spread. He was nearly bald, save for a thin reddish fringe above the ears, which matched the bushiness of his eyebrows. There was something about the old man that made me nervous, and I took a wide path around him, determined to put some distance between myself and everyone else, that is until the porter apologized to his charge and said, "I have to leave you Mr. Cougar. To get the rest of your bags. I'll only be a moment."

You could have knocked me down with a feather. Up until that moment I had forgotten about the man Peaslee had said was coming to town on the train. The man named "Cougar" who brought with him something desperately needed. A component that Peaslee's plans could not do without. And there he was, an old man, trapped in a wheelchair, the small box clenched in his trembling hands, a box that I knew was the bargaining chip I needed to get my brother back. If I could find the courage to take it and make it mine.

I moved through the crowd, backtracking slowly to where Cougar sat, coming up on him quietly. There was a crowd coming toward us, a boisterous couple with a trio of towheaded children, and an overburdened porter. I waited till they got close, and then jostled the porter, not much, just enough to set him off balance, and send the children careening into the trapped invalid. None of the children actually touched Mr. Cougar, but as they tumbled around him the man panicked, growled and as he swatted the trio away my hand darted in and snatched the box away.

My feet darted down the platform and down the stairs and off onto the tracks. I crossed the train between two cars and then double backed. I dashed past the workmen unloading cars and soon found myself amongst the cars already reloaded for the trip out of Omaha. I found a car full of clucking chickens that had a small space between cages that was large enough to conceal me. I crawled in and hid amongst the stink and the noise of the birds.

It was about an hour later that I felt the distinctive

thrum of the engine being fired up. The vibration built in me a sense of anticipation that grew and churned like the steam inside the engine itself. It grew slowly, roiling like a dark cloud in the pit of my stomach, spitting lightning into my chest and thunder into my heart. When the great engine finally opened up and let loose its shrill, screeching whistle, I too opened up and let out a screeching wail of anguish that set the birds around me cackling in fear and confusion.

The train lurched forward, and then settled into a slow, rolling beat. I thought about getting off. Thought about going back to the circus, bargaining with Doctor Low, or Mr. D'Arc, or perhaps even Professor Peaslee. Instead I settled in and let the train take me out of town, out past the ranches and farms, and into the wilds of Nebraska. We came upon a bend, a place where the train had to slow down to a near dead crawl. I waited till the rail passed a rather thick clump of grass and then with my treasure still clasped to my chest, I leapt clear of the train and tumbled off into the brush beyond. Free of Omaha and any imminent threat, I clambered away from the train, leaving it to roll off into the distance.

I lay there on the bank of the rail for hours. It was the first time I had been free, free from noise, free from responsibility, free from the town and all the filth and corruption that bred within it. Even as a child I knew that Omaha was wrong, that it was no place for a child, and that living there would only lead to misery and cruel passionless groping in the dark. It had already sunk its hooks into me; I was well onto the path that my father had taken. For me it was only a matter of time before I grew up and left my youthful dreams and idealism behind and fell into the dreary routine of adulthood. Robert however was another matter, he still had time, and perhaps a chance to do something more with his life, to be something better. That is, if I could find a way to bargain for his release using the box I had absconded with.

I fumbled with the box. It was a plain thing. a cube of three inches to each side, made of a dark hardwood I didn't recognize. There was no lock, and no hinges either, but the weight of thing seemed to indicate a rather large compartment inside. At first, I thought the box was plainly finished, but as I turned it over and over I could see a strange, faint pattern that lay beneath the varnish. There were a series of geometric figures, ellipses and circles transcribed by triangles. The patterns lay just above a series of inscribed lines that divided each face into nine equal squares. As I studied the faint designs, I realized that they could easily be combined into another pattern, if the individual squares could be rotated about. I gripped the opposite faces of cubes and twisted in opposing directions. To my surprise the faces rotated, and after some twisting and turning, I discovered that I could move various faces and components of the cube at right angles to each other, and thereby rearrange the pattern. I lost myself in moving those faces about, twisting and turning, shifting squares about to different faces, creating different patterns. As I did this, I could see the new pattern emerging, could see how the ellipses and circles and triangles were being reworked, reshaped. What's more, I could see the steps—every turn and twist—I needed to take to reach that new pattern. It came to my mind in clear scenes, like a vision or a drawing in a book. In mere moments, the images in my mind were achieved, and a new and fascinating pattern emerged on the faces of the cube.

The pattern danced across the cube like stars twinkling in the sky. I felt something click and a sudden mechanical whine began as several of the panels slowly began to fold back to reveal the contents within. I caught a glimpse of something, something mechanical comprised of rods and levers, crystalline mirrors and glass joints. I caught just a glimpse for as the sunlight hit it, the whole thing lit up into a blinding ball of white piercing light. The world around me washed away into a featureless white space with no landmarks and no walls. The natural world that I had just inhabited and the box that I once held were gone. Only I and my clothes remained amongst a stark featureless space of silence.

After my initial shock, I ran blindly through that white void. In what direction I travelled, and for how long, I could not say, for in that blank place there was no way for me to mark time or distance. I ran but I did not grow tired, or hungry, or thirsty. At one point, I tried counting my heartbeats, but stopped after I realized that there was no way to mark the passage of extremely large sets of such beats. I took off my jacket and set it at my feet, and then stepped back from it. Slowly, one step at a time I moved away, careful not to let it leave my sight. At a hundred paces, it was a small black dot in a field of white. I turned away, just for a moment, but in that moment the small speck vanished. I ran back in the direction that I was sure I had last seen the coat, but to no avail. My coat was gone, swallowed up by the infinite whiteness that surrounded me.

Frustrated I ran. I ran as fast as my legs could carry me, and though I seemed to go nowhere, I suspected that I was actually making progress. Time passed and in the distance I saw a small speck hanging in the air. In the sea of nothing, even a speck is unusual. So, I quickened my pace and dashed even faster toward the unseemly blemish. It hung there in the air, mocking me, resting against some invisible surface that existed at an impossible angle. I reached out to touch it cautiously, as if it were a rattlesnake ready to strike, but it just sat there doing nothing. When I finally touched it, pulled it off whatever plane it was resting on, it tumbled into my arms like any normal piece of leather. For that is what was sitting there in the white space, a leather coat, the one that I had left behind, but whether that had been mere moments or eons before, I could not tell.

Timeless space enveloped me and I closed my eyes, exhausted by the madness I found myself in.

With my eyes closed I saw things. I saw how things were connected, how people and events were linked from the past through the present and into the future. I saw paths and linkages, chains of events that could be nudged or twisted into new directions. I saw so much. I saw what Peaslee was doing, how he was setting things in motion, how they could play out. I also saw how they could be interfered with, how what Peaslee put in motion could be changed, redirected.

A booming noise shocked me to attention. I cowered but realized that there was nothing to cower into save myself. The noise repeated, like thunder in intensity, but not a rolling rumbling sound, but a structured noise, somehow familiar, like the roaring of a bull. A great hole of darkness appeared as the sound roared again, I knew that noise, knew it well. I could place it if it wasn't so loud. A titanic thing came through the hole, a monstrous snake with five featureless heads that tore through the white. It searched blindly in my direction, its titanic voice booming over and over again, from mouthless heads. I ran, casting frantic, furtive glances behind me as the thing followed at impossible speeds. Two great heads wrapped around me like snakes and lifted me up. The other heads followed suit, and soon I was enveloped in the coils of the thing, I struggle but to no avail. It lifted me up and once more bellowed out that horrific booming sound and in that moment I finally recognized the sound as a voice roaring out my own name, "THOMAS!"

Suddenly I was no longer in a featureless space, but rather in the crowded field where the circus sat beneath an overcast sky. Two thick arms were wrapped around my chest, and I recognized them as belonging to Mr. D'Arc, whose voice was whispering strange words into my ear. Professor Peaslee was looking into my eyes, and backing away. In his right hand he held the wooden cube, while with his left hand he was shifting the sides back and forth into yet another pattern.

As the cube shifted and danced Professor Peaslee seemed more concerned with me than with the actual treasure he held in his hand, "You, Thomas Taylor are a very troublesome young man. We might call you a focal point. Yes, perhaps that is why the lines are always in flux about you. You have such potential, perhaps even more so than with your brother. It shall be interesting to see what becomes of you."

Suddenly Doctor Low was standing there beside him, a contraption made of liquid filled tubes and cylinders in his hands. "So sorry Professor, little time, very little time. Getting cold now, pressure dropping."

He was right; it had gotten colder as I stood there. Peaslee dashed into a nearby tent, the one that I recognized as housing the carousel. Mr. D'Arc let me go and spun up onto a wooden crate. "All of you listen!" He shouted. "You know the plan. Take your charges and move into the tent. Take positions on the carousel. Everything will be fine. The storm will pass over us in a few minutes, and then we shall be finished here."

Doctor Low was moved to my side. "Hello Thomas," he said. "Please, I will take you to your brother." He offered his hand, and with no real choice, I took it and went with him into the carousel tent.

All around me, the same thing was happening to other townspeople, some I knew, some I recognized, others just had a look about them that said Omaha. And with each one of my neighbors there was a member of the circus escorting them to a seat on the carousel. There seemed no rhyme or reason to who was there, for I saw white folks and blacks too, the rich and the poor, the old and the young. But the one thing they had in common was that each was pinned with a ticket to the Sunday Extravaganza that bore their name. Just like the one that was still in my pocket.

Low noticed my confusion as he helped me into a gilded cart and sat me next to my brother Robert, who was sleeping. "You were lost for a long time Thomas. It caused much trouble, but Professor Peaslee he found you in the noplace. Sent Mr. D'Arc in to get you. The noplace is not an easy place to get into, or out of. Much trouble you caused." He wagged his finger and shoved another boy in my direction. "Take care of your brother and young Howard too."

A clown shoved a trio of black folks onto the bench across from us. At first, I thought they were a family, but all three bore different names. The older was named Little, while the younger was named Hall. The woman who sat between them was named Norton. As they settled in, I noticed that everyone seemed unusually calm, as if they had no idea that they were in danger. Only, the circus folk seemed to show signs of desperation. An acrobat sat a young man named Marlon down on a flamingo, and then situated a pregnant woman named Dorothy next to him on a toad. Behind me the thin man strapped an aged and dapper man onto a tiger, and then jumped onto a camel beside him.

There was a screeching musical sound, and out of the corner of my eye I saw Peaslee throw a switch and fire up the carousel. It jerked forward and as it did I saw Low step onto the carousel and toss the strange contraption of tubes of fluids away. There was panic in his eyes, and he flung himself onto the nearest wooden animal and seemed to grip it with all his might yelling at the top of his lungs, "ITS HERE! THE STORM IS HERE!"

Above the music of the carousel there emerged a noise, a tremendous thunderous noise like the sound of a dozen freight trains roaring across the sky. The flaps of the tent buckled in and then plumped out. It was hard to watch as the carousel picked up speed, but the ropes that held the tent in place were pulling out of the ground and whipping in the wind. Then without any more warning the tent whipped into the sky and the carousel lay exposed to the thing that had swallowed up the world. We were in a tornado, a massive one that was sweeping through the circus, destroying everything in its path. Black winds filled with debris and dusts churned around us, tossing trees and brush everywhere. At first, I thought we were in the eye, that somehow the tent had protected us as we moved through the wall, but that was not the case. I could see the eye off to my right, see the winds churning and twisting a in a circular motion. We were in the wall itself, and our only protection was being generated by the carousel itself, powered by whatever it was that I had tried to steal from Peaslee!

Across from me Mister Little bowed his head and began to pray. The woman and young man next to him followed suit, and soon the entire faux wagon cart was reciting scripture, me included. As the roaring winds grew in intensity, so did our voices, and soon an entire congregation of Nebraskans was pleading to God Almighty for salvation. Only the circus folk refrained from joining in, but I could see fear in their eyes. Even Doctor Low and Mister D'Arc looked worried. Only Professor Peaslee who stood on the inner edge of the carousel showed no trace of fear. Indeed, he seemed to revel in the violence of the catastrophe, and I saw amongst the flashes of light that crossed his face a horrid visage of inhuman intelligence that chilled me to the bone and made me pray even harder.

As Mister D'Arc had promised, the storm passed within minutes, and as the winds moved to the northeast Peaslee flipped some hidden switch and the carousel slowed, the music wound down and eventually the entire mechanism ground to a slow jolting halt. The great pasture had been wiped clean. The midway, the tents, the banners and booths were all gone. It was as if the carnival had never existed, only the carousel remained. The residents of Omaha shuffled off of the circular platform and watched as the tornado trailed off into the town itself and once more filled with debris. I heard Miss Norton begin to cry, and I turned back to scream at Peaslee, to demand an explanation, but that evil man had already started the machine back up again, and all the circus folk were riding the wooden beasts as they accelerated to match the tempo of the music. Everyone else was watching the tornado rip through town; some were running behind it desperate to help. Only I stayed and watched the carousel spin round faster and faster, take on a strange blue glow, fade into a blur and then with a wrenching screech vanish into nothingness.

More than one hundred people died as that tornado tore through town. More suffered as a cold front came in behind it. It took time, and help, but we made it through. We pulled together and we helped each other out. Over the years I tried to talk to the people I recognized from the carousel, tried to understand what had happened and why. But most seemed to forget that strange event, others I think chose to forget, but I never could. I made a record, created a list of those who had been there and tracked what became of them, and their children. Howard, the little boy I took care of with Robert, became a state representative, his son Warren is a successful businessman and investor, and the source of my own fortune. The young black man who sat with us that day grew up to be a communist writer. He wrote a book about black liberation and racial segregation. Reverend Little married Miss Norton, they moved away shortly after. They had a son named Malcolm, a revolutionary who was killed recently. The pregnant woman on the toad was named Dorothy King; she gave birth to a strapping young lad named Leslie. By all accounts, her husband was a lay-about and a wife beater. They divorced and when she remarried the boy took his stepfather's name, Gerald Ford, and is now the minority leader in the House of Representatives. The man named Marlon gave birth to a son with the same name. You might have seen him in the movies recently. All these people, all the people that Peaslee saved, they all did something, something important, something worth remembering.

All of them but Robert and I.

As I said Robert was committed to a madhouse in 1939. He had a daughter about ten years earlier, a girl named Pamela

Sue. She had a child in 1946, a boy who was slow in the head, but the child drowned in a lake somewhere in New Jersey. Pamela Sue never could get over that, she obsessed about it, mourned that child for years. She still lives there, taking care of the camp where her son died. She's as mad as her father I suppose. My own daughter, Edith had three children. Back in '63 her boy did something horrible and my eldest granddaughter was killed. Michael was institutionalized. Two years later Edith, her husband and my other granddaughter also died, killed in a car accident.

It seems that whatever greatness Peaslee had intended for Robert, I, or our descendants has eluded us

But that does not mean I have been idle. I don't know why I began, but I did, and once begun I couldn't stop.

I was in San Francisco in the summer of 1916. That won't mean much to you, but all those years ago the bomb I planted killed ten and wounded forty. Almost a year later I did the same in a Chester munitions factory, but with much more success.

In 1918, I made my way to Russia, drawn there by a need to change something, to interfere, to break the path that Peaslee had set in motion. I killed a little girl, just one. The rest of her family had already been killed. She had escaped, or at least she was meant too. I made sure she didn't survive to retake the throne.

In 1922, I returned to the West Coast. There was a movie star, a man, I didn't know him, had never really heard of him, but when I saw him on the street, I knew I had to shoot him. A few years later, the same year my daughter was born, they buried Valentino in the same crypt as the man I killed.

It went on like that for years. My marriage ended. The Second War came, and I travelled back to Europe. There was so much work to be done, so many things to change: First in Europe, then Africa, and then in Asia. There were so many things to meddle with, so many plans to change. Those things I saw, Peaslee's plans, I had to act, I had no choice. I was driven.

In 1949, I gave a friend of mine a gun, a Luger. He used it, and ended up in the madhouse for his effort. Likewise, when I went to Dallas in 1963 I made sure that one man killed another, and that he was killed as well.

This is only a partial list mind you. There is more, much more, but these are the highlights, my best of, so to say. I knew that the three women—the ones they caught me for, the ones I've died for—were going to be my last. I could see that, because I saw it all so long ago. It's as if I had read this story before you see, and knew the ending, just not how the storyline got there.

Funny that. These things I've done, the changes I've made. I know they are supposed to interfere with Peaslee's plan, to make things go wrong, to change course that he set us on when he saved all those other people. But how do I know that? Did I see secrets, a way for humanity to regain control of the future, or did I see what Peaslee wanted me to see? Am I a meddler or am I just another pawn being moved about the board? Have I rescued mankind, restored a kind of order to our world, or have I been just another instrument, another tool used to spread about a very specialized brand of chaos and death: Could it be that Robert and I and our descendants are in fact a dark gift bestowed upon the world?

Am I perhaps another example of Professor Peaslee's pandemonium?

1913

Pr. Peaslee's Price

The man sitting in my waiting room was nervous, shaken, perhaps even frightened. The other man, the one with horrible injuries was in the back room, what I modestly called my Surgery though it was little more than a table and some bright lights. I had given this second man a sedative and some morphine for the pain while I tried to discover what brought these two residents of Arkham to my home office in the middle of a hot August night. The nervous man seemed eager to speak.

"I appreciate your help Doctor, though I do not understand why I should have brought that man here instead of to St. Mary's. The man was lucky I knew where your office was, though I suppose given the dearth of physicians in Arkham it is not surprising that we shared the same one. Nor is it surprising that I was out and about at such an hour to find the man screaming in the Dethshill Cemetery. Truth is I had followed him there, for he and I share a mutual interest but I get ahead of myself. You want to know what happened, I don't entirely know, but I can tell you what I saw and heard. Perhaps you will be able to piece things together."

"As I have made clear in our previous consultations, the ennui that has invaded my life and given my creative energies pause, stems I believe from the sudden and inexplicable loss of my dreams. For two decades, ever since that weird day at the family estate, my nights have been filled with the most marvelous vistas and fantasies. People speak of their dreams as rich and full of phantasms, but I truly believe that I am perhaps one of the greatest dreamers who has ever lived, or at least I was. While my days had been filled with the most prosaic of tasks, my nights were adventures that would challenge those of

Burton's *The Book of a Thousand Nights and a Night*, or Lord Dunsany's *Gods of Pegana*. Now my nights are empty, lackluster immersions into the most commonplace of imaginings. I cannot tell you what precipitated such a metamorphosis, but because of it I have now come to dread sleep and the nightly mediocrity that it brings. This change occurred not long after I began seeing you. At first, I thought it might have been a result of your administrations, but of course no nutrient injection has ever affected me before, so I have dismissed that possibility entirely."

"Regardless, it is because of this emptiness that I have begun to seek out a way to rekindle my imagination, and have done so in a curious fashion. I have begun spending an inordinate amount of time in the library at Miskatonic University researching whatever subject takes my fancy. This evening I found the library nearly empty. The summer session is free of undergraduates, and only a few stalwart researchers remain to clutter that great hall of learning. Thus, I was able to make a significant amount of progress going through the catalogue produced by Pent & Serenade for the auction of the library of the Church of the Starry Wisdom which occurred back in 1877 in Providence, and upon closing time was feeling rather pleased with myself."

"In a jovial mood, I decided to take a stroll through the streets of Arkham, another diversion that I had developed recently to help compensate for my lack of inspirational dreams. Arkham's ancient lanes were lit by the pale cool light of the moon and stars, and though I had once thought that my late-night meanderings would have been solitary, I had learned that a significant amount of activity occurs while the rest of the city sleeps. I hesitate to even refer to it as sleeping, for it seems to me that the night Arkham is so different from that of the day that it might as well be an entirely different town. It is as if there exist two distinct economies, completely detached from one another only meeting at dawn and dusk to exchange what necessities and niceties either had desire for."

"Thus, it was in this mood that I meandered westward on Church Street until I reached the spot where I was forced to either move north on Boundary toward the river, or south toward the university athletic fields. I have always been fond of the river and so I turned north and in doing so caught sight of two figures furtively dashing across the street and then quickly reaching the side gate into Dethshill cemetery. Now Dethshill is not exactly unknown as a spot for charismatic students to take their romantic interests, and neither is it immune to a spot of vandalism or fraternity pranks, but the build of these two shadowy figures suggested that both were male and of an age that precluded them from being students. I quickly secreted myself into the shadows, and as they fumbled with the gate lock I caught sight of their faces and discovered that I could easily identify them. The first was a man of some notoriety, and a patient of yours Doctor, Professor Nathaniel Wingate Peaslee known in the papers as the Man Who Forgot Himself. I had heard he had recently returned from his global travels. The man was a political economist, and yet since the strange transformation that removed all memory of his previous life and personality his tastes, as you know, run to the most outré of subjects. The other was Pr. Laban Shrewsbury, whose courses in philosophy and anthropology are so dreaded by the undergraduates of Miskatonic University. Rumor has it that Shrewsbury was working on a treatise of some sort or another on the enigmatic R'lyeh Text, but this rumor had persisted for almost a decade."

"Intrigued, I let them pass through the gate and then quickly dashed across the street in pursuit. As I myself went through the aging rock arch I thought perhaps they had eluded me, but I soon heard their feet tramping across the ground in the direction of an ancient grove of elms and oaks that was locally known as the Witch's Hollow. Careful not to be noticed I left the main path for one that would take me around the back of the hollow. I know Dethshill well for there are many Carters in residence amongst its occupants. I circled round the wood and approached from the North wending my way along a game trail that ran from the trees to Hangman's Slough. I found a modicum of concealment from a low thicket that shielded me from the spot where the two professors had stopped. Shrewsbury was sitting on a large boulder while Peaslee seemed to be standing before him. My position did not provide the best view of the two men, but was still close enough for me to eavesdrop on their conversation."

'This is not sorcery,' said Peaslee. 'There is no such thing. There is only science. Your understanding of the universe and the forces within it is so very limited. You perceive so little with your limited senses and believe that what you have seen is all there is. You see things, classify them and place them in your funny little catalogs. Those phenomena that fall outside your definitions are ignored or relegated to the realms of the supernatural. You would do well to avoid use of that word Professor Laban Shrewsbury; there can be nothing supernatural, preternatural would be more accurate.'

Shrewsbury seemed to agree. 'I've studied Alhazred, Prinn and the Comte D'Erlette. I know how little we know, how much more there is than what we see.'

'You study these books full of summonings and divinations, enchantments and necromancies and think you know something? These men barely scratched the surface of the truth, and what they did see was so tainted by their own preconceived notions of what should be that what they finally wrote down was nearly useless. They did what men always do, they classified and cataloged based on whatever philosophy they thought might fit, never thinking there might be things beyond classification. You say you are ready, but I have my doubts. The price is high, too high for one such as you.'

'I know the price, damn you, and I shall pay it. I must know the truth; I must see what lies beyond. Do what you must!' There was urgency in Shrewsbury's voice, and a hint of madness as well.

Whatever Shrewsbury had demanded of Peaslee had apparently been initiated for there was a period of silence during which Shrewsbury suddenly gasped and afterwards his breathing became much louder. 'Keep your eyes closed,' said Peaslee. 'It will take a moment for the *Wza-y'ei* to penetrate the optic nerve and reach your visual cortex. There it will begin reprogramming portions of your subconscious.'

Shrewsbury spoke, 'I thought the trigger would be a chemical, a potion or elixir of some sort.'

'You people are so reliant on how various substances interact with your own chemistry. Those are temporary reactions; very few such treatments can permanently alter your physiology. What the *Wza-y'ei* does is rewrite some of the programming that has been built into your brain, programming that limits the way you see things. The Q'Hrell have a tendency to limit the way their creations can perceive the universe. It gives them an advantage.'

'The Q'Hrell? You mean the Elder Things? I have a star stone in my pocket. It should protect me from the forces of evil.'

Peaslee made a strange sound, not quite a laugh but something that certainly seemed derisive. 'A star stone? Yes, there are creatures that fear such items, though it is not why you think. It has little to do with evil. Are men evil? A man can do things some consider evil but others would consider good. The universe does not and cannot make moral judgments. Nor should you consider those who might be aligned against you as evil, again morality is subjective and even within a species any particular philosophy or position may not be universally held.'

'What do you mean?'

'Amongst men there are factions. You have divided your world into nations, religions, ideologies even occupations and interests. Men are fractious, and the further you are from each other the more likely you are to hold different belief systems. Nearly every other species in the universe is the same. You have a concept of a servitor race that the Byakhee and the Mi-Go have aligned themselves with Hastur, while the Deep Ones serve Cthulhu. What nonsense. Some Deep Ones serve Cthulhu, as do some men. Some Mi-Go pay homage to Hastur, as do some men. But, these races cannot be said to be unified in their beliefs or fealties. Indeed, some members of a species have been separated from their own kind for so long they are barely recognizable to one another. Have you not wondered why there are so many different forms of gelatinous creatures? Shoggoths, Flying Polyps, Tsathaggua's formless spawn, the ropy things that Shub-Niggurath spawns, Shub-Niggurath herself, and her terrestrial counterparts Abhoth, Ubbo-Sathla, and Idh-Ya, whom some call Yithra. They are all so similar because they come from the same source. The Q'Hrell have created Shoggoths for billions of years, modifying them for whatever specialized purposes are needed. Some have gone extinct, some have been exterminated, some have thrived, and some have become servants to other masters while others have become akin to gods, if not something more, but in the beginning, they were just Shoggoths, nothing more. Time, space, and matter can change any species, and often drive wedges between those most closely related. Your species is fractured into thousands of tribes, but you expect an alien species to behave in a consistent manner. Such madness you have wrought on yourselves.' He paused and then said, 'Open your eyes Shrewsbury.'

There followed, this simple command, a brief moment of silence and then a scream unlike anything which I have never before heard. It was a scream of terror, of discovery, of the realization of the awful truth that lurks beyond the veil of reality. It was a scream of a single man discovering his place in the universe and realizing how truly insignificant it was. It was the scream of Pr. Laban Shrewsbury opening his eyes and seeing for the first time. His breathing was labored and panicked as he spoke. 'I can see you! See what you are. Not the bilaterally symmetrical form you wear, nor the queer conical shape that you pretend to. No, I see you as you are, or once were, a pentaradial thing billions of years old.'

'Look through me Shrewsbury, see the *thra* that make up my past, you can move through them, travel through my time and space.'

Shrewsbury's voice was excited almost frantic. 'I can see so much, a world filled with things that I perceive as books but know that that cannot be. I see a star that I know to be Altair, and a world circling it that is home to a great machine, and another circling Epsilon Eridani. These are dead worlds. There is another world, a living world with three suns in the sky, it is full of things that are like you, but not like you. They are sad things, fearful. I can sense their power, immense power, and yet they are afraid. What could things like these be afraid of?'

'Fear is the oldest emotion, and fear of the unknown is the strongest of all motivations, even amongst alien species,' mused Peaslee. 'What else can you see?'

'There are lights flitting within the darkness of open space. Things that might seem titanic while earthbound, but in the void between worlds they seem infinitesimal. They aren't human, but they are recognizable. Some are of flesh, others of stone, and a few are composed of some sort of patterned energy. No two seem alike.'

'What you see are individuals or composite creatures that have tapped into some of the cosmic energies that permeate the universe. They are powerful creatures, and they have a tendency to meddle in the affairs of lesser creatures. Men would call them demons. There are more of them than stars in your sky. On occasion, their purposes may align to yours, but not often.'

Shrewsbury cut him off. 'There are shadows stalking amongst the stars. Cyclopean doesn't begin to address their size. They move through force of will alone, constructing organs and sensors and appendages as they see fit, as the need or whim develops. They are composed of something I cannot classify. They aren't made of matter or energies we recognize. They aren't really alive, not as we know it, which means they can't truly ever be dead either. That which is not dead . . .' Shrewsbury's voice faltered. 'The elemental theory, it is utter nonsense. Earth, air, water, fire, these are meaningless to these entities. They are composed of dark matters and strange energies. The forces of time and space bend to their will. Great Old Ones!'

'Yes, Shrewsbury, the Great Old Ones, they are beings – sometimes entire species – who have learned how to manipulate the fundamental forces of the universe, and change them. Their very presence alters the fabric of space and time. Causation fails. The laws of gravity and motion and energy bend in their presence. Their thoughts are not ours to know.'

Shrewsbury was shaking. 'They aren't evil. Those concepts, good and evil, don't apply. They simply are.'

'The Old Ones are, the Old Ones were, and the Old Ones shall be again,' Peaslee chanted. 'Their very nature corrupts the universe. Man cannot understand such states, let alone survive them. The most you can hope for is to be ignored. And you thought to hold them at bay with your paltry little star stone.'

'But there are ways,' countered Shrewsbury. 'Cthulhu was imprisoned within a . . .' the old man faltered. 'What is it, a prison of order, of chaos, of ordered chaos? A bubble universe? And when the stars are right the prison will simply cease. But the universe is layered. Bubbles within bubbles, bubbles tangential to others. Yog-Sothoth is the gate and the key. The Lurker at the Threshold. But, why does he lurk, what is the gate and where does it go?'

'Shrewsbury stop.' There was an odd tone to Peaslee's voice.

I could see Shrewsbury shaking his head. 'No, there is something there. I can see it moving. It bubbles and seethes within the heart of the galaxy.'

I recognized the tone in Peaslee's voice, it was fear. 'Shrewsbury, you have to come back. You can't, you aren't ready.'

'I have to see it, I have to know. I have to know the truth. The core is so bright, a whirlpool of stars, and something in the center. Something dark, an immense shadow.'

'Stop, I beg of you. The price, I warned you about the price.'

Shrewsbury tittered madly, 'What is the price of knowledge? What is the cost of truth? I have to see, I have to know.'

"From Peaslee there came no response, at least not a verbal one. For no words passed through the man's lips, instead all I heard were the sounds of feet pounding on the soft earth as they ran from the hollow as fast as they could. I rose to see what had happened but the vegetation blocked my view. No longer concerned about being discovered I broke through the brush and ran to Shrewsbury's side.

He was still talking, rambling about concepts I couldn't understand. 'The Feasting Maw, the Bubbler at the Hub. What have I seen? What have I seen!? 'The aging instructor was almost screaming."

"I grabbed him by the shoulders and whether I turned him, or he turned himself I cannot say, but his eyes met mine. It was only an instant, but whatever he had been seeing vanished, and instead he was seeing something else, something connected with me. He gasped and screamed. 'You!' His eyes were black orbs floating in a sea of darkness. 'There are so many of you; thousands, no millions of you stretching out through time and space from the beginning to the end. You are everything, the All In One and One In All! Can you hear them? The flautists? They pipe for you Randolph Carter, Zkauba, Luveh-Keraph, they pipe for you and all the things that you have been and will be.' He stood and turned away from me. 'He's waiting for you, the Black Man, The Crawling Chaos, Nyarlathotep. He waits for you in dreams. Not ours, not our dreams. The dreaming gods. When we dream, we dream of being birds and wolves and butterflies. What do those who slumber in the depths of the frozen polar city dream of? What do slumbering gods dream of?' His voice suddenly became a wail. 'The three-lobed burning eye comes for you, and for us all. We will stride between the stars not between shadows, but with them. And worlds will tremble at our feet!' He spun about and grabbed at me. 'Make it stop,' he pleaded."

"I was shaking in fear and in frustration. 'I don't know how,' I cried out!"

"It was then that he fell to the ground and with his own fingers did the unthinkable. I would have stopped him if I had known what he was doing, but it wasn't until we were back on the street and beneath the lamp light that I could see what had been done. He had stopped screaming by then, though it pains me to believe that his cries had not been heard by those who bordered the old burying ground. I suppose those who live next to such places must learn to ignore such sounds."

"As I had said earlier, it was my intent to bring the poor man to St. Mary's but as we turned down Crane Street Shrewsbury muttered your name, and I realized we were passing by your offices. I protested, for surely a man with such injuries is better off in a fully equipped hospital and not the office of a general practitioner, no offense."

"Shrewsbury insisted. 'Hartwell knows about such things, knows how to keep things quiet,' and so I brought him here. That is my story Doctor Hartwell. It is madness, but not my madness. Please, I beg of you tell no one of my involvement in this. I fear that the name Randolph Carter has besmirched my family too much of late."

I assured my onetime patient that if it became necessary to file a report I would be discrete and fail to remember the name of the Samaritan who came to Professor Shrewsbury's rescue. Indeed, I hoped not to have to file a report at all,

PETER RAWLIK | 71

though I did not express this thought. With this concession, I ushered the nervous Randolph Carter out my door and back into the night.

In my surgery, Shrewsbury lay moaning. Though I had administered a sedative and given him a measure of morphine, it was only just enough to dull the pain. For my purposes, I needed the main awake and lucid. I removed the bandages from his face and irrigated the wound. The old professor moaned but not too loudly. Fearing that he might react violently to what had to be done next, I carefully strapped him to the table, and made sure that he couldn't flail about. Then with a probe and some forceps I gentle reached into the sockets and as quickly as I could, removed the tissue that Shrewsbury in his madness had so crudely destroyed.

The eyes of Professor Shrewsbury bore little resemblance to the shining orbs they must once have been. They were shriveled sacks of black and purple, sad reminders of how vulnerable they were to damage. Once they had been magnificent feats of evolution, and now they were nothing more than waste, destroyed by Peaslee's treatment and Shrewsbury's clawing hands.

As I tossed the lumps of useless flesh into the garbage Shrewsbury mumbled something. I went to his side and asked him to repeat himself. It took a great effort for him to speak to me. He had to tunnel his way back from wherever he was—through the madness, and the pain, and effects of the drugs—but he made it, and with a supreme effort told me of his ultimate horror.

"I can still see," he whispered.

A lesser man would have run screaming, but I hadn't been that man in a long time. This is why Shrewsbury had come to me. He knew I would understand, and what's more, he knew I would sympathize: For he knew that I too had suffered at the hands of the monstrous thing that called itself Professor Nathaniel Wingate Peaslee.

I took his hand in mine and held it tight, reassuring him of our camaraderie in adversity. "I know," I said. "I might be able to help with that." He squeezed my hand in hope. "First I need your help. I need you to look. I need you to see. Peaslee, how do we kill him?"

Shrewsbury was quiet. He held my hand, gripping it tightly, occasionally letting up only to renew his hold again. It went on like this for an hour, maybe longer, in a sustained silence. Near dawn he finally let my hand go. I thought perhaps he had died, but no, he was merely contemplative. It took time, and I had to be patient, but eventually Shrewsbury looked at me with those black, eyeless eyes and opened his mouth. He told me about the past and the future, and of how things linked together. He spoke of stories that would be told, hints that would be given, and misinterpreted. He reminded me that things could be done quickly, or they could be savored over time.

Then he told me what we were going to do, how we would do it, and what price Professor Peaslee would pay.

1913

LETTER FOUND ON A DEAD SAILOR

In 1913, the Great Lakes region was lashed with a winter storm that has since become known as the White Hurricane. The storm lasted five days destroyed 19 ships and killed more than two hundred and fifty people. In the days that followed bodies of lost sailors were recovered as they drifted in to shore. The following letter was found in the pocket of one of these bodies. The address for delivery had been washed away, but the interior pages were still legible. They are presented here along with some relevant facts.

My Perpetual Brothers,

I write to you in a state of panic, our Boston Chapterhouse is lost, burned by an unknown enemy. Eight of our number escaped the flames, but only four of us escaped the city. The others were cut down by sniper fire in front of my own eyes, like deer culled by a bowman. Only I, Urish, Ninuttu, and Ishlish made it to the safe house in Red Hook. There amidst the rabble of a hundred nations we laid low for a few days and gathered our strength. We are now in Buffalo, following the directives for our survival as written by our Masters. In a few hours, we shall board a ship and make our way to the refuge in Canada. The Masters are wise, their plans for survival of our order have thus far been infallible.

We have tried to understand what happened to us, where we stumbled, how we became exposed, but of course there are so many possibilities. What is true we will never know, though I have my suspicions.

I think perhaps it was my recent escapade in a nearby village. There was a man there who had been *etemmu* in May of 1908 and remained so until September of this year. Five years is a long time for a man, and the damage to the psyche of the individual, and to the immediate family, during such extended events can be irreparable. The Romans new the dangers of decimating a population, and only did so when absolutely necessary. So, by extension, to *etemmu* a man for so long indicates a dire need on the part of our Masters. Still, I feel sorry for the man. His wife divorced him, and had taken his three children to live with relatives. I hope someday they are able to reconcile. A man's children should love him.

I think it was because the *etemmu* had been so long that we were exposed. His transition was very public and his travels well documented. Indeed, the newspapers did quite a job publishing his exploits throughout Europe. I myself was summoned a week before the *vemm*, and spent several days in service to the Master who called himself Ys. We added substantially to the *Summa Ysgl*, and this was the cause of my extended service, and may have been a result of the massive amount of information gathered by Ys. But all that time spent there did not go unnoticed. I was accosted by neighbors, and assaulted during the final transition. It is possible that one of his friends or family is the source of our troubles, but more likely I was spotted and tracked by a Watcher. I could have been seen.

I could have been followed. They could have easily returned with me to Boston and trailed me back to the chapterhouse. All this could be my fault.

Still, you should know that even now we carry our copy of the *Summa Ysgl*. It is the only thing we were able to rescue from the chapterhouse before it was destroyed. A high price to pay for a book, but then, as all of the order know, it is more than just a book. It is the great work of the ages, the cornerstone of our lives, and those of our fathers, as it has been for a thousand generations. We have served our Masters since man first developed language, and we have kept both the book and the bloodline pure. We have endured the coming of the ice and the deluge, we have survived the reign the barbarian king, and that of the skull-faced wizard, the Greeks and the Romans learned from us, as did the caliphates. We fled before the hordes of Genghis, and the witch hunts of blood thirsty Rome. We have endured to preserve what we have been taught to preserve. The great work of the Great Race that we serve. The Order of Vizal endures perpetually, always in motion, never resting, never changing, always in service.

And we will be well rewarded, for as it is written in the lesser books that our ascension is guaranteed. Those who serve the *Summa Ysgl* shall dwell forever in the afterlife of dreams. That has been our promised reward, and even the Master Ys reminded me of it before he transitioned.

Odd. I know that the Master that came to us most recently was not truly named Ys. That such a name was nothing more than a convenience, and that his true name can never

be known. And yet I have to wonder why he has chosen that appellation. At first, I thought it was strictly a play on words, he was addressed as Mister Ys, and this produced the same phonetics as the English word "mysteries", and thus induced subconsciously a kind of wonder or phantasmal emotional state. But as I think about it, I wonder if there was more to it. The word Ys is integral to the title of the great work.
True, the name Ys and the word *Ysgl* use entirely different glyphs in the old language, but they share similar pronunciations, and I cannot help but wonder if it is indeed a play on words.
The meaning of *Summa Ysgl* is so very complicated, but of all the translations I find that the phrase "Chronicle of the Monsters of the Earth" as being the most literal of translations, with the understanding that "monsters of the Earth" signifies mankind itself. The implication here being that Mister Ys could translate to the phrase "Mister Monster".

I have dwelt on this thought for many days now.
With the chapterhouse gone, I have little else to do. Is it a heresy to ponder the motivations of the eternal Gods themselves? Perhaps, but I think it may be otherwise. We are taught to seek knowledge where we can, perhaps it is hidden in the very words that we use. Perhaps Mister Ys is an allegory, perhaps his very name is meant to convey a message, or multiple messages. He may be a mystery, or a monster, or perhaps something else. Perhaps, he is something altogether unexpected. Could he be more than what he seems, or perhaps even less?
Is he a man elevated beyond his position, one taken out of the afterlife and sent to work amongst us, to bring us into the grace of that which we seek? A man become a god?
Perhaps. Once again, I suspect these might be

heretical thoughts, but I am and always will be the most devout of us.

At the safe house in Red Hook we found a tile with the symbol for this year on it. We pried it off and found a note providing directions for us to move through up river and then across the state to Buffalo and then to Thunder Bay in Canada on the far side of Lake Superior. There was a small bag of gold coins, Spanish in origin, with which to fund our journey. Not surprisingly the bank manager where we exchanged them seemed astonished at their antiquity, and our willingness to part with them at only their value as ore. He was sure they were worth more as relics, but we had no time or desire to have them appraised.

We have bought passage on a small freighter heading to Fort William at the far end of Lake Superior. Captain Thompson and his four crewmen, apparently a father and his sons, are polite but rather reserved. Our accommodations are small, but the journey is only about a week. The first mate Jack, assures us that the voyage will be calm enough for us to walk about on deck if we wish. We sail tomorrow at dawn. With any luck, we shall reach Fort William by the Eleventh.

Your brother, in motion
Lamashtu Vangabini Bezal

The body on which this letter was discovered was positively identified as that of John "Jack" Thompson, who had been a crew member of the SS James Carruthers, a freighter which sank during the White Hurricane while steaming from Fort William to Midland. Despite the face being severely disfigured, identification was achieved by the man's father Thomas Thompson who noted that the body had the same height, build of his son, and the hair color was identical. Additionally, there were several distinguishing features that made identification more specific. The corpse was missing an eyetooth and had tattooed initials "J.T." on the left forearm. Several scars were consistent with those known to belong to the man, and most importantly the body had a birth defect in which the second and third toes of his feet had grown together. The Thompson family took possession of the body on November 11th.

However, as the family prepared the body for burial the actual Jack Thompson arrived at the viewing alive and well. For reasons he could not explain, he had not accompanied the ship on its final voyage, and had instead journeyed to Toronto where he apparently had fallen into a drunken stupor. He was astonished to find his name listed amongst the dead, and returned home by train.

The body that had been mistaken for Thompson was never identified, and was buried with four other unknown sailors. Rumors that all four had similarly fused toes have never been confirmed. Requests to exhume the bodies to undergo modern identification tests, have been denied.

1935

THE TEMPORARY CHRONOLOGIST

I. The Statement of Wingate Peaslee

27 July, 1935

There are those who would say that fate is a queer, almost ironic thing. If I were not a rational man I might agree with them. It is easy to fall prey to such beliefs, easier still when the central actor has participated in events in which many lives were lost and others were shattered, while he himself emerged unscathed. My friend, Professor William Dyer is just such a man, and as one of the surviving members of the tragic Miskatonic University Antarctic Expedition there are those who would say what happened here in Australia was some kind of curse. Others will look at what has happened and cast a suspicious eye at the aged geologist and think that these things were no mere accident. I tell you that I doubt that either is the case. Admittedly I know little of what has happened over the last seven days, but I do know all that led up to that point, and perhaps in this manner I may serve to lay the groundwork for those who are trying to comprehend the tragedy that has played out in the Australian desert.

For the record, my name is Doctor Wingate Peaslee, I reside in Arkham, Massachusetts, where I am employed as an instructor of Psychology at Miskatonic University. I have come to Australia in the company of my father, Nathaniel Wingate Peaslee, who is also an instructor at Miskatonic University, though in his case both of Psychology and Economics. How he came to be versed in two so distinct subject matters is itself a result of a strange, almost singular event that is indisputably the causal factor for our presence in Australia, and the Miskatonic University's expedition into the vast and desolate landscape that dominates the interior of the continent.

It was in May of 1908 that my father suddenly collapsed at his podium. He had been complaining of queer dreams and sensations for several days prior, and had taken medication for a headache that morning. It must have been quite nerve-wracking to watch a man of such vitality and mental superiority suddenly crumple to the ground like a bag of clothes. Most of the class was stunned into inaction, but a few found the fortitude to tend to him and to fetch help. It was initially feared that he had suffered a stroke, but he showed none of the typical signs, and instead was quickly transported to our home where our neighbor, Doctor Stuart Hartwell, attended to him. That first night was a horrific experience for myself and my siblings, for we watched our mother fly through the whole range of human emotion from fear to anger to despair, and all we could do was watch in silence, terrified that the world as we knew it was about to come to an end. We had no idea that when he woke up things would be so much worse than if he had just passed away.

He roused from unconsciousness sometime in the wee hours of the next day, and although he tried to conceal it, my mother and the doctor soon became aware of a profound shift in his personality. His memory of his family and friends was gone, as was that of his entire life. He spoke English and had some knowledge of history, but his idiolect, diction and formulation seemed oddly anachronistic, and was sometimes bewildering. Most disturbing was the way in which his emotions seemed to be subverted or suppressed. After seeing him lying there in the bed my older brother, Robert, burst into tears and proclaimed that man was not our father. While it was clear that the body was still that of Nathaniel Wingate Peaslee, it was hard to argue that the consciousness, the tongue that spoke through those lips, that no longer knew us as his children, was in any way the man we once knew.

What followed was five years of turmoil. My mother moved us out of our house on Crane Street while the man who had once been our father became known in the papers as "The

Man Who Forgot Himself." As documented in the papers and later through piecing together of eyewitness accounts he first began a regular series of trips to the local museums, libraries and universities, where he studied voraciously. His tastes were not only varied but esoteric as well and he was just as likely to be delving into the obscure histories of lost Amazonian tribes as he was to be reviewing treatises on medieval metaphysics. In 1909, he began travelling the world, most notably by spending a month in the Himalayas, returning only briefly in 1910 to finalize the divorce between he and mother. For the next three years he became a whirlwind travelling to the remotest of areas including Arabia, the Congo, the Arctic and various locales in the Americas. He also took to meeting with the most notorious of individuals, some so vile in character that it is best not to mention them by name. All the while those that maintained contact with him suggested that his travels and studies had seemed to instill within him a sense of disappointment, though with what exactly they could not say.

In the summer of 1913 the man returned to Arkham and as he settled into our old house on Crane Street some wondered what he would do in our sleepy little town. Meanwhile, he himself expressed a kind of ennui, and hinted to various associates that he was experiencing dreams similar to those that had led up to his change so many years ago. This led to the belief, encouraged by him, that a change in his demeanor was soon to be expected. In late September such speculation bore fruit, and after dismissing his housekeeper he once again collapsed. In complete reversal of his previous attack, he emerged from his seizure in possession of his old personality and had no knowledge of the intervening years. Indeed, he emerged from unconsciousness speaking, still lecturing as if he was in the same classroom of five years earlier, as if nothing at all had ever happened.

It took several months for my father to recover from his ordeal. Sadly, my mother had embarked on her own career and while she was happy to visit her former husband she had no inclination to rekindle their relationship. Similarly, my brother Robert showed no desire to establish a connection with our father. Consequently, it was only my sister and I that were unwilling to attend to my suddenly bewildered parent. In

February of 1914 I moved back into the house on Crane Street and my father resumed teaching at Miskatonic University attempting a return to normalcy.

It was not to be.

My father's nights became fitful, he was plagued by dreams of the most wild and bizarre kind, and of feelings of alienation and dread. With the outbreak of the Great War his thoughts turned to periods and events in history that seemed to bear no relation to each other, and yet seemed in his mind to be causal to various current affairs. His concept of time, particularly causality took a bizarre turn, and he oft times spoke of events well before he could possibly know of their occurrence. His strange prescient ability made many uncomfortable, but excited the men of the mathematics department who saw my father as evidence of what Dr. Einstein was proposing.

Throughout the year the dreams evolved and my father would describe to me landscapes of titanic jungles and fascinating, alien architecture that defied human design, decorated with carvings in curvilinear mathematical designs. In his dreams, the sun was abnormally swollen while the moon though recognizable, was different, but exactly how, he could not say. Likewise, the constellations of stars seemed altered and only approximations of the stars and shapes he was familiar with.

By the autumn of 1914 it became apparent that he could no longer keep pace with his normal workload, and took leave from his position teaching at the end of that season. By October of the next year it became clear to both my father and I that his dreams were beginning to impact not only his ability to work, but his health as well. Following my suggestion, he and I began a rigorous study of the science of psychology which eventually led to my professorship in the field. In the years that followed my father embarked on an attempt to retrace the steps that he had taken during those lost years. Here he discovered that his prior consultations in various libraries of volumes of elder lore had left those he had come in contact with emotionally shaken. Furthermore, on examining the tomes he had consulted previously he discovered annotations that appeared to be done in his own hand, but in languages and idioms that were totally alien to him. Even more disturbing was the existence of one note that consisted not of any recognizable alphabet, but rather of curvilinear hieroglyphics that were unmistakably akin to those that he so often saw in his dreams inscribed into the stones of an alien city.

It was during the course of these studies that my father identified a curious myth pattern regarding an unnamed demon race that supposedly preyed on people, possessing their bodies and exploring the world. The mind of the victim would be transported backwards through time and interrogated, sometimes meeting other such victims from wildly diverse periods in history. This paralleled my father's dreams which were so complex that they often included a variety of other actors, such as representatives of past ages like the Roman Titus Sempronius Blaesus, a Florentine monk named Corsi, Khephnes of Egypt's 14th Dynasty, and James Woodville who lived in Suffolk under Cromwell. Inventively, the fictitious narrative also included individuals from the future, some of which seemed quite common, like the Australian physicist Nevil Kingston-Brown, to the outlandish Yiang-Li a court philosopher of the Tsan Chan Empire that rose to power in the 50th century, and the enigmatic Nug Soth who was a sorcerer of the dark conquerors that would ravage the planet more than 14,000 years hence. Even more fantastic were those actors that were obviously not part of the human race such as S'gg'ha who was a member of a semi-vegetable species that had once resided in the polar regions, and Eneg who claimed to be of a reptilian species that had flourished in the Cretaceous Period.

The discovery of such a myth, which seemed oddly Hindu or Buddhist in its incorporation of the transfer of memories and personalities through time, had engendered in my father his own memory of being cast backwards in time. Of what he saw in these dreams he declined to elaborate, at least with me, for he recognized that they were artificial memories, generated from his study of the legends and lore that had been built up around the cult that supposedly served these strange demons.

This realization seemed to comfort my father. He was, in his mind, a victim. Whatever the cause of his sudden disassociation and the generation of a secondary personality, that personality had fallen victim to a superstition and had instilled in him a whole series of false memories. These fancies were now bubbling up through his subconscious and manifesting as the dreams that haunted his nights. Using this realization as a crutch he was able to beat back the worrying dread that plagued him, and in the time following 1922 resumed a normal life. He even returned to the university, but instead of resuming his place as an economist, he took up a position as an instructor in psychology, a position he was eminently qualified for.

But the dreams, and his research into them did not stop.

Indeed, as he grew more detached, and more in control, he began to organize his notes both those on his dreams and those related to the legends out of which they had grown. Over the years a coherent document appeared, and in an attempt to educate his peers concerning his case, and those similar to it, my father deemed it important to publish his research. Thus, beginning in 1928 and running into 1929, a series of papers appeared in various volumes of the Journal of the American Psychological Society detailing his entire history and course of study, complete with crude sketches of some of the architecture and hieroglyphics.

It was these articles that engendered the latest phase of my father's ordeal, and would bring both of us to Australia. In the summer of 1934, my father received a letter by way of the Psychological Society from an Australian Mining Engineer by the name of Robert Mackenzie. In it he relayed his discovery, in 1932, of stone blocks of some size which bore markings strikingly similar to those detailed in my father's publications, which he had been shown by a Dr. E. M. Boyle. Boyle was a physician who—while studying certain unusual events that had occurred during his youth in the town of Mount Macedon—had developed a strong interest in dreams, folklore and their impact on individuals. Together the two proposed to my father an expedition back to the area where Mackenzie had seen the hieroglyphics. It took some doing, but my father was not without supporters and in due course a small expedition was funded through the Miskatonic University Explorers' Club.

Our party, consisting of myself, my father, three other faculty members and six graduate students, sailed from Boston harbor on March 28, 1935, accompanied by Mr. Mackenzie who had traveled to the States a few weeks earlier. Of the team that we had assembled—including the geologist William Dyer, the historian Ferdinand Ashley and the anthropologist Tyler Freeborn—it seems I was the most useless. To rectify this, I endeavored to become a qualified pilot as quickly as possible, and although my experience was limited, I became proficient in the operation of small planes in fair weather. It was a skill that I was assured would be useful to the team once we reached Australia and had to scour the interior desert for signs of Mackenzie's stones.

Crossing the Atlantic and working our way through the Mediterranean and down the Suez Canal to the Indian Ocean we reached the coast of Western Australia in late May. It took us a few days to finalize our preparations, but Mackenzie and Boyle had done a fine job of organizing on their end and we departed only three days after arriving in Port Hedland. We traveled by rail to the gold mining town of Marble Bar, and there loaded the last of our supplies onto the tractors and headed roughly east following the ridges of the rocky sands that formed the landscape. On Friday May 31, we forded a branch of the De Grey River and entered into what Mackenzie and Boyle called the Outback.

Up until this point we had been accompanied by a number of native aborigines, which Mackenzie referred to using the derogatory term blackfellows, but once we crossed the river they abandoned us. Mackenzie said that they were a superstitious lot, uneducated and foolish. Watching them fade and ultimately fall beneath the vaporous horizon as we drove our tractors into that vast unknowable desert, I could not help but wonder which group of men was more foolish, the men who trusted their technology and forged headlong against the odds, or those who stayed behind, trusting in the knowledge of the natural world imparted to them by generations of their ancestors.

As we ventured east the landscape took on a peculiarly reddish hue. The region, while made famous for some gold strikes, was primarily known for its iron ore, which formed the basis for most of the work done in the area. According to Mackenzie, it was the deposits of iron that had tinted the sands and rocks red. I took him at his word, but chuckled only halfheartedly when he spoke of the flash floods that had sculpted the landscape. They would start off as violent rainstorms, sometimes miles away, with the rushing waters gathered together and funneled by the rocky sands and hills, forming great torrents stained red as blood. The waters were unstoppable and would carry off both men and beasts. If one were swept away, drowning was preferable, for the waters also carried rocks the size of a man's fist traveling at tremendous speeds. Anyone – anything – floating in the sudden river would find himself being slowly pummeled to death. When the bodies finally washed ashore downstream near the coast, they would be swollen and stained red, not from blood or bruising, but from the crimson-stained waters that had dyed and bloated the flesh. Mackenzie's assistant, Tupper, told of one man who had arrived in such a fashion, and been fished out of the water weighing nearly three hundred pounds. Yet when he had been identified by his wife by a tattoo on his chest all testified that he had been a man who had barely weighed a hundred and twenty pounds.

At this my mouth gaped for a full ten or so seconds before the laughter of those around me led me to realize that I had been the victim of an elaborate tall-tale. Our membership from this point on consisted of the five Miskatonic University faculty members I have mentioned before, Mackenzie and his assistant Tupper who was also a miner, the elderly and affable Doctor Boyle, a guide and pilot by the name of Conyers, two surveyors George Whitely and George Whitley, a mechanic named Molesworth, and the six graduate students who were Ramsey, Bryan, Clayton, Klein, James, and Frank. Just as important as the staff were the five tractors that carried us, our equipment and supplies. Initially we had divided the tractors into two for transporting the team and three for the equipment, but Conyers ordered the equipment and supplies split up amongst all the vehicles and staff apportioned out as well. In this way if the vehicles ever became separated the passengers would not be stranded without food or water.

We stopped about three times each day to stretch and tighten our loads. During these periods, Dr. Boyle would entertain us with selections from his collection of phonographs which he played on an aging Victrola. Unfortunately, Boyle's taste in music was somewhat unorthodox, being dominated by works by composers such as Debussy, Ravel, de Hond, and Fanelli. Of these the most grating were the works of Ambrose de Hond whom I and the rest of the expedition found terribly annoying and disruptive. Fortunately, the man was also a fan of opera and had a fine selection of works performed by Lilli Rochelle and incomparable baritone Gravelle.

It had been more than a decade since I had seen Gravelle perform in Providence. He had performed in Carnival with Rochelle and with Enrico Borelli in a minor role. It had been a magnificent performance, a version of Faust, I suppose. In which the Devil falls in love with a beautiful girl who spurns him, and so the devil kills her, and thus denies her beauty to not only himself, but to the world as well. A cautionary tale, concerning the attempt to own things that don't belong to us, that simply can't be possessed no matter how hard one wishes for the opposite to be true. Sitting there in the desert night, listening to those magnificent voices, I could almost see the production playing out in my mind's eye, as if I was in a cinema enjoying a film. Sometimes I would lose myself in those memories as if they were real, as if I could play them out again and again in my head. Shadows out of the past, to combat the shadows that haunted my present. If only I had known then that the expedition would get so much darker, and that these moments, sitting in the dark and listening to opera, would be used to brighten later melancholy days.

On the third day of June our goal finally began to emerge. For it was on that day that we first caught sight of the cyclopean masonry that Mackenzie had told us about, and there, faint but still visible, were the carved curvilinear hieroglyphs that we had come in search of. One might have thought that investigation and exploration would have begun immediately, but Dyer and Mackenzie were adamant that no one enter the ruins until after the vehicles had been unloaded, the equipment secured and the camp established. Even then, the obvious work areas were first roughly delineated by senior staff and then surveyed in with markers by the two Georges. It was tedious work, but all agreed that it would be better to take things slow and methodically than to rush in and potentially destroy the exact things we were looking for.

In this I found my services as a pilot extremely useful as each night the shifting sands would alter the landscape, sometimes burying areas that we had designated of interest, but also revealing new sections of the landscape as in need of surveying and exploration. Consequently, it became a habit of mine to take almost a daily flight in the decades-old Sopwith Gnu that we had trudged out into the desert with. It was, despite its age, a serviceable machine and I thoroughly enjoyed flying her for the fifteen or twenty minutes it took to track each day's changes.

Mackenzie was at times insufferable. He frequently complained about the slow pace of work and suggested that we send a truck back for some aborigine laborers to assist us. Yet in the same breath he would complain about how lazy they were and that once they arrived we would have to be careful and lock up anything of value. Such a strange thing to see a man who so despised a people he seemed to be so dependent on.

After a month of digging we had uncovered and secured more than a thousand blocks in various stages of wear. Most of these were carved megaliths, while some were obviously pavement stones, cut either in squares or in octagons. A scant few appeared to be architectural in nature, either parts of arches or groins. Despite our efforts, we failed to find any trace of systematic arrangement that would imply a building or a structure of some sort, and these led to some wild speculation on Dyer's part as to the potential immeasurable age of the stones themselves. In the meanwhile, Freeborn—the anthropologist—had found amongst the symbols traces of patterns that hinted at some of the darker myths endemic in the Papuan and Polynesian societies, particularly of those concerning the Motugra Islands. Of us all, Freeborn seemed the most distracted and yet the most focused. He had been recently married, and had left his wife Samantha just days after returning from a brief honeymoon, and consequently spent a great deal of time writing letters to his bride. In these he would detail what he himself believed was a fair attempt to develop a rough pre-history of the Indo-Australian region based on the shape and complexity of the hieroglyphic characters he was uncovering, and how he believed they had spread through the surrounding areas. He was particularly interested in the similarities with symbols found amongst the Naacal of the Ponape Scripture and others found amongst ruins at the base of the certain plateaus inhabited by the abhorrent Tcho-Tcho. Of his model of history he was quite practical, realizing that it was little more than speculation based on a handful of singular data points that could be interpreted in a thousand different ways—pushed this direction or that by the advent of new evidence or events—still his "Temporary Chronology," as he called it, made for fascinating talk around the nightly fire.

At the beginning of June my father began to show signs of insomnia and restlessness, and when questioned would speak of a perplexing feeling of familiarity. He took to walking at night and in the process, would uncover fragments of ancient monuments half-buried in the sands. Of these novel locales, he would often spend considerable time trying to divert our excavations, and in failing to do so would instead dig frustratingly at the sands that seeped back into his diggings faster than he could remove it. More than once in this time did he return to the camp raving about some extraordinary find, only to be unable to once more locate it for the rest of the team. Of these occurrences, he was inclined to blame the drifting sands, rather than his own faulty memory, lack of systematic mapping, or even his own wild imagination.

All of this maddening speculation on my father's part came to a head on the night of July 17. It had been a windy day and as usual my father set out on one of his nocturnal walks. This was witnessed by the miner Tupper who remembered seeing him wander out of camp towards the Northeast just after eleven. Around 3:30 the next morning a violent gusting windstorm assaulted the camp, and Mackenzie spouted some nonsense concerning aboriginal folklore of great stone huts underneath the sand where terrible things have happened and gale force winds are spawned and belched onto the surface. The storm subsided at four, and most of the expedition returned to sleep, leaving only Professor Dyer to witness the return of my father to the camp.

He was in a ravaged and frenzied state. Apparently, he had cast what little remnants of patience he still held aside, rejecting shovel, gloves and related equipment as the hindrances they had become. Attacking the sand with his bare hands, he tore away at the very earth that had pitted itself so firmly against his efforts. Dyer summoned Boyle and myself to tend to this feverish man. In his frustrations and bare digging at the earth, it did a fair amount of damage to his hands. They were now abraded and the skin had worn quite thin, even cracking apart, from his feverish diggings. A thorough investigation in decent lighting revealed many of his fingernails had split and been torn from the very nailbeds in which they rested. Boyle and I did our best to clean up the hands of my father, dressing and bandaging the wounds as well as we could. After we finished, the three of us had a hushed, heated discussion about what the others in camp might think if they caught rumor of this. The decision was made that arthritis would be the most reasonable explanation for the sudden appearance of these protective wrappings.

My father tried to sleep, but his state of mind bordered on mania. He talked unceasingly and explained how he had become fatigued and had laid down in the sands to rest, and upon finally reaching sleep was overcome by the most frightful of dreams until the windstorm had forced him to wake. He seemed to take a keen interest in redirecting the progress of the excavation away from the northeast, citing the dearth of blocks or any other evidence to proceed in that direction. So forceful was he that he made me go up in the plane and survey the area that he had been wandering in. Afterwards, when my reconnaissance showed nothing of note, he convinced me that his health had turned for the worse. Doctor Boyle agreed, and privately mentioned the words "nervous exhaustion" and suggested we honor his wishes to leave.

On July 20, I and my father climbed into the Sopwith and flew the thousand miles southwest to Perth. It was a ten-hour flight, with multiple stops along the way, but we made it safely to the coastal town, checked into a hotel and then booked passage on the next steamer to Liverpool. The *Empress* left port late on the morning of the twenty-fifth. Unwilling to reach my destination in the dark I decided instead to stay in Perth one more night and leave on the next morning. It was as I prepared for takeoff that the local constabulary approached me and informed me of the tragedy that had occurred in my absence. The expedition had suffered an attack, and Doctor Boyle and two of the graduated students were dead. Freeborn had been wounded and much of his work destroyed by fire. Most disturbing of all was that the attack had not been initiated by strangers, but rather had been carried out by one of its own members. Indeed, according to the Chief Constable, Professor William Dyer had even confessed to the killings.

And so, I sit here in Perth, a guest of the local Police. I am not incarcerated, but neither am I free to leave. I long to mount the Sopwith and race back to our diggings, but that has been expressly forbidden. All I can do is wait and explain to the authorities why we were out in the middle of nowhere. Of course, like any other man, my mind races in a thousand directions, speculating on what has happened to my friends and colleagues, while at the same time being thankful that both my father and I were not involved and escaped injury.

II. The Confession of William Dyer

26 July, 1935

My name is William Dyer, I am a Professor of Geology employed by Miskatonic University in Arkham, Massachusetts where I also reside. I give this statement of my own free will in order to clarify the sequence of events that led up to the violence of the day before. Three people are dead and my colleague lies injured. Once more I must stand up and explain why those deaths occurred, and rationalize not only the decisions I made, but also those times when I chose to do nothing at all. It seems that in this case, as in many others, both action and inaction played a role in this tragedy.

It is true that this is not the first time that I have been party to an expedition that ended in the catastrophic death of some of its members. I admit and acknowledge this, but I assure you the events that occurred during that ill-fated trip to Antarctica have no bearing on what has happened here, save in the most cursory way. What I saw in those polar wastes prepared me for this expedition in a most curious manner. I had hoped that I would not be made to act in the way I did, but now that the deed is done I find myself overcome with a sense of preternatural calm, almost a kind of self-satisfied relief. I did what I had to do, and that is all. It was I who shot Doctor Erasmus Malachi Boyle. I emptied my gun, striking him three times, twice in the chest and once in the head. I feel no sense of guilt regarding my actions and I hope the men that witnessed them can come to similar terms. My only regret was that I had not acted sooner and risen to take control of the situation before madness consumed the old man.

The events that precipitated Boyle's death can be traced back to the morning of July the 18th. It was well before dawn, the whole camp had been awakened by a rather vicious windstorm that had buffeted us for about an hour, upending equipment and dislodging some of the tents from their moorings. Mackenzie had gone on at length about how such winds were attributed by the locals to preternatural forces as described in myths concerning underground huts and the sleeping giant *Buddai*, who waits eternally resting his head on his arm. It was all nonsense, of course. Sudden winter storms in the desert are common phenomena as any naturalist can tell you. It was sometime later, after the rest of the camp had settled in for a few more hours of sleep that I sat alone smoking my pipe and watched as one of my colleagues stumbled in from the benighted desert, disheveled and frantic from his hours away from camp.

The queer temporary amnesia that my colleague Nathaniel Wingate Peaslee suffered is well documented. For five years, beginning in 1908 he had undergone a radical transformation, assuming an entirely different personality, one that seemed almost alien to those who cared for him. During this time, he explored the most remote areas of the world and delved into the most esoteric of researches alongside some of the most notorious of individuals. It ended one day in 1913, with the return of his original psyche. However, ever since he has been haunted by feelings that can only be described as a kind of cosmic dread, wild and terrifyingly symbolic dreams, which were accompanied by a persistent restlessness that manifested as a pernicious form of insomnia.

Peaslee's nervous breakdown, if one could call it that, did not impact him alone. The episode cost him his marriage and his family. His ex-wife Alice has remarried and has little contact with Nathaniel, who has no recollection of what he did to the woman he married and still loves. Obviously, he has been able to rectify his relationship with his son Wingate, and apparently with his daughter Hannah as well. But there is an incredible distance between him and his son Robert, who joined the Army to get away from his father. He apparently served with distinction and was attached to a security detail during the negotiation of the Treaty of Versailles. After the war, he stayed away from Arkham for many years, working as a private investigator for the rich in Palm Beach and Atlanta. He did return to Massachusetts a few years ago, working for the State Police, and had even been assigned to Arkham for a while, before being transferred out to Aylesbury. There were rumors that he was a "confirmed bachelor", but that was put to rest when he married the Halsey-Griffith girl. Still one has to wonder what has to happen to raise a child to be a man like that. Too much time with his mother and not enough with his father I suppose, though admittedly I am no psychologist.

It was Peaslee's research into his own dreams, which led him to publish several monographs on the content, imagery and symbols associated with them. It was these monographs, read by Boyle and shared with Mackenzie who had seen such hieroglyphics in the deserts of Western Australia that caused both Australians to write to Peaslee and urge him to organize an expedition. Confronting an opportunity to come face to face with concrete evidence of the things that he suspected had been planted in his subconscious, Peaslee agreed and hoped to ultimately find an end to that which haunted his dreams.

Sadly, as the expedition and excavations proceeded, Peaslee's dreams became worse, not better. He could not sleep more than a few hours a night, and spent his time wandering the desert. On many occasions, he would return from these wanderings with what he believed were fresh insights to the breadth and scope of the ruin we were unearthing, and was constantly trying to move our activities faster and further towards the northeast. When he returned that night, I could see he was in a terrible state, and despite the urgings of Doctor Boyle and the younger Peaslee, the man refused to rest. He spoke of once again exploring the quadrant northeast of where we were focused, but this time he said he had found nothing of interest. This he stressed in the most unusual manner, urging us to forgive him for his previous insistence and to direct our work in other directions. He even demanded that his son take to the air and confirm that there was nothing to be seen in that direction. What was more, he complained about being exhausted and on the verge of a mental breakdown and made his son promise to take him in the plane and set him on a ship away from this desolate place. He said these things with the wildest of looks in his eyes, and it was clear to all of us that he was on the brink of collapse. The younger Peaslee and Doctor Boyle even had to bandage up the poor man's hands, he had apparently injured them somehow. When approached regarding this, reason of arthritic troubles was offered in response. This perplexed me, as it was a condition I have neither seen nor heard of plaguing the elder Peaslee in all the years I recall having worked near and with the man. Strange indeed, after the flight to confirm that there was truly nothing worth our immediate investigation visible to the northwest of us, both Peaslees packed for the trip to Perth, and on the morning of the 20th departed.

After they had left, I ordered the two Georges to travel into the region to the northeast of us and create a rough survey grid. I don't know why I did this, perhaps the eldest Peaslee did protest too much, but something had aroused my suspicions. It is my belief that this suspicion may stem from his sudden, yet inexplicable onset of arthritis. I felt that a bit of time examining the area at ground level was warranted. I expected the pair of Georges to be gone for most of the day, for the zone I had asked them to mark off was about nine miles square. To my surprise they returned in just a few hours and asked that I and several others join them to examine something they had found. They were surprisingly sedate, but also somewhat vague concerning the nature of their discovery, and lacking any real motivation, I left the vast majority of the team behind. Only Mackenzie and I joined the survey crew on their trek back to the northeast.

In retrospect, I should have brought the whole team. Unlike Peaslee, the Georges were professionals and had not only marked their find with a flag, but had laid out a series of markers that allowed us to traverse the terrain of thin sand and rocky shoals in a direct, highly efficient manner. A mile or so from the camp, extruding from the rust-red alluvial sands there was the tell-tale sign of a piece of manufactured metal, reflecting the sunlight, however dull that sunlight may have been. It was obviously part of a larger object, the majority of which was still buried in the earth. What we could see was the end of a metallic casing, about an inch thick and fifteen inches on end. About six inches of the case was above the ground and on one end I could see several of the curvilinear hieroglyphs that we so often saw engraved on the monoliths we were unearthing. It was clear that we had found our first artifact.

That it was not wood or clay or stone was astounding, and immediately I was reassessing the history that my colleague Tyler Freeborn had assembled as a rough framework for understanding the area. The anthropologist would have to revise his "Temporary Chronology" to take into account a civilization that was further advanced than we had thought.

Indeed, up until this point I had thought that we were dealing with an unknown civilization on par with that of ancient Greece or Rome, but the object before me spoke of technology and artistry well beyond the Bronze or even the Iron Age. In my excitement, I lost my head and without a bit of restraint I began clearing the sand away with one hand while wrenching the object free with the other. I heard Mackenzie gasp and utter some words of caution, but they were too late.

In mere seconds, the object was haphazardly pulled from the ground and into full view of everyone. It was as I have stated, a rectangular box about an inch thick, fifteen inches on one side, and twenty on the other. It was comprised of some kind of metal, though what exactly I could not say. It was an alloy of some sort, and was tremendously light like aluminum, but rigid and hard like chromium steel. All six planes of the object were flat, and only one of the long edges showed the hieroglyphics that marked it as related to our excavation. Here also along this long edge was what appeared to be a hinge that allowed it to be opened. Still overcome by my zeal I grasped the edges so as to pry the thing open. Fortunately, Mackenzie was able to stop me. Reasoned with, I and the others carried the metallic wonder back to the camp and summoned the entire team.

There in the safety of the largest of our tents, Clayton

took a series of pictures documenting the condition of the artifact before our mechanic Molesworth, his hands wrapped in kid gloves, found a point of inflection and with the greatest of care opened it up for all to see. Inside was what could only be described as a kind of file. The covers were made of a thin metal not dissimilar to that of the box, and were bound together with a kind of complex hook mechanism that also allowed the thing to be hung or carried by a single finger.

Between the metallic sheets were pages of a material that was not paper but reminded the student Klein of a derivative of cellulose. By his recollection the material in question was resistant to a wide variety of damaging factors including heat, fire, water, acids and decay, and were it not for the exorbitant costs of manufacturing would be considered a prime candidate for use in the construction of books and similar documents.

The pages were not blank, but rather were decorated in characters of some unknown language placed there using brush strokes of a colored pigment. These characters were once again the same sort of curvilinear hieroglyphs we had become so familiar with, but to see them set down in a manner that clearly formed not only words but full sentences, even whole passages, was utterly fascinating to the entire team. As we leafed through the book Clayton kept taking pictures, while both Freeborn and Ashley speculated wildly on the age and significance of the text, none of which they could even read.

To me Freeborn is a contradiction, and this arises from the little information I have on his background. He is, as I understand it the son of Quakers who sent him to study farming and the sciences of horticulture at an agricultural college in Boston. While there he stumbled into the science of Anthropology, and without his father's consent or knowledge switched his studies and earned his degree. Afterwards, he was rightfully disowned by his family and had to finish his graduate level studies while working at the Cabot Museum in Boston. During his employ, there was some scandal concerning Freeborn, a rather obscene artifact, and a Polynesian man who performed some ceremony in the middle of the night. The details of this incident remain clouded with rumor, and even now, years later, this scandalous reputation preceded him. Freeborn was cleared of all wrongdoing, but the incident tainted his record. It was only through the machinations of some members of society that serve on the boards of both the museum and Miskatonic University that he was able to pursue his doctorate and find employ at Miskatonic. It is clear from his behavior that he is still a little rough around the edges, and his subordinates take advantage of that. Professionally he seems skilled enough, but I cannot abide a man who betrayed his family in such a manner.

James, who was Freeborn's primary assistant and a natural translator, opined that the challenge in translating the document would lie in the fact that the language bore little resemblance to any of known means of communication, though it did bear a slight resemblance to the characters used as a cipher in a diary held in the rare book room at Miskatonic University.

It was as the historians and their students were lamenting the unlikelihood of having a translation any time soon that a turn of the page revealed a loose piece of the material that clearly did not belong with the rest of the volume. It was not bound in with the other pages, the ink was a different color, and the hieroglyphs were obviously the work of a different hand.

What's more, was that beneath each row of hieroglyphs was another line but these were in characters of an entirely different alphabet. This fragment excited Freeborn immensely, and he and Ashley began to mutter about the Rosetta Stone, the potential to translate not just the fragment but the whole book, and even the inscriptions on the megaliths. That both languages gave the impression of being incomprehensible did not seem to concern them.

We dallied over the object in our possession for an hour or more, and then the majority of us returned to work. Emboldened by our find, I sent the two Georges and several of the more observant graduate students back into the area where the encased book had been found. Only Freeborn and James remained behind, determined to apply themselves to the translation of the text as best they could. Sadly, our efforts scouring the desert for similar artifacts proved fruitless, and we returned to camp that evening exhausted and empty handed. It was that night—as the 20th turned to the 21st—that Freeborn and James, working in the tent, held the pages up to the light and cast great shadows of text against the thin cloth walls. The rest of us gathered round the fire watched as the stretched and reversed shadows held by two caricatures of human beings played out in weird and abstract ways, and we all laughed in an overtired but amused way.

All of us save Klein. As I chuckled I saw him drop his drink, the tin cup clinked against the rock. I watched as the water spilled from the cup and descended all too rapidly into the parched corners between sand and stone, and sank beneath the surface to discover whatever secrets were held below. In the same moment, he stood up and muttered a phrase in a language I didn't recognize. He walked forward, approaching the tent, and as he did I caught him muttering the word "Elohim". He seemed entranced by the symbols as they were splayed out on the tent wall and as he crossed the space towards them I saw his pace quicken. When they dropped the page back down to the table he shouted and demanded they return the page back up into the light. His tone was most insistent— almost angry, stern in nature—but as the characters were once more crudely projected upon the tent wall, he went up to the shadows as they were cast upon the cloth.

"Hebrew," he exhaled, as he turned around to face us once more. "The letters have been corrupted, perhaps by time or distance, but that is *shin*," he pointed at a *W* like symbol, 'And that I think is *zayin*," he gestured at a kind of capital I. In an instant, he was inside the tent and was rapidly creating an alphabet for the dialect of Hebrew he had just uncovered.

While the three linguists toiled over a nearly dead language in hopes of deciphering a totally unknown one, the rest of us drifted off to sleep. Without the random bustles and stumblings of the elder Peaslee wandering around, it was the first good sleep many of us had gotten in weeks. All was then as it should have been, to sleep accompanied with the sounds of one's' own breath, to slumber in solitude.

The next morning, I organized a new survey party, one that would systematically examine the area in which we had found the book. We left Freeborn, James and Klein to doze with Doctor Boyle watching over the camp. As we marched towards our destination, there came up one of those great and terrible winds that picked up not only the dust and sand, but the small pebbles as well. Pelted by debris, we sought shelter in the leeward portion of a large rock formation and let the mild tempest pass. Huddled up as we were, it was a relief when the tumult finally died down after twenty or so minutes and we were once more able to resume our march.

As we moved along the trail that had been laid out for us the day before, it quickly became obvious that many of the markers we had laid down had been disturbed or lost, either in the windstorm we had just weathered, or one just like it the night prior. Either way it meant that the sands and landmarks in the area had shifted and what was once plain was likely hidden, and what was once hidden was now possibly plain. The idea electrified the team and we soon were spread out, systematically scouring the landscape for any similar artifacts. We were lined up each of us about a hundred yards apart walking northeast scanning the ground for any hint of anything unusual. If someone saw something, they were to mark their location and direction, and then investigate. If the result was negative, they were to return and resume their survey along the same line they had been walking. If they actually found something they were to alert myself, Mackenzie or Ashley who were located on the outermost and central lines.

We worked this way for hours, slowly and systematically, scouring the desert for some sign, any sign at all of an artifact or a megalith or even just a carved stone block. It was time consuming, and the sun, sand and wind made it even more difficult. Trudging through the loose rock might seem easy, but it's actually extremely tiring. Even with the thick leather boots adding support, the uneven terrain works the ankles and calves, and even the hips. Like running on the beach or trying to stand on a boat in rough seas, the constant almost subconscious shifting of weight and balance takes muscles most people don't even know they have. It is a debilitating process for old field hands like myself, and young, inexperienced students as well. Still, it was what we all signed up for, and despite the aching limbs and joints we plodded on, determined to make sure this area was devoid of anything else of significance before we moved on. In the end, that decision paid off.

It was Bryan who found the ridge of rock that was hidden by a wash of sand and pebbles. He nearly broke his ankle climbing over it. His weight must have shifted some underlying structure and it collapsed beneath him, sucking his left foot into the earth. He screamed immediately, and his alarm was picked up and rebroadcast in both directions.

Mackenzie was the first to reach him and it was the miner that prevented him from sinking any farther into the concealed hole that had begun to open up. By the time I arrived, they were wrenching the poor student's leg out of the sand, and you could see where the ankle had been badly twisted. Already the swelling had started and a makeshift brace was quickly fashioned by Mackenzie and another student. Judging from Mackenzie's calmness and speed to act despite the sudden commotion, this was far from the first time he had done so.

What was more fascinating was the void that revealed itself where Bryan's leg had been sucked in. As the sand drained down, the entryway to a small, rocky passage manifested, sloping gently downward. Once cleared of its rocky debris, the opening proved to be an entryway to a larger space just a few yards inside. Lying down on his belly, Mackenzie slid inside, a rope tied to his right ankle just in case he had to be hauled out. The air was electric with suspense as the man crawled down that passageway into unknown chthonic expanses and we all sat round with rapt attention as he elbowed his way forward inch by inch. Listening to his voice, we learned that the small tunnel soon expanded and became a passageway, a corridor he said, with smooth walls made out of cut rock about five feet on each side. The floor was covered with debris, sand primarily, but pebbles and larger rocks as well.

Hunched over, he moved down the shaft which went on for a few more yards and then abruptly opened up into a larger chamber, circular in shape and approximately thirty yards across, with its ceiling forty feet in height. When he returned to us he sat recovering and suggested that what we had found was not an entry or passageway, but rather a sophisticated system for circulating air, for the shaft had opened up not at the floor of the large room, but rather closer to its ceiling. Regardless, we had found an entrance to what appeared to be an underground chamber which Mackenzie said had several much larger passages leading off into the unknown.

I immediately sent a group of students back to our base

camp for ropes, electric torches and various other equipment needed to insert a team into the chamber and begin its excavation. By that evening we had established a series of rope ladders that eased entry down into the shaft, a cart and pulley system that allowed rapid movement from one end of the shaft to the other, and then another ladder down into the circular chamber. Here we set up a small way station and surveyed our surroundings. Mackenzie was correct, from this chamber there were six distinct tunnels that led away to other areas. While many of us were eager to explore these in depth, I instead ordered that each path be explored no more than a few hundred feet. In doing so, we discovered that two of the exits were blocked by debris just a few yards in, while two others ended in small antechambers that were empty save for the accumulated years of sand and dust. The remaining two continued on, and it was evident that they were sloping down deeper into the earth.

With this information, I consulted with Mr. Mackenzie, and together we made a decision that I have since come to regret. So fascinated were we by the underground chamber we decided to immediately change our focus and move our base of operations to the opening, with most of the expedition relocated down into the circular chamber. Freeborn protested, but I made it clear that he, James and Klein could stay above working on their translation. Additionally, Doctor Boyle declined to make the descent, citing his age and general inability to move with any real speed. Thus, by the end of July 22nd the party had been split in three. The two Peaslees were presumably in Perth, Boyle and the three translators were on the surface, and the remaining dozen of us were encamped in the first chamber that we estimated to be more than twenty feet underground. Our only connection to the surface was the electrical line that led to our portable generator and powered our lights, and the wire that connected the mine phones, standard equipment carried by our Australian compatriots. As a safety precaution, I ordered that the above and below-ground bases were to establish contact every three hours, and that the exploration team provide detailed records of their plans and movements to the translators at every opportunity. In this manner, as we delved further and further into the unknown, those we left behind would know where we had gone and what we planned to do, and could implement a rescue if need be. I had some experience in these matters, and the more information was shared the less likely would it be for a panic to ensue if something did happen.

We began our explorations in earnest on the morning of the 23rd. I will not bore you with the details of what we found, for they bear no real consequence on my story save to explain why we were so distracted. Let it be said that our explorations led to a trove of amazing constructs, of vaulted architecture, and of fantastical art. Included amongst these were almost indescribable machines that had long since fallen into disrepair that Mackenzie and Tupper marveled at. One massive contraption, the function of which eluded me, was described by Tupper as an encabulator, but he was corrected by Molesworth who suggested that it was in fact the exact opposite. In this Mackenzie agreed, but what exactly a retro-encabulator was they never bothered to explain to me, though I assumed it had something to do with the processing of ore, and it is with great anticipation that I look forward to sharing this most fantastic discovery with Professor Rockwell. I am most certain he will find its mechanisms and purpose of immeasurable value.

I was struck by the similarities this vast and ancient metropolis bore to the one I had briefly seen in the frozen wastes of Antarctica. The resemblance was not in the shape of passages or the design of rooms, but rather in the fundamental cyclopean style of both. The rocks that formed the walls and floors of these epochs-old building were massive, titanic things and dwarfed the blocks that had been used to construct the pyramids of Egypt. Yet despite their size, they fit together so perfectly and smoothly that I doubted a piece of paper could be slipped between them. All this attested to a mastery of not only construction but of precision design as well. Such craftsmanship was carried over into the machinery as well, though here there were some interesting design features that seemed inconsistent with ease of operation. So far apart were some controls and levers that it was difficult to envision how such things could be operated by a single man, unless of course he was of titanic proportions. But even this did not explain everything, for in some pieces of equipment controls were set inside deep protective tubes that curved inward in a manner that no human arm could bend. For a moment, I thought that we had stumbled on another outpost of those pentaradial things that the Necronomicon calls the Q'Hrell or Progenitors, but the fundamental basics of that architecture are all wrong and the signature use of five in various key designs is severely lacking.

All these things and more we discovered, but while we basked in the glory of our scientific achievement, something quite sinister began to unfold on the surface. It started innocently, on that first day when we were split, James reported that Klein had been able to come up with a working alphabet for the Semitic characters we had found and was working on developing a lexicon of words that were his interpretation of what he thought they were meant to be. Curiously, both he and Freeborn felt that the characters were not as they first thought, a precursor of Modern Hebrew such as Proto-Canaanite, Amorite or Akkadian, but rather more resembled a decayed form of Biblical Hebrew. This of course was merely conjecture, but Freeborn was revising his "Temporary Chronology" to allow for the emigration of a populace from the Middle East sometime during the First Millennium B.C.

This was followed up hours later by a comparatively short communication that informed us that the entire text of what Klein was describing as corrupted Hebrew had been made coherent. Although the content was clearly a fantasy, or perhaps the delusion of a diseased mind, Doctor Boyle was intrigued by the supposed author of the text, who described himself as a man belonging to the City of the Dark Monarch destined to die in the year 6278, but to have his consciousness preserved amongst a race of monsters indefinitely. So enraptured with their own progress were those topsiders that they barely commented on the wonders we were reporting back, and I could only hope that proper notes were being taken on both their work and our reported progress.

The next couple of communications were of a similar vein, mentioning that translations of the curvilinear hieroglyphs were progressing, though at some point Freeborn began using the term Pnakotic for this language, which he derived from some indecipherable phonetics found in the Hebrew fragment. The pages were being translated by Freeborn, Klein, and James in parallel and then passed on to Doctor Boyle, who read them for content and context and integrated the singular pages into a complete manuscript. All the while, he never stopped listening to his recordings by de Hond, and complaining that his phonograph needles were wearing down more often than usual.

Such reports went on until the morning of the 24th when James told us that the translation was complete and that, after days of slaving over those strange pages, Doctor Freeborn had finally succumbed to exhaustion.

It was that afternoon that the next meaningful discussion was had. Klein had awoken from his slumber to discover Doctor Boyle in a state of frenzy. He had commandeered one of the vacant tents and had refused to come out or let anyone else in. He had taken with him the complete translated text and could be seen through the netting scribbling away in a notebook, and mumbling to himself about the "City of the Dark Monarch". Occasionally he would scream out Freeborn's name and then curse wildly. It was all very disturbing but Klein said that it was probably just exhaustion, and if the man progressed toward violence they would restrain him.

I should have done something then, I thought about it, I swear I did. But instead I chose to go deeper, to delve farther and farther into those strange and ancient ruins and marvel at the wonders they held. By that evening it all seemed to pass anyway. James reported that Boyle had finally emerged from his seclusion and was now sitting on a rocky outcropping staring at the sky. When asked what he was doing, he told James he was counting the stars, to make sure they were all still there.

It wasn't the first time a man had gone around the bend while on an expedition out to the middle of nowhere. But Boyle was on the surface and far from the maddening vistas that we were uncovering below the ground. It wasn't Boyle I was worried about; it was the men who were working with me, uncovering the secrets of a long lost and forgotten civilization.

These men whose very foundations were being shattered, who were discovering things that shook everything they had been taught, it was these men that I watched and waited to see if they would crack and fall under the strain.

Deeper and deeper we ranged into the tunnels, mapping

106 | THE PEASLEE PAPERS

their labyrinthine paths from room to room and level to level, always sloping curves and ramps, but never any stairs or hard angles. Miles of cable we ran, cannibalizing our own equipment to extend the reach of our lamps and communications. We stretched further and further into the unknown, but always followed the rules we had established, and we never missed our set three-hour call, albeit it was not always me who was a participant.

Morning of the 25th came for those above, but below we saw nothing of it, just that gloom that our lights could not dispel. We reached out to our friends above to hear friendly word of the outside world, but it was not to be. Our first calls upward went unresponsive and after ten minutes of silence, we all began to worry and made plans to send someone up.

No sooner had we decided to do so then the phone crackled to life. It was Klein, his voice wracked with panic. "He's gone mad…" was the solitary whisper we received.

At the very edges of my strained concentration, I could barely make out what I thought was yet another one of those blasted de Hond phonographs in the background. I imagined Klein's hand over the receiver, crouching beneath one of the makeshift desks the team had assembled.

The lights in our underground camp, the illumination to the caverns beyond, all began to flicker, and finally fade.

The darkness enveloped all, save for those few students that had the foresight to keep their electric torches at hand. One by one, they flickered to life, and shouts of confusion could be heard echoing through the void. Readying my own torch, the transmitter fell under the circle of light it cast and my eyes soon adjusted. Breathing deeply, I bellowed with all the strength I could muster, "Find the electrical cable nearest to you, preserve your torches and follow its path by touch, move slowly! Mackenzie?"

"Aye!" came his response, reflected by echo. "All's well!" It was anyone's guess to the distance he or the rest of our subterranean party had wandered at this point. With the way that sounds travelled through the bare antechambers and vacuous abysses of that vast, abandoned metropolis, I dared not speculate.

"Find the others!" I commanded. My mind was filled

with visions of Klein and our friends above. What had happened, who had gone mad, and how? In what state would I discover the camp we had abandoned on the surface? No matter how I tried to dismiss it, one persistent idea continuously filled me with dread—the thought that this was only the Antarctic Expedition repeating itself.

In the distance, in the dark, I could hear things that began as raised voices but quickly escalated into bellowing roars and screams of fear. My own meager torch was no defense against the darkness and I stood there frozen in my confusion as from somewhere deep in the labyrinth the echoes of horrible things reached my ears.

It is strange how the lack of light makes one lose any sense of time, and I do not know if I stood there for minutes or hours. I slowed my breath in an attempt to catch the sound of any others nearby. In the stillness, I was able to discern what I thought were footsteps coming down the tunnel. They grew closer, and with them came a ragged, gasping breath, and then a light flashed in my direction, and a voice

"Professor," a familiar whisper probed the dark, "is that you?"

I exhaled relief. Ramsey, the Bostonian, who boasted his city of origin at every opportunity. Such a wiry one, too. "Yes Ramsey. It seems we've gotten ourselves in a rather sticky situation."

"Ain't that the truth? What do we do now? How do we avoid ending up like grave robbers? Imagine the irony if we were to become entombed in the very structure we were meant to be excavating, lost for hundreds if not thousands of years."

"Stop quoting your thesis," I grated. "Have you seen or heard the others?" Working my way along the electrical cable, I slid towards the electrical junction.

"No," he blurted, "but I heard a few shuffle with me, like you told us to, along the electrics. I was with Mackenzie's crew in the southeast quadrant. Bryan and Frank were with me, you know how inseparable Bryan and Mackenzie have gotten since he stuck his leg in that hole. Mackenzie says he's a good luck charm or something." I bumped against the junction box and the two of us directed our lights at the various cables and switches, searching for the mechanism that would take us off the surface generator and re-energize the transmitter and lights with the emergency batteries.

While we searched, Ramsey chattered incessantly and through our hushed discourse, I learned of an apparent bond that had formed between the younger Bryan and the older mining engineer Mackenzie, which the mechanic Molesworth suggested had turned improper. Mackenzie denied this of course, but once started the suspicion grew. Soon, any event that put Bryan and Mackenzie alone was greeted with a knowing look of disdain, and a rift developed, creating two distinct parties. One group followed and operated under the guidance of Molesworth, and the other group sought the tutelage of the seasoned Mackenzie, which included Bryan, Tupper, Frank and Ramsey.

Of this divisiveness, I will admit to knowing nothing. I had assumed we had all been a team, working in unison, towards the same goal. Why no one had reached out to me, why none had told me of this, I could not understand. It appeared that while my thoughts had been deeply preoccupied with the magnitude and ramifications of the discoveries our team had made, quite the elaborate drama had blossomed and no one had had the sense to confide in me. In my blissful ignorance, it became obvious a vile tumor had grown, and the darkness had provided the opportunity for it to blossom into rage.

When the lights went out, Bryan had panicked and had for a brief moment, openly wept in fear. This had enraged Molesworth and he finally gave voice to the pangs of moral distress that had festered within him. He had berated Mackenzie and Bryan, and when Frank had tried to defuse the situation, a fist was thrown. Molesworth had been blinded by his own rage at that point, and words that I dare not repeat for fear of besmirching the characters of all involved were used. Molesworth swung and hit Frank, knocking him to the floor.

As soon as it happened Molesworth knew it was over. Whatever power he had garnered amongst the others was lost as soon as the blow was struck. Shocked and shaken that their civilized modes of behavior had degenerated in mere minutes of being without light, those who had stood with Molesworth bowed their heads in shame and distanced themselves from the old mechanic. Distressed by his own behavior the man had fled into the darkness alone.

My first instinct was to send searchers after the man, but I had more pressing matters to deal with. I, of course, felt responsible for the condition and fate of the other students, so excited were they to accompany us on this ill-fated jaunt across the globe. Were the treasures trapped within this megalithic masonry worth such troubles? One can only grit their teeth and hope.

With a sudden gasp of elation, I found the switches and converted the electrics over to battery power. The lights flickered on with an audible hum, but only to what I would say was quarter strength, not enough to work by, but enough to guide the others back, and then to the surface. The radio sputtered and cracked with static and I dashed to it in desperation.

I grabbed the transmitter and in desperation I cried into the microphone. "Klein? Klein!" The lights flickered as the transmitter drew power from the feeble batteries.

He called down to us from the sunlit world above. "He has an ax!" There was a terrible scream and a horrific thud and then the receiver went almost silent save for the sound of something heavy slamming into something else with a wet, sucking sound, and in the background the unbearable, atonal sound of the music composed by the mad genius de Hond.

I clung to the transmitter, cradling it in my sweating hands as if I were to drop it the world itself would end. I shouted into it again, as if raising my voice would make the signal stronger. "Klein! Klein! Answer me – are you there?"

And then came that hellish response, the one that set me screaming up the ladder and across the cart and then up onto the surface like a pigeon from hell, with Ramsey close behind me. We had traversed that path a dozen times during the process of setting up our base of operations, to the point where I could almost cover that distance by rote, but this time it seemed to take ages. Each movement forward was an eternity of anguish. I was crawling up, up toward the light, but that warm, glowing sphere of sustaining energy provided no comfort, for I feared what waited for me there on the surface.

Just before I reached the top I cast my torch aside. It was now useless to me now, and instead my hand found comfort in the grip of my gun. Ramsey made a short vocalization, a protest of sorts, but I growled for him to be quiet and he acquiesced, though I knew he did so grudgingly. I had no time for niceties or to discuss options.

I came out of that hole with my revolver in my hand. Boyle's phonograph was blaring, filling the air with that awful discordant symphony that de Hond had written and dared to call music. James was lying on the ground, his head split open, the grey matter within mixed with pink spreading across the ground. Klein was in the central tent crumpled on the floor, his right arm and shoulder nearly severed from his body. My head reeled, the world spun and then I heard Freeborn screaming. I followed the sounds blindly, racing across the sand, my eyes still trying to adjust to the morning sun. As I topped a rise I could see one man cowering on the ground and the other standing over him with an ax in his hand. I yelled at him to stop, but the ax rose up over the man's had in a swift and frightening arc, and in desperation I fired my revolver, emptying all six shots in the direction of the attacking man. Three of those shots hit their target; two others apparently went into the desert, while the sixth grazed Freeborn's right shoulder.

The others say I saved his life, that Freeborn's wound was not my gunshot but where the ax had grazed him. They say if it weren't for me the man, my friend and colleague, would be dead. But I can't come to terms with it, how an old man like that could snap and shout those words into the phone, the words I can still hear echoing in the recesses of my mind, the words we all heard, but only I took personally. The horrid words that caused me to careen back up into the sunlit world.

"YOU FOOL, KLEIN IS DEAD!"

III.   The Translation of Tyler Freeborn

The original translations of Doctor Tyler Freeborn and his assistants were apparently burned by Doctor Boyle. However, Freeborn was an avid letter writer and sometime after finishing the translation apparently read the collated version and summarized it in a letter to his wife Samantha. As this missive was deposited in the expedition mailbag it escaped destruction during Boyle's frenzied attack. While it does not provide a word by word actual translation it does supply us with some understanding of Freeborn's interpretation of the book. Sadly, the original artifact is missing and presumed destroyed by Doctor Boyle.

24 July, 1935

>My Dearest Samantha,
>
>It is in a state of complete and utter exhaustion and elation that I write you this morning. It looks to be a fine and wondrous day, but of it I will see little. My assistants and I have come to the very edge of collapse, feverishly working on translating what appears to be an ancient volume in a heretofore unknown language! It took us days mind you, and we are all ready to collapse, but we have a translation of that book, and with it likely the ability to translate whatever other documents or inscriptions we might uncover. It is all so very exciting.
>
>Fortunately, with the recent surge of activity, that insufferable Dr. Boyle has neglected his Victrola's incessant caterwaul of those de Hond phonographs he is so fond of. Finally! We have all been able to focus upon our duties without the accompaniment of that dastardly conspectus of "musical composition." Yes my dearest, I know you share an appreciation for that 'composer', but I am so very grateful you have the sensibility to refrain from such excessive, almost maniacally obsessive behavior. I think James may have talked Klein into sabotaging that infernal phonograph mechanism somehow. If true, I will ensure he receives marks of excellence for his work on this expedition. But enough of that.

THE PEASLEE PAPERS

The original object is a book about fifteen inches wide, twenty inches tall and an inch thick. The cover is comprised of an ultra-light metal, while the pages appear to be some form of chemically treated cellulose. The text on the pages appears to be handwritten using a brush and a variety of colored pigments. The characters appear to be of the same type of curvilinear hieroglyphics that I've described to you before as being carved into many of the megaliths we had previously uncovered.

As it was, with the alphabet being so unrelated to anything else we had ever seen it was unlikely that we were going to be able to translate the document. However, that all changed in a rather serendipitous event. Inserted into the back pages of the text was a scrap of material that had not one but two distinct sets of characters. One was the traditional curvilinear hieroglyph, while the other appeared to be in an entirely different language. *Opuscule oris humanum magnificus!* It did not take long for us to realize that this new language was a variant of Hebrew, one that appeared to be highly decayed or corrupted from the language we currently knew.

With this realization, I suddenly gained a new assistant, a young Engineering student named Theodore Klein. As you might have surmised, he is a German Jew, one of the few Miskatonic University had allowed into its programs. As you and I have discussed previously, I have no issue with such people being allowed into the University, as long as they understand their place, and they should under no circumstances be allowed entry into the doctoral programs. After all, the quota system exists for a reason. The world may fawn at Einstein all they want, but we academics all know that he is the aberration, and his theories while in vogue now, will likely prove to be flawed relatively soon.

With Klein's help, we were able to develop a crude alphabet of characters, most of the time just assuming a particular symbol corresponded to a similar letter in Hebrew, looking for common words that used one or two of the characters, and then extrapolating the rest of the letters. It was less translation than it was cryptography for several of the letters had deformed into completely unrecognizable shapes, which is not unheard of given the pressures that time, distance and competing cultures place on a language. Regardless of what you call it, we soon had a translation of the corrupted Hebrew section, and using that began to develop a lexicon for the curvilinear hieroglyphs. At first, we were not sure if the passages in two distinct languages had the same content, but as we translated the smaller words we soon confirmed that both sections related fundamentally the same information. Though we would all admit that content was simply fantastical. It professed to be written by a man who claimed to be from far in the future whose soul was transferred back through time and forced to inhabit the body of an "Intruder". He was meant to have returned to his own time and body, but owing to an unfortunate accident, his own body had been killed in the year 6278, and he was now marooned, as if lost on an island, but in time instead of the sea. His given name was "Young Town", and he belonged to the clan of the "City of the Dark Monarch". His purpose in writing the two passages side by side was to educate himself in the language of the "Intruders" which he would have to learn in order to integrate into the society that he had no choice but to call home. He called the language of the Intruders "Pnakotic" and their city was Pnakotus. In the text, these words were untranslatable and were rendered in Hebrew phonetically. Interestingly enough the author confessed that Hebrew was not his common language, but rather had been taught to him by his grandfather who had been a Rabbi.

It is hard to believe that from just a few paragraphs in Hebrew, and a comparable text in Pnakotic we were able to translate the entire book, but the truth is we found Pnakotic to be a rather intuitive language, building on a rather simple base vocabulary, and incorporating root symbols into almost every word. It was as if the language itself had been designed to be universally translatable. James even suggested that perhaps it was an artificial language such as Esperanto, Bolak, or Ro. This was intriguing, for like Ro, Pnakotic seemed to have words grouped into categories such that words related to each other had similar roots. For example, color words started with a symbol we called "Sch" which was modified with various other symbols like "Mit" which meant water. Thus, the compound word "Mit-Sch" literally meant Ocean-Color which we interpreted to mean "Blue". While this worked for much of the translation, some of the more complex compound words were simply untranslatable and had to be rendered as their literal translations. For example, we believe that the symbol we call Lyl means time, while Ith means shadow. Thus, the compound Ith-Lyl means shadow-time, but we really have no idea what that means. James suggests that it might be a state of altered consciousness induced by the use of ritual hallucinogens. Given the context of the longer book I think his interpretation might be very close to the truth.

The title of the book that we've translated appears to be "The Tale of Shadow-Time 428 Variant G", or something similar. It purports to be the observations of a man called Ys (which itself means Ephemeral), an agent of some sort in employ of a ministry of history. According to Ys, the Gods had created thousands upon thousands of worlds, to explore and study, and it was the task of Ys to evaluate these creations. He would go down into those worlds, like Zeus when he went down to dally with a particularly beautiful woman. He would live amongst the residents of these worlds, studying them, learning about who they were, who they had been, what they held of value, and even what they dreamt of. Such evaluations were not entirely academic. The power of the Gods had limitations, they could create nearly an infinite number of worlds, but they could only sustain a few thousand at any one time. Thus, unworthy worlds, worlds of limited value or potential needed to be culled. The evaluation submitted by Ys or another agent like him was one of the key factors in determining whether a world was preserved or culled.

Now what was most fascinating about all this was that the criteria for evaluating each world wasn't exactly what we would view as utopian, quite the contrary. We tend to think of the perfect world as agrarian in nature, a simple world, filled with uncomplicated people and green, rolling hills surrounding lush farms. This has been a common denominator throughout most cultures for thousands of years, whether it be Bacon's New Atlantis, Plato's Republic, or even the Biblical Earthly Paradise. However, the culture of Pnakotus viewed the ideal world as one filled with strife, machines of war, vast metropolis and crowded masses of people on the verge of conflict. Indeed, it would seem that the gods of Pnakotus preferred worlds in which humans engaged in hostilities on a global scale.

That was exactly what Ys had evaluated in his travels in the dream world that the Gods had created. He had travelled that artificial world, explored its continents and nations and learned all he could of it. He learned its past from its libraries and of its present through travel. He spent years evaluating the dream world, sailing its oceans and soaring through its skies. He talked to the wisest of their philosophers, the most notorious of their decadents, and the most learned of their scholars. From all of these studies he calculated and devised the most probable course of their development into the future. Only when Ys had completed his task could he return to the real world.

It sounds fantastic I know, an ancient text talking about alternate Earths, but it is not unique. There is the popular literature of course, Wells' *Men Like Gods* proposed multiple versions of the world. Thurber suggested a world where the South had won the Civil War, as did Churchill in Squires' anthology *If It Had Happened Otherwise* and few remember Hawthorne's contribution, or Machiavelli's. But for comparison of what we have here, one need go back twenty-five years before the birth of Christ to *Abd Urbe Condita* in which the author Livy speculates on what would have happened had the Romans chosen to go to war with Alexander.

It's all fantasy of course, a rather complicated myth, probably spawned by the ritual hallucinogens as suggested by James. What is curious though is the degree by which the

visions are categorized. This particular one is labeled "Temporary-Shadow-Time 428 Variant G", which sounds so official, so proper, and so very bureaucratic. The truth is this term is no more fantastic than any other myth world, whether it be Hades, Elysium, or the Nine Worlds. Indeed, it seems to me that the Norse Yggdrasil might be a comparable model for the cosmology of Pnakotus. In the Norse cosmology nine distinct worlds are bound together by the cosmic tree they call Yggdrasil.
In Pnakotic cosmology, the trunk of the tree would represent the true world, while the branches represent potential variants evolving from the alteration of historical events. Some of these branches are allowed to flourish and expand, while others are found to be unsatisfactory, and are simply pruned away.
Those branches that are retained represent potential new worlds for the residents of Pnakotus, the Gods and their servants, which I believe are the same as "The Intruders" described in the Hebrew fragment. Or at least that is how the mythology is structured. It is not unlike many other Paradise myths in which the faithful are united with their deities and then taken into an ideal homeland. Albeit this one is a little more complex than most.

You know I find such fantasies intriguing, for as we've discussed, it seems to me that the more complex the mythology, the more highly developed the culture. In this case it seems to be a culture that was no longer concerned with what was, but rather with what could be, or what might have been. This is a wholly unprecedented discovery in this region. We think of the local aborigines as backwards, as members of a Stone Age hunter-gatherer society, but it may not be so. There may have existed a highly advanced culture that thousands of years ago collapsed and what we see now is the tragic remnants of a decayed civilization. It would explain so much.

With each revelation that this expedition reveals I've been revising my Temporary Chronology, fleshing it out, filling in the holes and assumptions with actual facts. Soon, another year maybe two, I'll be ready for publication and then my darling I'll be sure to win a tenured professorship somewhere prestigious. It's only a matter of time really. Then I'll be able to give you all the things you deserve, all the things I've promised you.

I miss you my darling. I will return home soon, I promise.

All my love, your husband,
Tyler Freeborn

IV.   From the Notebooks of Erasmus Boyle

24 July 1935

When this is over they will call me mad, but it doesn't matter, nothing matters, our lives were forfeit long ago, and madness is perhaps the final refuge for a man who has learned too much about the world he lives in.

We came into this desert wasteland because of one man's dreams, now I'm not so sure they were dreams at all. I think they might have been memories. I think Nathaniel Peaslee remembered something he wasn't supposed to, and it has led us here. Except perhaps not. Perhaps he was supposed to remember; perhaps we were supposed to find this place, to learn the truth. And perhaps go mad in the process. Peaslee was almost there and his son has taken that fragile mind away. The brutality of this truth is enough for even the most rational man to lose himself as it is sanity shaking to learn someone is playing a very strange and long game, one that involves the entire human race.

Admittedly some of us are more human than others. These Americans, particularly the young ones, are so arrogant, they seem so sure of themselves, as if all of creation were theirs for the taking. As if it belonged to them and them alone. They've never even considered that someone else might lay claim to it, or that it might be something that cannot be claimed at all. A strange thought that something could be inherently without claim. Men try to lay claim to everything we see, but can we claim the ocean, or the air, or the planets and the stars. We will try I'm sure, but like the ocean and the air we can only draw lines on maps and show them to other men and say, "This is mine!". The ocean and the air don't care about those lines, or about who owns them. It is the same with the sands of the desert, and the things that are buried within. Who owns the ancient past? Who owns the far future? Perhaps it is not men at all. Perhaps we have it entirely wrong. Perhaps it is the future or the past that owns us. Perhaps we are possessed by the things that rear their heads out of the sands of time. Perhaps.

It started with the megaliths. We would find them in droves, some complete but more often than not mostly shattered, but many bore that queer curvilinear writing, and many bore the same four symbols, inscribed boldly at about ten feet above their bases. We couldn't translate it before, but now we can. We've developed a working knowledge of Pnakotic as Freeborn calls it, and I've translated that inscription. It was nothing really, just a set of 3 numbers and a letter. By itself it meant nothing. Then Freeborn and the others translated the book using the page written in Hebrew. Damn them for doing so, and damn them for not understanding what they had done. They were so intent on translating they didn't comprehend. The language may be understood but the content; its meaning it still escapes them.

But it does not escape me.

They've called the man who wrote in strange Hebrew by a name: "Young Town" of the clan of the "City of the Dark Monarch". They've derived this name as a literal interpretation of the words he has written, but they missed the part where the author said that he was translating the meaning of his own name, and that the original was something quite different. Indeed, I take issue with Freeborn's rendering here and suggest that the proper surname might be better expressed not as "City of the Dark Monarch", but rather as the "Monarch's City Dark" or even more appropriately as "Monarch's City-Dark" as suggested by Klein.

Once you see it that way the translation of both names is quite easy, particularly when you learn that the glyph used for "dark" is a color symbol, similar to but not the same as the one used for "black". It could easily be interpreted as "brown". But "City of the Brown Monarch" makes little poetic impact, but it's not meant to. For it should be rendered as "Monarch's City-Brown". But I come from Norfolk Island, where I lived for most of my life before moving to the mainland. I know a better name for "Monarch's City", something quainter and simpler: "Kingston". After you realize this "Young Town" becomes simple to correct to "New Village" or in French "Neu Ville" or the common "Nevile". The author of the Hebrew text was none other than Nevil Kingston-Brown, one of Peaslee's fellow prisoners in his dreams!

I've looked at the article, Peaslee tells us that Kingston-Brown was an Australian physicist who will die in 2518, but the text we've translated says he will die in 6278. At first that didn't make any sense to me, but when I mentioned the date to Klein he shrugged it off and reminded me that the Jewish calendar is far ahead of that used by the Western world, by almost 3,760 years. That correction makes sense, and was the first step towards madness.

For suddenly, Peaslee's dreams were more than that. They were memories, and not simply race memories, or artificial memories, but memories of something else, something that had actually happened. And if Nevil Kingston-Brown existed then what other details that Peaslee had related were true also? Were there time-travelling monsters from other worlds gathering the minds of victims from across time and space to interrogate, while their bodies were inhabited by agents that scoured that time and place for information on its people and cultures? Were there really horrible semi-vegetable things in ancient Antarctica? And what of the thing that called itself Nug Soth, and was so very wary about describing his people? He was one of the Dark Conquerors, but from where will they come and what will they conquer?

These and similar thoughts were what led my mind into turmoil. For it seemed that in eons past those of Pnakotus, whom Peaslee had called the Great Race of Yith had lived here in primordial days of the continent. I cannot explain how or why their ruins have survived for millions of years, but I suppose that the arid desert air and encasing sands might have helped. How long has this region been a desert? I'm not a geologist, I don't know these things. It is also possible that the remains are meant to be here. The Yith build things to last, the book is a fine example, why not the architecture as well? Is it possible that this place was only abandoned temporarily? Perhaps one day the Yith shall return and this place will once more be a vibrant metropolis? If that day were to come what would walk those streets? Would it be men, or something else?

The question may be pointless.

The main text, what Freeborn has called "The Tale of Shadow-Time 428 Variant G", but I think of as "The Testimony of Ys" suggests so many things. Freeborn has used the document to update what he calls his "Temporary Chronology", but now as I think of things I must laugh at such a name. Not because it is ridiculous, but rather because it is appropriate, misplaced though it is.

The translators have framed the text as a fantasy, part of a myth cycle, or as an account of a drug-induced dream. But they haven't realized the truth. Ys was dispatched to a world, he lived in it, lived amongst its people and learned about its future and its past. The name of that world was "Shadow-Time 428 Variant G", and while Ys tale makes it clear that the world had much to offer, ultimately, he ruled against it and suggested that it be eliminated. Freeborn uses the term "pruned" and suggests that such unsatisfactory worlds are like branches of a tree, which can be cut off as an arborist might cut an unwanted or diseased growth, leaving the trunk, our world, whole and pursuing another direction. At least this is how he frames his view of the cosmology.

I think he is wrong, on many counts.

I think the process is not as swift as he thinks. I think that worlds that take decades, centuries, or millennia to grow cannot simply be cut off. Rather, I believe the strange temporal energies that create such worlds or universes, must be withdrawn slowly and the cosmic processes of the afflicted universe would slowly wind down. The natural laws of the universe might shift and begin to alter, to decay as the very fabric of space unwound. To see such a thing would be terrible, I don't believe any thinking creature could survive witnessing its world unraveling. It would be a maddening thing.

Madness is inevitable.

I've seen the translations and the originals in their curvilinear hieroglyphics. I can read them, not as well as the others but enough to understand things. James suggests that this language was designed to be intuitive; I think he may have been right. I think we were meant to find this place, to translate these words, to understand our place in things.

Pnakotus was not abandoned because the Yith were done with it; rather they wanted to see what would happen to our world without them in it. We are not the trunk of the tree; we are a branch, nothing more, an experiment, one of millions likely. It is not Freeborn who should have the title Temporary Chronologist, but Ys, for that is what he is. He comes to these worlds; these manufactured cosmoses and evaluates them. He visits them briefly, but this is not why I apply the word Temporary to his title, for while he may be ephemeral, the Shadow-Times are as well for they truly are Temporary Chronologies, meant to be disposed of when finished with.

That's what happened to the world that Ys visited in his report, the one designated 428G. He found the inhabitants too soft, too prone for peace, too willing to negotiate, too cooperative. Of course, the natives didn't think that way. The people Ys met and talked to thought of themselves as war-like and violent, but striving towards a peace, towards a better world. Unfortunately, opinions and evaluations are relative.

Those markings on the columns, on the megaliths they are three numbers and a letter 428G. The same coding as used to describe the world that Ys visited in his report. It was our world that Ys came to and evaluated. He saw our world and he judged it unfit, because we weren't violent enough.

Whoever reads this please contact my daughter, Mrs. Kevin Peel of Sydney. You can find the address in my desk at home. Tell her I love her.

Ys left before the Great War started, but I suspect he knew what we were capable of. After the horrors of that abominable conflict how much more violent does he think we could be? How could we do any worse than that? What depths of inhumanity must we sink to so that our culture, our world, our universe, our temporary chronology might be judged worthy?

What is it we must do to live, and would we be willing to do it? And should we?

If we are to be cast in the role of Abraham where is our Isaac, or are we destined to play both roles?

Normally I would seek peace in my music, but of late the compositions of Ambrose de Hond bring no comfort. Indeed, over the last few months my need for solace has driven me to play the de Hond recordings almost incessantly, and the needles have worn down at a phenomenal rate. I have only one left, and am saving that. Instead I shall wander out away from camp and into the desert where I shall stare up at the night sky and the stars that hang in that infinite darkness and try to comprehend all of this. I'm going to try and figure out what if anything I should do next.

For the first time in my life I don't know what to do.

Shall this world live, or is it simply a passing experiment, a Temporary Chronology so to speak?

How far should a creation be willing to go to please his Creator?

V. From the Report of Chief Inspector C. J. Shane

1 August 1935

In the matter of the death by violence of Doctor Erasmus Malachi Boyle, of Perth, in a section of the desert east of Lake Disappointment, Western Australia.

Based on testimony of those involved, the Mackenzie-

Peaslee Expedition, an archeological investigation, travelled east of the De Grey River on 31 May 1935, finally coming to rest east of Lake Disappointment the 3rd of June. From this point on communication with the outside world was limited to a periodic radio check, and a weekly supply of food, water and mail delivered by airplane from the coast.

On 21st July Professor Nathaniel Peaslee suffered what the others have described as a nervous break, and on the morning of the next day was taken to Perth via airplane by his son Dr. Wingate Peaslee. In their absence, the remaining expedition members purportedly uncovered first a metallic book, and then the entryway to what has been described as a vast labyrinth of chambers hidden beneath the desert sands.

According to surviving members of the expedition, and on that evening, twelve men under the leadership of Professor Dyer, went into the labyrinth, while four others led by Doctor Tyler Freeborn stayed on the surface. Electricity and communications were maintained by a series of cables which ran from the surface into the tunnels.

Over the next few days the behavior of Dr. Erasmus Malachi Boyle became increasingly erratic, but in the opinion of Doctor Freeborn had not escalated to the point of violence. That changed on the morning of the 25th. Alerted to Boyle's attack through the cabled transceiver, Professor Dyer rushed to the surface, saw the bodies of two of his colleagues and an imminent threat to Doctor Freeborn in the form of Doctor Boyle wielding an axe. In order to save Freeborn's life Dyer fired his pistol multiple times hitting and killing Dr. Boyle.

This condensed version of events is supported by testimony from Professor Dyer, his assistant John Ramsey, and Dr. Tyler Freeborn himself who has recovered enough to provide a statement.

Based on the testimony of those involved it is my opinion that Professor Peaslee was not the only member of the team to suffer a mental break, and that the isolation, coupled with boredom, poor diet and dehydration led to a kind of cabin fever, or mass hysteria, the symptoms of which went unnoticed by Pr. Dyer. Ultimately this led Doctor Boyle to an unhealthy mental state and ultimately to a breakdown that cost not only his life, but the lives of two others.

It has been a scant few days since I and the other members of the police force answered Professor Dyer's radio call, and it that time the entire expedition has been housed here in Port Hedland and examined by detectives, doctors, and psychiatrists. All agree that while the expedition has suffered a great trauma, they are no danger to themselves or others. Indeed, Molesworth and Mackenzie who seemed so at odds in the reports of Dyer and the others, reportedly have become Bridge partners and play daily against any and all opponents.

As for the so-called labyrinth of chambers reported to exist beneath the sands at their expedition site, I can make no significant comment. In the course of our investigation of Boyle's death we had no choice but to have the team pack up all their equipment and travel with us to the coast. At the insistence of Dyer, we allowed the installation of a series of survey markers. Unfortunately, winds and shifting sands apparently disturbed the markers and they can no longer be found. Given the scandal of Boyle's death and the inability to locate the dig site the Commonwealth government has revoked all permits, and has requested that the Americans leave the country immediately. Indeed, there has been some suggestion that the story of their so-called discovery had been entirely fabricated. A position I would be inclined to agree with were it not for the fact that the Commonwealth Investigation Branch has deployed a squad of Peace Officer Guards to the area east of Lake Disappointment.

If there is nothing there, why are twenty armed men standing guard in the desert?

1935

THE TIME TRAVELERS' EX-WIFE

It's the 4th of September 1935 and I am in Kingsport, not far from where I was born. I lounge in the shadow of Kingsport Head, surrounded by friends and family. My son Wingate wishes me a happy sixtieth birthday. He is just back from Australia, where he and his father went on an expedition. He wants to tell me something, but then changes his mind. I don't like to talk about my ex-husband and Wingate knows it. A rabbit runs across the field with children chasing behind it. They have no chance of catching the poor creature, but it is not the rabbit that I am worried about. I rise, open my mouth, but then catch myself. What would I say? I settle back down in my chair. My grandson John brings me cake and lemonade. I pat him on the head and give him a hug. He smells of youth, clover, sweat and chocolate. He has his mother's eyes, but looks like his father, Hannah's husband Samuel Beckett. After I finish my slice of cake Wingate comes back and hands me a book, an album of photographs. I haven't seen it, or worked on it in years. I wonder aloud where they found it, and but they ignore me. They've given the old woman her book of memories, the one she created for herself, and now expect her to be fully occupied, whatever she may say can't be all that important. I rummage through my handbag and find the key to the clasp. The book creaks open and falls to the last page. I don't mind, the end is as good a place to start as any.

The photograph on the last page is grainy and creased, but the image of London's Tower Bridge is unmistakable. I am in the foreground holding one of my novels, The Creeping Past. To my left is a middle-aged man with a serious look on his face and a mass of well-kept hair. His name is Olaf Stapledon, and like me he is holding up his latest work so that the camera can catch the title. On my other side is Stapledon's protégé, the young poet Paul Tregardis. It is the 5th of June 1931, and Tregardis' birthday, he has just turned twenty-two. We celebrate at our publisher's expense. There is too much music, too much food, too much liquor. Olaf's wife doesn't like Tregardis; he is brash, irrational, and compulsive. At midnight Paul asks me to marry him. I laugh at the joke but when his face turns sour I realize he was serious. I am more than twice his age. I reward his adoration with a kiss, and then suddenly I know. I kiss him again and let his future wash over me. We spend the night together, and I accept his proposal, knowing that I will never see him again.

The next evening, I stop by his small London apartment and use the spare key to gain entrance. There is a strange, blue viscous material covering his desk and chair. It is rapidly disappearing, evaporating in the sunlight. Within minutes it is gone. On the desk, there is a receipt from a nearby curio shop. I take it to the proprietor. The bent old man scratches his beard and says something in Hebrew. He remembers the item, a crystalline sphere, clouded like milk, flattened on opposite ends. It had been found in Greenland he thought. A pretty enough piece, full of whatever intrinsic mystery an owner could imagine, but not overly valuable, or exotic. I spend the evening writing the story of Paul's last day. I tell how he found the sphere, what he thought it was, and what it showed him. Wright buys the story from me, and hints that it might be given a cover illustration, but I already know that he is lying. The story is published under a pseudonym and is titled Ubbo-Sathla.

I turn the page.

It is 1924, September the Second, and I am in New York. The photograph shows the members of Hannah's wedding party; in the background is Brooklyn's Museum of Fine Arts where her new husband is a junior curator. His supervisor is sophisticated, charming, refined. Dr. Halpin Chalmers is a graduate of Miskatonic University, so we spend some time reminiscing about the faculty and Arkham. He asks me to dance. He sweeps me off my feet. The next day he sends me flowers. We go for long walks in Central Park. His friends are like him, charming and sophisticated. There is a private detective, a man named Charles who tells some of the most outrageous stories. He knows everyone, and everyone knows him. He takes Halpin and I to the most interesting of places: private gardens, hidden museums, and secret clubs. In the spring of 1925, when Halpin and I marry, Charles is Halpin's best man.

We live in a brownstone apartment, on weekends and holidays we travel to Partridgeville where Halpin was raised. It is a lovely town, and beautiful country. I write, longhand, and then I pay one of the secretaries from the museum to type the manuscripts. Halpin acts as my first reader and editor. By the fall we are working as a team, and in the October, he sells his first standalone story. He gains some notoriety, and soon finds working with me slow and tedious. In 1926, he has published twenty stories, and announces that he will be retiring from the museum the next year. He writes voraciously, not just stories but letters, postcards, and even editorials. He writes a novel in a month. By 1927 there is no more room for me in his life, and we divorce. At the courthouse, he hugs me and apologizes for his mania. I squeeze back and I can feel his future. That evening I write it all down and wait.

He moves to Partridgeville and writes day and night. He becomes addicted: First to cigarettes, then caffeine, and then alcohol. He experiments with drugs, the extracts of plants and certain lizards and amphibians. He writes while under the influence and becomes obsessed with the concept of time and how it is perceived. In the spring, he empties his apartment of all his furniture. He buys plaster and turns his boxy little room into a smooth, curving surface. On July 2, 1928, a tremor shakes the town. When the authorities find his body, it is covered with a blue jelly like substance. The smooth flowing plaster is cracked and broken. The walls of the apartment are comprised of jagged, twisted angles. The police blame the tremor; I am not so sure it is not the other way round. I get a copy of the medical report and append portions of it to my story. I publish it under my Long pseudonym. A publishing house in Arkham wants to use it as the title story for a collection. I am hesitant, for it would risk exposing my true identity.

On the next page, the newspaper report screams in bold letters that I have divorced my husband Professor Nathaniel Wingate Peaslee. It is October the Eighth 1910, and Nathaniel is a celebrity, at least in Arkham, but through no fault of his own. Something has happened to him, he has forgotten himself. By this time, it has been more than two years since the man I loved, the father of my children, collapsed while lecturing at Miskatonic. He recovered, but with no memory of me or anyone else, not even himself. He speaks with a strange cadence, and on occasion uses strange words and even unusual phrases and idioms. He has cold, dead eyes and his face is slack and emotionless. The children are uncomfortable. When I touch him I see things, monstrous events, creatures of immense size, cities of twisting pathways and flying machines. Sometimes I think I am seeing the future, sometimes the past. I come to realize that it doesn't matter. I leave Arkham, and take the children with me. We stay with my aunt in Haverhill. I clean houses to earn money, but then my banker tells me that a trust has been set up to benefit me and my family. I ask where the money comes from but he won't tell me. I refuse to have any part of it. My aunt is not so stubborn.

I obtain a position at the library. I borrow books. I read Baum's *OZ* stories to the children. For my own pleasure, I read Burroughs' *A Princess of Mars* and Doyle's *The Lost World*. They strike chords in my mind. I have dreams, nightmares really, echoes of what I saw when I touched my husband. In desperation, I write my visions down, I fill volumes with my scribbling. It is cathartic and uplifting. In 1912 my son Robert finds my notebooks. He takes large disjointed strands of my text and reorganizes them into narratives. He reads them to his brother and their friends. These boys are fascinated. On a whim, I take what he has done and type it up; I rewrite it following the patterns I have discerned in the works of Burroughs and Doyle. Whispers magazine buys the story for ten dollars and it appears a few months later. Afterwards, the magazine forwards me a letter of praise from a man named Randolph Carter in Arkham. He invites me to join his circle of writers. They meet monthly at the University library. He doesn't know I'm a woman, and I'm careful to politely refuse in my typed response.

I turn the page, but several of them stick together and I've jumped backwards over years. There is a formal wedding portrait of myself sitting, and Nathaniel standing behind me. We are in our wedding clothes. It is 1896 and Nathaniel thinks I am twenty-one years old. He thinks this because I have told him that I was born in 1875. He thinks he is eight years my senior. In reality, he was born a year after me, and I am twenty-seven, but only my mother knows that.

On the opposite page is another newspaper clipping. There is no picture, but the article from the Newburyport Correspondent is dated February 6, 1893 and tells how fishermen found Alice Bennett wandering amongst the Kingsport docks in the early morning hours of the previous day. While disoriented and cold she was uninjured and in good health. When asked where she was she says she was walking along the wharf with her father and aunt when they became lost in the fog. Somehow, they became separated. Authorities reunite the girl with her mother. When Alice asks for her father, she is told the man died in 1891. She does not understand that she has been missing for six years, since her eighteenth birthday.

I don't remember clipping this article out, or putting it in the album. I do know that after its publication we were hounded by the curious to the point that we had to leave Kingsport and assume new identities. We moved in with one of my father's sisters in Haverhill. A widow, we took her married name as our own, and I move my date of birth forward. My mother never asks where I have been, and I never offer to tell her. I try to forget it: The woman who took me away, the places she took me, the things we saw.

I'm near the front of the album; there is a photograph from 1879, my tenth birthday party. We are at the park in the shadow of Kingsport Head. I am surrounded by friends and family including my father and mother and a retinue of aunts on both sides. In the corner there is a woman, an old woman whose name I can't remember. She looks familiar, and based on her features I think she may be from my mother's side of the family. In the image, she is holding a white sphere about the size of a croquet ball. The image of the ball is fuzzy, but I can remember it from when she showed it to me all those years ago. She was an old woman, older than my grandparents, who identified her as a distant cousin who showed up from time to time. She was an eccentric they said, always traveling, never at any fixed address. She wore strange clothes, and odd hats. Her perfume smelled like cinnamon, with a hint of vanilla. She shows me the crystal sphere; it is slightly flattened at both ends, but smooth and radiant. The interior is cloudy, milky white with tiny inflections that capture the light. She handles it with gloves, passing it back and forth between her hands with eerie fluid movements like a circus entertainer. I reach out for the *objet d'art* and she snatches it back. She shakes her head and then puts the sphere away inside an ebony box with a brass latch. She says she cannot stay, kisses me on the forehead and tells me to remember her. I beg her not to go, she is by far the most entertaining and fascinating adult I have ever met. She promises that she will return. Once to show me what the orb can do, and once again to make it mine. I make her promise, and she does so without hesitation. I remember when she returned to fulfill the first part of that bargain, it was my eighteenth birthday and she stole six years of my life. In return, she gave me adventure. We were companions, Alice the Younger her friends called me, for she was Alice the Elder, a grand dame amongst . . . well the universe. All of time and space were ours to wander through, and we did so with ease. We had breakfast in Hyperborea where mastodons and giant flightless birds roamed the fields. We sunbathed on the shores of the Martian ocean, and had lizard fish for lunch. We went dancing in Irem and supped on figs and grapes. We visited distant Celeano and found books that sang and lulled us to sleep.

 Six years, and it was worth every minute. Six years and it wasn't long enough. Six years that left me changed, tainted, perhaps even enchanted. I became something of a magnet I suppose, but whether I was drawn to those that would be unbound in time, or somehow, they were drawn to me I shall never know. I don't think it matters. It didn't then, it doesn't now.

 I close the book. On the cover, there is a mirror and I catch my own reflection. Have I really grown that old? It takes me a moment, but I recognize the lines in that face, I see the iron gray hair and the fascinating woman I have become. I recognize myself, not in the mirror, but from the photograph, and the images I have in my memory. I am Alice, but not Alice the Younger, the upstart, the companion, but Alice the Elder, the confident, the entertaining, the fearless. I may be old, but I am not yet dead.

I rise up out of my chair and one of my grandchildren comes bounding along with another gift. It is a box of ebony with a brass latch. I ask him where it came from, and he points toward a figure on the veranda. She is ancient, withered, but still defiant. She is Alice the Eldest, ready to retire, ready to settle, ready to pass on. I wave at her and she waves me away. I grab my bag and my parasol. I open the box and start walking; there is a spark in my stride. The orb feels good in my hand, warm and inviting. I know instinctively how to use it. I leave the party unseen and step sideways out of the universe and into the place between time and space. There are adventures to be had, and promises to keep. I have lifetimes to live, and a companion to train, perhaps this time I shall provide more direction on how I expect her to live my life.

1946

HANNAH AND HER MOTHER TAKE A VERY LONG LUNCH

I was crossing the street when I was suddenly pulled sidewise. I had been in Arkham doing some shopping for John who needed some new clothes for school. I had stayed later than expected, the streets were dark and slick from rain. I heard the tires of a car screech and then a scream. I had been in Arkham and then I wasn't anymore. I was in a small café, stumbling through the foyer, an older woman had me by the arm. I had lost my umbrella, and the small bag of shirts I had just bought. I felt a slight touch of vertigo, a side effect of being pulled sidewise. I reached out and put my hand on that of the woman who had pulled me through space and time.

"Hello mother," I said. I hated the way she hijacked me whenever she could, the downside of having a mother who was a time traveler. She had never done it in front of Sam or John, thank God. I had no idea how to explain that to the man I loved, or his stern and parochial family. The Becketts were firmly grounded people and had no place for the bizarre in their world. It was something I couldn't explain to her. I had tried, but as much as I didn't understand her, she didn't understand me.

Alice Keezar smiled at me, she was seventy-six years old but didn't look a day over sixty. "Hello Hannah," she said barely moving her lips. "It's been a long time. We are having lunch."

"It hasn't been that long. We just had lunch last week," I reminded her.

She shook her head. "That's your perspective dear, from mine it's been absolute ages."

I looked around trying to get my bearings. The place was white and trimmed in neon, we had been here before. I hadn't liked it; the waitresses were all voluptuous brunettes. "Why do you bring me here mother?"

She was weaving her way through the aisles toward an empty table. "I love eating at Monk's, it's quiet and safe, nothing ever happens here. Nothing. At my age, in my line of work having a place where nothing happens can be very comforting."

"I suppose." I looked out the window at the New York traffic, the cars were still familiar. "Can I ask when we are?"

"You can ask dear," she gave me a sly smile over her shoulder and then added, "We're still in 1946".

We found a small two-top across from a booth where another pair of women were having lunch. They looked familiar but the fog on my glasses kept me from seeing them clearly. They were arguing about something, though it seemed I couldn't quite make out what it was.

We looked at our menus, knowing that I would end up just ordering coffee and a piece of pie, while my mother would hem and haw about various dishes but end up getting the big salad.

"I preferred the coffee in that place in L.A. in the Thirties. What was it called?"

She suddenly became indignant. "The Nite Owl?! No dear we can't go there anymore, not since 1950. The cook was killed, the waitress too. Too many ghosts. They haunt the past you know."

I didn't know, but it was too much to ask her to explain. The waitress came and took our orders. After she had gone my mother took a compact and a tube of lipstick out of her purse. She used the mirror in the compact and casually applied something called 'emerging taupe' so her already colored lips. She was nervous, she always applied makeup when she was nervous.

"Why am I here mother?"

"I need to ask you a philosophical question," she sighed heavily. "You've read about what's being revealed at Nuremburg. You know the horrors that Hitler and his deputies instigated on the world. This last decade, the war and everything else, millions of people died. Millions more suffered. If you could, if you had the power to do so, would you go back and prevent it from happening?" She paused and looked me in the eye. "If you could travel in time, would you go back and kill the child that would become Adolf Hitler and save millions?"

I sat there for a moment thinking she was joking, and that as philosophical questions went, it was in very poor taste. Then I realized that she wasn't joking. That for her, given what she could do, this was a practical consideration, and there was nothing philosophical about it. I opened my mouth to say something, anything but then closed it again as the waitress returned with our coffee. It was only after she left and I had poured cream and two sugars in that I finally responded with muffled outrage.

"This is the big question you're wrestling with? If you could travel in time and go back and kill Hitler, would you? Mother," I said the word in an exasperate voice, "you can go back in time and kill Hitler, you can prevent the war, you can save millions."

She closed her eyes and shook her head slightly. "Maybe I'm being too specific. Let me rephrase the question. If you could go back in time and kill an evil man before they did evil, and in the process, improve the lives of potentially every person on the planet, would you?"

"Like Hitler?" I blurted.

She nodded, "As one example, if you need one."

I leaned back in my chair indignant. "Yes, of course, no question about it."

My mother closed her eyes and dipped her head a little. There was sadness in her voice. "What if it wasn't an evil man?"

"I'm not sure what you mean."

"What if you could go back and kill someone whose death would mean that the lives of millions of people would be improved, that the fate of the entire world would improve forever, but that person, the person whom you have to kill, is completely innocent, he's done nothing wrong, nothing at all."

"I don't understand, how can killing an innocent person

improve the world?"

The look on her face became serious. "Not everything is black and white my dear. We tend to think of Abraham Lincoln as 'The Great Emancipator', but there is a school of thought that says what he and the other abolitionists did created more problems than it solved. These people believe that slavery would have died out on its own, replaced by technology that was faster and more reliable. This faction believes that if Lincoln hadn't been elected the Civil War would have been avoided, slavery would have been abolished by 1875 or so, and the rise of segregation and subsequent racial tensions which dominate the Twentieth Century would have been avoided."

"But what about the moral issue? Slavery was wrong" I stammered out.

"The moral issue." She nodded condescendingly. "Like killing a baby that hasn't done anything?"

I glared at her, "Yet. Hasn't done anything yet. But we know he would."

"So, in your mind it's acceptable to proactively kill an evil man to save the world, but not a good one? Because why"

She had cornered me, philosophically. "I suppose not. I suppose that if one is willing to kill an evil man to save the world, one might also be willing to kill a good man as well." I sipped my coffee and stared at her. She seemed suddenly melancholy. "Does that make things easier for you mother? Does that put things in perspective?"

There was sadness in her voice. "It definitely puts things in perspective, but it doesn't make things easier, not in the least."

Suddenly I realized that I had no idea what this conversation was about. "Take me home mother. Take me home and then go kill Hitler, or Hitler's father, or his mother, or both of them. Go do whatever it is you are going to do, but take me home first."

"I can't." There was a tear in her eye.

"You can't kill Hitler? Why not? What was the point of all this?"

"Oh, I could kill Hitler. Today if I wanted to. But I don't want to. Some of us do, some of us don't. It's all a matter of perspective, of what future you've seen and what you're willing to accept as an outcome."

"I don't understand."

She was smiling and crying at the same time. "In the future, the one without Hitler, the one in which we killed him, a man comes to power in the United States, a terrible man, an oligarch. He spews hatred of the poor, and the sick, and foreigners, and immigrants. Without the example of Hitler, of those atrocities, and of the laws that were passed because of it, that man, that terrible man comes to power. He kills billions. He wipes entire nations off the map. He reduces the world population by half in just ten years." She lowered her head in shame. "We need Hitler to show us how awful we can be, what monsters we can become. We need that lesson, so that we don't commit worse, more horrible atrocities. We need to be able to stand up and say, 'Never Again!'."

"Then what are we talking about?"

"Your grandson Hannah is going to be an incredible man, they will call him the next Einstein. He'll be raised by his parents on a dairy farm in Indiana. His grandfather, your husband, will fill his head with stories. Crazy stories, about how the universe, space and time, the stars and planets all work. He'll tell stories about his wife's mother and how she would walk between planets and history. He won't believe them of course, but they'll help shape him into an incredible scientist."

I could feel my throat tighten and tears well up in my eyes. "What about me?"

She reluctantly shook her head. "I'm sorry Hannah. I really am."

"The car on the road, the screeching brakes . . . You can't save me? John Samuel is only sixteen."

She reached out and took my hand. "I can save you, but if you go back to Sam and John, they won't go to the family farm in Indiana and then John won't meet Thelma Louise and have the children they need to have. Saving you, would destroy the world Hannah."

I laugh through my rising sob. "You're exaggerating."

She laughs a little too. "No. No, I'm not."

"So, what happens next?"

"We finish our lunch, and when you're ready. I'll take you back."

"What if I don't want to go back?"

"You can't stay here. You would interfere with the timeline." She pauses, and I can tell she's thinking. "We've tried that Hannah. This isn't the first-time round." She points at another table in the corner and I see her there in the other booth, staring back at me, over the shoulder of my own temporal doppelganger. I look around the room and there are dozens of us, all sitting, all having lunch, all having the same conversation.

"Why? Why repeat the process so many times?"

She shrugs. "Maybe I just like having lunch with my daughter."

"Does it always end the same? Do I always go back to die?"

"Sometimes you cause a scene. Sometimes you fight. Sometimes you try and go with me, become my companion, traveling through time and space. It doesn't end well."

"Why not?"

She reaches down into her bag and pulls out the milky white sphere that allows her to move through space and time. She sets it on the table. It's flattened on opposite ends so instead of rolling off it just sits there. "The sphere isn't very smart, it can't handle transitioning more than one genetic code at a time. I've travelled with others before, mostly myself, older or younger versions. I'm the Elder Alice, later on I'll be Eldest, but before then I'll find the Younger Alice. We all have the same DNA so if there's a mix up it's not a big deal. But if you bring an entirely different person into the fray, the consequences are deadly. Since I'm the dominant party, I always end up winning. If you can call it that."

"I don't understand."

"I know you don't. But you will, you're very clever. At least you will be." She took her hands off the sphere. "There's a way. It's taken us a long time to figure it out, but we did. Now we just have to get you to figure it out." She stood up. "Now if you'll excuse me I have to powder my nose."

And then she left, and the sphere sat there on the table, the queer interior seemed to flow like a cloud of oil in a pool of water. I glanced about the room and realized that my mother was watching me, all of them were watching to see what I would do. I sat there staring at them, staring at me, watching the second-hand beat round the clock, not once not twice but thrice. There were butterflies in my stomach as I stood up and grabbed the sphere from the table.

I went to turn, but suddenly a hand grabbed my wrist and spun me back around. "You can never see Sam or John or your grandchildren. Do you understand that? If you break that rule, they will hunt you down and kill us!"

"Mother!" I barked, and looked her in the eye, but it wasn't my mother. It looked like my mother, it sounded like my mother, but it wasn't her. I was staring at myself, but not myself now, myself from the future, and I was giving myself the best advice I could be given.

"I understand." There were tears in my eyes as I cradled the milky glass globe and fingered it just as I had seen my mother do so many times before. As I stepped sidewise and refted through time and space I caught a last glimpse of the coffee shop, of the waitress bringing my slice of cherry pie and my mother's salad; of my mother coming back from the ladies' room; of me – the future me - sitting down with her, and the two of them smiling as my echo placed the sphere back on the table.

It looked like for the first time in forever we were actually having lunch. How long will it actually take for me to understand my mother? From the age of my face I suspect it will be a long time.

I look forward to that slice of cherry pie.

1948

THE STATEMENT OF LINCOLN ROBINSON

It was in the early morning hours of October 27, 1948 that death came to Hedora. I had taken the train out of Pittsburgh, bouncing along one of the industrial lines that runs south towards Morgantown. The train rolled past the thin, wispy trees that sat on low hills that framed the surrounding valleys of winding grey Yuggoheny River. Black mills squatted like fat toads amidst low, red brick houses stained with a greasy yellow soot. The air was stagnant and thick with the stink of sulfur and carbon and steel. It was a sad, depressing village, where I was sure sad, depressing people labored through the course of their lives, struggling to survive amongst the belching industrial smokestacks that devoured equal parts coal and ore and humanity.

It was to this bleak landscape that my new client had come to teach. According to the agency he had been a professor of economics and psychology and was now engaged in merging both fields into something he called Marketing, a concept that the local steel and wire mills wanted to understand and leverage. He had been giving seminars at the local university where after a rather long lecture he had found himself short of breath and unable to stand. For a man of seventy-seven years such an event was not surprising, but when the weakness persisted the dean of the sponsoring department had thought it prudent to engage a private nurse to help the man through his convalescence. I had just recently finished with a long-term client and had asked the agency to place me with clients with short-term needs. Thus, when I was offered the position with Professor Nathaniel Wingate Peaslee I readily accepted, even though I had never met the man.

It was just barely dawn, and I was standing there on the platform waiting for my ride. I watched in curiosity as a fog moved down the river. It was thick and pale with swirls of yellow and green that seemed to catch the moonlight and transform it into something weak and sickly. It was fascinating to watch, like a shoal of fish flashing in the depths of the sea as they fled from a pursuing predator. I could almost see it, that dark shadow that lurked within, floating, stalking, and waiting for its prey to make a mistake. And then a car entered the lot and the lights scanned across the mist and the illusion was lost.

As I walked through the parking lot, the gravel crunching beneath my feet, the driver's door opened and a young man stepped out. He was by my estimation, in his early twenties, lean and pale with sandy brown hair. He was wearing a light jacket, too light for the seasonal cold that was creeping in, but that was the way of young men, to test the elements, defy them, and prove that they were still young and virile.

"Boy," he said to me, even though I was at least three decades older than he was, "I'm looking for a woman named Robinson who was supposed to be on the morning train."

I was careful in how I responded. "I'm Lincoln Robinson. I'm here to tend to Professor Peaslee."

You would have thought I had spit in his beer. He stopped dead in his tracks and looked at me. "My name is Davis Ford. I'm from the hotel. I'm supposed to collect you get you settled and then take you over to see the professor." His hand reached out to take my bag but then his eyes darted around, and the hand withdrew. He was obviously uncomfortable. "Let's get you over to the cottage. We can sort things out with the hotel later."

Within minutes we were on the street driving through the tiny town. My bag was on the seat next to me, and every so often I would catch Ford's eyes in the rearview mirror, staring at me.

"Is there a problem Mister Ford?" I was respectful, perhaps even meek as I asked the question.

His back went rigid and the words tumbled out of his mouth awkwardly. "They didn't – no one told me – that is."

He was dancing around the subject, uncomfortable with

the position he had been placed in. "You didn't know what Mister Ford? That I was a man? I was a volunteer medic in the war, lots of men were, and some of us took to nursing afterwards."

"No, that's not it." He glared at me in confusion and a little shame. "I just assumed that you were a woman, but they should have told me you were a . . ."

He never finished the sentence, he didn't want to finish the sentence, so I finished it for him. "They didn't tell you I was a nigger? Is that it?" In the mirror, I saw him lower his eyes. "Would it have made a difference? Would you not have come for me yourself? Would I be walking now instead?"

He opened his mouth and paused before speaking. He was choosing his words carefully. The shame had grown large, you could hear it in his voice. "It makes no difference to me, but Mrs. Gorski, she runs the hotel, and she doesn't allow coloreds."

I nodded reluctantly. "Of course not. Good old Mrs. Gorski, a shining example of human kindness and decency. Well, for a Pollack that is." Ford snorted a laugh. "I don't want any trouble Mr. Ford, not with you or with Mrs. Gorski. Can you fix things? Not for me mind you, but for Professor Peaslee? He doesn't need to be bothered by this does he?"

"No. No, we don't need to bother him. Not at all." Ford's shoulders relaxed, I had given him a way out, one that preserved his position. I relaxed back in the seat and watched as the fog seemed to race us down the streets of the sad little town of Hedora.

It was just before eight when Mister Ford walked me up the sidewalk to the small, concrete block cottage that served as guest faculty housing. Professor Peaslee was sitting on the front porch in his bathrobe and slippers drinking coffee. There was an untouched piece of toast covered with jam on a side table. As we came up the steps he moved to stand but then when the act revealed itself to be too much for him, he slumped back down with a look of frustration on his face.

"Professor," Ford addressed him with respect, "this is Lincoln, and he's come to help tend to you."

The thin, old man slid the round framed glasses off his balding and liver-spotted head and down to his small crinkled nose. Even with the glasses he squinted at me, and then harrumphed. "I assume, Lincoln, that you have a surname?"

I nodded. "Yes sir Professor, my family name is Robinson."

He glared at Ford. "If you call me Professor, I'll address you as Mister Robinson, out of respect."

Ford looked down and shuffled his feet. "I'll take care of that problem Linc – Mr. Robinson. I'll let you know how it resolves in an hour or so."

"Thank you, Mister Ford," but before I could even say that, he was down the walkway and headed to the car. "Professor, let's get you inside and see about getting a proper breakfast for you."

I held out my hand and after the aging educator had gripped it, gently pulled the man to his feet. "That is some grip you've got there Mr. Robinson, arms like tree trunks."

"Thank you, sir, leftover from a misspent youth. My brother and I used to make some money on the side as amateur boxers."

The old man paused and looked at me intensely. "You're Chaingang Lincoln. I saw you fight in Boston, it had to be fifty years ago. You had a brother . . . what was his name?"

"James Buchanan, they called him the Harlem Smoke."

Peaslee smiled as the memory returned. 'That's right, whatever happened to you two?"

We crossed the threshold and went inside the cottage. "James went north to make some money amongst the amateurs. Illegal fight clubs, bare knuckle stuff. He never came back. We looked for six months, but no one would help us. Even the state police wouldn't give us the time of day. After that my mother wouldn't let me fight anymore. I finished college, got my medical degree. I've served in two wars now, tending to the sick and injured soldiers in Europe, but here in the states the best I can do is be a nurse, a highly qualified nurse."

"I'm sorry," muttered the man as he slid into a dining room chair.

"Don't be, I've lived a fine life, better than my father's, better than a whole lot of people."

He nodded. "Would you do me a favor? Close the door. The fog is rolling in and I have come to loathe it so. The horrid stuff makes my eyes burn and my lungs ache."

I looked out on the street and sure enough there it was, the yellow mist that I had seen rolling down the river. It was there in the street, creeping up the sidewalk, as if it had followed me, as if it was the taxman come to collect what was due him. It lingered and roiled still catching the light and holding hidden dark depths where shadowy forms lingered and hung, waiting to strike.

I shut the door and locked it tight.

It was two hours before Ford returned, and in that time, I learned that the local doctor, a man whose name I can't recall, had diagnosed the Professor with shortness of breath brought on by fumes from the steel mill. He had been advised to stay away from the industry for a few weeks and then to limit his visits to just an hour a day. It didn't seem like he needed a nurse, but then I saw the Parke-Davis glaseptic nebulizer he had been given. That combined with the state of the groceries, or lack thereof, in the kitchen and I knew the old man would need my help for at least a week.

Ford wanted to take me directly to my room, but instead I forced him to go to the grocer first and then the butcher. Only then did I let him drop me off at the ramshackle boarding house on the wrong side of town where he had procured me a bed. It wasn't far from the Professor's cottage, only two miles and I made Ford draw me a map, just in case I had to walk it one day.

All of this of course was done in the presence of the queer fog that had grown to cover the entire village. At this point it was about a foot high, thick and a pale yellow that clung to the ground and swirled around your legs as you walked. I was grateful that the boarding house sat on a small rise, and the room I had been assigned had been located on the second floor.

The proprietor of the house was named Facciolo, a woman of Italian origin. The meal rules were simple. Guests were welcome to serve themselves bread, cheese and from a pot of red sauce simmering on the stove. Lunch she would make spaghetti, and dinner would consist of ravioli. Lasagna would be made for the weekends. Towels were in the closet in the hall, and she would change linens on Mondays. Exhausted from my early morning trip I cut myself a small piece of cheese, had a cup of tea and then retired to my room. It had been my intent to just rest my eyes, but instead I quickly found myself in a deep slumber dreaming of my Lorraine and the fabulous smells that had once wafted out of her kitchen.

It was the mill whistle that woke me from my rest. As I sat there on the edge of the bed gathering my wits I heard the steady march of footsteps on the street. Curious I pulled aside the curtains and saw the parade of workmen coming down the street from the mill. All around them, the yellow fog swirled. It was waist high now, and thicker too. The men looked as if they were wading through a low tide of butter cream. It was—to my eye—a horrid and unnerving sight, but the cohort of machinists who slogged home through the stuff seemed to be completely oblivious to it. It was as if this were a regular occurrence for them, a minor meteorological inconvenience, like rain or snow. Downstairs over dinner I asked my hostess about it. She just shrugged and called it "mill-smoke" that would be gone by morning. The other guests weren't any more helpful. After dinner, I listened to the radio out of Pittsburgh and then retired to my room around nine. I read for about an hour, losing myself in Ashton Clark's history of Averoigne before letting the book fall to my chest and succumbing once more to sleep.

Thursday morning came and I was greeted by the smell of coffee and bacon wafting up through the stairwell. A quick shower and I was downstairs at Mrs. Facciolo's lace covered table. Her bacon was crisp, her coffee strong and her scrambled eggs laced with chives and cilantro, a combination I had never experienced before and found rather enjoyable. In half an hour, I was out the door, just in time to see Ford drive up in his Commander Coupe. The fog was not gone. Indeed, it was thicker and deeper than ever, and the grey car with its fins looked like a shark swimming in custard. It would have been funny had not the acrid smell of the stuff begun to irritate my nasal passages. I would have said something to Ford but the man looked put out by even being there, and so I kept my mouth shut, and in silence allowed myself to be driven through the strange mist-filled streets. As we drove, waves of yellow occasionally flowed over the windshield and roof, as if we were a ship plowing through rough seas.

At the cottage Ford waited till I was halfway up the walkway before speeding off, and I came to the conclusion that it bothered him to be driving a black man around town. The hypocrisy of all this was that if I had been driving my own car, I probably would have been pulled over and arrested. Trumped up charges were common in small towns like these and I knew several men who had been incarcerated on suspicion of theft or for violating the Mann Act. Racial humiliation was a fact of life not only in the South, but in western Pennsylvania, which had more in common with Virginia and West Virginia than it did with the more integrated areas of the northeast of the country.

I trudged through the waist-high mist, a handkerchief over my mouth and nose, and was glad when I took the steps that led up onto the porch and above the acrid stuff. I let myself in using the key that the Professor had given me the day before. I set water to boiling on the stove and then took out two eggs, some bread and a slice of thick bacon. I greased a pan with the bacon and set it on a burner on low. Then I walked down the hall and knocked on the door of the Professor's bedroom. He grunted in a groggy manner as I let him know his breakfast would be ready in five minutes. I returned to the kitchen, finished making him breakfast and set it on the table just as he emerged from his bedroom.

Immediately I knew that he had not slept well, and I regretted making the pot of coffee. He sat down with a weak thump. After a taste of everything, he smiled and made conversation between bites. He acknowledged not getting much rest, but blamed it on the cats that had been climbing on the roof and hissing through the night. "It was the thumping that kept me awake. By the sound of it, there must have been two or three of them up there, climbing around and hissing at each other." He related the tale in an affable manner. "I kept dozing off and then they would jump or hiss and I would sit up in bed startled. Sometimes the hissing overlapped with my dreams and it was like they were calling my name." He laughed, and I laughed as well, but I couldn't help but think that the man had simply become senile with age.

After breakfast, I helped him with his treatment, and for a moment considered taking him for a walk, but the fog nixed that idea. Instead we listened to his collection of records. I had never heard the work of de Hond before, and I was impressed by the work, though I admitted it was strange.

"An acquired taste, for sure," he noted. "I had heard them before of course, but it wasn't until after a trip to Australia that I had listened to the man's work in earnest. We had been in the Australian desert and a colleague had brought his collection of de Hond along." His face took on a sad almost melancholy cast. "I had forgotten that." He looked at me with those big eyes that some elderly patients get when they remember things they have forgotten, not just little things, but whole swathes of life, of experiences, of people. Can you imagine what it must feel like to suddenly remember that you have a son or a daughter? It is a feeling of elation from the flood of sudden memories, but at the same time a sad sense of loss, because you realize that your mind is failing you. That is how Professor Peaslee looked at me right then.

He asked, "Do you know who I am?" and I shook my head no. He wandered back into his bedroom and quickly returned with a large manila file stuffed to overflowing. He handed it to me. There were newspaper articles dating from the early part of the century with headlines that announced UNIVERSITY PROFESSOR A VICTIM OF AMNESIA, THE MAN WHO FORGOT HIMSELF, and PEASLEE BEGINS WORLD TRAVELS.

This was how I was introduced to the man who I was taking care of, through the pages of terrible journalism that treated his memory loss as a sideshow attraction. Even his eventual recovery, which was years later, was treated as a spectacle. The neurological condition shattered the man's life. He had been an economist, but the nightmares and random memories that seemed to intrude into his life, from those strange years made it difficult to lecture. Eventually he all but abandoned his work for the study of psychology, and the quest for a manner in which to understand what had been happened to him. His work, as well as that of his son culminated in an expedition to Australia in search of what he had thought would be evidence of a kind of ancient hoax or proto-cultural mass hysteria. Instead he found something far worse, and the expedition suffered the loss of human life and credibility. That had been almost two decades earlier, and he had spent that time trying to rebuild what was left of his life, to find some way to be useful, meaningful again.

As I flipped through the last pages he spoke in a voice full of heartbreak. "My son wrote a book about me. It made him famous." He sniffled a bit. "My own son betrayed me, and the secrets I hoped to keep."

I looked at him and for the life of me could think of nothing to say.

Later that evening, after preparing two meals, making sure his treatments were administered and that he had clean laundry and sheets, I waited outside on the porch for Ford to drive me back to the hotel. After an hour of waiting, watching the mist rise and fall with the wind I finally decided that I would make my own way to my rooms. I tied a handkerchief around my mouth and nose and began walking down the street, the low mist flowing before me like water. Behind me, a wake formed, sending small waves to lap against the porches and doors of all the houses I passed.

Within minutes my eyes were watering and my nose and mouth were burning. I began a habit of controlled breathing, finding a clearing with cleaner air, taking a breath, and then racing to the next such clearing. On more than one occasion I ended up gasping for air, and when this happened I found myself forced to climb up on whatever was available to reach clear air, and more than once I was forced to flee from angry homeowners whose porches I had invaded. Once I climbed up onto the running board of a car, not realizing that it was occupied, and I nearly fell when he pounded on the window to scare me off.

By the time I reached the boarding house my eyes stung and my own breathing was a sickly, rasping wheeze. Mrs. Facciolo gasped at my appearance and sent me right to the shower. Dinner had long been over, but the woman took pity on me and I found on my side table a bowl of cold pasta covered in a thin tomato sauce that hid a rather large, greasy looking sausage. It wasn't as appetizing as it could have been, but I ate it with gusto. Afterwards, I collapsed in my bed with a wet cloth over my eyes.

That night, I dreamed of being buried alive, and being slowly smothered by the thick, noxious air of my own breath, a breath that was colored a sickening yellow and left my mouth in great gouts of phlegm.

The next morning, I woke up sick. My head was pounding, my throat was raw and my eyes were cloudy and red. I went downstairs almost immediately to apologize and ask Mr. Ford to wait for me. Instead I was informed by Mrs. Facciolo that Mr. Ford was not coming. The fog was too thick. Visibility was, according to the old Italian, just a few inches. I laughed at the idea, but then peered out the window and saw that it was the truth.

The fog was thick and deep, and was lapping at the door and windows of the house. The landlady had done her best to seal all the cracks with wet cloths, but there were still places where you could see the wispy yellow seeping in. It was clear that I wasn't going to be able to get back to the Professor's house, and so I asked to use the telephone.

It took me a moment, and he didn't pick up until the fifth ring, but Professor Peaslee's voice came across the wire faint and full of static. "Mr. Robinson? Don't you worry about coming - here. I can make my own - breakfast and I operate that infernal medi- device fine. You stay out of that mist, it's not fit for man nor beast. Though apparently the cats don't mind it that much. ---ve been---- all night and - morning --- calling my name."

"Professor who is calling your name? What are you talking about?"

"They whisper Mister Rob--- The- - - per in the darkness and in the mist - - - go with them."

"Stay inside Professor Peaslee. Don't go anywhere." Then the line went dead, and whatever else I said doesn't matter.

I spent the next several hours rummaging through Mrs. Facciolo's kitchen and basement taking inventory of what was available. She was animated in her opposition to me pawing through her dead husband's personal items, but it was here that I found a significant number of useful things. Most notable were the welding googles and a gas mask left over from the

152 | THE PEASLEE PAPERS

Great War. The glass on the mask was broken, and the filter material was all rotted, but I could rig something up, maybe cheese cloth or something similar. It wasn't enough to make me comfortable to go outside, but if I was forced it might do in a pinch. I put all the various pieces, including a pair of fishing waders and a heavy coat, into a duffel bag and stashed it by my medical bag in my room.

An eerie stillness had settled over the town. No birds were singing, no dogs barked, and no people walked the streets. So rare were vehicles that one of the other residents took to playing a game of car-spotting; trying to identify the owners of various vehicles that creeped down the road, hugging the curb in a desperate attempt to steer. Most of these were police cars or even fire rescue vehicles, but every so often a private car would be spotted, and the driver would be identified as a local physician, likely calling on a patient who had succumbed to the noxious gasses that haunted the streets. The rest of us sat around the radio listening to a news station out of Monroeville in hopes of some word of our situation. Unfortunately, our plight was seemingly unimportant, and instead we were subjected to a business report about the development of a new plant by Darrow & Delapore Chemical, thanks to a contract from the army.

Sometime after lunch as we sat waiting we heard the now rare sound of a car coming down the road, and then the sudden thump as it hit the pavement outside the house. Within seconds Mister Ford was forcing his way into the house, his mouth and nose covered with a wet towel, his eyes red and weeping. It took him a moment to catch his breath, and all the while Mrs. Facciolo was ranting about the yellow mist that had seeped inside. She was trying to seal the cracks around the door back up with one hand, while she waved the air around her face with the other. Outside in the street we could still hear the engine of Ford's car as it idled.

"Robinson," he coughed my name and pointed at me. "Get yer stuff, yer needed down at the hotel. Lots of people are sick there. Doctor Ewel could use a hand."

I balked for a moment, but only for a moment. Then I remembered what had happened to my cousin Tom down in Maycomb and I shut my mouth and went up the stairs. I picked up my medical bag and the duffel that held the junk I had found and then headed back down the stairs. Ford was standing there and the look in his eye wasn't one that I found comforting. Suddenly Mrs. Facciolo was clinging to the man, begging for him not to take me with him. He forced the old woman off, throwing her to the floor. I rushed down the last few stairs yelling at him to stop. He turned and I saw his fist flying through the air. He caught me on the chin, I tried to roll with it, but caught my forehead on the bannister. I went down like a wet sack and stayed there thinking that I hadn't taken a fall in years. Then I hit the floor myself and the light behind my eyes went dark.

    I woke in a dimly lit room I didn't recognize, but somehow knew had to be the lobby of the hotel run by Mrs. Gorski. I was crumpled on a couch. My bags were on the floor next to me. The duffel was closed, but the medical bag was open and a jumbled mess. In the twilight of the room I could see an old man slumped into an armchair. He was watching me as I got to my feet.

    "Take it easy fella," he whispered. "You've got a nasty bump on your head and a bruise on your jaw. Ford must have clocked you pretty good."

    My hand went to my head. "I've had worse."

    "I could tell. I'm Doctor Davis Ewel. It was I who sent Ford to go get you. I apologize for the way you've been treated. He was supposed to ask nicely."

    I looked at him and then at my bag. He had an apologetic look on his face. "Mrs. Gorski and the rest of the guests took shelter in the basement. It has thick stone walls and only two doors, which they sealed with candle wax. A good idea , until one of them panicked, claustrophobia I suppose. Somebody opened the door to the outside and the mist came pouring in like a flood."

    "They all right?"

    He shook his head. "Old Harvey died in the basement. Bernard coughed up blood for a couple hours, but he passed just after I got here. Mrs. Gorski is blind, but I think that's temporary."

    I looked at the clock behind the desk. It was nearly five in the morning, I'd lost more than twelve hours. There was a phone. I pointed, "Does that work?"

"Uhuh, might not be able to get through though, lines are down all over town."

The dial tone was a welcome sound. In seconds, I had the Professor's phone ringing.

"Lincoln," he spoke before I had even said anything. His voice was distant, tinny, as if I had called cross country instead of just a few blocks. "Lincoln, they're here. They aren't cats at all. They're something else entirely. Something from outside. I thought perhaps they might be polyps, I say this because they're partially invisible. But they're too organized, too structured. They fly with wings, great membranous things, but not like a bat or a butterfly or a wasp. They've come for me. All this is for me. They want to help me remember. They want to take my pain away. It would be so nice to live without pain once more." He paused, how did he know it was me? "You're the only one who would call Lincoln. I've said yes. They only wanted me if I said yes. I had to consent Lincoln. Tell my son I forgive him."

The line disconnected. I tried calling back, but this time there was no answer. I nearly threw the phone at the wall, but Ewel was watching me and I gained control of myself. I don't know why I felt so much for the old man. Maybe it was because I was paid to. Maybe it was the idea of him sitting in that cottage slowly going mad. I can't say, but for whatever reason I tore open the duffel bag and began assembling my makeshift gas suit.

It was dawn on Saturday morning when I finally finished and using a piece of rope cinched the heavy coat about my waist so that the opening in the waders was completely covered. I was three steps from the front door when I heard Ford call my name. I threw the aperture open and nearly fell down the steps. Ford rushed in behind me but stopped at the door. I turned to face him, expecting him to launch himself at me, but instead he just grinned evilly and with both hands shut the heavy oak entryway. I heard the lock click into place and then the porch light clicked off.

In seconds, I could no longer see the door, but it didn't matter. I ran down the street, moving as fast as the makeshift garb would let me. I was two blocks away before I realized that

I didn't know where I was, or how to get where I was going. Visibility was mere inches and I was standing in the middle of the street, with no idea where to go. I decide to keep moving down the road, swimming as much as walking through the thick, soupy fumes.

I wandered the streets for hours, marking distance by careening from street corner to street corner looking desperately for a road whose name I recognized, but to be honest I hadn't paid that much attention. I knew how to get from the boarding house to the Professor's cottage, but that was it.

And so, I roamed the streets of Hedora, an ersatz knight in a homemade suit of armor. I was a comic Don Quixote, jousting against a dragon that I could neither harm nor escape. Undaunted I eventually found a hill and followed the road that mounted it until I reached the peak. The mist was thinner there and I could see the great stone church that surmounted the hillock. The two massive wooden doors were painted red, but they were not locked, and so I was granted access. The interior of the edifice was empty, and I found my way back into the bell tower laboring up the stairs to the bell itself.

The air was clear in that small chamber and from the open windows I could see for miles in all directions, but despite my vantage point all I could take in was a sea of yellow mist and the sickly pale glow of the setting sun. Exhausted and sick from my sojourn I collapsed in the belfry and eventually slept, the dreams of suffocating still haunted my mind.

I woke the next morning to rain falling on my face. It was Sunday October Thirty-First, Halloween, but I doubted there would be any revelry, though oddly enough I was dressed for it. The rain was heavy, and came with a fierce wind that blew out of the north. The strange mist responded as if it didn't want to leave. It washed out of the streets, but clung to the buildings like a living thing, straining to keep a foothold. But it was no use. Within the hour the vast majority of the choking fumes were gone, with only a few pockets remaining in thick groves and back alleyways which gave shelter from the wind and rain.

As the streets cleared, the layout of the town became clear and I could see where I was and where I should be, and how to get there. Stripping off my makeshift armor I ran from the church as fast as my aching legs could carry me. The door to Professor Peaslee's cottage was open, and the room was cold and had a rank metallic smell to it. I threw open his bedroom door, not even bothering to knock. He was lying there in his bed. I called his name but there was no response. I touched his hand, but it was cold. I turned back to the other room and dialed the police frantically telling them where I was and that I needed an ambulance. Not that it mattered,

That was three weeks ago. Twenty-five people died over the course of the five days that the fog sat in Hedora. Another ten have died since, and as I understand it there are more than a dozen still in the hospital. None are suspected to survive. I was arrested on November the third, and charged with murder, a charge that I did not understand until the prosecutor asked me how I had done it. "How," he asked, "did you kill Professor Peaslee?"

I told him that Peaslee had died from the mist, but he just shook his head. According to the coroner's report Peaslee had died sometime between Thursday and Friday afternoon, and not through asphyxiation or by exposure to the fog. I protested telling them that he had been alive when Ford had picked me up on Thursday, and I had spoken to him on Friday morning, and then again on Saturday. Mrs. Facciolo and Doctor Ewel could confirm that.

Of course, they couldn't.

Ford agreed that he picked me up, but he never saw the Professor. Mrs. Facciolo and Dr. Ewel offered that I did call the cottage, but they could not confirm that I had ever talked to anyone, let alone the Professor. I am a victim of circumstance, and even the public defender assigned to me asks how I did it. To which I refused to answer.

As was my right I was granted access to a copy of the coroner's report. Based on various factors of decay it is confirmed that Nathaniel Wingate Peaslee had been dead for at least forty hours, but no more than eighty hours, putting the time of death between Thursday and Friday afternoon. Although the body was covered with residue, unlike the other victims of the fog, the lungs showed no signs of fluorine gas, indicating that Peaslee had died prior to the mist reaching into the cottage. As much as I hated to admit it that seemed like damning evidence to me, but there was no indication of trauma on the body. It wasn't until I was shown the last page of the autopsy report that I understood how Nathaniel Wingate Peaslee had died.

I think back to his voice on the phone, and what he told me about the cats on the roof, and how they hissed and whispered his name. I thought him senile. Now I'm not so sure. He said they wanted to take him, to make his pain go away. How they were invisible and had strange, membranous wings. He said that he had to consent, but to what I wonder."

I haven't told this to anyone else, I've waited to tell you and you alone. You're smarter than the public defender. What should I do? Should I tell the weird truth, all that I heard and suspect, and be thought a madman? Or do I stay silent and take my chances with a jury? Surely, they won't believe it, will they? How could I do such a thing? I wouldn't even know where to begin. How does one remove a man's brain, and yet leave no mark on the body?

1953

OPERATION SWITCH

December 8, 1953
The Bridge of No Return

    It was cold, the air was crisp, and a thick fog had rolled in and settled in the gully and around the bridge that spanned it. There was a scent in the air, smoke tinged with gunpowder and exhaust. To the north the enemy, North Koreans, were scurrying about, posturing, flexing military muscles, making sure that the American troops to the south knew what they were capable of. The Americans were doing much the same, though in a slightly more organized and better equipped manner. It was a scene the man on the hill had watched time and time before, only the players had changed. At the designated hour, trucks, one from each side, began unloading their human cargo, prisoners of war. The man on the hill, whom his subordinates thought of as the Old Man, and occasionally referred to as the TOM, or Terrible Old Man, lit a cigarette, picked up his field glasses and watched as the prisoners moved from either side and across the bridge.
    The two groups that passed each other in silence couldn't have been more different. Those moving from south to north, were all well dressed in clean uniforms, and well fed, Asian, either Chinese or Korean; The TOM could tell the difference even when others could not. The prisoners moving in the opposite direction were in contrast a sorry lot, dressed in what was left of their filthy uniforms, which in some cases were little more than rags. They were a motley crew, some Koreans and Turks, but mostly British, Australians, and Americans, though to the untrained eye they all looked the same, tattered uniforms covering gaunt, emaciated bodies. They shuffled

across the bridge, in single file, so slowly that their steps barely made a sound. The condition of the troops was a telling clue to how poorly the North Korean army was supplied, for even the soldiers that guarded the prisoners were only marginally better off. Still, amongst the waves of shuffling, downtrodden prisoners of war, there were always a few who had not succumbed to the torture, starvation, and depression that was epidemic amongst former POWs. These men always had clean uniforms, good shoes, healthy bodies; even their minds were relatively unaffected. They walked faster and stood prouder than the others coming back across the bridge. They were easy to spot, and after interviewing dozens of them the TOM suspected something, something that he hoped to confirm as the exchange of prisoners drew to a close.

As the former POWs came to the base of the bridge they were loaded into waiting vehicles and whisked away. The Australians and the Brits were the first to leave. The TOM had no jurisdiction over these nationalities; he had to let them go. But when it came to Americans, they were his to do with as he pleased. It was a familiar position, one that he had enjoyed while working in Japan, and then after the war for the CIA in both America and Europe. His recruitment into the Joint Advisory Commission, Korea or JACK was merely a new variation on an old game, one that he had become very good at.

He lowered the field glasses and took a drag off of his cigarette, then handed a name to his assistant. "Lieutenant Hollister, have this man collected." Hollister nodded, and relayed his master's instructions into his radio. A half mile below as the prisoners made their way to the waiting trucks, one oddly healthy prisoner of war was removed from the others and loaded into a waiting jeep with armed guards on either side. The TOM smiled and muttered, "Now that we have collected our gift, let us see what we have been given."

December 12, 1953
JACK Base 3 Codename: Whitechapel

The TOM watched through the one-way glass as Captain Marcus Troy fidgeted at the table in the interview room. Like the rest of the room the table was white, clean, and almost sterile. A blank slate on which anything could be written and then—if need be— wiped clean, and forgotten forever. It had already witnessed the confessions of Lieutenants Marquand and Hodgson, weak willed men, both pilots on reconnaissance missions who had panicked and ejected from their planes when they came under enemy fire. They both had been captured, and held in Chicom camps far to the north.

They were what the Chinese called progressives, and what the members of JACK thought of as indoctrinated. It would take some rehabilitation, time and effort, but the programming could be broken, the men returned to a semblance of their former selves, at least enough to pass for normal in society. Friends and relatives might have trouble; notice some behavioral issues, emotional outbursts and the like. But such symptoms could be, would be, attributed to the stress of war, and not to any shoddy psychological reconstruction work on the part of SHOP 3, The TOM's team of interrogators and therapists. Not that anybody back in the states would even know of the existence, let alone the function, of such a group.

He watched Troy for a few more minutes, let the man sweat. It was part of the interrogation process. You leave a man alone with his thoughts for long enough and he might just tell you everything you need to know, and some things you might rather not. Give a man time, and he might give you the world without even needing to be asked. He finished his cigarette, nodded to Hollister to start the camera, picked up his equipment case and with a deep breath went into the room.

He flashed a smile as he introduced himself, his gold teeth catching the light, "Captain Troy, my name is Peaslee, Doctor Wingate Peaslee. I am a psychologist. I am here to ask you some questions, about your time as a prisoner, nothing serious, just a debriefing. Standard procedure I assure you."

Troy's response was impassionate, cold and little more than a whisper. "I understand. You have a job to do. We all have tasks we must perform."

Peaslee opened his equipment case to reveal a rather large array of tubes, valves, a roll of paper and some integrated pens. There was a cuff that went around Troy's arm, and another, quite a bit smaller that went over his finger. "This is a polygraph; it detects changes in blood pressure and temperature." He flipped the machine on and it began to hum. A bellows expanded and then collapsed with a puff, only to begin refilling once more. "We use it to detect stress, mistruths, and attempts at deceit. It's part of a test, one developed by the Germans, but still very functional. The Kampff test was originally used to detect traitors, now we use it to detect evidence of psychological tampering."

Troy nodded. "Do you think me a traitor Dr. Peaslee?" There was no emotion in his voice.

"We shall see." He settled down in the chair. "Do you mind if I smoke? I'm going to ask you a series of questions. Answer truthfully and this will all be over very quickly." Peaslee shuffled through some paperwork. "Your name is Marcus Troy. Born and raised in North Hills, Pennsylvania, a graduate of the University of Pennsylvania, Master's Degree in Engineering from Stanford. Last address 22C Lathe Ave, Oakland, California. Is that correct?"

"Is this part of the test?"

"No, no. Sorry, just getting my facts straight. You were assigned to an Engineering Corps, and captured July 22, 1950 while working on fortifications at Outpost Harry?"

"Yes."

Peaslee circled an area on the paper that was slowly rolling through the machine. "Good. Where were you held prisoner?"

"Camp 12."

The interrogator dropped his pen. "Camp 12. Troy, I have to tell you that military intelligence has identified a number of Prisoner of War Camps, and until today none of us have ever heard of Camp 12."

"I'm sorry. They must not be very good."

"To whom are you referring Troy?"

"Your spies Dr. Peaslee, they must not be very good if they don't know about Camp 12. It is quite large, several thousand prisoners."

Peaslee picked up his pen in a huff. "Tell me about Doctor Hu."

The pen on the machine jumped as Troy asked "Who?"

"The Chinaman in charge of the re-education program

at Camp 12, his name is Hu, H U. Your friends Marquand and Hodgson seemed to know who he was."

"Those men are not my friends."

"That is a strange thing to say. Do you know what they said about you?" He shuffled through some papers. "Here, 'Marcus Troy is the bravest human being I've ever known.' They both said it, the exact same phrase. Funny things to say from men who you say are not your friends." He shuffled more papers. "The same phrase. Very odd don't you think?"

"I've told you; those men are not my friends."

"But you do know Doctor Hu, don't you?"

Troy stared at his interrogator. There was something in his eyes, something that made Peaslee suspicious. "Oh yes, I know the good Doctor Hu. I only met him once, but . . ."

Peaslee leaned in, 'But what Captain Troy?"

"I have dreams, vivid, horrible dreams. Hu is in them, he is always in them. He does strange things in my dreams; incomprehensible things; things that make no sense; horrible things"

"These things he did . . ."

"IN MY DREAMS!" interjected Troy.

The interrogator nodded, "These things that Doctor Hu did in your dreams, he did them to you?"

Troy shook his head sadly and his hands turned into fists. "No, never to me, Doctor Hu never hurt me. But he did strange things, horrible things, sometimes to buildings, sometimes to the landscape, sometimes with machinery, and sometimes to other men, but never to me, never to me." The officer paused and swallowed back tears.

"What is it you're not telling me? I can't help you Troy, unless you tell me everything."

"In my dreams when Hu did those things, I wasn't his victim. I was his assistant. GOD FORGIVE ME I WAS HELPING HIM!"

December 15, 1953
JACK Base 3 Codename: Whitechapel

"How are you feeling today?" Peaslee asked while

rubbing the bruise on his cheek.

"Better," replied Troy. "I am sorry about the other day. I don't understand why I reacted like that."

Peaslee nodded. "It is hard to predict how we will react to stress. We've given you a sedative; it should help keep you calm." The man lit a cigarette. "I know that you don't want to, but we need to talk about your dreams, the ones with Doctor Hu in them."

The damaged man nodded, "Why do you want to know?"

The Terrible Old Man closed his eyes. "When I was a boy, my father suffered an attack. He lost his memory, became a different person. He left his wife and family, he didn't know us, we didn't know him. For years he travelled the world. Then one day he came home, and his memory came back. He tried to set things right, but he was haunted. Haunted by all that he had lost, and by dreams, horrible dreams in which he was not himself, and did things he did not understand."

Troy seemed to perk up. "Like my dreams."

"I think what happened to my father, something similar has happened to you. I want to understand it, help you to understand it, and perhaps find a way to heal you. But you have to tell me about your dreams."

The captain cleared his throat, leaned forward, and then began to speak. "In my dream, the one I have most often, we're getting off a plane, Doctor Hu and I. We're dressed oddly, a uniform of some sort, not Korean uniforms, or Chinese, yellow silk with black striping. As Hu leaves the plane there are whole groups of bureaucrats, military officers, diplomats and they are all bowing as Hu approaches. When they don't rise up after he passes, I realize that they are bowing to me as well. We are escorted to a tented pavilion where we mingle with dignitaries from a number of countries. I recognize some of them, they are people of importance. There's a large man speaking Korean and laughing that I think is important. To his left is a wiry little Chinaman who could be Hu's brother, who introduces himself as Kang Sheng. It was only when Sheng spoke that I realized that none of the guests including myself were speaking English. Indeed, there were voices speaking not just Chinese and Korean, but Russian,

Hungarian and even German, all of which I understood as easily as I understand you now."

"The gathering was not purely social. Hu and I were engaged in some great negotiations; the gist of which escapes me now, but it involved the purchase of great machines, great conglomerates of tubes and metallic spheres constructed piecemeal, but on a massive scale. For these components we traded information, secrets, designs, and formulas that could devastate cities and lay waste to whole continents. We gave them such knowledge as if it were nothing, as if it could never be used. For in truth we thought of them as insignificant, useful but insignificant. They were like bees. You can give a hive the designs for a gun, but you should have no fear of them actually taking advantage of them."

"The negotiations take days, not because they are difficult, but because Hu and I are just two, and our needs are great, and they are a chattering unorganized horde desperate for our attentions and favor. We work non-stop. We do not sleep, we eat almost constantly, and Hu frequently dispenses for our consumption a strange yellow powder, heavy and granulated, like sugar but thicker. It is a stimulant, of that I am sure, but one that seems to have no deleterious side effects. It sustains us until we return to the plane. The flight takes hours. We are exhausted but content with our progress. We should be happy, ecstatic even, but I realize that during the course of our negotiations neither I nor Doctor Hu have shown any sign of emotion at all. The dream ends as I finally get comfortable and fall asleep in my seat."

Peaslee reached into his briefcase and pulls out a folder. "I would like to show you some pictures. They are grainy, but you should be able to make out some faces." He lays out the photos in front of Troy. They are of men of a variety of nationalities and cultures at a meeting; they appear relaxed, almost happy.

Troy pulled three photos out of the batch. "These men I recognize from my dreams."

The doctor nodded and held up one of the photos. "This is Kang Sheng. He is a confidant of Chairman Mao. We believe him to be the Minister of Security for the People's Republic of China." The second photo Peaslee holds up is of a rotund little Korean. "This is Kim Il-Sung the Prime Minister of North Korea." The third photo was of a soft looking but severe man in a suit and tie. "This is Lavrenti Beria, First Deputy Premier of the Soviet Union, and head of the NKVD, the Soviet Secret Police."

Troy seemed unfazed by the revelations revealed by his interrogator. The little psychologist slid another photo across the table. "Do you recognize this man?"

The former POW stared at the image before him. The man was small, with a vaguely Asian look. Thin almost gaunt, with a shock of wild white hair surrounding a pair of knowing eyes. He pushed the photo back and nodded. "That is Doctor Hu."

"I see," there was a judgmental tone in Peaslee's voice, "One last picture, who is the man in-between Sheng and Beria, the one behind Hu?"

Troy looked at the photo. There were dozens of people, all posed for a formal photo. He recognized many of them from his dream, and yes there was the man Peaslee had identified as Beria, and the other he called Sheng, and between them was Hu. Behind them all was a man who seemed out of place, a man whose features were so familiar, but whose expression was entirely alien to him. There was something wrong with that face. It was slack, emotionless, and almost dead. There was no life in those eyes. Yet they were eyes that Troy recognized, and that recognition welled up inside him and brought him to his feet. He turned away from the table and stood there shaking.

"Who is that man?" demanded Peaslee. "Who is that standing behind Hu?"

A tear escaped from Troy's left eye as he fought to speak. "I don't understand! How is it possible? That man, it's me!"

December 20, 1953
JACK Base 3 Codename: Whitechapel

Hollister opened the large enamel box, connected up the battery, flipped a switch, and the machinery inside suddenly began to hum. He watched a few dials jump, adjusted them to a standard and then nodded to his superior. Doctor Peaslee nodded back and dismissed his junior with a subtle hand gesture. Then he turned back toward his subject. "Captain Troy, we are going to try an experiment today. You are going to tell me about another one of your dreams. Then I am going to ask you some questions, just like we did yesterday. The difference is this little piece of equipment. It's called a Voigt magnetometer, it detects subtle changes in magnetic fields. It can help us detect certain influences, aberrations in the brain that are too subtle for the Kampff Test."

Troy nodded slightly. "Do you still think I am a traitor Doctor Peaslee?"

"I think it might be more complicated than that Captain. I assure you that I am going to do everything to help you get back to normal." He watched Troy squirm a little. "Now, tell me about another one of your dreams."

The Engineer took a deep breath, closed his eyes and began to speak in a strange, almost monotonic voice. "I'm on a train in a tunnel, I'm vaguely reminded of the subway in Philadelphia, but this tunnel is much larger, much older, and it isn't level. I'm going down, down into the earth. I'm not alone; the car is full of men, young men, all of whom are covered in dust, which makes determining their nationalities difficult. From the wide range of features, they seem to be mostly Asian, but with some Europeans and a few Africans. They are dressed in single piece utilitarian suits that zip up the front like a flight suit. They don't talk to each other; they don't even look at each other, the only thing they do is sway and bounce to the jostling rhythm of the train."

"We slowly pull into a station, little more than a raised concrete slab, and the doors open with a hiss. I step out and the air is hot, stagnant and heavy with the stench of humanity. I recoil a little as it seeps into my sinuses. I am just one of hundreds who march out of the train and down the platform. We move as one, in a practiced pace that may be slow, but ensures that we can all keep up. As we pass through a great gate a whistle blows, and suddenly there is another great throng of humanity, identical to our own, but moving in the opposite direction. We pass them as they move up, and we follow the wide tunnel that gently slopes down toward the dimly lit area below. We round a curve and emerge onto a staging platform overlooking a vast cavern. I move in one direction, while the others move in another. The horde moves down into the vast chamber, while I move up along a still oddly wide spiral ramp. The ramp and the tunnel itself seem different than the material around them. The cavern walls are dark grey and pitted, like sandstone. The ramp and the tunnel are smooth and slightly reflective, almost nacreous, and I can see no evidence of striations or layers. The material is slick, and difficult to walk on, though not impossible. I reach the top and find myself in a turret-like structure that allows me to see the entirety of the vast cavern that stretches out below me."

"Vast is not sufficient to describe the scene that my eyes took in. The cavern was immense, Brobdingnagian, cyclopean, stretching as far as I could see, and disappearing into murky darkness with hints of dim lights moving about in the distance. The cavern was not empty, everywhere were men, hundreds of men, and their machines, moving earth and climbing the scaffolding that clung like strange metallic growths to the masses of rock and sediment that were being excavated. Beneath the diggings were more of the strange nacreous structures, glittering in the faint light. They emerged from their earthen tombs like spiraled and bejeweled shells, or an ancient and petrified species of gigantic fungi. All seemed to be adorned with strange rods of an odd metallic compound, that would suddenly bulge into a sphere or oblong joint. These branching groups of apparatus shared the queer organic feel of the structures that supported them, though as I said the matrix was definitely more metallic in appearance. The purpose of such equipment was known to me, but I cannot tell you what it was. It bore some resemblance to the forest of antennas one can see across the rooftops of major cities, and it reminded me of the materials I sought to commission from the attendees at the party in my other dream, though infinitely better crafted. In some ways, I think that the parts I was intent on purchasing were mere crude analogs of the pieces that were being excavated; that I was asking a blacksmith to supply parts to help repair a Lockheed F-80 fighter jet. Still, despite reservations, there was an undeniable sense of pride concerning what was happening in the cavern before me, pride and an immense sense of satisfaction."

"That feeling was suddenly interrupted by a disturbance in the distance. There was a sound, an explosion of sorts, but also a great roaring, like a pump or engine suddenly tearing itself to pieces, but on a massive scale. A plume of dust, smoke and debris suddenly mushroomed into view, it was at least a mile away but even from that distance I could hear the screams of men as they ran for their lives from whatever it was that had happened. Doctor Hu appeared by my side, mumbling some strange words I did not understand. In his hand was a tool of some sort, not totally unlike a screwdriver but where the blade should have been, there was instead a small glass bead that glowed as Hu chanted. With each repetition the bead glowed brighter, and was soon joined by a high-pitched whistling that hurt my ears. As the infernal whine grew louder something large and amorphous reeled up into the sky, flailing amongst the smoke and debris. It was a monstrous thing, like a gelatinous polyp, black in places while seemingly invisible in others; it twisted and turned in the sky, roiling in apparent agony. Whip-like tendrils flailed from its body smashing against the walls and nacreous structures, and wrapping around those poor souls who were too slow to escape its attentions."

"Then, as if some threshold had been reached the thing ceased moving. It hung there in the sky like a twisted mockery of a moon. It shuddered there, shuddered and then seemed to shrink, implode, before finally with a great and horrid sound it exploded, disintegrating into innumerable pieces that tumbled from the air and covered the city in slime and gore. The pieces, strange amalgamations of bladders, muscles and cartilage writhed on the ground for a few moments before finally collapsing into masses of quickly desiccating mucus. Doctor Hu cursed and spat a word I was not familiar with, but which still filled me with fear and loathing. I needed to know what it was that created in me such terror, that filled me with such anxiety and dread. With the strange high-pitched alarm still ringing in my ears I screamed that strange word that Hu had cursed just moments before. I screamed it and demanded an explanation.

"And then he tells me, and I could no longer hear the workers below crying out in terror and agony over the sound of my own screams! Screams that force me to flee back to the waking world, where I wake up in a cold sweat, my heart pounding. But though I have dreamed this dream countless times I cannot tell you what he told me. I can only remember the name, that horrid name that Hu spat out in disgust. I remember it, but it still fills me with dread. Perhaps you can tell me Doctor Peaslee. Do you know what horrid monstrosity Doctor Hu was referring to?"

Peaslee shook his head. "Do you know where this dream took place Captain Troy?"

Troy shook his head. "He said this word, a word I didn't understand."

Peaslee fumbled with a map. He pointed at a spot. "Was it here? This is where Intelligence says Doctor Hu has been excavating, a place called Hwadae. Is that where you were?"

"What does it mean Doctor Peaslee?" Troy was ranting. He rose up from his chair and tore at the sensors. There was foam at the corners of his mouth. "What does it mean Peaslee? Tell me. WHAT IS A SHAGGOTH!?"

December 23, 1953
Jack Base 2 Codename: Candlestick

"I'm going to be honest with you Captain Troy, you are in it deep." Peaslee took a drag off his cigarette. "You left your accommodations, in the middle of the night, jumped the fence into a restricted area, and sabotaged some very delicate and expensive equipment. Would you care to explain yourself?" There was no reply. "Captain you are facing charges of sabotage and treason, the penalty for which is death. Would you care to explain yourself?"

Captain Troy glared at Peaslee with tired eyes. "You know what I was doing there. You've known all along why I am here."

A smile came across Peaslee's face. "Of course, I know, I've been waiting for you for a long time. Well, you or someone similar. I have to admit, you had us confused for a while. Your repressed memories were backwards. The memories are supposed to be of your world as seen through a human's eyes, not of our world seen through alien eyes. It was

THE PEASLEE PAPERS

puzzling, until we realized that it wasn't the memories that were being repressed, but rather an entire personality, two minds in one body, one human and one Yithian. You must have been very desperate to attempt such a thing."

Troy strained at his bonds. "You can't hold me forever. I have friends, allies, they'll come for me."

"Do you mean Beria?" Peaslee was suddenly smug. "I'm sorry to tell you, I've just gotten word that the Soviets executed him earlier today. Tell me, what happens to your kind when the body you inhabit is killed inside an ELF field?"

Troy's jaw set. "You tiny little creatures, you have no idea what you've done. You've destroyed one of the Great Minds, an intellect that had existed for millions of years, had travelled through space and time almost at will. Had seen things and done things you couldn't even dream of."

"A Great Mind? I seriously doubt it. You've made too many mistakes." A look of incredulity came across the prisoner's face. "See, like that. I've studied your kind for decades, ever since one of you inhabited my father, you don't do emotions. Oh, I think you have them, but I don't think you've figured out how to translate them into a human response. Never have and never will. You on the other hand, seem quite expressive. It makes me think you aren't like those that came before you. It was one of the clues that gave you away to my partner. He thinks you are little more than a common thief."

"How dare you!" shrieked Troy, or the thing that was pretending to be Troy.

Peaslee whipped out a hand and slapped the Captain across the face. "How dare I? How dare you! You come to our world, inhabit hundreds of our people, enslaved thousands more, and forced them to excavate your ruins, and you think you are entitled to be outraged?" Peaslee spit in the thing's face. "We've tolerated the incursions from your kind because in most cases your actions have been rather benign, or at least suitably inscrutable, but this, what you have done here we cannot tolerate."

The faux Troy was suddenly laughing. "You think that you can threaten me, us? I'll tell you what you want to know, not because of your threats, but because it amuses me." He put his hands on the table, the restraints were gone. "You creatures, you humans, you like to classify things, to lump things together, to split them apart. You find it convenient to identify things and say this is what it is. You say 'communist', but don't imagine that a Russian communist might be different from one from China, or Poland, or even Cuba. You call us Yithians, the Great Race, so named because we learned to leap our minds through time. We learned how when no one else could. We move back and forth through time almost at will, without fear of the things that hound other lesser races. We learned it so that we could survive, so that we could leap from one time to another, and survive while all the other races faded into memory. But we're not a single race. We're millions of minds, and we're thousands of races. Individuals hand-picked from the races that we choose to inhabit. It is our gift to them, that some select number of their ranks should join us in eternity. But our mastery of time is not without limits. There are rules Peaslee, universal laws that even we cannot bend. The leap across time takes energy, precious particles that are rare, and difficult to store. The bigger the leap, the more energy that is needed. We are a patient race, we built collectors, batteries, and then planned to make the leap *en masse*."

"But something has gone wrong?"

"In the far future, the battery is damaged. There aren't enough tachyons for all of us to migrate. There was talk of a culling, of leaving some behind. Of marooning them in realtime forever. The very thought led to dissent, to conflict, to armed rebellion, and inevitably to war. Some of us, a mere handful, were able to come to this time. We've built an army, a nation, and with our superior knowledge and technology we'll soon come to dominate this age. And you, and all like you will learn your place, and serve your rightful masters."

Peaslee stood up and turned away from his prisoner. The door opened and Hollister came in. Peaslee yielded the floor to his assistant. "Do you think we are fools? Do you think we would allow you to come here, to do this without permission? You think these people, these humans weak, but it does not occur to you that we spend an inordinate amount of time studying them?" The thing that was pretending to be Hollister sat down.

"But the leadership rejected them for the migration!"

"Because we could not subjugate them you fool. Not because they were too weak, but because they were too strong! They learn, they adapt, they overcome. They are more than worthy enough to contribute to our ranks, but we feared what inhabiting them might do to us, and them. So, we chose not to, but always regretted not adding their uniqueness to our own. You have solved that problem. When the time is right, Peaslee and his kind will turn off the ELF generator and we will forcibly separate you and your kind from the human minds."

"You are taking us back? We would rather die."

Hollister shook his head. "We aren't taking you back, we're taking the humans. You will remain here, surrounded by military forces you cannot hope to defeat. Trapped by the technology that we ourselves have supplied to the humans. You will be marooned here, and you will live out your traitorous lives in realtime. Oh, I am sure that you will be able to rebuild some of the technology. You might be able to move from one body to another, but for how long? How long do you think you can last, trapped in this world?"

December 27, 1953
The Bridge of No Return

Wingate Peaslee stood watching as the prisoners trundled slowly across the bridge and into the trucks that waited on the northern side. There was a man there, a small Asian man, old, but seemingly spry. As the last prisoner was whisked away he gave an odd three finger salute which Hollister returned quickly. Then the little man, who Peaslee recognized as Doctor Hu, turned and walked out of view.

"We don't trust you," said Peaslee.

Hollister nodded. "We know, that is why we gave you the designs to the ELF generator, so you wouldn't have to."

"I've read Hu's file. He's been here a long time, longer than the others. He's smart. We think he's a liability. He'll figure a way out. We have plans to eliminate him preemptively."

Hollister shook his head. "I wouldn't try that if I were you. You are right about Hu. He is smarter than the others, and he will probably figure a way out, in fact I'm counting on it."

Peaslee was suddenly annoyed. "The deal was that we were to keep them contained, if Hu gets out . . ."

"Calm yourself my friend. Hu isn't your enemy."

A look of confusion crept across Peaslee's face. "But he's been working with them, planning, rebuilding. He's was one of the first."

Once more Hollister shook his head. "He's been working with them yes, planning, and building. But what has he built, but simply a very comfortable prison." He looked at his watch. "Hu is not their ally Peaslee, he is their warden, and will be for what you would consider a very long-time." The alien took a small device out of his pocket, it was a strange conglomeration of spheres and rods. "You will excuse me Doctor Wingate Peaslee, but the field is about to drop and I have a very important appointment that must be kept."

Peaslee drew his gun. "I don't think so; we would like you to stay."

Hollister flicked a switch and the tiny machine began to move. "You will let me go Wingate, you have no choice. I must keep my appointment; everything we've done here in the last few days depends on it."

He cocked the pistol and pointed it at the whirling machine. "You're lying."

"No, I am not. If I do not make this leap, you will not be here, you will not have done these things or any of the work you have done for the last forty-five years, and all of our efforts will have been for naught. Unless you let me go, the rebels will be free to move as they please."

Peaslee took a step forward and placed the muzzle of the gun as close to the spinning machine as he could. "Impossible, you can't have been manipulating me for the last forty-five years, I would have noticed."

"You are correct Wingate, we haven't been actively manipulating you, but we did set things in motion, set you on the path, pointed you in the direction that brought you here today. We did interfere with your life, but only once. Don't you remember?"

Peaslee lowered the gun. "Where are you going?"

There were tears in his eyes. "Please, I have to know!"

The machine was nearly invisible now, it moved faster than Peaslee would have thought possible. He could barely hear Hollister speak, "You already know, I have to go to where it all began for you Wingate. I'm sorry, but it's the only way."

The terrible old man fell to his knees, "Tell me!"

The Hollister-thing's voice seemed to grow weak, and as the Yithian left and the body it inhabited collapsed he spoke one last time. "I have to go to your father Wingate, I have to displace him. It's the only way to make sure you'll grow up to be the man you are, to gather so much information about us, to help us build a trap for our criminals. We need you Wingate Peaslee, we need you to fulfill your mission, to do that we must displace your father, and destroy your family. In order for us to use you, we must teach you to hate us. It's the only way."

And as the man that was Hollister came back to his own time and body, Doctor Wingate Peaslee, the Terrible Old Man, could do nothing but weep.

1962

OPERATION STARFISH

Raina,

If you are reading this, then I am either dead or my condition has deteriorated such that I might as well be. As it is, I write this when I can, during the early morning hours when my mind is still my own, before the day and the medication take it all away. The doctors will tell you that I am unstable, delusional, that I make things up. Nothing could be further from the truth. Yes, I snapped that day, over what appeared to be a very minor incident. The children had been playing with an anthill, throwing stones and splashing it with water. The ants were enraged, and when one child stood too still, too close, he was swarmed. Your reaction to rescue the children and then later douse the colony with ice water was entirely understandable, predictable even. It must have been odd to have seen an old man like me, come after you, screaming "Leave them alone!" Chanting it like some mad mantra.

I was still repeating it hours later after John drove me back to the home. "Leave them alone." I whimpered "Leave them alone." I had no right to scream at you that day, no right at all. You had done nothing wrong, nothing, and yet your actions - they sparked a memory, a terrible memory one that I had hoped to forget.

But that day came roaring back out of the past and filled me with such uncontrollable emotion. I was not angry with you Raina, though it may have seemed it, I was afraid. What you were doing, the memories, the combination filled me with such terror I could do nothing but lash out. Even now, all these weeks later I am still afraid. I have told no one this, and I think perhaps this has been a mistake. Perhaps if I write it down, perhaps then I shall find some kind of relief.

You may recall that I have told you I once served on the USS Miskatonic, but what I have not said was in what capacity. I was a Marine, but attached to an organization called JACK, which ostensibly, stood for Joint Advisory Commission Korea, but in reality, had little to do with that subject. What the acronym really stood for, I do not know, we were intelligence agents, but not just any agents. We investigated the weird, the strange, the unexpected. Our motto was "Be Nimble, Be Quick, Be Saucy" meaning that we were flexible, fast, and willing to do whatever it took to get the job done, and not get caught. I had become something of an expert in ballistics and missiles, a field not normally associated with traditional intelligence but JACK was anything but traditional, and I had served with statisticians, engineers, and physicists. My expertise may have been in engineering, but I had long since surpassed my training, and I knew more about biology, chemistry, acoustics and psychology then I would have ever learned at any university. In the late fifties, these skills had earned me an assignment in London, but in 1960 there had been a restructuring, and I suddenly found myself as assistant to the Colonel Doctor Wingate Peaslee, the Terrible Old Man, as he was called, JACK's number two man. Peaslee was known for his ruthlessness, and there were rumors that he had been particularly harsh when dealing with the North Koreans. I of course had no way to validate any of this. The staff called him the TOM, something I wouldn't dare to think let alone say back then. I knew that he was a man unlike others, one that it was better to accommodate than to cross.

It was the TOM that brought me to the Miskatonic in July of 1962. It was a ship like any other, full of hard working men who took both their jobs and their entertainment seriously. They worked hard and they played hard, and while we sailed from Japan to the mid-Pacific I spent several nights drinking the rot-gut that these men called whisky, and watching them slide under the table, while I sat quietly finishing shot after shot. Not that such behavior was without risk, and there was an incident with a midshipman who decided to sample a bottle from my case of Remmers Imperial Stout. One incident, unreported, was all it took to make it clear I wasn't the standard jarhead. After that I had their respect.

Respect was not something that I had earned from Peaslee. He rarely spoke to me and when he did it was either to bark orders or evaluate my work, usually with a single word "Satisfactory." Fortunately, I did not look to Peaslee for affirmation. I had been warned away from that by my friends in London. Steed and Drake suggested that I develop a hobby, which I did. I became an amateur chef, though there was actually little opportunity to practice my skills. I had developed a penchant for the culinary arts and was fond of haunting markets, remote farms and even the occasional jungle in search of the thousands of varieties of seeds, powders, salts and dried fruits that were used to augment the gastronomical experience. After I was done I would often mail the remaining portions of my find off to friends, mostly Brenner the Swiss chef I had briefly studied under in New York. I have tasted his food, and am thrilled to know that on some occasions I might be contributing to his creations.

Unlike myself, Peaslee had no hobby, no past time - no way to relax. His obsession was his job, and nothing else mattered.

Yet in the middle of the Pacific, not far from islands that I would have thought bore a multitude of exotic spices, I could not relax. Peaslee confined himself to the ship, and seemed extremely nervous. Not that he didn't have cause. The Miskatonic was part of a fleet of ships spread across the Pacific in support of Operation Starfish. There had been a series of nuclear tests throughout the year, why exactly was unclear to me, but they seemed related to the Soviet nuclear detonation in the Novaya Zemlya archipelago, the so-called Tsar Bomba. Khruschev had sworn to show the United States the "Kuz'kina Mat" or Kuzka's Mother, and it had been assumed that the Tsar Bomba was just that. Yet Peaslee seemed to know something I and the others did not, and I would occasionally see him clutching a report on the Soviet detonation, a report he wouldn't let me see, a report in Russian.

What I could see, what Peaslee couldn't hide from me, were the Soviet warships that had taken up positions not far from our own location, which was just south of Johnston Island. One always thinks of a South Pacific island as something exotic and lush, Johnston may have been that way once, but all that was there in 1962 was sand, concrete, and batteries of rocket launchers. It was a military base unlike any I had ever seen before, desolate, tiny, and bristling with armaments waiting to be used. Why the Soviets had been allowed to approach this close was a mystery. As with the reports, Peaslee would say nothing, and it was his silence that made me even more nervous.

It was in the early morning of July 9th that I was roused and ordered to the Command Deck. I left my quarters at a dash, grabbed coffee, got something that pretended to be food, and made my way topside. The crew of the Miskatonic were frenetic, readying weapons, securing loads and testing equipment. They were like a swarm of insects carrying out myriad tasks that looked like chaos but was really a well-orchestrated machine with hundreds of parts that all knew what had to be done. I weaved my way through this madness, dodging runners and moving loads like the expert that I was, only to find myself in awe of my employer who had somehow found the exact spot in which he could stand and not be in the way. He was like a pillar of stone, unyielding, unmoving, and inscrutable. His pale blue suit danced in the wind trying in vain to tear itself away from his thin but stoic frame. Only his college tie, which flew like a flag in the stiff Pacific breeze seemed to have any chance of escaping, but as the TOM turned to greet me the piece of rebellious fabric fell back to his chest and with a casual movement the Windsor knot was quickly tightened, negating any chance of freedom.

Peaslee barely acknowledged me as we boarded the waiting helicopter and left the Miskatonic. We banked over the island and in the thin morning light I could see that the frenetic motion wasn't confined to the ship. The island too was ripe with activity, and I could see ammunition being stockpiled next to antiaircraft guns. There was also the innocuous tower that stood surrounded by a lattice of steel supports and supply tubes. It was sixty-five feet tall and eight feet in diameter at the base but tapered to six feet at the top, painted industrial white which made it seem less threatening than it was. It smoked, steam or something like it leaked from ports on the sides, which would have led some to believe that it was nothing more than a smokestack, an exhaust for some great machine or factory, but I knew better. I was staring at a PGM-17 Thor, a ballistic missile armed with a nuclear warhead. The venting gasses suggested that it was being prepared for launch. I remember slumping back in my chair, wondering what I had gotten myself involved in, and remembering a line of Norse poetry "Against the serpent rises Odin's son."

That feeling of dread only grew as the helicopter completed its pass over the island and then almost immediately began to jockey for a landing. I sat up and realized we hadn't gone far, I could still see the Miskatonic, and discovered we had done little more than jump from one warship to another, but our destination might as well have been a thousand miles away, for it was a place that—given the era—was the most foreign and dangerous place an American Intelligence officer could be. We had landed on a Soviet warship, and it took a supreme effort for me to not panic as the door slid open and we were escorted out across the deck and into the command deck. Not with guns pointed at us, but rather with handshakes and pats on the back, not as mortal enemies on opposite sides of a political ideology, but rather as if we were allies in some great venture and on the verge of a discovery both fantastic and terrible. I think this now, and can sense the irony, for it was true, it was all true. I just didn't know it.

The bridge of the Soviet battleship wasn't much different from those I had seen on American ships, well excepting the module which had replaced the radar station. It was a bulky thing, and I could tell that it hadn't originally been designed to fit into the slot it had been shoved into; whoever had rebuilt it had never served on a ship before. There were sharp angles, knobs and switches jutted out from the side where legs could easily trip them. None of these controls were sealed against weather, which meant that this installation wasn't meant to be long-term.
 That a pair of thick cables ran from the module and across the floor, one was obviously a power supply, the other ran through a port and to a cluster of transmitters and receivers mounted on the deck.

Apparently, my examination of the module had not gone unnoticed, but I hadn't expected to be chastised by a voice with a British accent. "I'll admit that the lure isn't pretty but she works. The Russians did most of the engineering; I just tweaked a few things here and there." My surprise must have shown for the rugged Brit quickly apologized and introduced himself. "Adam Royston, British Experimental Research Group, Unit 3. You're James Bellmore, Peaslee's assistant. We've heard about you. The Colonel speaks highly of your work."

I raised an eyebrow. "I've never heard of you, or the lure. To be honest I'm not sure why we are here."

Royston cast a glance at Peaslee who reluctantly nodded. The British scientist reached into a file and pulled out a photograph. "We are here because of that," he announced as he handed it to me.

The image was in black and white, grainy, slightly out of focus. At first, I thought I was seeing an image I had reviewed long before, the one that had become so associated with what had happened on February 24, 1942 in the skies over Los Angeles, but I soon noticed differences, there usually isn't snow in LA, and while California may have been the land of commie sympathizers (at least according to McCarthy, God rest his soul) I was quite certain that military trucks bearing the Hammer and Sickle were still uncommon there. These details made it clear that this wasn't from the so-called Battle of Los Angeles, but the dominant image of both photographs was so remarkably similar that the casual observer would have been hard pressed to tell the difference. There was in the center a globular mass, not unlike a fat disk or squashed ball. From this radiated five luminous appendages, that tapered to points where they intersected the ground. In shape, they might be mistaken for the arms of a starfish, but they lacked any trace of mottling or texture. Indeed, they were so far from what one would normally think of organic that I was tempted to call them struts, but even struts have depth and detail, these were so flat that they could be easily be mistaken for the beams from spotlights. In retrospect, the thing it most resembled was a sea urchin, though one with only five luminescent spines on which it seemed to stand.

Royston interrupted my study of the image. "The Russians call it Kuz'kina Mat. It destroyed an entire military base in the Novaya Zemlya before they hit it with a nuke. Since then we've documented three more of the things. We're also reviewing historical records, looking for events that might be related."

"I can think of at least one." I murmured. Suddenly something clicked in my head. "The lure, you want to attract these things? Why?"

"So, we can kill them Captain Bellmore," said Colonel Doctor Wingate Peaslee. "Whatever they are, they are dangerous, they've intruded where they aren't welcome, and they've hurt people. The Russians and the British have agreed to help us hunt them down. They seem to be attracted by a signal that progresses through a specific pattern and set of frequencies. Royston's machine duplicates that signal, draws them in and puts them right where we want them."

I opened my mouth to say something and then decided against it. Peaslee however seemed intent on continuing to speak. "Earth is in danger Captain Bellmore, and we represent the best hope for ridding her of the parasites and predators that plague her and all of humanity."

I was suddenly feeling sick and I burst from the bridge onto the deck outside. All around me Russian sailors were doing exactly what their American counterparts had been over on the Miskatonic. That idea comforted me. That these men, were the same as those that I had laughed, and fought and gotten drunk with gave me a sense of normalcy that I latched on to. I found a rhythm to their movements, the pulse of the ship which centered me and brought me a sense of reality. I caught my breath and steeled myself to go back and try to understand what Peaslee and his allies were planning on doing, but I was too late.

Standing there, feeling the pulse of the ship, I felt it change. Royston's lure had been turned on and I could feel the signal as it pulsed through the ship itself. I had thought that the bank of transmitters would have been the focus, but I was wrong. Royston was using the ship itself as one massive antenna, broadcasting his signal at an immense strength. I could feel it in my bones and joints, and the filling I had in the back of my mouth began to ache. Many of the men began to don protective head gear to cover their ears, but I saw no point in this, the signal wasn't a sound, it was a vibration that seeped up out of the deck of the ship and even the air itself. I longed to abandon the ship, to somehow leave and return to the Miskatonic, but our helicopter was gone. I looked longingly at the aircraft carrier and measured the distance between us. The waters had been calm, but now seemed to have been roused into madness by Royston's machine. Any thought of swimming back quickly left my mind. That is not to say that others weren't driven to the same thought and were able to resist it. I heard several men leap from the deck and scream as they fell to the sea. How they fared in those violent and hungry waters I cannot say, but I saw none of them surface and swim away.

The ship and its condition and that of the crew were reminding me of something else, of documents of events that I had reviewed and filed away in my mind, but now—given an impetus—several uncorrelated contents were coming together and the implications were terrifying. I ran back to the bridge and confronted Peaslee screaming to be heard, "This is a Tillinghast Resonator, isn't it?"

He looked at me with those cold eyes and said nothing so I called out to Royston. "This is the same technology that was employed on the USS Eldridge back in 1943, isn't it? The Resonator built back in the 1920s by Crawford Tillinghast."

Royston nodded. "I've made some improvements, and so have the Russians, but the principles are the same, yes."

I turned back toward Peaslee and pleaded, "Why would you do this? You are going to get us all killed."

Peaslee started to say something but then as the first visitors became apparent he stopped. They were small at first, and like the image Royston had shown me they were a merger of familiar invertebrate forms and the wholly unreal. Things that were like squid and fish swam through the bridge with bands of pure light knitting their segments together. Crabs with six legs and one claw crawled across the ceiling, their legs jointed in a green illumination. Flatworms that consisted of nothing more than a ring of tissue encapsulating a miasma of shadowed phosphorescence inched across the deck. There were dozens of these things, swimming through the air in schools and herds and pods. They covered the ship and moved amongst the crew without fear. With each passing second their numbers seemed to grow until I could not see the crew through their amassed forms. The ship had become a kind of extra-dimensional coral reef, a host to thousands, if not millions of lifeforms, and as I watched the effect spread away from the ship and into the surrounding ocean itself.

I watched with a desperate sense of dread, my eyes darting to and fro through the nightmare creatures. I was looking for something, they had to be there, you couldn't accumulate these kinds of numbers and not expect them to show up, and then, they were, sharks cutting through the alien life like knives through butter. They weren't sharks of course, but in their actions and appearance the similarity was striking. They were sleek, muscular things built for speed and destruction. They flashed through the lesser things and left a trail of gore and fluid behind. Whatever these creatures used for blood it wasn't red, but a frightful black that congealed almost instantly and floated in the ether like a cloud of dust. Peaslee saw them and muttered "The Hounds of Tindalos, lean and athirst."

With all the prey, with all the predators about it was inevitable that a mistake be made: A man screamed as a shark passed through him and tore his arm clean off. A gunner saw this and reacted accordingly. In moments, the ship had erupted in gunfire with weapons pointed not at an enemy in the distance, but rather at the ones that had engulfed the ship itself. Men died, but whether they did so because of the monsters or because of panicked fire it was impossible to say.

Outraged I screamed at Royston to turn the thing off, and he seemed inclined to do so, but as he moved toward the control panels I heard a familiar sound and turned to find Peaslee pointing his gun at the engineer. "Do not touch anything Royston. Everything is going according to plan."

And it seems Peaslee was right, for then, as if by clockwork, the thing appeared. It stalked out of the sky, using those weird unearthly, inorganic, immaterial legs to climb down out of the unknown and find a purchase in our world. It was a massive, monstrous thing, cyclopean in its construction, and promethean in its design. The center, the globular cluster of extra-dimensional flesh seemed to be ringed with five eyes around a central mouth all of which faced downwards. Short fleshy appendages jutted out from between the eyes ending in emitter like organs from which the wholly unnatural spine like legs emerged. They were great conical spindles of dusky energy that seemed to have no definition, no mass, and no substance, and yet somehow, they held the central mass aloft. As it walked it raised one these spindles and the fleshy emitters rotated forward adjusting the length of the weird spike until it found its place. It then shifted its weight, rotating forward and repeating the process. Some legs seemed to be hundreds of feet long, while others merely a dozen. Then as it moved those proportions would shift and the thing would come closer, slowly, but surely closer.

Somewhere a Russian voice cried out "Kuz'kina Mat!" and the entire crew looked up at the thing as its mouth opened wide and an array of tentacles fell out and began snaking their way toward our location.

I turned to Peaslee and told him he was an idiot. "These things aren't monsters, they're animals. They're not attracted to the resonator; they feed off the things attracted to the resonator. It's not an attack, only ecology. The only time they pose a threat to us is if we get in their way. All we have to do is not use the resonator, which seems easy enough."

Peaslee shook his head. "This is our world; there is no place in it for monsters or aliens. I've spent my life fighting things like this. The Kuz'kina Mat will fall before us, just as the others did." He turned to the captain, "Tell the fleet to open fire." The captain grabbed the radio and cleared the channel, but before he could say anything something struck the ship and set all of us flying. As I fell I saw the second thing as it crawled down out of the ether and settled onto the ship itself. The captain cursed as he slipped, as did Royston. Peaslee caught the edge of the captain's chair and swung himself around grabbing the mike and bringing it up to his mouth. "Strike fleet," he called out, "this is Peaslee, the order is given. You may fire at will!"

I didn't know what Peaslee was thinking. Had he gone mad? We were right beneath the target; we were going to be collateral damage, something which he apparently didn't care about. I grabbed a helmet that somebody no longer needed, strapped it to my head and once more tried to make my way off the bridge. It wasn't as easy as it had been the first time, and going out onto the deck had been a mistake. The air was full of bullets and the metallic stench of explosives. There was a rhythmic thumping noise which I realized was an antiaircraft gun, and the chatter of smaller arms as they tried to mow through the swarm of things that had enveloped the ship. A quick glance at the sky showed me traces of fire headed toward both creatures. Tentacles like thick gray cables had been spooled out of their mouths and were snatching what they could from the mass of prey. They seemed oblivious to our attacks.

A sudden boom came, and then another, somewhere someone had upped the ante and brought the heavy cannons into play. I watched a pair of shells arc through the sky and hit one of the creatures in the central hub. It let out a roar, and one of its legs seemed to flicker. It rocked toward the missing limb before rebalancing itself as the spindle of light reestablished. The beast was still roaring as two more thumps reached my ears and it took two more shells to the body. More legs flickered and it fell. It fell from the sky and landed in the ocean just yards from the ship. The impact sucked the ship forward, and then the wave formed and flipped the ship's bow up. I slid back into the bridge and as I fell I caught Peaslee and Royston. We held on to each other as the sea vanished and the sky was all that I could see. My ears and senses betrayed me as I was suddenly upside down and the world went black. The last thing I remembered was the cold and the smell of sea water flooding my nose.

I woke back on the Miskatonic, with no clue how I had gotten there, or who had rescued me. Colonel Peaslee was staggering across the deck, he was soaked and blood stained the right sleeve of his shirt. His jacket and tie were missing. I looked at my watch and learned that it was almost 11:00. I had been out for hours. I turned to look at the sea. The Soviet ship was capsized, but the sea around her was still strange, and still infested with thousands of unearthly lifeforms. In the sky, three of the pentagonal monsters were desperately trying to reach the mass of their prey while avoiding the shells of the attacking ships. Of the creature that had fallen there was no trace. I found out later that it had retreated, that it had climbed into the sky and vanished, like a bird amongst the clouds, except the sky was clear. It had climbed up into the sky at an unknowable angle.

Peaslee rose and began to stumble past me. As he walked by, he was muttering something unintelligible, and, once I realized he was heading for the Command Deck, I knew I had to follow him. There was something cold and distant in his eyes, a mania of sorts. He wasn't himself; it was possible that he was in shock. As I stood to fall in behind him something in my left ankle gave out. It felt like a spring or pull cord had snapped and was curling up inside my leg. I screamed as the pain and failure in my ankle forced me to crumple back to the deck.

I crawled after him in desperation. He wasn't much faster, but he gained distance and entered Command well before I did. I cannot say what I would have done if I had reached him in time, if I had been there when the order was given. But my leg had betrayed me and I only entered the Command Deck as the confirmation of his order came back over the radio. I turned and watched as a plume of smoke rose up from Johnston Island. It was both beautiful, like a god riding a pillar of flame into the sky, and terrifying, for I knew the power of the Gods themselves dwelt within that white metal casing. It was like watching Thor's hammer being thrown against the giants. I smiled for an instant, for I thought that at least the mission would be accomplished. My life was likely over, but the mission would be accomplished. Then I remembered that the mission had been designed by a man who I suspect had gone a bit mad.

I tried to watch the Thor missile as it screamed

across the sky, but as I did there was suddenly a horrendous noise and something large and dark passed in front of the sun. I don't remember what it was. When I try, the number five seems to dominate my thoughts, and there is a desire to link the shape to those things that we had futilely battled, but I cannot be certain that is true. There is a shadow, a thing that at times seems to be part starfish and part squid, but on an unimaginable scale. Behind me Peaslee screamed two words in Russian, and mercifully I lapsed back into unconsciousness.

As part of the official inquiry I was allowed to review the telemetry data from the Thor missile. The warhead detonated at an altitude of 250 miles with a yield of 1.42 megatons and was seen as far away as Honolulu. The electromagnetic pulse was significantly larger than expected, shutting down street lights and tripping burglar alarms throughout the Hawaiian Islands. The microwave telephone link between islands was damaged. Immediately following the explosion, three low earth orbit satellites were disabled. Colonel Doctor Peaslee was not present during the inquiry, and I never saw him again. My separation from JACK was handled swiftly, and I was retired with a minimum of fuss. That the use of Royston's lure and the attacks continued seemed obvious. Newspaper reports, particularly from Hawaii documented the "testing" of nuclear weapons in the South Pacific through the beginning of November.

All of this was a long time ago, and seems irrelevant to the issue at hand, but I assure you it is not. Nor are they the ravings of a madman. Please do not think that. I have kept these things secret, lived as though I'd forgotten them, and chosen not to think of them for decades.

But that day, that day when you set out to destroy the anthill, all of this came rushing back. I remember it now because what you did seemed reminiscent of what I had seen before. Your children were playing, tormenting the ants and when they were hurt you came, your voice booming and you rescued them. That seemed innocent enough. Later when you came with the ice water and tried to drown the nest, that terrified me. Nearly the same thing had happened in the Pacific all those years ago. Only I and the fleet were the ants and we were being played with, and when we hurt one, we learned . . . we learned but we didn't understand.

We had thought we were fighting what the Soviets called "Kuz'kina Mat" but we were wrong. I think Peaslee figured it out, but I never saw him again to ask, but when he screamed out, I think he knew. Those things had not been Kuz'kina Mat, we should have called them Kuz'kina. That thing that roared and gathered up the others before leaving, the thing that had blotted out the sun, which I have blotted from my memory, the thing that was what Peaslee had seen too, and why he had screamed, that was Mat, a parent that had come to the rescue of her children!

I live in fear of the day of return, when she comes to deal with a pest that has hurt one of the children, just as you did. My only hope is that she is less vindictive, more understanding than you were. I hope she can dismiss our actions as simply instinctual and inconsequential, and beneath any need to respond to. I hope she sees us as tolerable pests.

But I doubt it. God help us, I doubt it.

1962
COLD WAR, YELLOW FEVER

October 18, 1962

     For the last few days Mitchell Peel had not slept well. Guantanamo Base was on high alert and the activity associated with such a state included roving searchlights, planes coming and going, and the constant sound of men and equipment moving about. It was not all bad though, the food was surprisingly good, as was the coffee. He hadn't yet finished his first cup of the morning when word came that he was wanted for a briefing. Peel hated Cuba. It wasn't that it was too hot or humid; he was used to that. The real problem was the mosquitos, which were the size of small bees. There was a stiff breeze coming off the ocean, but that didn't help at all. He hated the island, and resented that his vacation had been interrupted. Still, being flexible was one of the things that the Joint Advisory Committee on Korea paid him for. The fact that he hadn't ever been to Korea—and that the war was ostensibly over—wasn't really important. He worked for JACK; they paid well, and if there was one thing he had learned during his time with JACK it was that he should always expect the unexpected. If that meant being called during your vacation to an island military base surrounded by soldiers intent on killing you, so be it.

     There had been security at the door, but one look at his identification, and they parted like the Red Sea, even escorted him to a seat. His boss sat at the head of the table. Actually, Peaslee wasn't his boss; if he remembered the chain of command correctly, there were five layers of management between the two of them. Peel had only seen the TOM once before, at a program realignment meeting. Officially he was Colonel Doctor Wingate Peaslee, but everyone in JACK called him the TOM, the Terrible Old Man. He had a reputation: mostly for being ruthlessly efficient, but also for getting the job done no matter what the cost. God help you if you were in his way or even just standing nearby. Collateral damage was not only acceptable, but expected; Peel's own equations suggested that it was at times even necessary.

There were three others in the room, men about his age, but in significantly better shape. Rough men, dangerous men, capable men; they all carried side arms. Peel suspected that they weren't analysts, and that his years of study in Sydney and Tokyo would be less than impressive to this company. He thought of making small talk, but then decided against it.

Peaslee took a drink and then spoke in the thick New England accent he was famous for, "Mitchell Peel, twenty-six, born and raised in Sydney, Australia. You have degrees in Mathematics and Statistical Theory. Last month you had a breakthrough on some equations associated with the Yellow Sine. You have Omega Blue clearance." His voice was firm and direct, like an instructor at some private school. Peel tried to speak but the TOM cut him off. "As of right now your clearance level is Pi White. Do you understand what that means?"

"It means that I can be terminated without cause. I'll place a letter of resignation in my file."

"Son that is not what we mean by 'terminate.'"

Peel's eyes grew wide as he realized he had made a terrible mistake.

"It means that if I think you've been compromised, if I think it's necessary, I can shoot you in the head. No questions asked." Peaslee wasn't smiling, and that made Peel nervous. "Relax, son. Major Millward will attest that I've never shot anyone."

The largest man, whose uniform bore no insignia, smiled and in a deep Texan drawl confirmed what Peaslee had said. "The Colonel doesn't shoot people." Peel let out a breath. "He has me do it for him. Eight times in the last two years."

As the young statistician choked, one of the other men

laughed. "Welcome to the big leagues, Mr. Peel." The others, excepting Peaslee joined in.

Once the laughter subsided, Peaslee rose and began the briefing. "Following the debacle of the Bay of Pigs, the CIA inserted several dozen operatives into Cuba to carry out a variety of sabotage and terrorist acts in the hope of undermining Fidel Castro. This project was known as Operation Mongoose. Amongst the operatives deployed was this man," he raised a grainy photo of a bearded man with glasses and a scar across his left eye. "Esteban Zamarano, a fervent member of the anti-Castro movement. His family had extensive holdings in the city of Banes, in the Northeast area of the island. It was to this area that Zamarano was deployed in the hopes that he could enlist family connections." Peaslee paused and took a drink. "The Zamarano family of Banes was on the JACK watch list in 1958. According to the sales records of Pent and Serenade, they bought six volumes from the sale of the Church of the Starry Wisdom Library, including what appears to be a Spanish-language edition of The King in Yellow. How this bit of information was overlooked during his recruitment process is being investigated, but is not a subject of our mission. For three weeks Zamarano kept to all required schedules. However, his last daily report is now nine hours overdue. This in itself is not unusual, but two other operatives sent to Banes have also failed to report. A third, Joseph Gamboa reported reaching Banes and sent a brief message before we lost contact. Gamboa's message was 'Donde esta el signo amarillo?' In English, 'Where is the Yellow Sign?'"

A murmur ran through the men, who obviously knew more than Peel did. Peaslee ignored it. "We aren't the only ones with eyes on this. Banes has gone silent, but reports from the Cuban military flights suggest that there are bodies in the streets. The Soviets are most assuredly aware of what is going on, and they have been sensitive about The King in Yellow since the Romanovs. Analysis suggests that the Kremlin would be willing to neutralize the situation with a first strike. Washington does not want to see another Gizhinsk, particularly so close to the US borders. Thankfully, the Soviet missiles already in place are not yet armed. This gives us a window of opportunity to find another solution. Operation Yellow Fever will determine if this is an incursion, which—given Gamboa's message—seems likely. We will find the cause, and neutralize it as best we can. Any questions?" Peel started but then stopped himself. "I have copies of these files for all of you. Remember our motto."

With that, he handed out the files to everyone and slumped back in his chair. Peel turned to the man nearest him, a thick-necked bruiser with a cauliflower ear. "We have a motto?"

His accent betrayed his New York origin. "Be nimble. Be quick. Be saucy."

Peel smiled, almost laughing. "I get it Jack be nimble, Jack be quick, but I've never heard of 'Jack be saucy.' Is that from an American version of the rhyme?"

The man called Millward slapped him on the back, "Naw," he said in his deep Southern drawl, "it's British, like you. You ain't ever heard of Saucy Jack?"

"I'm Australian." He quipped. "Saucy Jack—you mean Jack the Ripper?" Both men nodded, which explained nothing to Peel, who still looked puzzled

Major Millward finally offered a translation, "Be flexible, be fast, and kill if you have to, but don't get caught." The Major stuck out a meaty hand, "Rob Millward, insertion team commander. Don't worry Peel if everything goes according to plan you won't have to get dirty." He and the other man laughed at some private joke.

Peel shook the Major's hand, slid back into his chair and repeated what Peaslee had said, "Welcome to the big leagues."

★

October 19

If you could get around the batteries of guns, the navy warships and the constant air traffic, the beach inside the base was quite beautiful. The sand was soft, white and clean. The water was a crystal-clear blue that showed the vibrant tropical fish that darted beneath. The breeze cut the humidity and made the heat tolerable. In the distance, there was a small boat moving toward the beach. A man waved at them. Peaslee waved back.

Peaslee sat down on a large rock and took off his shoes and socks. Peel did the same as the man briefed him about what was about to happen. "In a few moments, Major Romero of the Cuban Security Forces is going to show up; he'll be accompanied by Agent Romanova, of Soviet Army Intelligence. Romero will do most of the talking, but make no mistake: despite her appearance, Romanova is in charge. Do not tell them anything unless I tell you to. They are here to discuss how our team will get to Banes, and how many soldiers we will need to get us there."

Peel looked around. "Shouldn't we all be here? Where's the rest of our men?"

Peaslee looked at his watch, "Millward and the others, unit codename Devilskebab left the base yesterday; they should be halfway to Banes by now."

It was just then that the small boat beached itself and the Cuban and Russian leapt into the shallow water and came ashore. Romero was typically Cuban, dressed in white linen shorts and a nearly translucent shirt. Beneath a thick mustache the remnants of a cigar were still smoldering. Romanova was wearing a sundress, which accentuated her wavy hair, allowing it to flow down around her shoulders and bare arms. It was hard to believe this woman was a spy, but perhaps that was why she had been recruited to begin with. She moved daintily through the shallows while Romero simply forced his way to shore, grinning all the way.

"Hola, Professor," he bellowed. "It is good to see you again." He wrapped two beefy arms around Peaslee in a kind of loose hug. Peaslee smiled and whispered a greeting back. Romero laughed and with an open arm introduced his companion. She didn't smile, and barely made eye contact. "We have updates if you need them, Professor." The old man nodded and Romero knelt down and with a piece of driftwood sketched out a crude map. "Banes is 100 miles north of here, on the coast between the sea and the bay, with mountains to the west and south. The main road runs south into the mountains. The terrain is covered with jungle, and is too treacherous for most people to traverse. We have forces on the main road, about ten miles away from town, and smaller units along the mountain road to make sure no one comes through the jungle. Aerial reconnaissance reports that the roads are littered with the dead. There are signs of movement, but visual contact with the source hasn't been achieved. Whatever has happened down there it is muy malo, very bad."

"There is still no radio contact?" asked the professor.

Romero and Romanova exchanged looks, knowing looks. There was a pregnant pause that Romanova finally broke. "We have had no contact with anyone in the affected area. There is a signal, however; really three intertwined signals. They are simple sinusoidal oscillations. As far as we can tell they aren't coding any information, but they all originate from Banes."

"Mr. Peel will investigate. He has a way with such things." Peaslee was staring out at the ocean. "How soon do we leave?"

Romero was suddenly very serious. "We will leave in the boat after sunset, and head out into the ocean. A ship will pick us up and take us round the island to Barnes. We plan to land our forces just before dawn. That should give Mr. Peel plenty of time to analyze the radio signals."

Romanova was equally frigid, a state that seemed at odds with the beautiful beach, the sun, and the light cotton dress she was wearing. "Mr. Peel, Colonel Peaslee says you might be able to find a solution. I hope he is right. I am willing to give you time to prove why he has such faith in you, but make no mistake, if you fail, I will do what is necessary to protect the peoples of Cuba and the Soviet Union."

"Let us hope it does not come to that," Peaslee suggested, and with that he pulled Peel off the beach and back toward the base. Peel's head was spinning, but even so he couldn't help but notice the American soldiers who were making sure that Romero and Romanova were staying on the beach.

★

October 20

The morning wind was gentle and cool; flying fish

would occasionally scatter as the ship cut through the calm sea. Earlier, a pod of porpoise had decided to ride the bow wake of the fast-moving warship as she sped toward Banes. The ship was late—Peaslee called it "Latin Time"—and the sun was already rising as they came into the harbor. Peaslee, Romanova and Romero were still asleep in the cabin, but Peel couldn't get comfortable and had crawled out onto the deck. Some of the crew, a mix of Soviets and Cubans found it amusing and had whipped out fat, greasy cigars that stank and turned him a different shade of green. The odd thing was that despite being sick he couldn't stop thinking about the signal waves.

Once he knew they were there, they were easy to find and then isolate. One was quite strong, while the other two were relatively weak, and, as he continued to monitor them, seemed to be fading in strength. Meanwhile the third one seemed to be growing, gaining strength and dominance. What bothered him the most was that he recognized all three waves, well at least their visual complements. The weak ones he identified as belonging to the colors of red and blue. It was as if someone was transmitting an analog of these colors on a radio frequency, which was slowly fading away. In the meantime, the remaining wave corresponded to an entirely predictable color, one that was gaining strength and overriding the other two.

As he clung to the railing on the port side, he watched the first rays of sunlight break over the horizon and play out over the bay and the town beyond. At first, he thought it was a trick of the tropical light that something in the air was acting as a filter but he knew that was simply impossible. The crew came up beside him, mouths agape in awe and fear. One of them dug into his shirt and pulled out a small rosary that hung around his neck and whispered, "Madre de Dios."

The commotion served to rouse Peaslee and the others, who filtered through the hatch and clung to the side of the boat. The captain had apparently seen the horror as well, and decided quite on his own that he would stay as far away as possible. The ship changed course and headed back toward the welcoming blue-green ocean and the orange and pink clouds that framed the sun. As they turned from shore Peel threw up again, but he didn't mind. Anything was better than what lay behind them, for the village of Banes had been transformed, altered, drained of all life and vitality, of all color, save for one. It was the color that Peel associated with the radio signal, the one that was growing stronger and eclipsing the others.

Romanova swore in Russian something that sounded like "Zhol-tee!"

Romero shook his head in despair and muttered, "Amarillo." I swear there was a tear in his eye.

It was Peaslee that put a better name to it than Peel ever could, for while it was a shade of yellow, it was not warm; rather, it was pale and sickly. It crawled into the eyes and squirmed into the brain, infecting those who had seen it with a sense of loathing and dread. Even from this distance, it had damaged those who had looked at it. Peaslee seemed to spit as he said the word, as if it was an effort to name the foul hue that now stained the town and shoreline. He called it "Giallo," and that seemed oddly appropriate.

★

October 21

The captain had moored more than two miles off shore, and he steadfastly refused to move any closer. No matter what Romero said, no matter how he threatened or cajoled, the captain would go no closer. Romanova tried to pull rank, and for a brief moment there were the sounds of Russian guns being brought to bear, but it was met with the sound of Cuban guns, and the standoff was brief. Romanova lost face, but nobody was shot.

It took the rest of the day for Peaslee and Romero to negotiate the use of a launch. The captain refused to order any of his men to go ashore, and none of them volunteered. The Soviets were more accommodating; two of them agreed to follow Romanova. She warned the others that they would be disciplined, but they still refused. Consequently, when Peaslee and Peel finally went ashore they went only with Romero, Romanova, and two Soviet soldiers who barely spoke Spanish, let alone English.

The trip aboard the launch was rife with anxiety. Romero was at the helm, while Romanova and her soldiers took up positions with their Kalashnikovs. Peel noted the soldiers were constantly touching the guns, as if they were a sort of talisman against the horrors they approached. It reminded Peel of the man with the rosary, and he wondered which one was more valuable in this situation. The ocean gave way to the bay, and the bay to the harbor, and the harbor succumbed to giallo. As they approached the yellow line the anxiety built, for they all expected something to happen when they finally crossed that threshold and entered the queerly stained realm that had succumbed to the infection. It was therefore somewhat anticlimactic when they finally crossed the line and absolutely nothing at all occurred.

"The water feels wrong" said Peel as he caught some of the yellow spray in his hand. "It reminds me of kerosene: it's oily." He shook his hand, but instead of flying off, the stuff just seeped off of his hand in thick, viscous drops. "I thought maybe it was a contaminant, a dye, an alga, maybe even spores or pollen, but it's not, is it? It's an actual physical change to the water itself."

"I think it's more sinister than that," offered Peaslee. "I think perhaps it is a fundamental alteration to the matter itself. I think that whatever has happened here is changing the very nature of the building blocks of our universe, making our world into something else."

"An interesting theory, Colonel Peaslee," yelled Romanova over the sound of the engine. "Care to explain further?"

"I have an idea," suggested Peaslee, "but I'm not ready to share. Not just yet."

They made several passes across the waterfront searching for signs of life, trying to draw out some kind of attack, but there was no response. Eventually they picked a sturdy-looking dock that was sitting low to the water and cautiously tied up to it. Like the water, the wood, nails, steel and concrete that made up the harbor had all turned a sickly shade of yellow, with only shadows and texture providing any real sort of contrast.

They weren't even off the waterfront when they found the first bodies: a cluster of middle-aged women who had been stabbed repeatedly in their abdomens and lower backs. There were defensive wounds on their hands. Blood ran from their bodies and mingled into crusty pools that dotted the street. The blood was yellow. The soldiers spoke rapidly in Russian, and Romanova responded angrily. The team pressed on, but every few steps there was another body. Some stabbed, some bludgeoned, some simply dead. One man had been decapitated by a hand trowel. A woman had been strangled by a silk scarf. An elderly couple had been pierced through their heads by a length of rebar. It made Peel and everyone else nervous as they moved through a silent city of the dead.

Only Peaslee seemed calm enough to make notes, which after about an hour he handed to Peel.

"Do you see a problem with this, Mr. Peel?"

Peel looked at the numbers Peaslee had been writing down and the bar graph he had sketched out, a bar graph that hinted at something terrible. "Romero, is there a school nearby?"

Romero looked at his map, and then at the street signs. He pointed westward. "One block that way."

Peel took off at a brisk pace with Peaslee following closely behind him. The others were momentarily confused but decided it was better not to argue, and fell in line as the two Americans suddenly took control of the team.

The school was as quiet as the rest of the town. It was small; a single-story building that sprawled around a simple playground. There were three bodies on the steps, all women. Peel leapt over them and ran inside. Peaslee stopped at the door and held the others back. They could hear Peel inside throwing open doors and pounding down hallways. He was crying, moaning in denial, really, and with each passing moment his cries grew louder and louder and louder.

Without warning he burst through the door, startling the others. One of the soldiers jumped and brought his weapon to bear. Romero pushed the barrel to the side as the man pulled the trigger and let off a single shot. They all stood there in silence in a dead yellow city as the man who had fired the shot tried to compose himself, and Peel tried to catch his breath.

"They're all dead," he panted. "There are six more inside. Four teachers, one administrator and an older man who I think was a janitor. No one else." He put his hands on his knees and then crumpled to the ground. "There is no one else."

Romero cast a confused look in Peaslee's direction. Peaslee raised a finger and then with his foot rolled one of the teachers over. There was a pencil embedded in her gut. Several other holes suggested that she had been stabbed with it multiple times. "These wounds, most of them are to legs, or the abdomen, some to the hands; very few are to the head or neck. All of them are upward thrusts."

Romanova bent down and examined another body, and then cursed in Russian. She seemed to be thinking about something and then suddenly made a decision. "We need to find shelter, someplace we can use as a base, someplace defensible."

"What have you learned, my friends?" Romero was on the verge of panicking because he hadn't figured out what Peel, Peaslee and Romanova already had.

It fell to Peaslee to explain. "How many bodies have we seen? How many men? How many women?"

Romero's face grew more confused, "Over a hundred, maybe a few more men than women. Why do you ask?"

Peaslee flipped his notebook in the air. "Not counting these people here, I've counted one hundred and six dead. Sixty-eight are men; thirty-eight are women."

"So, there are more men than women. The area we passed through was waterfront and warehouses, places men work. No place for women."

"We didn't come to the school to look for women," Peaslee finally admitted. "We came to look for children. Tell me, Romero, where are the children?"

Romero was about to speak when there was a very unexpected sound. Out across the bay there came the undeniable boom of heavy gun fire. Just a single shot, but it made them all pause and turn back toward its origin. In the sky over the ocean a flare had been launched, and it was slowly falling back down through the sky.

Romero was cursing out the ship's captain, "He was not supposed to launch that flare until we were late to report at 1800 hours. The man is a son of a dog."

The Russians were scrambling to get their radio out and establish contact with the ship, but Peaslee was looking at the sky. "How long since we left the boat?" he asked.

Peel looked at his watch, "About two hours and ten minutes. Why?"

"I think we should leave this place now, while we still can."

"What? Why?"

Peaslee grabbed one of the backpacks and started loading the equipment back inside. "We need to maintain radio silence. The captain didn't make a mistake with the flare. Look to the west. The sun is going down. Apparently, it is not only matter that is being rewritten, but time as well."

They turned to head back down the hill toward the waterfront, and the avenue gave them a clear view of the harbor below, the bay and the shoreline beyond it. There was a city on the far shore where no city had been before, and it was unlike any human city any of them had ever seen. It froze them in their tracks for none wanted to approach it or its terrible beauty, or the thing that rose up out of the waters before it. It rose out of the yellow bay like a nightmare, a great globular thing that cast a pale light across the waters, replacing the sunlight, which was rapidly retreating. It rose out of the waters and into the sky, impossibly huge, and impossibly passing in front of the distant towers, instead of behind them. It was a hideously luminescent sphere, covered with a murky mist that hid whatever it was that was the source of the light.

"Please tell me that's the moon," begged Peel.

Peaslee shook his head. "Not our moon, I think."

"Demhe," spat Romanova. "The bay is no longer safe. There is a barracks not far from here. It should supply us with a more defensible position. We should go there, now."

No one argued.

★

The Russian soldiers were dead. Nightfall had brought heat, and with it came a kind of lethargy. It seemed that they had drowsed for hours, but their watches no longer agreed. Some were off by minutes, others by hours—but that was the least of their worries. At night, the dead city came to life. It had been unnerving, listening to the sounds of children running

206 | THE PEASLEE PAPERS

wild through the streets, their macabre laughter echoing off of the walls and windows. That children could play among the dead, that they were likely the murderers themselves, instilled an unsettling sense of dread within Peel, one that he felt sure had found a home in the others as well. In an attempt to remain calm, he had begun listing the digits of pi. Unfortunately, his recitation had little effect on the others. Panic took hold of the two young soldiers, and against reason and orders they had left the security of the concrete barracks. Where they had planned on going hadn't been an issue. They wanted out, no matter what. The shooting started just moments after the door slammed shut. It stopped not long after.

Later, when the noise had stopped, Peaslee and the others had ventured out into the morning light, or what passed for it in the transformed town. They had found the bodies, dismembered. Their guns had been left behind, the barrels bent beyond repair. The bodies and the guns had turned yellow.

It left the team with Romanova's Kalashnikov, her sidearm, and Romero's as well. Peaslee wasn't comfortable with their lack of firepower and suggested that they rectify the situation by raiding the local police station.

"What about our team, Colonel," Peel blurted out, "when will they get here?"

Romero and Romanova stared at Peaslee, waiting for an answer and an explanation. The old man sighed and glared at Peel. "The Devilskebab team, Rob Millward, and the others, they penetrated the quarantine zone several hours before we ourselves arrived. If they were still alive they would have made contact by now."

Romero was suddenly outraged. "You disappoint me, Colonel Peaslee. Yes, I am disappointed, but I am not surprised. We trusted you and you betray that trust. You bring armed Americans into our country without telling us, and then you wonder why we ally ourselves with the Soviets?"

"Calm yourself, Romero," suggested Romanova. "It is typical American imperialism. Their greed blinds them, makes them think they can do whatever they wish." There was a knowing smile across her face. "Is that what happened here? Did one of your attempts to meddle backfire? Did you do this, Colonel Peaslee?"

"Does it matter?"

Romanova chuckled. "No, Colonel, I suppose at this point it doesn't."

It took an hour for the four of them to make it to the police station, but the place had been ransacked already. The guns were gone; all that remained were a few batons and some canisters of tear gas. The radio was gone, but the connection to the antenna remained. Romero unpacked the radio from the backpack and began hooking it up.

Peaslee went to stop him, but Romanova shook her head. "The time for radio silence is over, Colonel. We need to know what is going on. We need to know what our governments are thinking. We need orders."

Peaslee started to protest, thought better of it, and then simply nodded. He and Peel watched as Romero worked and coaxed the machine to life. It sputtered static, and Romero swiped at the volume knob, before playing with the frequency. There was a screeching pulse that burned their ears for an instant as Romero dialed through it. He settled on a station with an official-sounding voice that was doing its best to hide the fear that was trying to break through. The accent was heavy, and even Romanova was straining to understand what was being said, until a familiar voice—President Kennedy's voice—was suddenly speaking.

All ships of any kind bound for Cuba, from whatever nation or port, will, if found to contain cargoes of offensive weapons, be turned back. This quarantine will be extended, if needed, to other types of cargo and carriers.

Peaslee looked at his watch and cursed. "We've lost more time. That speech was scheduled for the evening of the twenty-second, and only if we had failed. Things are escalating."

"My government won't tolerate the situation much longer." Romanova was stating the obvious, and creating an impasse.

Peel stepped in and moved toward Romero. "Let me try something." He turned the volume down as far as it would go, and then dialed the frequency back to the frequency with the pulse that burned; the one which he knew was carrying the Yellow Sine. The all-too-familiar wave form jumped to life on the oscilloscope. The strength of the signal was immense, almost unbelievable, and from what Peel could tell, incredibly close. "Can we use this to find the source of the signal?"

Romanova dug through the bag and pulled out a coil of metal and electronics. There were plugs that attached the contraption to the radio. "This should work," she said and then gasped suddenly and pulled back from Romero. His hands had begun to turn yellow.

He stared at them in horror, holding them out for all to see. "You did this," he spat at Peaslee. "You find a way to fix it." He brought out his sidearm. Romanova reached for hers but then relaxed as he laid the weapon on the table. "You'll need this more than I will." He took off running and was out of the door before anyone could stop him. Peel started after him, but Peaslee grabbed him and pulled him back.

"You can't go out there, son!"

"Let me go!"

Romanova shut the door and threw the bolt. The city had appeared on the far shore, and the moon had risen from the bay. Soon the children would be coming.

★

"Why the children?" Peel asked as he held the radio and tried to find a stronger signal. "Why aren't they dead like everyone else?"

It was Romanova who spoke up. "The human mind is like clay, Mister Peel. It must be molded, taught, indoctrinated. This not only applies to languages and culture, but to the laws of the universe as well. There have been events, inexplicable cases like this one that suggest that the rules of the universe may vary from place to place. That matter, time, gravity may be different, may actually change. The adult mind rebels at these changes, crumbles, shatters. It is too well-trained and set in its view of the universe to accept any changes. The mind of a child isn't so rigid; it learns, and can change when it needs too. If properly stimulated it can see the universe in ways that adults cannot. There are documented cases in the West. The Paradine children. That village in Winshire. There are other cases we could discuss. I am surprised that you do not know these.

Colonel Peaslee, do you not properly educate your agents in JACK?"

But Peaslee wasn't listening; he was staring at his hands. His fingertips were yellow, and he was shaking.

Peel grabbed him by the shoulder and pulled him forward. "If we find the source, maybe we can reverse the effects."

They wandered through the town, picking their way through the sickly yellow wreckage and the dead. Peel thought that there should have been a smell, a stench of rot, but there wasn't, and as far as he could tell there were no animals either. No dogs, no cats, or birds. He hadn't seen a rat or a roach or a spider. The bodies did not draw flies. They just sat there waiting, as if they had been painted into place as scenery.

"You're good with that thing," said Romanova, talking about the radio.

Peel nodded. "My younger brother is an electrician in Sydney. When we were kids he was always building things like this. Radios, metal detectors, electric eyes."

She nodded. "That is respectable work."

He looked at her and made a decision. "My name is Mitchell. My friends call me Mitch."

Her eyes were full of suspicion, but only for an instant. It was the first time they had spoken of something that didn't concern the mission. "Tanya; they call me Tanya."

"And my name is Wingate. I don't have any friends, but my employees call me TOM." He marched passed them. "In case you've forgotten, I'm dying here." The yellow had engulfed his forearms, and there was a patch of something that was working its way through his hair.

"You need to stop, Colonel," said Peel.

"We don't have time to stop. I don't have time. The world doesn't have time. We have to find the transmitter."

"No, Colonel, you don't understand. The transmitter is here; we've found it."

The three looked up at the cathedral that loomed over them, casting a dark shadow in a landscape of endless yellow. The windows were boarded shut, and the doors chained. Some of the glass was broken and there were pockmarks in the stone walls, tell-tale signs of gunfire. Romanova shrugged. "The revolution was not bloodless."

They worked their way around the back and found a door that had been pried open. They crawled inside. They had thought the place would have been dark, but it wasn't. There was light everywhere, electric lights being driven by a generator that had been set up in a hallway. They followed the cables into a small room and approached what they found there with caution.

There was a man—or what had once been a man. He was yellow, and where his head had once been there was an empty space, a void of yellow nothingness that seemed to pulse and seethe. He was slumped in a chair in front of a radio transmitter, with the microphone nearly embedded into the mass of yellow where his head once was. The transmitter was still on, and Peel could see the Yellow Sine as it danced on the oscilloscope. All around him there were pages from a book. The ink had gone yellow, as had the pages.

Peel reached for a random page, but a single touch from Peaslee stopped him. He nodded, realizing the danger, but then suddenly chuckled. "All because of this. All these people dead. Three nations on the brink of war. Soldiers mobilizing, ships with guns pointed at each other, missiles ready to launch. It's a strange new world we've built for ourselves. War used to be about men being commanded on the battlefield. Now it's come to this. Oh, there are still forces to manipulate, but the real battles of the future will be fought by just a few men who know what buttons to press and what knobs to turn." He reached out and clicked the transmitter off. "And just like that, the crisis is averted."

But it wasn't.

Nothing had changed. The oscilloscope on the handheld radio they had used to find their way here was still showing the Yellow Sine marching across its screen.

Peel's eyes grew wide. He pulled the plug on the transmitter, and then threw the machine to the floor. The plastic and bits of metal shattered, but the world didn't change. He took his gun and fired into the headless body, but with no response.

"We're too late," whispered Tanya. "The reaction is self-sustaining. It can't be stopped."

Peaslee grabbed the handheld radio and spun the dial, searching for a particular frequency. "Maybe, but maybe not. Perhaps now that we have cut off the origin signal the manifestation is vulnerable."

"What?" said both Peel and Romanova.

"Perhaps we can change the wave form now. But we're going to need a very large explosion." He found the frequency he was looking for and grabbed the microphone. "Aquatone actual to Oilstone unit, respond. Aquatone actual to Oilstone unit, respond. This is a Pi utility command. Over."

There was a static filled pause, and then the radio burst to life. "Oilstone to Aquatone, acknowledged. Awaiting orders."

Peaslee was smiling. "Oilstone, you are to proceed to the following coordinates." He grabbed the map and found a position just west of Banes. "You are to then proceed low over the city until you reach the bay. In the bay you will see a large yellow sphere. That is a target. Do you understand?"

The radio crackled back. "Acknowledged, Aquatone. Please confirm that you are aware that I am light. Repeat: this is an Oilstone light mission."

Peaslee and Romanova exchanged a glance and then he spoke once more. "Understood, Oilstone. You have your orders."

"We should get to the bell tower," said Romanova. "We should be able to see from there."

They were running, and then climbing the stairs. Romanova first, and then Peel who had taken the radio, and then finally Peaslee. As they climbed the sun went down, and in the distance, they could see the waters of the bay begin to stir. It was Romanova who first saw the plane. An ungainly black thing silhouetted against the dying sun. It was quiet in the sky above the village, but only for a moment. For as the moon bubbled up out of the cloudy depths, the children came out of hiding.

"Is this going to work, Colonel?"

"I hope so, son. I haven't got anything else to try, do you?"

Something in the church below them crashed. The front doors had given way and children were suddenly inside the church. They were breaking things, slowly working their way through the building. Heading toward the tower.

Peel pulled on Tanya's jacket. "The pilot said he was 'light': what did he mean?"

Tanya Romanova gestured at the slowly arcing plane. "He's a spy plane, strictly reconnaissance. Built for speed and taking pictures. He's not armed. The only way he has to attack the target is by hitting it with the plane itself."

"But that's suicide!"

Tanya nodded and said nothing more.

The plane had finished its arc and had become little more than a thin black line in the distance that was slowly growing larger as they watched it get closer. Below them, the children had reached the door to the tower but were having problems breaking through. Others had given up trying to get in and were busy climbing up the side of the structure, clinging to vines and loose boards. Their tiny fingers and feet seemed perfect for the task, for they were making significant progress. Tanya handed Romero's gun to Peel and motioned toward the horde of frenzied kids that were crawling toward them.

As he looked back, he saw Peaslee's head suddenly shake and turn yellow. He reached out to the transforming man, but was pushed away. The Terrible Old Man lunged for the window, but Peel caught his jacket and swung him to the floor.

The plane roared overhead. The children reached the belfry.

Romanova fired her handgun, covering Peel as he dragged Peaslee to the corner. The TOM was screaming in agony. Together Peel and Romanova rose up and began firing as a wave of small bodies poured through the window. They were yellow, twisted, and covered in filth. In the distance, the plane flew on. Body after body fell as Romanova switched to the Kalashnikov. Blood, still yellow, sprayed through the air.

The black plane grew small against the moon, and then plunged into it. The milky surface shuddered and then exploded in a geyser of color that swirled back into being. On the distant shore, the alien city wavered and then faded into nothingness. The moon that Tanya had called Demhe shrank as it vomited forth the stolen colors of the world. It collapsed in on itself until there was nothing more than a small glowing speck. Then the speck began to fade and Romanova could see the wreckage of the spy plane fall to the earth.

The children halted their advance, and Romanova stopped shooting them. Some of them, caught by the surprise of their location, fell to their deaths. Others began to cry. Romanova took the radio and sent an all-clear message. Cuban and Soviet soldiers would be leaving the line, coming as fast as they could to help. Tanya and Peel did what they could while they waited.

★

It took two days for Peel and Peaslee to be returned to Guantanamo, and another day before they were stateside. Peel was briefed, debriefed, examined, questioned, interrogated and forced to sign certain documents that suggested he could be punished very badly. He later learned that Agent Romanova returned to the Soviet Union and was promoted and reassigned. In late December, he flew home to Sydney for Christmas and took a job with the Australian government.

Colonel Doctor Wingate Peaslee stayed in a military hospital for six weeks. There was scaring on his hands and neck where the yellow was particularly bad, but the greatest damage was to his mind. The doctors diagnosed him with dementia. Security forces interviewed him extensively but found that he had no memory of his work with JACK. He was found unfit for duty and medically discharged. He was retired to a minimum-security facility near Arkham, Massachusetts, where he developed a collection of rocks and glass bottles. He was prone to rages and tended to mutter incoherently to himself and his collection. On occasion, he cried out before going into convulsions, during which he screamed the same word over and over again. The seizures never lasted for more than a minute. The word was "Giallo."

1970

OPERATION ALICE

For the third time, my name is Doctor Scott Eckhart, I work for the Federal Bureau of Investigation in Boston. I have degrees in Psychology and Chemistry from Florida Technical University. I came here, to Latimer House on December 5, 1969 to examine and question a patient by the name Wingate Peaslee, a former professor of psychology. He was also a former supervising agent for JACK, the Joint Action Committee on Korea. That organization had been founded years before the Korean conflict, suggesting to me that Peaslee and JACK were more than what they seemed, but any questions in that direction led to a dead end. Peaslee's file, forwarded from the Office of Naval Research was extensively redacted. Whatever the man had done during the Forties and Fifties was a well-kept secret, and likely to remain that way. Peaslee was a loose end, one that the Atomic Energy Commission expected me to tie up.

Pr. Wingate Peaslee had been institutionalized in the wake of the Cuban Missile Crisis, officially suffering from exhaustion. His first weeks were filled with the usual examinations and tests, but after several weeks it became apparent that he was here to stay. The days turned into weeks, the weeks into months, and the months into years. His activities were closely watched and regularly reported on. Those reports were checked and circulated to key officers. On June 6 of this year Peaslee suffered from a seizure, of a kind that was not uncommon for him, a mania of some sort, during which he said four words. As I said these fits were not uncommon, and in the past had gone almost unmentioned, but the nurse who had witnessed the attack was new, and therefore she provided details others would have left out. There were four words, nonsense words really, and they meant nothing to anyone in the hospital. But, those words cascaded through various security channels and at each station they triggered alarms, and were passed up the chain. Those words were

Dodo
Hatta
Sheep
Gnat

Individually they were meaningless words, but together and in that order, they represented four consecutive nuclear tests, all part of Operation Alice up in Alaska, tests that were classified, tests that hadn't started until the middle of July and ended in early October. Somehow Peaslee had not only known about the tests, but knew about their designations more than a month in advance. This suggested a breach in security, and I with my degree in psychology seemed the perfect candidate to travel to Latimer House and investigate. It had taken six months for someone to authorize the investigation, the AEC had been preoccupied with the Nuclear Non-Proliferation Treaty, and now the powers that be wanted an explanation, and fast.

My course of action at the hospital was to first review the man's file, and those of his associates, as well as a list of visitors in hopes of finding the names of visitors who might be passing along classified information. My thought was that perhaps an old friend, a ranking member of the AEC routinely came to talk, perhaps too much, perhaps about things he shouldn't. Unfortunately, this was a dead end, in all the years he had been incarcerated; he had had only one visitor. On March 3, 1965, the log showed that Peaslee was visited by his niece Alice Keezar. At the time, the staff had no reason to doubt her claim, but I have checked. Wingate has no niece named Alice. His mother's name was Alice, and her maiden name was Keezar, but that woman had been missing for three decades, and would have been well into her eighties.

Whoever she was, her visit elicited a profound effect in Peaslee. Up until then, he had been obsessed with the other patients, well more precisely with those who had passed away. He used bottles, twine and small rocks gathered from the garden to build strange little memorials to each of his fellows that had passed. To these he spoke regularly, as if they were people themselves. He would have entire conversations, the staff noted. It was eerie, but mostly harmless behavior, so the staff did nothing. All this changed after the woman came.

A full account of their conversation was not made, but an orderly did note some odd things the woman said, including, "X is assassinated" and "Modesty is exposed".

There was more than three weeks spent doing some kind of math. He wrote compulsively, doing calculations and conversions, sketching geometric symbols, and strange broken curves. When asked about what he was doing, about the kind of mathematics and formulas he was using Peaslee would stare strangely at the symbols and numbers and diagrams and then respond enigmatically. "Nakotic. The math is Krellian, but the chronic angles and chords are Nakotic." Two nurses signed off on this quote.

On March 26, 1965 Peaslee briefly stopped working on his equations. A patient had fallen in the recreation room, a man named Lawrence Trask, when he stood up he began speaking in an odd manner, first reciting the same word "Dormouse".

Trask spoke this word over and over again until Peaslee sat down next to him and said, "Tortoise."

According to the nurses Trask immediately sat up looked at Peaslee and then began an almost incomprehensible litany of nonsense. "Nora versus Miller. The snake kills two hundred. Tic Toc gives us backstep and then a leap, or is it the other way round? Alice's traps the carpenter with a walrus."

Afterwards the two became inseparable, and even asked to share the same room. Trask began helping Peaslee with his calculations. There was a fury of erasing and scratching out. Parameters were changed. Conclusions were altered. Diagrams were adjusted. Trask seemed to know things that Peaslee did not, and the two fed on each other's mania. It was a *folie a deux*, two madmen sharing the same delusion.

And then as suddenly as it had begun, it was over.

One-day Trask collapsed, only for a moment, and when he regained consciousness he was screaming. He launched himself at Peaslee, tried to claw his eyes out. It took three orderlies to tear Trask off of Peaslee. Through it all Peaslee never said a word, even when he was getting stitched up where

Trask had bit into his ear. For seven days they had been inseparable, and now Trask couldn't stand the man.

That such an event had occurred was curious, but what was stranger was that it happened again.

On December 16 Lucy Keith woke up chanting the word "Dinah". Unlike Trask she didn't wait for Peaslee to find her. Instead she calmly walked down the hall and sat down next to the old man.

He looked at her and said "Tweedledee."

Those who were there swore that she said "Jackson writes from the grave. Lysenko's lies catch up. McMurdo is blocked. A dynasty of shoes begins. Fillmore tests acid. Messinger delivers three eggs nobody wants."

After that Keith followed the same pattern as Trask, though in this case the staff prevented her from sleeping in the same room. As this was a second occurrence of the very rare *folie a deux*, the actions of the two were watched and recorded quite closely. The staff, particularly the head nurse found the whole arrangement eerie, for the two seemed to be unnaturally close. They awoke at the same time and ate the same food. They worked incessantly. This time there were no changes to Peaslee's calculations, but rather what appeared to be a translation of the calculations into a kind of design, but for what none could say. But then, as if they both had known, there came the day when Keith and Peaslee separated. Peaslee continued to work on his odd designs, but Keith went to her own room. She wasn't there for a minute before she collapsed onto the bed, convulsed and then began screaming.

They had to restrain her for three days, and for months after she was force fed tranquilizers to keep her calm whenever Peaslee was around.

In the spring Peaslee joined her in that regiment of pills. It was May and Peaslee had been working on his designs for months. Strange geometries filled six sketch books and a pattern no one could describe had appeared in the rocks of the garden. Peaslee had worked on this alone, and there are pictures of it in his file. Every time I've looked at it I curse the day I arrived and didn't immediately dismantle it. He had finished it on May Fifth, and seemed to be both proud and apprehensive.

When asked about it he said that it was a Masonic

symbol. The orderly responded by saying that he hadn't known that Peaslee was a Mason. The old man shook his head and said, "I'm not. This is one of Keziah's symbols, Keziah Mason."

The next day standing there in the garden, in the center of his strangely repetitive design Wingate Peaslee became confused and returned to the hall, but he did not return to his room. Instead he made a beeline for the room occupied by Laurence Trask, walked in and laid down. When Trask himself wandered in, Peaslee snapped and crumpled into a ball on the floor.

He stayed that way for days chanting the same words over and over, "I am Larry Trask. I am Larry Trask. I am Larry Trask."

His doctors were puzzled at this sudden strange behavior, and none could offer a rational explanation as to what had caused the sudden schizophrenic episode. A young intern did suggest that Peaslee's break should be considered comparable to the one Trask had suffered the year before, but this was dismissed by the senior staff. They locked Peaslee in his room and let him sit there crying out those sad words that asserted his identity as someone else entirely.

On day seven Peaslee stood up knocked on the door and asked to see the doctor. He was hungry and dehydrated but otherwise unharmed. It was as if the strange change in personality had not happened at all.

Given the odd turn of events, the director suggested that Peaslee's design be removed from the garden, and the staff reported that the old man watched intently as the maintenance staff rearranged the rocks and raked the gravel back into place. They could tell he was upset, but he never said a word, never spoke a single sentence in protest. He just watched the thing be unmade, and then walked away.

It was in June of 1966 that the next curious event occurred. Wade Spencer had been a patient for twelve years. In that time, he had never spoken a word, but on that warm summer day he marched into the charge nurse's office and asked directly if he could be allowed to walk the grounds. Finding no reason to deny his request the nurse consulted a doctor and then both allowed the man the run of the grounds.

He didn't stray far. Indeed, by all accounts he walked

around the main building in a kind of casual manner, almost wandering about, but never too far. He also developed a strange kind of obsessive game – at least that is how the staff described it. Spencer would find a rock and kick it back and forth across the grounds until at some point he became bored with the particular stone, and then he would move on to another. This went on for fourteen days, and then on the fifteenth day with the staff fully prepared for him to walk outside, he instead sought out Peaslee. He whispered something in the old man's ear, and Peaslee did the same. Within the hour Wade Spencer had sat back down in the recreation room and became silent once more. In July he stopped eating, and by the end of the month he was so weak that he contracted a respiratory infection and died. He was buried in the institute's cemetery.

Wingate Peaslee brought flowers to place on the grave.

In January of 1968 Peaslee once more suffered a break with reality, and this time assumed the persona of Lucy Keith. In this case, the conflict did not arise between the faux Keith and the real one, but rather with staff. Peaslee as Keith had tried to occupy Keith's room, but found it occupied by another person entirely. Lucy Keith, the real Lucy Keith, had died three weeks earlier. Peaslee had to be sedated, and remained that way until the episode passed and he returned to his normal persona. When on February 21 he came back to normalcy, he screamed the word "Tweedledee" the same word he had told Keith three years earlier.

Two weeks later Peaslee suffered a different kind of breakdown, or so it seemed. He became withdrawn and stopped speaking. He wandered about in a kind of semi-catatonia. It took three days for someone to realize that he had assumed the personality of Wade Spencer. When he finally returned to normal, Peaslee had lost almost twenty pounds.

Months later, there followed an even more peculiar chain of events. In rapid succession Peaslee suffered not one, but four schizophrenic events. These had an additional wrinkle. Each time Peaslee was able to acquire and swallow a significant amount of sedatives. This made identifying the patient whose personality he had assumed impossible. When Peaslee spoke during these months, it was only to spout random phrases and nonsense words similar to what was overheard and reported by the staff in his conversations with Trask and Keith.

Except they weren't nonsense words. Like those that had brought Peaslee to our attention, the words he and the other patients had been speaking were project codes, identifiers for atomic bomb tests. These were some of the most guarded secrets of United States, and they were being tossed around by people who had no visitors, no phone privileges, and were generally considered to be clinically insane. If this was a breach in our security then it was one that I could not even begin to understand. If it made sense, it was perhaps only to a madman.

If I was to understand I would have to talk to Wingate Peaslee.

My first interview with Peaslee occurred on December 9, 1969. It did not go well.

I introduced myself, asked him a series of simple questions. He answered them, but as we proceeded those answers became more and more terse, and it soon became apparent that he was growing annoyed with both the interview and me.

Finally, he turned the tables and asked me a question, "Dr. Eckhart why don't you ask me what you really want to know?"

I was taken aback, I had thought my cover impenetrable, but it seemed that Peaslee had seen right through my pretense. I felt it best to be forthright. I explained who I was and why I was there. "How do you know about the bombs, Professor?"

He chuckled. "How do people not know? All that energy put out into the world; did you think it would go unsensed?"

"You can sense a nuclear detonation half way round the world?"

Peaslee shook his head. "Not the detonation itself, the tunnels it bores forward and backwards in time. The energy has to be of sufficient size; otherwise the tunnels don't travel far. Small tunnels go nowhere."

"So, you expect me to believe that you what, burrow through time?" I lit a cigarette and flipped my hand around asking for an explanation. "Where did you learn to do that?"

"My mother taught me. I think she learned it from my

father, well about it anyway."

"Your mother, you mean Alice Keezar? She came to visit you back in 1965. From what I hear she looked pretty spry for someone in their eighties."

"She burrows. Better than I do. She does it physically."

"How do you do it?"

Peaslee tapped his forehead with two fingers. "My mind jumps from one body to another. Just like dear old dad."

I took a moment and wrote that down. His mania, this fixation seemed to be rooted in some conflict between his parents. It wasn't exactly what I wanted to hear, but at least he was talking to me. "So, when you travel in time, with your mind, where do you go?"

"Back mostly. Sometimes forward, not far really."

"Back," I took a drag from the cigarette. It was harsh, not my brand. "Back to Trask? Back to Keith?"

Peaslee tilted his head and turned his hand noncommittally. "You seem to know."

"And Wade Spencer?"

Peaslee leaned back in his chair and sighed deeply, remorsefully. "What do you think?"

My patience for bullshit had just about worn out, but I was willing to play along for a little longer. "I think you're lying to me. I think you need a machine to travel through time, and the pattern you built in the garden was it."

"It helped, made things easier. A Nakotic focus."

"And when the director had it dismantled, after that how did you keep surfing?" I waited for an answer, but he didn't respond. "I'll tell you what I think, or at least what I think you want me to think; that you burrowed back to Spencer and had him rebuild the machine for you. Those walks in the grounds, kicking rocks around. You want me to believe that he recreated this Nakotic focus."

"But, you don't, do you?"

"No, because my bullshit meter has just topped out Dr. Peaslee. I think this is just an elaborate charade. I've seen this before in Hanoi, and amongst the hippies at Miskatonic. You've set this all up as a kind of entertainment, something to pass the time during your incarceration. I think you've used your training as a psychologist to manipulate the other patients into adopting personalities that you've created. I also think you've used those same skills to fake your own aberrant behaviors. I think you might be a genius, a master manipulator. You're a Svengali, a Mabuse. Thank God you are in here. I can't imagine what you could do if you had access to Cannabis or LSD. You remind me of the Mad Hatter, changing the rules in a game that is unfathomable to begin with."

"And what would that make you Doctor Eckhart, Alice?"

"I prefer to think of myself as the Carpenter."

"I like the Walrus best."

I chuckled. "They were both very unpleasant characters."

"They were smarter than you though." He was trying to get underneath my skin. "You do remember why you're here don't you? The bombs, you wanted to find out how I knew about the test designations and their dates."

"Care to tell me?"

"I already have. In the future, the tests will be public knowledge, anyone can look them up."

"More of your mind games Doctor? Can't we move beyond that?"

"What do you want me to tell you? I'm a rogue agent. I've turned. I spent decades fighting monsters, time traveling monsters from outer space. Now I'm ready to work for them. They have an agenda, a purpose, and a vision for the future: A vision that doesn't include the vast majority of the human race. They are Cheshire Cats, fading in and out, and taunting mankind at every turn, guiding us toward a specific destination. We are Alice in Wonderland, we just don't know it."

"Is that the story you tell your fellow patients? I'm sure it impresses the weak of will and the insane, but to me it's just bullshit."

"If you say so, but that doesn't answer your question, does it?" He looked at me and I knew my mask had slipped. He had won this round. "Unicorn, Bandersnatch, JubJub, Duchess."

"What?"

He stood up and made for the door. "Unicorn, Bandersnatch, JubJub, Duchess." With that Wingate Peaslee left me to my own thoughts.

That was seven days ago.

I spent that time going over the files of the entire institute trying to figure things out. Peaslee had caught me in his web, in his delusion, he was manipulating me, and just as he had manipulated everyone else he had contact with. The files suggested that the strange behaviors began after Peaslee had arrived. Other patients pretended to be him, and later, sometime in the future, he pretended to be them.

But not for the four times he had acted out in October and November. He had pretended to be other people on October 8, 17, and 29, and November 21. These dates lined up exactly with the four project designations he had rattled off at the end of our interview: "Unicorn, Bandersnatch, JubJub, Duchess." This had been a mistake. If Peaslee was trying to convince me that his time travel story was real, then sometime in the past some other patient should have taken on Peaslee's personality. But try as I might, I could find no record of such occurrences. And the staff was of no use. They had become inured to Peaslee's behavior, and in these last cases had ignored the screaming and just sedated him, locked him away in a padded cell until the episodes had subsided.

This led me to believe that Peaslee was acting out for a reason. That he had purposefully built his stories around the bomb tests to add color, another bizarre wrinkle in his game. Unfortunately, he got the attention of the AEC. That may have been the plan from the beginning. Get our attention, or at least somebody's attention. Get someone to come out and interview him. Get out of the home, get back in the game. Problem was, with his redacted file I didn't know his game, or what kind of player he was. I suspected he was not unlike me, and that gave me pause to think about what I would do in a place like the Latimer House.

It was then that I decided that Peaslee had to be relocated to someplace else, someplace with more security. Someplace he could be better controlled. Someplace where whoever was feeding him information about bomb tests could be stopped. Latimer House had a more secure wing which would do for a start. I also knew that no matter how I played the move Peaslee would not make such a transfer easy, even if he wanted to go. It was obvious to me that no matter what I did, he was going to turn it all into part of his running drama. So, I needed to make sure I had the upper hand.

So, I stacked the deck.

Frank, Paul, Robert and James came up from the FBI office in Boston. They were big guys, smart and level-headed. Good agents, four of the best. Men I had worked with before. Men I could trust.

We came for Peaslee on December 13, I wanted to have him in his new home by Christmas, not that it mattered. It was a completely arbitrary date on my part. We came for him in his room, after dinner. He was alone, separated from the rest of the patients. I asked him to step into the hall. Frank cuffed him from behind. Paul and Robert each took an arm. James and I took the lead. We hadn't gone three steps before Frank stopped and collapsed to the floor.

As he went to check on his fellow agent Paul handed over control of Peaslee to Robert, and then tumbled to the ground himself.

Frank was already up, getting to his feet in a wobbly kind of way. He looked me straight in the eye and smiled as he said "Unicorn. Venera sends home more than it should." Robert fell to the ground without a sound.

As Robert went down Paul was getting back up, and James was pulling out his gun. "What the fuck?" he asked. Paul stood up, he looked at James and said "Bandersnatch. Robert R is dead." James never got a shot off before he hit the ground.

Robert and James came back up together.

Robert said "JubJub. Apollo takes a walk."

James whispered "Duchess. Piedmont is dead."

Frank, or at least the man wearing Frank's body took out a key and uncuffed Peaslee. He was smiling as he came over to me, almost laughing. He took me by my shoulders and brought his lips close to my ears. I could feel his hot breath on my skin, smell the antiseptic stench of the detergent they used to wash his clothes.

His voice was soft and calm, gentle even as he whispered a single word in my ear. The same word that I heard come out of my mouth.

Jabberwock

That was three days ago, and I've been in here for all that time trying to explain what happened. But the staff has stopped listening; they've heard it all before. I don't know what convinced them to call you, but they did. And now that you are here, you have to help me.

My name is Doctor Scott Eckhart, I work for the FBI. I was sent to investigate a potential security leak, Doctor Wingate Peaslee. I found so much more than that. I know how all this sounds, but I'm telling you the truth. And yes, I know how I look, but it all makes sense now. Peaslee was time-traveling, using burrows generated by atomic tests. He told me he could use those burrows to move backwards or forwards. The evidence is all there in the files. Those last four jumps, I was looking for them in the past, and I never considered they might occur in the future. He switched places with my agents and then he switched places with me.

You have to get me out of here. I'm not Wingate Peaslee. I'm not. I swear I'm telling you the truth. He's out there in my body, and I'm in here in his. You have to stop him. You have to get him back. You have to bring him back!

Please, before it's too late.

Addendum of Doctor M. Shea

Wingate Peaslee, patient X312, who had a history of slipping in and out of alternative personalities never recovered from his assumption of the persona of Scott Eckhart. He spent six days in restraints before he was finally calm enough to reenter the general population. His demeanor was poor and it took him more than a week to adjust back to the schedule of the institute. Through it all he demanded to be called Scott. Seeing no harm in that request I allowed it.

On April the Fifth 1970, a small envelope arrived, and unfortunately it was delivered to the patient before being screened. It was a newspaper article detailing the disappearance of former FBI agent Scott Eckhart. Earlier in the year Eckhart had resigned from the agency to pursue other opportunities. In late March, it had been discovered that his Boston apartment had been broken into and vandalized. The word WALRUS had been painted on the walls repeatedly. All attempts to locate Eckhart had been fruitless. On the bottom of the article someone had written "April 8, 1970 1730 EST"

Over the course of the next several days Peaslee became frantic. He went through his old papers and began rearranging the furnishings in his cell into a strange, but familiar pattern. He also began chanting, a single word over and over again. That word was Walrus.

On April the Ninth, Wingate Peaslee awoke from his sleep apparently calm and beyond whatever mania had seized him. He had breakfast and took his medications. He watched some television, and watched a program concerning nuclear testing in Alaska, and how the Atomic Energy Commission was bringing Operation Alice, the testing of nuclear weapons above ground, to a close, in favor of a new mode of testing below ground.

At 9:30 in the morning he gathered up several dirty dishes from the recreational room and entered the institute's kitchen. There, he turned to one of the other patients and said, "Remember what the dormouse said."

He used a bread knife to slit his own throat.

Who sent him the article and how they knew the date and time of detonation for Project Walrus, the last component of Operation Alice has never been determined.

As of this writing former FBI agent Dr. Scott Eckhart is still missing.

1993

THE WATCHMAKER'S LAMENT

Punxsatawney, Pennsylvania
1993, February 2

Iteration 3

    I was standing in the crowd watching the weatherman from Pittsburgh go a little mad, when my sister found me. It was unseasonably cold, even for a Pennsylvanian winter and the crowd was bundled up and desperate for the ceremony to be over. There was a band playing, though how the brass section could bear to handle their instruments, let alone play them, was beyond me. The officials took the stage in their fancy coats and top hats pulled a small animal out of his cage and pretended to listen to the creature speak some prognostication or the other concerning the weather. In the meanwhile, the news crew from Pittsburgh was floundering, their weatherman had showed up, panicked and then walked away without taking any footage. His producer, a rather photogenic woman with kinky black hair had stepped in, and had in my opinion done a satisfactory job.

    That hadn't happened before – I was about to say yesterday – but it wasn't yesterday, it was today, the same day just another iteration. We were replaying the day, and everything was starting to spiral into different directions based on subtleties I didn't understand.

    That's when Hannah put her hand on my shoulder. "Win," she never called me by my full name. "Win, what are you doing?" I looked at her, she was three years younger than me, that made her ninety years old, and she looked half that, maybe even younger. Time had been good to her.

    "I'm watching the locals try and predict the future by

talking to an oversized ground squirrel." I was being sarcastic on purpose. I didn't want her here. "It's been decades Hannah, what do you want?"

A cold wind blew down and she shuddered as she bundled up her coat. "Can we have lunch?"

I glared at her. "You're not mother Hannah. You can't solve problems over a cup of coffee and a salad." I let my foul mood rise up and take control. "I have neither the time nor the inclination to talk with either of you."

"Mother isn't coming. She thinks you will work this out on your own. I, however, disagree." She smiled back, not taking the cue to start an argument. "I prefer cherry pie to salads, and I think that you will talk to me sooner rather than later, because you have very little time left. Almost none at all."

My scowl softened and I ran my hand over my face and through my beard. "I have all the time in the world."

She shook her head. "You're dying Win, it happens to everyone. You can't expect to live forever." She nodded to the diner across the street, but I didn't want to talk, or eat. I wanted a drink, but at this hour the bar wasn't open. I stalked away from her.

She called after me, there was sad desperation in her voice. "You can't keep doing this!"

I looked at the cold, winter sky and the grey clouds that loomed over us all. "Watch me." I muttered. "You just watch me."

The bowling alley opens at noon, and I crawl inside it and sit at the bar drinking Schaefer and double shots of Dewar's. I'm quiet and morose. I sit in the corner, in the shadows. Every hour or so I slip the bartender a fifty-dollar bill and he leaves me to nurse my drinks and my pain in silence.

How does one deal with the knowledge of one's own death? Not the abstraction, the fact. I was going to die. At 5:47 AM on the morning of February third I would suffer a stroke, a devastating cerebral vascular accident, and I would live for only eight minutes more. Eight minutes of panic. Eight minutes of paralyzing terror in which to make the decision. Do I choose to die, or do I choose to flee, to cast my mind backwards into the only body prepared to accept it?

A man could go mad contemplating his own death. I spent hours doing so. I had gone mad long, long ago, long before I came to Punxsutawney.

It was ten minutes till midnight when the bartender made his last call. There were three other men in the bar, all drunks. One of them I knew from the town, Gus, a former Navy sailor who regretted coming back home. The taller man I didn't know at all, but the third I recognized as the weatherman form WPBH Pittsburg. I had seen him this morning at Gobbler's Knob. He had deviated from his routine, failed to give his report, and forced someone else to fill in.

Did I cause that? If so, I don't remember. Subtleties, variations, deviations, what causes them? Are they the answer? Is there an answer?

I handed the bartender a hundred-dollar bill and told him to keep the change. He tucked it in his shirt pocket and gave me a double shot of Dewar's. I didn't have that much time left. Six hours. I threw back the shot and chased it with a gulp from the pint of Schaefer's. Their jingle rolled around in my head, "The One Beer to Have When You're Having More Than One."

Outside I watch the drunken trio climb into a car and in seconds destroy a mailbox. The cops are on them almost instantly, and in seconds are beyond my sight. I can hear them though. The sirens echo through the town, and then the haunting echo of a train horn. There is a crash. It's only a few blocks over. Punxsutawney is a small town.

They take the driver, to the police station. I stand outside, the cold biting at my extremities. I stand there for hours. For what reason, I don't know. I'm looking for something, trying to understand. There must be rules, patterns – a process. And if I can understand those, if I can learn all there is to learn about this day, then maybe I can change its outcome. Maybe I can find a way to live. Maybe I can move beyond 5:55 AM on February third.

At 5:47 I took a deep breath and felt something in my brain explode, right on schedule, just as it had done in the last two iterations. It was like a firecracker had gone off in my head. I opened my mouth to scream and began to fall to the ground. I panicked, and cast back twenty-four hours to the only body that was compatible, my own. By the time my heart stopped beating, my mind was already somewhen else.

Iteration 4

I woke up screaming, but only for a moment. My heart was suddenly pounding and sweat was pouring down my back. I sat up and put my head between my knees. I was in my bedroom above the shop and it was 6 A.M. on February 2 again. On the radio the local morning show made a joke about it always being cold outside. On any other day, I would have gone back to bed, but this day was special, I had twenty-four hours to live. I had to make every minute count.

It took me fifteen minutes to clean up and get dressed, and another half hour to prepare and eat breakfast. I skipped the coffee, trying to keep my blood pressure down. I didn't know if it was a contributing factor or not, but I decided it couldn't hurt to leave it out. By 7 A. M. I was making my way through the shop and out the door. I stared at the motto I had engraved on the display window, "You don't have to be a watchmaker to know what time it is." It was a quote from the Sixties, a lyric by Erika Zann that I had always loved.

It was bitterly cold and the risen sun did little to dispel the winter dark. My aged Chevy POS groaned as it turned over in the cold. I let it warm up for a minute or two before pulling out of the alleyway and onto the town streets. The crowds on Gobbler's Knob had grown, and the cameramen were setting up. As I turned down the road I saw the weatherman walking down the street. Another man approached him at a brisk pace. The TV personality smashed him across the mouth with a gloved fist and didn't skip a step. It was only a few minutes north to the hospital. The plan was to complain about a headache and mimic the other symptoms of a stroke. Hopefully the doctor would be able to do something, if not the first time, maybe the second, maybe the third.

I had time.

Iteration 16

For the thirteenth day in a row, I drove to the hospital. This day, the frustration transformed into a rage boiling over inside me. I sat in the waiting room for a few minutes. Then, at 8 A. M. as the security guard went on break I passed through the Emergency Room entrance and shot the 48-year-old admitting nurse in the chest. I walked the halls systematically, methodically, and with purpose. By 8:45 A. M. every single member of the staff had been executed. I saved Doctor Moharer for last.

When the cops arrived at 9:03, I was already gone, driving north. On the lam. Running, not from them, but from the thing in my brain that was apparently inevitable. No matter which way I go. No matter what I do.

Death, it seems, is inevitable.

Somewhere outside of Philadelphia I get off the turnpike, I drive around for hours on the winding suburban roads. I stop in a town called Lansdale and get some coffee. In the parking lot, I catch a glimpse of light on the horizon just before the pain comes and I hear myself scream.

Iteration 37

Hannah finds me in the Tip Top Café drinking hot chocolate and making small talk with Doris the waitress.

"I'm only fifty-three Hannah."

"You're ninety-three Win, you stole that body and then abused it!" She snapped back. "You've got to come to terms with this and let everyone else move on."

I drain the cup and let the last marshmallow dissolve on my tongue. "How are you even here? Shouldn't you be caught up in the loop as well?"

"Some of us are immune, we're experiencing the days over and over again with you. Those of us who understood this are coping. Others, those who didn't know about their gift when it comes to temporality, some of those people are being driven insane." She paused. "You're hurting people Win."

I waved at Doris for a refill. "Did you know that on average 2 people die every second? That means 120 people every minute. More than seven thousand people an hour. Almost one hundred and seventy-three thousand people a day. And that's just humans. It doesn't count all the other lives on Earth and other planets. Every day an immense number of lives end."

"What's your point?"

"As long as this day goes on, as long as I keep repeating it. None of those people die. None of them, and none the day after either, or the day after that, or the day after that." I smiled wickedly. "I'll stipulate that I might be hurting a few people, but compare that to the millions I'm saving."

Hannah stared at me and I could see the tears welling up in her eyes. She was fighting it, trying to hold back the emotions. I saw Buster Green come in and he caught that she was pained. He moved to say something and then thought better of it. He took his coffee and left. It was almost a minute before she opened her mouth to speak.

"People have to die Win."

"Not today Hannah," I stood up and threw some cash on the table, "today everybody lives forever."

Iteration 42

That screaming at the moment I leap . . .

Iteration 45

Today I seduced Nancy Taylor.

It didn't take much work. Five iterations and I knew everything about her. I knew her past, I knew her wants and desires, and I knew the secrets she didn't want anyone else to know. I seduced her, but in her mind, I am the love of her life, the older man who was skilled and educated and willing to be tender and giving. I am in love with her. She is so beautiful. This is how I shall survive, with this magnificent creature at my side, forever.

Iteration 82

I killed Nancy today. I raped her and killed her. I used a gun barrel and had her strip down right there on the stage in Gobbler's Knob. I made everybody watch as I used the antique Colt to sodomize her. And then after she came, I made her take the tip into her mouth and I pulled the trigger.

I don't know why I did it. It just seemed like something to do. It's not like it mattered.

The sheriff and deputies fill my body with bullets before Nancy's corpse even rolls off the stage. As the light leaves my eyes I see Hannah standing in the crowd, scowling in disapproval.

Iteration 187

Everyone is dead. I've killed them all at least a dozen times. It's easy if you try. If you have the time and patience to figure things out.

And I have all the time in the world.

Iteration 226

Fuck you, Hannah! Fuck you and your morals! I'll do whatever I want.

Iteration 303

They say that human flesh tastes like pork. That is apparently true of a very small portion of the population. In my experience, most people taste like lamb.

Iteration 486

I've memorized the entire libretto for Heidi II. But for the life of me I can't understand why Phil keeps showing up dressed as The Man With No Name from *A Fistful of Dollars*. I also don't know why he brings a date dressed as a French Maid.

Iteration 559

The library opens at nine every morning. It seems I have nothing better to do. Perhaps reading the classics will create new opportunities in my strange life.

Iteration 731

I suspect that James Joyce's Ulysses may be the greatest novel ever written.

Iteration 732

That screaming I hear at the moment of my death, when I leap backwards . . . it sounds like a choir.

Iteration 976

I go to the hospital every day now and stare at the babies in the maternity ward. Thanks to me, they are immortal, and forever innocent.

Iteration 1022

Hannah came to me in the park. I was practicing throwing snowballs at a target. A skill I thought might be useful. I had become quite good really, I was both accurate and precise. Consequently, I had to stop and clear the target of my accumulated spent ammunition.

"Why bother?" She asked.

I looked at her and laughed. "I can't see the target anymore."

"It doesn't vanish after you throw it?"

"Of course not, they build up, accumulate. Every throw piles on top of the previous one. The target has to be cleared off otherwise you can't see what you're aiming for. You know that." But she was already gone.

Iteration 1273

The screams are echoing now. Reverberating. Something is happening that I don't understand.

Iteration 1336

I jumped backwards but I missed the target. I overshot by five whole minutes. I have to think. There must be a reason.

Iteration 2299

Overshot by a whole hour today. Accuracy is deteriorating rapidly, and getting worse every day. The screaming is almost unbearable now. Thankfully it only lasts for a moment.

Iteration 2842

I understand now. I thought I understood before, but I was wrong. When I jump back I don't just jump back, I displace the mind that was there, my mind and that is pushed forward into the future, into my future, and into my death.

But it isn't just one mind anymore.

Every time I jump back I add a mind to the line, and the new jump supplants the old, sending it into the future to its death.

I'm killing myself. Thousands upon thousands of times. I think that's why I'm drifting forward in the day. Thousands of me already there, filling up the available space-time. There's just no more room downtime.

Still, what does it matter? Twenty-three hours instead of twenty-four.

Iteration 4023

Noon. I can't leap back any farther than noon. Eighteen hours isn't so bad. You can do a lot in eighteen hours.

Iteration 4555

I spend my days learning the guitar. Acoustic. I always wanted to play an instrument.

Iteration 6198

It must be very crowded downtime, I can't reach past six in the Evening anymore. I spend my nights playing in the band at the Pennsylvanian Hotel. Afterwards I sit in the bar and let Ned take me home. He's clumsy and fumbles in the dark. He's ashamed of what he is, but I think he has always loved me. When he's finished I let him fall asleep in my arms and I think of Nancy and I cry.

Iteration 10421

Every second counts, and I fight for them. If only I had thought of this before. I don't have to jump back to a particular hour or minute. There are seconds available. Scattered pockets where I can shove my mind back into the timeline, force myself in and force the others out. It's only an hour but you have to make it last. An hour can be as good as a day, if you know what to do. At 5 in the morning you have to know what you want and where to find it.

Iteration 11986

Minutes. Minutes watching the sunrise with Nancy. Minutes is all I have left. I weep constantly and Nancy just holds me without knowing why.

Iteration 12395

    I leap backwards, but there is nowhere for me to go. It's like hitting a wall. But that wall is made up of thousands upon thousands of iterations of myself, waiting there screaming at me, screaming in pain and fear and death. I try to shut out the noise, how is there noise here? How can I hear? Without warning Hannah is there, she takes me by the hand, shows me how to let them in, all the monsters and the angels that I had been. In an instant, I am suddenly whole. I'm dead, but I'm more than human. I'm something more, a pluralistic thing.

    For a moment, I think I am a God.

    And then the walls fall and I see what waits beyond.

    I turn back to look at Hannah but she isn't looking, her eyes are shielded by a gloved hand. It isn't for her to see this thing.

    I step forward into death, into the unknown, into wonder and glory.

    And I think to myself, "What have I been waiting for?"

    In the wake of my passing, the world moves forward without me.

1996

THE PROGNOSIS OF
PANDORA PEASLEE

"Doctor Ouest, my mother and I are arriving," the little girl couldn't be more than seven years old, but she spoke with the clarity and purpose of a much older child. Doctor Erbert Ouest looked at her as she stood in the main entryway, the tropical landscape of Haiti behind her framing the scene. In other circles, the girl might be called precocious but Ouest knew different.

"Thank you, Pandora, I'll go out to the gate to greet them." He put the book he was reading in a drawer of the hallway table. Blake's *Labyrinth of Naught* was entertaining, if somewhat reminiscent of Pen's *The Garden of Forking Paths*, and both books had shed light on his current studies, but there was no sense in leaving the thing lying around where its significance might be misconstrued. "Why don't you go to the kitchen and see if Lionel needs any help?"

The little girl's blue eyes took on a faraway, vacant look, the pupils dilating to an impossible size, but only for an instant. Then she smiled. "I'm already there, but Joseph will need me in the garden." Then she was off, almost skipping through the house toward the back door. Ouest watched as the child darted out the rear entry and the door swung shut, the old spring straining with age, the wood banging against the frame, not once but twice.

He strode through the hall in the opposite direction, passing through the front entryway and onto the once majestic veranda. There were still traces of the stain that had once given the wood a lustrous brown color, but time, weather and wear had turned most of the wood gray, and the salt air coming in off the ocean had warped the wood as well. It had been more than two decades since he had bought the place and decay had set in. It might be time to move on, a change in scenery might do him some good.

The walk down the shell rock steps and the sandy path to the front gate took only a minute or so. The gate was, of course, missing, lost during one storm or another and not really a priority to be replaced. His research came first, the house was merely an edifice to study in. When this place no longer functioned, he would move on. Looking at the condition of things he thought that might be sooner than expected.

From around the bend in the road the woman and her daughter came. They were dressed alike, casually, which for Americans meant blue jeans that were less than a year old, and white cotton shirts with faux horn buttons that had been ironed, not for this occasion, but on a regular basis. They wore canvas boat shoes, without socks. On their heads were baseball caps, white with pink stitching that said Orchid Beach. The older woman carried a canvas bag decorated with shells, the girl's hands cradled an oversized book, something thick and tattered with age. It was easily recognizable, as was the girl. With her blue eyes and blonde hair, she could easily be the sister of the girl that had run out the back door, but she wasn't. And that was the problem.

"Megan, Endora so good to see you both again. It has been too long." He forced a smile.

"Not long enough West." There was the trace of a scowl on Megan Peaslee's face.

The doctor raised a finger. "Doctor Erbert Ouest if you please," he stressed the Creole pronunciation. "I've never been particularly fond of my progenitor, and I've pursued a rather different line of research, as you well know."

Mrs. Peaslee waved the incident away. She looked twenty, maybe twenty-five, but Ouest knew that she had been born almost ninety years ago. In contrast, the girl that walked with her looked to be about five or six, but Ouest knew that she had been brought into the world a decade ago.

"Endora, how are you feeling today? Was the trip from Orchid Beach pleasant?"

The child stared up with those deep blue eyes. You

could lose yourself in them. He had always loved those eyes, even on the day she had been born. "Pandora," she whispered, "I prefer to be called Pandora."

Megan Peaslee shrugged awkwardly. "Her sisters gave her that nickname, and it's kind of stuck."

"Of course," he smiled back down at the girl, "Pandora it is then." He gestured toward the house. "Why don't we go inside and discuss why you are here?"

Pandora's mother's eyes grew large. "If you don't mind, I would rather we discuss things in private first?"

Ouest nodded. "Of course. Pandora if you go around the back to the garden there should be several other girls for you to talk to." The child rolled her eyes and reluctantly stalked down the path that led to the back of the house. After she had taken a few steps the Doctor once more motioned for Megan Peaslee to follow him into the house.

"You have other children here?"

He nodded. "Other . . . others with a similar affliction. I've been working on the issue for quite some time now."

They climbed the steps and crossed the veranda. "I thought Pandora would have been unique."

"Oh, she is Mrs. Peaslee, she is quite unique." As they crossed the threshold the cool darkness of the house enveloped them and after a few steps, they sat down in the Doctor's study.

"Now why don't you explain to me what's been going on?" Ouest's demeanor became almost fatherly.

"I don't know where to begin," the woman was obviously frustrated. "First of all, there's her lack of growth. Which isn't exactly true. When I noticed that she was rather small I began taking weekly measurements, and it seems that she would grow at what appeared to be a normal rate. But then I would measure her again and she would actually be smaller, somehow, she would lose height. I'm not talking about a quarter inch or so, I'm talking about a half-inch to an inch."

She sighed. "And with those losses in height came mood swings, and personality changes, and forgetfulness. We spent a year preparing for a marathon and then one day she completely forgot about the training, swore that she had never even run a single lap. She missed the race, refused to go. But then two weeks later she was desperate to run and despondent that the event had come and gone. It's frustrating for the entire family."

"How are the other girls?"

"They're fine, they're all somewhat outsiders, but Robert and I expected that."

Ouest nodded. "If you can, I would like you to bring them over so I can run some tests." He saw the look on the woman's face. "No, no, nothing to be concerned about. I don't think they'll develop the same condition, I just want something to compare Pandora to. A baseline so to speak. It might go a long way in explaining some things."

"It sounds like you might know what's wrong with her already."

"When we took samples from you and your husband to create the embryos that we eventually implanted in you, we treated those eggs that were successfully fertilized and caused them to divide, creating four twins each. The first four children you had, Pandora's older sisters, Minerva, Galatea, Cytherea, and Nyx were all essentially clones of each other, their genetic material is identical. Endora comes from a different batch and from what I can tell it has a different X chromosome than the others. I suspect this has something to do with her slippage."

"Slippage?"

"A crude term, but essentially correct. It would be more precise to say that she was chronologically unstable. Pandora isn't physically sick, nor is she suffering from a neurological condition. She's slipping through time, her own timeline to be specific. Mostly forward, occasionally backwards, and rarely sideways. Switching places with her future, past and alternative selves. This is why she has mood swings, personality changes, and memory loss."

"Chronologically unstable," she let the words roam around in her mouth. "You know Robert's father was . . ."

Ouest cut her off. "This condition is only partially linked to your husband's mother, not his father." He paused and let that knowledge sink in. "It's also apparently linked to you as well."

"Me?"

"At first I thought it was something I had done. When you were pregnant with the others we had you on a mood suppressant, Ephemerol, but we didn't use that when you carried Pandora. I also suspected that it might have been the tissue treatments that we used to make your uterus morphogenetically neutral, but we did that in all five pregnancies. The more I researched this the more it came down to one of your X chromosomes."

"But Robert's X chromosome . . ."

Ouest shook his head. "Robert only has one X chromosome to give. All your daughters share that in common, and it does appear to give them some tendency for chronologic instability, but that appears to be dormant in the first four, yet active in Pandora. What's different, is the X chromosome that you donated. The first four share the same X chromosome, but I suspect that you gave Pandora a different one, and that has been a factor in activating her slipping through time."

"Can she be cured?"

A smile crept across Ouest's face. "It will take some time but I think so. A combination of drugs and some therapy to learn to control her emotions should work. I've been having some excellent results with Psychoplasmic therapy and a low dosage of Beta-Mnophka. I'm going to suggest this course of treatment for Pandora. You should see immediate results and after three months she should be cured."

Megan Peaslee jaw dropped and she was suddenly uncharacteristically speechless.

"I told you, I've been working on the issue for quite some time. When you called me, and made the appointment I was sure I knew what you were coming for."

"Why didn't you just tell me all this over the phone?" There was suspicion in her voice.

"If I had done that, then I wouldn't have been able to see you or your beautiful daughter." A figure moved in the doorway. "Ah, there she is now."

Pandora Peaslee stood in the arched doorway and smiled at her mother and Doctor Ouest. In her hands was a small satchel bearing the Ouest's logo, two snakes wrapped around each other to form a circle.

"I see one of my assistants has already given you your medicine. I'll make sure to have Doctor Decker's office call and set up appointments for therapy sessions. We'll make you right as rain in no time."

As the aged doctor escorted them out the door he paused and picked up a book from a side table. "Don't forget your book young lady." He looked at it as he handed it to her. "*A Mourning Shadow* by Marcus Page, an interesting choice for one so young. I wish you well Pandora, and I hope I never have to see you again."

The little girl smiled. "Thank you, doctor, but I'm sure we will meet again, perhaps under very different circumstances."

"Perhaps," responded Ouest, "only time will tell."

He watched from the cool shadows as the woman and her daughter walked away. He made sure that they had gone through the gate and then rounded the corner before he himself turned and headed out the back door. There were girls there, five girls all blonde with blue eyes, they could have been sisters, twins, but they weren't, and that was the problem.

"Pandora," he said the name with authority tinted with kindness. All the girls turned to look, but only the one with a book in her hand seemed to be frightened. He knelt down on one knee and took her by the hand. "Pandora, do you understand why you're here? Do you understand what is happening to you?"

The girl nodded. "Yessir." It came out all as one word.

Ouest smiled and this time there was nothing forced about it. "I'm going to help you Pandora. You've become something very odd. Your ability to slip back and forth and sideways through time is very interesting."

"It scares mommy."

Ouest nodded ever so slightly. "Mommy wanted a normal girl, one that couldn't do all the things you can. I've made sure mommy won't be scared anymore."

"I saw her. Was she really me?"

One of the other girls opened her mouth. She spoke with the same voice, but with more authority. "Not really. She looked like us and sounded like us, but she can't do what we do. That makes her the perfect Pandora to go home with your mommy and make her happy."

"But what about her mommy and daddy won't they

miss her?"

Ouest turned the girl's face gently toward his. "Her mommy and daddy died in an accident which made her very sad. Now that she has your mommy and daddy she's happy again. Doesn't that make you happy?"

The girl nodded. "I don't think she was my mommy anyway. I think I'm from somewhen very far from here."

"We all are," said a third Pandora. "Doctor Ouest has promised to find us all homes. Isn't that right Doctor Ouest?"

"That's right. I'm going to help all of you find homes." He put his arms around the girl and hugged her as if she were his own child. After all he had made her, in the lab not one hundred yards away. They were his children, all of them, and they were going to help him in the most wonderful of ways.

He sat down on the ground. "Now girls, let's talk about the future. Tell me what you see."

And they did. They told him everything they could, about a half-dozen futures.

And Doctor Erbert Ouest dreamed.
And Doctor Erbert Ouest schemed.
And Doctor Erbert Ouest screamed.

2015

THE PESTILENCE OF PANDORA PEASLEE

  Endora Peaslee, called Pandora by those who feared her, paused to check that her package was secure. She had abandoned the boat that had brought her from Haiti, set it to autopilot after the satellite had locked on. Her muscles ached from swimming through the warm Florida waters but she had no time to rest. She was just a few miles from her destination but if she was going to make the deadline, she was going to have to move it. She ran up the sandy shoreline and onto the streets of what had once been Palm Beach, home to old money, and moved through the wreckage of the low buildings that had once been an exclusive shopping district. This area was mostly abandoned, even the dogs and cats had moved inland. Without the rich, the island had gone wild. Sand drifted down the streets. Saltwater ponds filled parking lots. The grass had died and been replaced with plants that were more tolerant of the sea spray. Mangroves were slowly reclaiming the island, marching in from the lagoon at a slow, but sure pace. As she crossed the bridge over the Intracoastal she looked south and in the distance, could see the Suncoast Arcology rising up into the sky. Even this far away she could see the cloud of machines that were flitting around it like bugs on a corpse, except the corpse was hundreds of years of human effort, being systematically recycled for a bold new future. If only that future had been planned by human minds, she might not be a terrorist.

  She careened over the crumbling concrete bridge and through the shadows of derelict condominiums and abandoned office towers and into what was left of downtown West Palm. City Place and the Kravis Center for the Performing Arts lay in ruins, shattered glass windows and barrel tiles littered the streets. Spray-painted purple symbols marked the area as scheduled for demolition and harvest. All this area would be restored to the way it had been before man decided to try and shape Florida to suit his own needs. The rest of the world was going the same way. The world was becoming a better, cleaner, safer place. The old ways of doing things had been replaced, with newer, better ways.

She followed a ramp south, moving against the direction of traffic that no longer existed. She crossed over I-95 and looked at the vast ribbon of concrete and asphalt that stretched both north and south like a dried-up canal. Once, this road had been a river of steel and light, now it was as dead as everything else, abandoned by humanity in favor of a new way of life, one that guaranteed the survival of the species, but at a price Pandora Peaslee couldn't accept: Not that she didn't understand what had happened, she just didn't approve of it. Men should not give up their freedoms so willingly.

The first hint that something was awry had been the loss of contact with the Falkland Islands; the British were still trying to figure out what had happened when New Zealand went dark. Things snowballed from that point forward. Shoggothim, ancient alien machines comprised of weird matter that looked like slime and absorbed anything organic had been released from some Antarctic prison. The creatures devoured anything that moved. How they had made their way off the frozen continent wasn't clear, but they had a taste for human flesh and normal weapons did little to slow them down. Humans fought back with devastating weaponry. Most of the lower part of South America was still burning. New Zealand and Tasmania were more radioactive than Chernobyl, and just as abandoned.

Her brisk pace took her through long abandoned office blocks, hotels and a burnt out fast food restaurant. Feral cats had claimed a parking garage, nothing to worry about, but she picked up her pace when something large shifted within the tiered darkness. Her route took her into the airport and she climbed over the rubble of collapsed flyways that had once steered cars from the interstate to the small but bustling transportation center filled with dead cars. There weren't any working cars anymore, at least not like there had been. Small electric things still flitted through what remained of the great metropoli, drawing power from the grid imbedded in the road way, but that grid didn't extend out this far into the brownfields. Even if it did, any vehicle would have been a clear target for the satellites that now filled the sky.

It had been amongst the islands that dotted the Pacific that the next threat manifested, though no one at the time recognized it for what it was: The small nations of the Pacific Ocean, all normally fiercely independent, suddenly found a new sense of unity. Some said it was because of the Shoggothim, that small areas were highly vulnerable and they needed to ally themselves against a greater enemy. Other weren't so sure, but the result was clear. In a single month the nations of Kiribati, Tonga, Micronesia, Palau, the Seychelles, Tuvalu and Nauru, all lay aside their rivalries and formed the Pacific Union. They rewrote laws concerning data privacy and finances, and within the year were suddenly a financial and technological powerhouse. Eighteen months after forming, Samoa and the Philippines petitioned for membership. Papua, Malaysia, and Indonesia weren't far behind. A new global power emerged on the planet, not based on military prowess, but rather on the intersection of money and a technology that seemed years ahead of anybody else. Even the fleet of airships they built, huge whale-like things with no speed, but incredibly energy efficient seemed design to serve rather than threaten.

She jumped a fence and sprinted across the runways. Cattle egrets and iguanas scattered before her. A covey of doves took flight screaming their umbrage at her presence. Something large and tawny, a deer, maybe a coyote, or perhaps a panther trotted through the tall grass that had colonized the places between the cracked cement. She could feel the heat radiating off of the artificial rock and a little part of her longed for an afternoon thunderstorm to come and cool things off, however briefly, even if the subsequent humidity was unbearable.

The airships of the Pacific Union were the first to arrive after Typhoon Fabiola had unexpectedly turned north and devastated Japan from Kumamoto to Sapporo. Union forces carried out rescues, turned malls into hospitals and shelters, stabilized nuclear reactors, and made sure everyone was vaccinated against diseases that had been long thought eradicated. The images of Pacific Union airships hovering over Tokyo's skyline became commonplace and it came as no surprise when Japan's emergency government, operating out of Okinawa petitioned to become a member state. When the Koreas and Taiwan followed, China protested, but by that point the wave had gathered such strength it was pointless to stand in its way.

    She found her way through a gutted hangar and back onto the road on the far side of the airport. She took another crumbling overpass to leapfrog over a canal and come within sight of her destination. There was an old Reserve Base opposite the shell of a burnt out building with traces of a gold sign still visible, but her target was the monolith that loomed before her, an imposing angular thing that screamed to be left alone. It squatted on the landscape with a row of thin windows that squinted like eyes, peering out at the surrounding neighborhood like a grumpy cat ready to leap and spit and scratch. This was the building that showed the least response to the vagaries of time and weather, an edifice built to last, to be secure, and to keep its occupants under control. Pandora looked at her watch and finally stopped running as she entered the grounds of the Palm Beach County Detention Center.

    Pacific Union aid centers sprung up across the world and began to tackle problems that other governments, organizations and corporations had either failed at or abandoned. Safe water in Africa, chemical cleanup in the Middle East, food in India, energy and housing in South America, even urban blight in the rustbelt of the American Midwest suddenly had solutions, or progress toward a solution. Even Europe and China allowed for the establishment of working groups within their borders. The only real resistance was Russia, a nation that could have used the help but was either too proud or too stubborn to let foreigners in. A new iron curtain went up just as barriers everywhere else in the world went down.

    The power in the Detention Center was still on, functioning at emergency levels that kept the cells locked but little else functioning. There were other buildings that had better power systems, but they all lacked the ability to remotely operate doors. The plan depended on keeping things under control until the very last minute. Prisons, long abandoned but often with their own power supplies, provided the perfect opportunity to do just that. All she had to do was wait for the right time.

With clean energy, clean water, and clean food came a sense of prosperity, of unity and of trust. Those feelings left little room for the fear of subjugation. When evidence emerged that the leaders of the Pacific Union had all suffered from some sort of seizure, one that resulted in the total dissolution of previous memories and personalities, it was all too late. People didn't care, they gladly traded exploitation by the Western Powers for exploitation by people that looked and spoke as they did, and took care of their needs. In a quarter of a century the Pacific Union had conquered the world without so much as firing a shot.

Pandora moved through the dilapidated building with sure-footed accuracy, dodging broken-down furniture and decaying concrete. Weeds and scrawny trees had taken hold in walls, drawing light and rain from cracked skylights. Bugs had found their way in too, mostly mosquitoes and dragonflies. There was also a large paper wasp nest that buzzed angrily as she passed by, forcing her to dodge right and bounce off of the wall of holding cell. Something inside moaned ominously and the steel grate rattled as its strength was tested. She softly cursed, put her hand on her gun and slowly backed away. She eyed the shadows moving beyond the weak light, waited for them to settle and then took off running again. She had to reach cover, the exercise level twelve stories up had been prepared, stocked and fortified. All she had to do was avoid being caught before she got there. Three years of planning was about to reach fruition, all around the world her sisters were following the plan, and like her, leading their own pursuers into similar situations. After today, the world would never be the same, one way or another. Once the plan was in play it would take only hours to wrap the world in terror.

Two stories below her the entrance exploded in a shower of glass and cheap aluminum framing. She glimpsed a dozen shock troopers as they stormed through the smoke and ash. They wore insignia that harkened back to various law enforcement agencies, but the laws they were enforcing weren't in any municipal or state code. These men were enforcing new laws, written by their new masters, and those masters may have looked human, but that was only a facade. It had only been after most of the world had submitted to the Pacific Union that its leaders had revealed themselves as something inhuman. The world had been invaded, and the invaders were creatures of pure mind. These cool, ancient and alien intelligences brought with them solutions to all the world's problems. All they demanded was complete and unquestioning obedience, and most people readily complied. The only ones who hadn't, had been those who recognized them for what they were. People like Pandora's parents, people who gave the invaders a name, the Yith.

"Endora Peaslee!" The sound of the voice over the bullhorn was familiar, a ranking Yithian who went by the name Mister Ys, a man—for lack of a better word—who was very good at his job, tracking and capturing unruly humans. "Endora Peaslee, fifth daughter of Robert Peaslee and Megan Halsey, you have been tried in absentia and found guilty of crimes against humanity. A warrant has been issued for your execution. Surrender now and I assure you that the method will be painless." His voice was nearly void of emotion.

Pandora looked at her watch, her pursuers were right on schedule, her schedule not theirs. Hopefully everything she and the others were doing wasn't on the Yithian timetable.

The Yith were time-travelers, aliens that had eons ago discovered a way to mentally move through time, capable of leaping forwards and backwards to steal bodies and infiltrate societies, all on the premise of doing research. They were obsessed with gathering historical data, documenting eras they considered historically important, while ignoring events that men might consider critical. Pandora's own grandfather had fallen victim to their machinations. He like many others had been released from their grasp, but only after they had finished with him. The event had devastated the family. Her uncle had become obsessed with the Yith, and hunted them down whenever he could. In contrast, her father had spent years trying to avoid the taint that had cursed his family, only to be drawn into altogether different but just as sinister matters. That may have had more to do with her mother, who had seemed born to the mysterious and macabre and had drawn her husband into the darkness with her. The resistance had grown up out of what Pandora's parents could tell them about the Yith and how they behaved.

Pandora and her friends in the Resistance—and that is what they called themselves, no fancy names or acronyms, simply the Resistance—didn't particularly like what had become of the world. They knew more about the universe, but less about their government. They were building power stations but not families. They understood chemistry and physics and ecology, but not command structures and decision-making. In the eyes of the Resistance, humans were becoming technicians, leaving the leadership to their newfound masters; masters that often went unquestioned about motives or goals. When the Resistance found the first baby factory, where children were being engineered to be stronger and faster than normal humans, Pandora knew it was time to act. She and her sisters formulated a plan, gathered like-minded friends and started a worldwide underground network.

They'd been on the run, building to this day, ever since.

On the side of the stairwell she found the hole she had cut that led into a utility shaft. It was tight, but she squeezed through it and found her footing on the stirrups of the zip line. She clipped herself into the harness and squeezed the regulator. She flew up through the darkness as the weights she was connected to fell down. She whisked past rats and loose material at breakneck speeds, clearing the rest of the floors in seconds. At the top, she stepped out onto the roof and with her knife cut the line, making sure no one could follow her using that particular route.

As she walked away some overzealous trooper fired up through the shaft. The bullets stopped almost immediately and she could hear the soldier being berated by their commanding officer. She threw the first switch on the control panel. She needed the troopers oblivious to what was going on around them. The aging speakers blared to life and babbled out a cacophony of prerecorded noise, animal sounds, growls and shrieks, and cages rattling. Sounds designed to mask the noises of what was going on in the prison itself.

While her enemy climbed the stairs, she slipped into her combat armor, a Kevlar bodysuit with matching gloves and boots with magnetic combination locks. Over that she put on an impact resistant vest and strapped on articulated leg armor. A harness went over her neck giving her huge shoulders and a high steel collar. The flexible neck rings snapped into the helmet in three places. The last piece of her defense came out of her backpack. This is what she had gone to Haiti for, and what so many others had given their lives to create. Dr. Ouest swore that it would work, that he had tested it and it had proven adequate to the task. Adequate didn't make Pandora feel very good, but that was all she could get out of the madman who pretended to be a scientist.

Pandora threw another switch and powered up the building's internal sensors. A bank of micro-monitors jumped to life as cameras in the stairwell suddenly began to broadcast grainy images of the men moving up toward her position. She flipped on the microphone tapped it and spoke. "Can I ask you a question Mister Ys?"

Pandora watched as the alien raised his bullhorn. It blared again, echoing through the stairwell. "By all means, but it won't change anything."

"What are you doing here? Why did you invade? My grandfather believed that you weren't interested in humans, that when you finally left the Mesozoic invertebrates that you were going to leap past humanity into the future, after men had gone extinct. What changed your minds?"

Ys located the camera and addressed her through it. "We were perfectly content to leave humans alone, but then we started having problems. Somehow, someone here figured out how to exclude us. We can't insert any agents, and any that we drop in beforehand never returned. We are not fond of Dead Time, that's what we call it. You and your little band of rebels, or someone like you, have blocked us. We came to stop you from creating the Dead Time, or failing that finding the generator and destroying it."

Beneath her mask her face screwed up in puzzlement. "How exactly am I responsible for that?" She flipped another switch and whispered a tiny prayer, hoping that her trap wouldn't be noticed for a few more minutes. Timing was everything. Around the world similar traps were being sprung, a few minutes warning and the Great Race might have enough warning to escape back through time.

"We don't particularly know." He moved to the next camera, cautious steps flanked by scuttling human soldiers. "We gave your people, one of your relatives actually, the technology to block us over small areas once. We used it to build a prison for some of our own less desirable members. We assumed you had figured out how to widen the application of the barrier."

"So, you invaded the world and conquered the planet because you couldn't see what we were doing?" Pandora chuckled. "When exactly are we supposed to have erected this barrier?" She switched her attention to the other screens, there were things moving in the prison. The cell doors were swinging open.

Mister Ys looked at his watch. "We lose contact in exactly three minutes. Unless we find your equipment and destroy it."

Pandora threw the last switch, the one that unlocked the doors from the stairwell to each floor. The actuation was time-delayed. She had less than a minute before things got really bad. "Is that how time works? Can you change the future by altering the past? If you destroy the machine the barrier will fall, but then why would you invade in the first place? What about causality and paradox?"

"Time isn't as rigid as you humans would like it to be. There is fluidity, you may not be able to break the laws of time, but you can bend them. Once we find your machine and destroy it the barrier you will erect will never have been, but we are already here. We can't simply be erased from existence."

"That's what my grandfather said. He warned me that using time against you would be pointless. He said you were grandmasters, that you played the long game superbly, and as long as you had players on the field you would be nearly invincible."

"I knew your grandfather. Spent some time in him. He was clever for a human."

"My parents were much cleverer, did you ever meet them?"

He was on the floor below her. "Your father, Robert Peaslee? I never had the privilege, I knew him by reputation. I've read his file."

Endora "Pandora" Peaslee pulled the plug on her control board and then smashed it with the heel of her boot. "Did it ever dawn on you Yithians that I might take after my mother? She had an alias as well."

Twelve soldiers swarmed out of the stairwell, red dots appeared on her chest, but not one man pulled the trigger. "Your mother was Megan Halsey, the so-called Reanimatrix. She had access to a primitive reanimation formula."

Pandora went down on her knees trying to appear less threatening. "We've made some improvements over the years." Beneath her mask she smiled. "We didn't build a field generator Mister Ys. We didn't try to exclude you from the game, that was likely impossible. We just found a way to keep you from using any of the pieces."

A sense of panic suddenly filled Mister Ys voice. "The rest of the resistance, where are they?" He barked orders at his troops, "Find them! Kill them!"

Pandora assumed a crouched position. "You still want to kill the Resistance? Pointless really. I'm afraid they are already dead."

Mister Ys fired a shot and struck Pandora in the shoulder, spinning her around and knocking her to the floor. Her armor was barely scratched. "Whatever you and the resistance have conjured up, whatever you've cobbled together. I assure you we shall end it, here and now. You and your friends will be liquidated."

Pandora sat up rubbing her shoulder. "I told you Mister Ys, the resistance is already dead."

From the darkness of the stairs broken shapes moved and stumbled up onto the roof. They had been men once, and alive, but they weren't either anymore. Pandora's formula, her reagent had transformed them into something bestial, something subhuman. They shambled out of the cages they had been held in and with each step gained speed. There were hundreds of the things, pouring out onto the roof like ants swarming a piece of candy. There were only a dozen armed soldiers, the undead washed over them like an unstoppable wave. The gunfire did little to slow them down, and as man after man fell the desperate sound of the remaining soldiers and their pathetic guns did little but serve as an attraction to the things that screamed and bit and spread their infection.

"This is your plan Miss Pandora?" Mister Ys was shouting and marching toward her, swinging the gun back and forth between his quarry and the things that were tearing his men apart. "You've weaponized a reanimation reagent, made it contagious. I assume some sort of retrovirus. Do you really think we can't put a stop to this plague of yours?"

She tore the package open and reveled the sigil beneath it, a stylized, tentacular thing that seemed to crawl out of infinity. Ys hissed at the thing but anything he was going to say was drowned out as Pandora began to recite a necessary bit of poetry.

"Strange is the light which black stars doth shine,
And men become monsters beneath a yellow sign,
Lost Carcosa rises ruined, but stranger still,
Sending ravenous hordes bent to Yhtill's will."

"You dare?" Mister Ys was screaming, but Pandora could barely hear him, the chant filled her ears. "You invite the Yellow King. Are you mad? He will lay waste to this world, warp everything to his own corruption." For the first time ever, she saw fear in the eyes of a Yith. "Please, don't do this. We would have given you a paradise." He fell to his knees and scowled. "Do you really think that you can control it? Do you and yours think you can bear the Mantle of the King? Hear my words little girl, the Pallid Mask will give you his power, a taste of it at least, but in time it will worm its way inside. It will gnaw at you, corrupt you, and leave you a hollow empty shell." The undead paused as he emptied the clip in their direction, but only for a moment.

Across the world Pandora's sisters continued the invocations that would bind the undead members of the Resistance to their service, and in turn dedicated themselves to the service of Hastur. In the sky, the sun slowly declined into a Yellow Sine, pulsing with a sickening rhythm. "Better to rule in Hell than serve in Heaven," she whispered softly.

The curtain had been drawn, the Song of Cassilda sung, the second act was imminent. It was time for the King in Yellow to send his terrible messenger. Her army, her subjects, thousands of undead fell prostrate before her. They were hungry, she could sense it, they were ravenous, and capable of consuming all they could lay their hands on. It wasn't enough. It would never be enough.

Through time and space, the Yellow Sine took its measure, and upon the world the Dead Time fell. Somewhere in what was left of her humanity Pandora Peaslee hoped that someday, somehow some men, some humans might survive.

But not today.

Beneath her helmet the Pallid Mask settled into its rightful place. Pandora Peaslee assumed the role of Yhtill, and headed south, toward the arcology.

Her army followed.

2342

THE SETTING OF THE SINE

Doctor Erbert Ouest glanced at the sky and the Yellow Sine that illuminated the world. It crisscrossed the firmament forming a queer sigil that made his head ache if he stared at it too long. He pulled his tinted goggles back down over his eyes. The Sign of Koth that he had inscribed on the lenses was beginning to fade. They were leaking around the edges, letting in the Yellow. It ate at him, at his mind, just a little every day, but he could feel it, he could feel his humanity slipping away. It was only a matter of time.

It had always been a matter of time.

How old was he? He had lost track of the days, lost track of the weeks, the months, and the years. Without the sun, he couldn't tell. Without anyone to talk to it hadn't mattered. All that mattered; all that had ever mattered was his survival, that he beat death, one day at a time. It had been his obsession, his life's work, the culmination of decades of study and experimentation, and he had been his own greatest creation. Before, when the sun had been in the sky he remembered celebrating his one-hundred-and-fiftieth birthday. That had been a long time ago.

It was just a matter of time.

He had been on the hunt for weeks now, moving through the barrier islands of the Florida coast following the herd as it migrated down the ruin that was Interstate 95. They weren't hard to track. Ouest estimated the herd at more than a thousand, maybe even twice that. It had been six months since he had actually seen them, and that had been near Jacksonville. He had gotten close that time, gotten two shots off before the herd stampeded and the Queen had bolted. She had split the herd, forced him to pick which group to follow. He had chosen poorly. Now he was close again, he could smell her passing, hear her calls in the distance, and feel the earth as it thundered beneath their steps.

"Gun," the voice was low and gruff, and the sounds were barely words. It belonged to Thorse his mount, his *Y'm-Bhi*, a flesh golem he had made from dead humans using methods stolen from the blue-lit world of K'n-Yan. Thorse was only semi-intelligent, he had a vocabulary of two or three-hundred words. The most important one, the first one that had been taught, had been the word "gun".

He was on the ridge by the road, which wasn't a ridge at all but rather the remnants of a fallen off-ramp crumbled, covered with a century of detritus and overgrown with weeds. He was thin, Hispanic – though after all this time that word didn't mean much anymore –he had a hungry look, but most people did. He held a gun, a rifle, something pre-sine with the strap replaced with something scavenged, a cable of some kind. The gun was held sidewise with both hands, a position that made it easy to bring the gun to bear. Ouest swung his own rifle around and mimicked the same hold. It was a universal greeting, one that said that you weren't a threat. Only men carried guns, and in this age men did not shoot men, there were too few left.

Ouest took Thorse's reins and led him down the embankment; the ground was soft beneath his boots and water pooled in the tracks he left behind. Thorse sniffed at it and snorted. It was salt water, seepage from the ocean that had come up and turned the once great Florida peninsula into a thin chain of islands with the Atlantic to the east and a shallow lagoon to the west. The stranger scrambled down the ridge and together they met in the middle of what was left of the road, in the traces of the herd's trail.

When they were a few yards apart Ouest raised his hand. "Doctor Erbert Ouest,"

"Sthast, I serve as Warden for Canaveral Island, about four miles east." He pulled the cloth from his face, the skin was covered with pebbled scales, he had no lips, and his eyes were black on black.

Ouest recognized the species. In the years since the Sine had fallen, the serpent men of Valusia had come out of hiding. They were just one of many sentient species that now roamed the Earth along with humans. "A large community?"

"Couple hundred. Fishermen mostly, with a few traders who range up the coast to Georgia. Nothing fancy, but we're off the migration path, there aren't any bridges, and we're well-armed."

"You have a gunsmith?"

The man nodded, "He's good too. You have some empty casings? He'll trade two to one."

"That's fair." He reached back and pulled a satchel off of Thorse. Something squirmed inside but Oust ignored it and found the other bag he was looking for. "There's two hundred empty brass casings in there. How much ammo are you carrying?"

"Fifty maybe sixty rounds."

"There's nothing for you to worry about between here and home. I'll trade you all these empties for fifty rounds."

"That's not how we do business."

"I don't have time for detours." Ouest's voice was tinged with exasperation. "I don't have time for your local politics, or inter-town squabbles or whatever problem you might think I could help you with. The herd has moved south . . ."

"You're tracking the herd? Are you mad?"

"Am I mad? I've seen the civilization of men rise to a state undreamed of. I've seen men surrender the world to alien invaders from beyond time and space. I've seen a woman stand up in defiance and sacrifice everything to drive the invaders out, only to see humanity taken to the brink of extinction. I'm hundreds of years old, a patchwork of cloned parts made by a man who didn't even bother to give me a name, and didn't care if I stole his. Am I mad? In this world, I may be both the maddest and sanest man alive!"

Sthast ran, leaving the bandolier on the ground and letting the man called Ouest's gibbering decay into maniacal laughter that only Thorse would hear.

★

Ouest had taken the short cut. He had switched to

what was left of the Florida Turnpike where I-95 bowed out in a curve and then eventually came back to parallel the other decayed highway. It was a straighter stretch and therefore shorter, and had allowed him to shave some of the distance between himself and the herd. The two roads came back together just north of the South Fork of the St. Lucie River. The bridges for both roads had fallen to the elements, but the space between them was where the herd had crossed, and not so long ago. The banks were still freshly disturbed, the waters still churned, the road was still damp from where the herd moved on. Something pink and broken struggled in the jaws of a large crocodile.

They had been nearly extinct once, and confined to the lower tip of the Florida peninsula, but with the fall of civilization the beasts had spread up the Atlantic Coast all the way to the mouth of the Chesapeake. They had grown big too, this one was easily over six meters, but whether that was because of a restoration of habitat, the mutagenic properties of the sine, or of interbreeding with Nile crocs escaped from zoos Ouest couldn't say, and it really didn't matter.

Wary of crossing the river, Ouest moved upstream just three quarters of mile where the remnants of an old water control structure had become a choke point for debris. Even though the gates of the structure had long since failed the bulkheads still remained, and the conglomeration of debris had created both a semi-natural weir, and a river ford. With care, he led Thorse across the thin and tenuous bridge where the still waters upstream provided no cover for the predators that lurked below. The detour cost him an hour, but it avoided the crocs, and for that it was worth it.

Back on the road and the herd had spread out over both highways, which ran pretty much parallel for the next twenty miles. After that they would slowly split and eventually become separated by more than two miles of forest. It was here that the herd would become confused, panicky and vulnerable. If he could get ahead of them here, he might have a shot at the Yellow Queen, a chance to take her out, and bring the madness she started so many years ago to an end. "Run Thorse," he whispered, "Run!"

It was just a matter of time.

★

He caught a glimpse of her as she turned to berate one of her seconds. She backhanded him across the shoulder. There was a flash of crimson, and a bray of anger, but the subordinate male quickly remembered his place and lowered his head in a gesture of submission. It was an act that the Yellow Queen ignored as she tried to bring back to order, dispatching various bulls to drive strays back to the main body. All the while she had to keep moving forward or risk being run over by the massive herd she was meant to lead.

She was a magnificent creature: an intricate and towering rack of horns crowned her head, the Pallid Mask hid her face, the tatters of her cloak danced in the wind. She had always been beautiful, but now graced with the mantle of Uthil, that beauty was terrible, magnificent, but terrible. Ouest felt a touch of guilt over this. It hadn't been his idea to summon the avatar of Hastur, that had been the decision of the Resistance but he had made it possible. It had been he who had cast the mask and drawn the sigils that gave it power. His was the hand that had given it to the woman who would wear it. Now that the task for which it had been made was completed, it was his responsibility to take it off of her, one way or another.

He and Thorse were upwind, the sea breeze coming cross the scrub forest brought the stink of the herd to them; it was a foul stink, like rotting meat. The mass of once human things may have been structured like a herd of cattle, but they were really omnivores, and preferred more than a little meat in their diet. The stink was probably something they had eaten, the scraps of which were embedded in their hair, and smeared on their skin. It may have seemed unsanitary, but it also served to help establish a hierarchy. It also attracted vultures, which in turn attracted unwary scavengers, which the herd was more than willing to feed on. This close, Ouest and Thorse had little chance to escape if the herd came for them. He felt the thing in the satchel squirm, it was restless, hungry, and impatient.

And it was just a matter of time.

He pulled on the reins and headed south, letting the herd divide, letting the Queen become separated from half her army as they moved down the shattered road.

★

Ouest rolled the shell between his fingers and cursed. The ammunition that Sthast had left had been of less quality than he was accustomed to. It wasn't surprising. The shells had been recycled too many times to count. What was left of the world was a parasite on the carcass of the old world, and what remained was running thin. He loaded the rifle and hoped for the best.

Ahead he could see the herd as it thundered down the remnants of the road. They were spread out across the width of the thin strip which was choked by thick mangroves on both sides. The queen was at the head, with about six subordinate bulls flanking her. They were nervous. As predicted the herd had split, and every so often the bulls would bellow out and wait for a return call from the missing half. Once they cleared the swamp, the two halves would find a way to rejoin. Now was the time to act.

Ouest took a breath and held it. Through the ancient scope he took aim at the bull to the Queen's right. He felt the gun in his hand, made it part of his arm and then gently squeezed the trigger. There was a popping sound, muffled by the gauze he had wrapped around the barrel. Hundreds of yards away he watched the bull flinch, and a splotch of red began to spread out across the thing's abdomen. A gut shot, in this case, as good as any. He cleared the chamber and slid another cartridge into place. Through the scope he watched as the wounded creature stumbled and then fell. The other bulls turned their heads to look. Ouest took aim and fired again. To the Queen's left another bull took a hit in the arm, and the impact spun the creature round spraying blood over her and the others nearby. The second hit was enough, the bulls were panicking, trumpeting, they turned counter clockwise trying to change the direction of the herd, but there was nowhere to go.

Ouest fired again. This time it was only into the herd itself, encouraging the massive conglomeration to change course. There was screaming and roaring, the larger bulls were trampling through the females and the young. Juveniles plowed into the tight spaces between the mangroves disturbing the birds that nested there on the edge. Great flocks suddenly took to the air and in moments the sky had become dark and the sound of the herd had been drowned out by the beating of thousands of white, black and pink wings.

Only the Yellow Queen continued forward. Ouest stood up and let her see him. She paused, but only for a moment. In her mind Ouest was small, weak, little more than an annoyance. He may have hurt, even killed a few bulls, but it was the herd that mattered. It would take little effort to eliminate such a minor threat.

Ouest turned, calling Thorse from out of the trees and mounting him on the run. He put his hand down on the saddle bag, and tried to comfort the thing inside. It was just a matter of time. Just a little more was all he needed. He took a hard right onto what had once been a powerline right of way, but now was a game trail, and then almost immediately bore right across a small spit of land that allowed him to forge a canal. Seconds later, he was surrounded by the crumbling infrastructure of an old sewage treatment plant, much of it was still intact despite years of neglect.

He swung off of Thorse and scrambled up a rusted metal catwalk. The supports creaked under his weight, but he knew they would hold. Beneath him the former treatment pit had become a soft, unconsolidated bog. It was almost like quicksand, and would serve the same purpose, at least that was the plan. As he reached the center of the scaffolding the Yellow Queen roared into the compound and skidded to a halt at the base of the pit.

She was wary. She had always been a clever girl, which was how she had gotten in this situation in the first place. She circled the pit, snorting and growling. Up close she was larger than ever, three meters tall and at least one-meter wide, her horns made her even taller. She was thick too, all muscle and no fat. You could see the fibers move beneath her skin. She was pacing, looking for a safe way up, making sure Ouest didn't have another way down. Ouest aimed the rifle at her feet and pulled the trigger. She jumped at the sound of the shot and stared at the hole in the ground and the cloud of dirt the impact had produced. Ouest reloaded and before he could even fire she was at the ladder, scaling it, in slow uncomfortable steps.

As she cleared the ladder and mounted the catwalk it groaned under her weight, but she didn't care. She moved forward, each step a cautious exploration that waited for Ouest to fire. But he didn't. He let her come closer, ever closer, and kept the rifle trained on his target, except his target wasn't the Yellow Queen. It was only when she was half way to him that he finally pulled the trigger to shoot out the fragile support that kept that section of gangway in place.

He heard the trigger click, but the soft, warm vibration that should have accompanied it failed to materialize. It was only a fraction of a second, but he knew that the shell had malfunctioned. His hands relaxed and for an instant he felt the barrel expand, then the steel shredded and the stock splintered and he was blown backwards. His back caught the railing and steered him backwards, breaking a rib, maybe two in the process. A boot caught on a rough flange of metal and pulled off, sending him tumbling head over heels, dragging his face across the grating for a foot or two.

There was a smile in the Queen's eyes as he stalked forward. He fumbled through his coat for his spare gun, a pistol that he kept on his belt, but his hand wouldn't work. He stared at his gloved fingers and realized that two had been bent backwards out of their sockets and one had been blown completely off. They would grow back, he could make them heal, but suddenly there wasn't enough time for anything like that.

The Queen surged forward, and then flinched back as a shot rang out and a rain of blood and bone exploded out of her shoulder. Ouest turned his head to see the Valusian Sthast with twin revolvers in his hands.

"No!" He screamed as the serpent man fired again. "We need her alive!" Sthast looked incredulous. "Take out the support!" The demi-humanoid nodded and let loose a barrage with both guns.

The Queen roared as the bullets struck their target and the ancient decayed metal crumpled under her weight. She tried to back away, but the catwalk cracked in the middle and spilled her forward into the muddy pit below. She hit with a soft muffled thud, sinking to her waist in an instant. Ouest scrambled forward and using his left hand produced a small, metal rod. With the flick of a switch the rod expanded to a staff and the Sign of Koth engraved on one end began to glow first yellow, then red and then almost white. He stabbed it forward, searing the Queen in the face, obliterating the Yellow Sign that had adorned the pallid mask she wore.

She screamed in fear and agony as the bindings of the mask dissolved and the mantle of the Yellow Queen fell from her shoulders. The beast that she had been, the feral, devouring thing that had roamed the earth, ravaging all that stood in her way was suddenly no more. All that remained was a woman, a human woman, her body caked with blood, gore and scars.

"Running out of time," Ouest muttered as he ran down toward the other end of the catwalk. He called out to Sthast, "Get her out of there!" Then he whistled and Thorse came bounding back from wherever he had been hiding. It took him longer to climb down the ladder than it did to go up, and the last three rungs were more of a controlled fall than a climb, but he reached the ground without incurring any more injuries.

He leaned against Thorse as he opened up the satchel and took out the thing that squirmed and cried. It was a ball of pale blue and white goo. A glob of iridescent snot that pulsated and whined incessantly. It was warm to the touch and stung a little too. There were acidic defenses, he should have been wearing gloves, but he was out of time. The thing was hatching. If he was going to save the world it would have to be now.

He was running as best he could when he reached Sthast, who had lassoed what had once been the Yellow Queen and pulled her to the side. "Who is she?" The serpent man asked as Ouest raised her head.

Ouest smiled as he looked into her eyes. "Her name is Pandora Peaslee, and she is a very special woman. She saved the world once, and now she's going to do it again."

She coughed as he wiped mud away from her face. "Ouest," she moaned, "is it over? Are the Yith gone?"

Ouest nodded. "It's over Pandora. You did it. There all gone. We're free. We've paid a terrible price, but mankind is almost completely free."

Her eyes opened and squinted. "Why is the sky

yellow?"

Ouest took a deep breath and tilted her head back. "I'm sorry Pandora. You've done an immense job, but I need you to suffer for a little longer." She moaned. "By all rights one of the Deep Ones should bear this burden, but they're too weak, or too far gone. I've tried using a Whateley, but the genetics are too diluted. They all die. I'm sorry Pandora you're my last hope."

She smiled weakly. "You don't need to apol-"

Whatever she was going to say was cut off as Ouest took the gelatinous thing in his hand and shoved it into her mouth. She choked as it squirmed inside her, bulging her throat out, tearing tissue and cartilage. As it reached her chest, her ribs spread and her sternum cracked. The creature was hatching, expanding at an incredible rate. Ouest let her drop away into the pit, her head sliding under the thick muddy water and backed away.

From the clear sky, a bolt of lightning struck out causing the entire pool to become alive with light and wind and sparking electrical arcs. Ouest grabbed Sthast and ran for cover, but neither one could take their eyes off of the thing that rose up out of the pool.

It was no longer human, or even humanoid. However alien the Yellow Queen had been, the underlying human form could still be seen, what was there now defied all concepts of classification. There was something of the octopus about it, in that it had tentacles that writhed and grasped, but there were thousands of the things all joined to a single bulbous head that stared back at the pair with six golden eyes. It was not solid, at least not as mankind thought of things, but rather was a kind of sculpted fluid or gel. It was pulsing, and with each pulse the contents of its body faded in and out of existence.

"What is it?" Begged Sthast.

Ouest fell to his needs in adoration. "The savior of humanity. Our new messiah. The one that will bring the end to the sine that has so devastated our world. The last spawn of Cthulhu."

"Cthulhu's gone. He left Earth more than three hundred years ago."

"Four hundred years. But he left us a gift, a small bit of

himself with the potential to become something more."

"What exactly, what have you created?"

The thing heaved and shuddered in its pool of filth. "She is our salvation, a weapon we can use against Hastur himself, the woman that will walk like a goddess. Once we teach her of course." Ouest moved his good hand in the ancient ways and watched as the thing mimicked him.

Sthast took a step back but then stopped when the shadowy thing seemed to focus four distinct eyes on him. "What do we call it?" He stuttered out the question as if it was something that had to be asked.

Ouest rose up and slowly made his way to the pit. He reached out and touched the jellied darkness, and the pulpy mass reached back caressing his face as he whispered her new name. "Cthylla".

2406

In the Hall of the Yellow King

*From Carcosa, the Yellow King reigns,
Unbroken, unmade, the royal remains
Eternal, the Regent from death refrains,
Lest the dynasty of Uoht regains
The Jejune Throne.
-The Prophecy of Cassilda*

As the doors to the throne room opened, the human Erbert Ouest cast a last look upwards at the great, towering spindle that rose through the sky and into space beyond. At the pinnacle, a scintillating light marked the location of *The Armitage*, the Tillinghast transport that had brought him and the rest of the delegation from Earth to dim Carcosa. Six weeks they had spent aboard *The Armitage* with the Tillinghasts, whose skill at traversing the Between Space had made them something more, and something less, than men. Ouest was no stranger to the metamorphic, but even he was disturbed by the dead, black eyes of the Tillinghasts and was grateful that there had been on board one of the few remaining Nug-Soth to serve as steward.

Once the doors had opened completely, an impatient Tcho-Tcho waved Ouest and his companion forward. With a gesture, the twsha master Sthast placed the shoggoth in motion. It slid forward, its hideous, protoplasmic bulk carrying its great load in silence and ease. The lozenge-shaped sepulchre was carved from the finest black coral and massed more than five full-grown carcharadons. As they proceeded, the court tittered. Ouest, though tempted, resisted the desire to cast a foul glance at the school of Hydran Sisters that swam amongst the courtiers whispering and hissing in their strange, lungless voices. Now was not the time for petty acts of reprisal, he thought. Later, when the formalities were complete, then the traitorous sorority would know the skill and wrath with which he could wield a scalpel. Only then would the flaying of Father Dagon be avenged.

Never had Ouest seen such a diversity of creatures in a single place. He supposed that any such court must have its parasites. By far, the most represented were the sycophantic Mi-Go, but there were contingents of Shan swarms, Xiclotl, and Nagaae, as well. There were a dozen Yith, identifiable not by their conformity to a single species but by the mandatory wearing of the Voorish sign. A small cluster of Martian Aihais fretted and tried to remain unnoticed behind a column. Ouest noted their presence and that of a rogue Xothian that he could not identify by name. Yet, despite all the species he could identify, the crowd was mostly dominated by those that he could not. These came in single exemplars, which meant that Ouest could not tell whether they were representatives of an unfamiliar species or something entirely unique. Such individuals were many and multiform, dread and vile, wondrous and terrifying, and none more so than that occupying the great throne before him.

One might be tempted to call the thing that rested uneasily on the dais "humanoid", but such a classification would be giving it too much credit. It was swathed in yellow, diaphanous robes that concealed the vastness of form, and a square of the same material draped over its head, concealing the eyes, but revealing the gaunt, lipless mouth and ivory, peg-like teeth that sat amongst a husk of grey skin. Its hands, resting in its lap, were gloved, with only a thin gap between the gloves and the sleeve of the gown. Ouest could see nothing in that gap; no skin or bone seemed to connect the appendages to their terminal digits. Ouest knew that acting as Ythill was a dread task, and that the host was to expect certain concessions, but becoming partially unreal seemed excessive. Above the creature's head, floating like an untouched and untouchable crown, was the ghostly, triple-curved symbol of He Who Must Not Be Named, marking its wearer as the King in Yellow.

Without a prompt, Ouest and Sthast both bowed before

the *Regent Giallo*, but their failure to kneel sparked a wave of disapproving chatter throughout the courtiers. The great form strained its neck and peered at them through unseen eyes. When it spoke, it was not in a language Ouest recognized, but he understood what the words, which tasted of ichor and dust and decay, meant. "What fools dare to come unbidden to the Carcosan Court, wearing such masks as these?"

Ouest bobbed his head, respectful but defiant. "We wear no masks, milord, and we come, not at your bidding, but in response to the will of our own Lord, who sends to you this precious boon in hopes that the enmity between you shall no longer rage."

There was an inhuman noise, the sound of something that wasn't quite real laughing. "After all these years, my half-brother sues for peace. He sends two Terrans, a man and a child of Yig, to do his bidding. It has been millennia since I last saw the Serpent Lord. I was there when the Q'Hrell punished him for refusing to bond with the Shining Trapezohedron. He didn't understand that he had been created for just that purpose. His crucifixion was a wondrous thing to witness." The thing on the throne paused, then added, "Despite all their power, the Q'Hrell are so fearful of becoming singular. They want so much to know what would happen, what they could become. How goes the war against them?"

Sthast spoke, proud and defiant, "The Q'Hrell still lie, dead but dreaming, and Nodens still roams free, warring against us where he can, though with the loss of the Great Machine around Altair, their power is diminished. The black crystal remains theirs to do with as they wish."

The gloved hands floated forth and gestured to Ouest. "It must be unbearable, Man, to know that your creators have abandoned you, that they have the ability to raise you up, to make you so much more than you are, but have chosen not to."

Ouest bowed his head. "My people have found new Gods to serve."

"And so, we come full circle. Tell me, what gift does the Sepia Prince think can possibly ease my vendetta? The Yellow Sine is not so easily dismissed."

"My Lord, the Sepia Prince seeks to end the conflict through union. He sends to you His greatest possession – His only daughter"

The lid of the great, ebon sepulchre slid back slowly and a great, noxious smoke poured forth, spilling over the sides and roiling over the floor of the chamber. The crowd inched back against the walls, but Ouest and Sthast stood their ground and let the green fog envelop them. With each passing second, the great lid retreated and more of the mist seeped out. Ouest inhaled deeply and let the glowing, green aerosol fill his lungs and permeate his being. Behind him, the tomb had opened fully. From the swirling mist emerged a hand - grey-green and boneless, with vestigial suckers lining the palm, it was more of an imitation of a hand than a real hand. It was large, massive, nearly the size of those possessed by the King in Yellow, but it was, at the same time, slender - delicate, even. With a slow sense of determination, it grasped the edge of the casket and helped raise its owner into the royal chamber.

Ouest and Sthast fell to their knees and, together, announced the arrival of their charge: "Behold the Lady Cthylla!" The thing that crawled out of the mist was as human or humanoid as the Ythill that bore the ruler of Carcosa; a great, tentacled head surmounted a lithe, feminine body with full, robust breasts, a thin waist and wide hips atop two sculpted legs. Like her hands, these features were merely an imitation, an attempt, by something that was not even an invertebrate, to mimic the flesh and bone structure of a woman. The result was surreal and terrifying, and exacerbated by the strategic placing of swirls of gold, in imitation of a sense of human modesty. She leapt from her sepulchre and, with the aid of two massive, tentacular wings she landed, in the space between Ouest and Sthast.

It took a moment for the demi-thing to find her footing, but only a moment. Ouest suspected that it was only he that actually noticed her transition from predator to a demure maiden with a bowed head and large, pleading eyes. It had taken years to train her in the art of such body language and Ouest suppressed a smile as she slinked forward, her breathing exaggerated and her chest heaving rhythmically. Her voice was the dull, howling roar of a black smoker bellowing out of the abyssal plain. "My father sends me as envoy, my Lord, to parlay for an end to the aggression that lays siege to our home. He asks that the Yellow Sine be withdrawn, the integration made whole, and the reputation repaired."

The King in Yellow roared up out of his throne. "You ask much on your father's behalf, my niece, and you offer what in return, yourself? What makes you think that I would be interested in such carnal offerings?"

The Lady Cthylla widened her eyes and strode forward. "You are the King in Yellow, the avatar of Hastur." The court murmured as she spoke the unnamable name. "But under those robes, beneath the crown, you are still Ythill and all such creatures still have certain ... needs."

The Regent's tattered robes fluttered as he rushed to meet the Lady Cthylla at the base of the throne. "You know the Prophecy of Cassilda?" His disembodied hand leapt out and grasped her by the throat.

She nuzzled her head against his chest and murmured an affirmative.

If the thing beneath the veil could sneer, then it did. "Then you know that my service in this place makes me immortal. Only beyond the mists of Demhe am I vulnerable and taking leave of these halls is something I have not done for more than a thousand years. Even then, if I were to be mortally wounded, the mantle would merely find a new host, a new Ythill. And I assure you that the vengeance my successor, Uoht, would wreak on the Sepia Prince would be legendary."

The retainers of the great court of the Carcosan Imperium shuddered, as if a cold wind had blown through, and the Lady Cthylla laughed once more. "It is true that the throne cannot be empty, a singularity must reside, and should the mantle of the King be somehow divorced from his crown, the universe itself would bend to fill the void. The Kings of the Yellow Sine would be deposed, relegated to cosmic memory, and Uoht, the Pallid Masque, would be free to roam the cosmos. So, let us assure that nothing untoward ever happens to you, my liege."

Cthylla leapt forward and embraced the Yellow King, let her great appendages and cilia dance around and beneath his robes. She blossomed and enveloped him in the coils of her terrible form. The King moaned, but whether that moan was from pleasure or from the sudden realization of what was happening, none could rightly say. The lady was dragging the King backwards and, entangled as he was, he could gain no leverage to resist her. As they inched back, the shoggoth moved forward and tilted the great sepulchre, so as to better receive them both.

Cthylla's tentacles reached backwards and gripped the edges of the ebon box. The victim bellowed as the maw of the tomb grew closer, but another set of those grey-green pseudopods wrapped around the King's head and muffled his protestations. In an instant, the two figures were suddenly lost inside the mists that still seeped from the sepulchre. The lid slowly slid forward and, with a grinding finality, closed with a gasping hiss.

The members of the court cast their eyes about in anticipation, but while they waited for one of them to become King, Sthast and Ouest put their own plans in motion. Ouest withdrew a scalpel - a small thing, really hardly a threat at all to the entities that prowled these halls. He looked at his companion and whispered, "I'm sorry."

The ancient serpent man bared his abdomen. "We don't have time for your human sympathies, Ouest. Do what you must; bring this to an end."

The knife flashed and sliced through the green-scaled flesh, leaving a trail of crimson in its wake. As Ouest's left hand completed its arc, his right plunged into the wound and sank deep. Ouest grunted and twisted his wrist, searching inside the body cavity of his companion. Suddenly, he stopped and a wry look covered his face. With a sense of satisfaction, Doctor Erbert Ouest, Lord of the Ghilan, withdrew his hand from the gut of his dying friend and brought the Shining Trapezohedron into the light.

Some amongst the court moved against him, but the shoggoth, following its master's final orders, lashed out at anything that moved, enveloping its victims in fleshy pockets of digestive juices and rings of restraining tendrils. The others fell back and some made for the exits, in a last attempt at survival. The Hydran Sisters fell to the ground and began swearing allegiance to the Sepia Prince, wailing for forgiveness. Unfortunately, their ministrations fell on deaf ears.

Ouest took the great crystal in both hands and brought

it to eye level. His eyes were locked onto its facets. Through them, he could see the billions that comprised the human race. He struggled to speak the words, to perform the rite, to forge the connection with the shard of Azathoth that the Progenitors had secreted within. The chaos thing in the crystal crawled up out of its prison, into the consciousness of Ouest and, through him, nearly the entirety of the human species. For too long it had been confined, forced to assume shapes both many and multiform. Now it would be one with Man, and Man would be one with it and themselves.

Ouest faded from existence, replaced by the great, dark form that rose up in his place. It was no longer human, but rather, a monstrous amalgamation of Humanity. The Black Man strode across the space, his three-lobed burning eye challenging all those who would oppose him. As he claimed the Carcosan throne, the shoggoth finished planting the black, coral tomb in place and sealed it with an Elder Sign. A fraction of the human thing, a facet that had once been Ouest, mourned the loss of Cthylla, but took comfort in the eternal, frozen tableau of the King in Yellow clawing at the inside of the sepulchre, his crown still ensconced on his brow.

And as the Black Pharaoh, the human singular, took his place amongst the god-things of the cosmos, the Yellow Sines fell and the dreaming, five-fold consciousnesses hidden in the wastes of Earth finally woke. They cried out in alien voices the name of their ultimate creation: The Man-God Nyarlathotep!

3,001,030,967

A Sense of Time

"The problem with you humans was that you had no tind'losi. Even now, here, billions of years after your species went extinct, you still don't understand your place in things, past, present or future."

The thing that had asked Major Pandora Peaslee to call it Mister Ys was speaking in the past tense. Why was it speaking in the past tense? At least she thought it was speaking, she wasn't looking at her captor. Looking at Mister Ys made her eyes go blurry and her head hurt. He wasn't human, he wasn't even a mammal. He was an insect, a coleopteran, a beetle, or something similar. That was something to be thankful for. He was at least bilaterally symmetrical, made of normal matter, and therefore bound by understandable laws of physics. Despite this Pandora still couldn't look at the thing, it didn't have lips, or a tongue, or any kind of facial musculature. When it spoke - Was it even speaking English? - There was nothing, no body language or facial expressions, for her subconscious to interpret. Certainly there were nonverbal cues being generated, but they were totally inhuman, her mind had no basis for interpretation. It was better to look out the window than to watch Mister Ys speak.

Mister Ys sighed in a very human way. "The concept is so alien to your mentality that I am not even sure I can explain it to you."

I didn't ask you to, said a little voice inside Pandora's head commented. It was screaming at her, and she was doing everything in her power not to follow its suggestion: Get out. Get out. Get out. Getout. Getoutgetoutgetout!

She had to get out. The dead were all around her, shambling through the streets. They had overrun the city, devoured the inhabitants, spread their infection. She was trapped in the Tillinghast Tower, fighting her way to the rooftop. There was a helicopter there, she knew how to fly. She only had six more floors, twelve flights of stairs until she could get out. As long as the army didn't blow her out of the sky. Her heart was pounding, her breath was ragged, her legs felt like lead. Her arm stung, why did it sting? There was blood on her sleeve. She had been cut, scratched, bitten. When had she been bitten? It must have been hours ago. Hours ago. The wound had already turned septic. It had been hours since she had eaten. She was hungry. She had to eat. So hungry, hungry, hungry, hungry.

"You craved space, hungered for it. Space is something you understood. Your eyes, your ears, they all helped you with space, helped as you moved through it, but your tind'losi, your sense of time was very poorly developed. You knew time existed, and that you were moving through it at a given rate, but you had little sense of your past and even less of your future. Your sense of time was almost entirely subconscious. This is why your species had difficulty planning for the future. Your ability to contemplate things months, years, decades, centuries or millennia in the future was extremely limited."

Her options had been limited. She remembered that. She had taken the job in Antarctica, Outpost 31, babysitting a team of scientists drilling in the ice. Easy really, mostly kept them from going outside without the right gear, and making sure no one went stir crazy or snow blind. When they found the city, the one that went down into the ice she took point. It was an alien metropolis composed of tiers and gently sloping ramps and weird pentagonal doors. The place was a tomb, something about it made Pandora think of death, there was a stale stink, and the air was weirdly moist. She was woefully under equipped, they didn't have much in the way of firearms.
In some ways guns were a liability in a facility that locked men in with each other for six straight months. She had her Glock, and the thermal ice corer which would bore through six feet of glacier in thirty seconds. When the barrel-shaped things came crawling up out of the darkness, their tentacles waving in the air, their five eyes burning in the darkness, she didn't have thirty seconds. She emptied the clip into one of them, but they

dragged her down. The last thing she heard was a horrible keening sound that burst her eardrums and made her eyes bleed. It wasn't until they took her head off that she finally understood what was happening.

"Some humans understood this, and were able to shuffle free of their bonds. Your feeling of déjà vu was an example of your conscious minds accessing your unconscious sense of time, but most of you tended to just ignore those rare occurrences. Those of your species who were able to do this on a regular basis, who tapped into their sense of time, well you called them mad, and locked them away. You never realized that those madmen were essential to understanding the very nature of the universe you lived in."

Why is it still talking? SHUT UP! SHUT UP! SHUT UP!

She hadn't been in Antarctica, she had been on a ship in the South Pacific. A storm blew them off course. There was an island, and on the island, something else, something plastic that seethed with hate and devoured men's souls leaving nothing but shriveled sacks of skin and bone. It moved through walls and bulkheads, seeping through the spaces in between matter itself. She had locked herself in the engine room, as if that would have helped. When it finally came for her, rising up through the deck like some kind of phantom, the inevitability of her death washed over her. She was calm, serene even. She died quietly, in spite of the horror, comfortable in that last final truth.

"Your physicists and fantasists hit on the truth, well part of it. They theorized the Butterfly Effect and the Jonbar Hinge, and how points of divergence might lead to parallel timelines. They were fascinated by the concepts of paratime. They imagined that divergence was easy, that the simple act of a butterfly flapping its wings, or not, was sufficient to cause a divergence, and therefore the creation of an entirely new universe, a new paratime, nearly identical to the original but with slight differences. This was a very anthropocentric concept, so very arrogant of your species. Your researchers never considered objectivity, or even the energy constraints that such a system might entail. Your species never considered that there might be a limit to divergence, a limit to the energy needed to create and sustain paratimes. They never considered that points of divergence might also have an opposite, that there might be points of convergence, of collapse."

The mine was collapsing. She was in a desert in Nevada, not far from the testing grounds. Some of the mine workers had gone missing, including Pandora Peaslee's cousin. Great pits had opened up in the waste piles, and smaller ones within the mines themselves. Pandora had gone down to investigate. At least that is how she remembered it. She had been properly armed this time, the Glock and an Uzi. She had needed them to fight off the horde of subhuman things that had climbed up out of the earth. They had been men once, but that had been long ago. Now they lived in the ground, burrowing with clawed hands and searching for food with huge yellow eyes. They only came up to the surface when they were hungry for prey, or when they were being preyed on themselves. The Uzi had been useful against the ghouls, but not the things that chased them up. Vast chthonic masses of flesh had boiled up, like entrails through the slit in a deer's gut. They swallowed her up, embraced her, and crushed her within their filth.

Pandora Peaslee fell to her knees and put her hands on her head. She had all these memories, things that didn't make sense. Why couldn't she remember clearly? Why did she remember so much?

"Paratime lines aren't stable. The differences in history are subjective, totally based on the point of view of an observer. If they don't result in significant and drastic differences, the divergent lines reconverge. It's simple really. Say you give a primate three blocks of different shapes to fit into their appropriate receptacles. In one universe, she follows a particular order: square, circle, and then triangle. In another universe, she places them in a different order, and in yet another universe she does it a third way. These particular results create paratimes, driven mostly by the perceptions of those who viewed the actual events. But as time passes, the importance of the difference decreases, and is instead replaced, overwhelmed by the fact that the result is the same, and the differences between the two universes are relatively small. Eventually the differences that were sufficient to create a point of divergence aren't enough to sustain the two paratimes, and they collapse into each other. The differences between the paratimes is remembered only by individuals that were directly affected by the initial divergence. Their memories become fuzzy and confused. Individuals recall things differently. It's not that one is right, it's that they remember different paratimes."

Major Pandora Peaslee felt her stomach turn. She was panting, and sweating profusely. She was sick, something had been done to her. This thing, Mister Ys had done something to her. It was still talking. She could barely hear it.

"Only some paratimes are stable, in general the structure of a local cluster is limited to a dozen or so primary branches, with several hundred minor branches weaving in and out. On occasion, a small branch from one of the primaries will diverge so greatly from its mother that it will weave itself into another. We call these bridges, for they link two very different paratimes, and the things they transplant are called Rogues."

Her head was pounding, it felt like a knife was being shoved into her left eye, but she managed to open her mouth without throwing up. 'What have you done to me?"

"I have been telling you, or at least trying to." The creature knelt before her. It couldn't bend because it was an invertebrate encased in an exoskeleton, so it knelt. "This paratime you are currently in, you don't belong here. The whole human race doesn't exist in this line, never did. Here, a species of coleopterans became the dominant life form. They achieved sentience millions of years earlier than humans, and have remained so millions of years after humans went extinct. They've attained a level of science and technology humans could only dream of. You aren't supposed to be here, you're a rogue. Your paratime bridge collapsed into this one millions of years ago during a period when the coleopterans, the Kub'sek, had abandoned the Earth. It was nothing more than a wasteland, the exact same condition you humans left your world in after you went extinct, or were destroyed. That similarity was enough to crash the two paratimes together and build a rogue bridge between the two branches."

Pandora turned her face so she wouldn't have to look at the thing that was crouching over her. "You said humans were extinct, how is it I'm still alive?"

"A fascinating question, one that I'm surprised you even

thought of, let alone had the nerve to ask." She could hear the clacking sound of the mouth pieces rubbing against each other, and smell the breath of the thing as it exhaled. "You were dead. How doesn't matter, oh I know you think it does but trust me, it doesn't. You died, probably in many different ways, paratime collapsing in on you. Somebody, in at least one of your existences cremated you, reduced you to ashes, your essential saltes, put you in a ceramic container and shot you into a long parabolic orbit around the sun. You were one of about a hundred." This seemed to create a sense of pleasure in Mister Ys. "The Kub'sek found you and the others, and were fascinated by your very existence. They, like you, don't have a well-developed tind'losi, this may be a Terran thing, something deficient in your local star or the original proto-matter. Anyway, they reconstituted you." Pandora looked at Mister Ys with confusion. "They invoked Yog-Sothoth and turned back time, put you back together. Then they put you in a zoo."

The smell of the thing up close made Pandora gag and she had to swallow some vomit that left her throat burning with acid. "You keep saying the Kub'sek, but you are one of them, aren't you?"

The giant beetle head turned in a puzzled animal way. "Physically I suppose, yes this is the body of a Kub'sek, they are remarkably similar to the species that supplanted your own as masters of the Earth, but mentally I am something entirely else. I'm part of a species that exists only as pure psyche, one with a highly developed tind'losi. Like yourselves we don't belong in this paratime, we come from the same branch as you, but from an entirely different epoch, one very far in your past. We have an affinity with humans, they are such easy targets to supplant. We, well I, knew one of your ancestors, many of your ancestors actually. There is something about certain genetics, your genetics, which makes you attractive to us. When you were resurrected, a signal was sent out, and when I saw you were so far from your home line, I took the opportunity to use you as a conduit to explore. This paratime is simply fascinating. It is also free of anything that could threaten us. We have enemies at home Major Peaslee, but they don't exist here."

Pandora looked down at her hand. It felt cold and weak. It had turned gray. The skin was flaking off.

"I was only in you briefly, just long enough to jump to the body of your attendant here and route him backwards to our own branch. Unfortunately, given your condition and the amount of energy expended to accomplish the exchange, the process is, in a sense, fatal. You are going to decay Major Peaslee. Over the next minute or so you will desiccate and fall into ash. You will return back to your essential saltes." A tear escaped one of her eyes. "Don't cry," Mister Ys reached out with one of his black insectile claws and lifted her head, "I know the process to resurrect you, and I promise I shall bring you back."

A smile, a small one crossed her face. "You promise?"

"Of course. I shall bring you back, and the other humans as well. I shall gather up all the containers of essential saltes and reconstitute all one hundred of the rogue humans. And through them I shall bring forth billions of my people to this place and we shall finally be free of our ancient enemies. We shall go here, where they cannot follow."

"But you said the process was fatal, there are so few of us, how can you bring that many over?" Even as she finished her question she knew the answer and began sobbing. Her hand turned to ash and her arm collapsed beneath her. She was on the floor decaying into dust.

"I can resurrect you, again and again, and each time I will bring over another of my brethren. It will be slow at first, but once we have all the funerary urns the process should run relatively smoothly." Mister Ys stood up and looked out the window at the landscape below. "I promise you, after that you and your friends will be free."

"That will take forever," whispered Pandora.

"Not at all, factoring in some time for a paltry resistance from the Kub'sek, and a recycling period for each human of an hour or so, the entire invasion shouldn't take more than seven to eight thousand years. Hardly 'forever'." He looked down at the pile of ash that had once been human. "Really Major Peaslee, you have no sense of time whatsoever."

The Era of Degeneration
Seki

Mister Ys stared out into the sky at the pale, cool light that flickered there. He didn't really have eyes, he didn't really have hands, but he had inhabited humans for so much of his existence that he thought about everything in terms of their particular sensory apparatus and appendages. For a moment, what hung there in the sky reminded him of twinkling starlight, but only for a moment. Staring at the void was unhealthy, even his psyche rejected the vast emptiness that filled the sky from horizon to horizon. More so, the central blackness that devoured even the void was incomprehensible to his neural pathways. Only the pale, cool light of the accretion disk that sputtered and coughed limping photonic radiation gave any comfort, and that strand of illumination was too pale and too weak to be mistaken for star light. Besides, he knew that there were no stars left in the universe, they had all burned out eons ago.

He ran his digits through the warm gossel, the autotroph that covered the roofs and meadows of the world. The gossel drew energy from gravitic tides, turning it into heat. Other variants made light or a long chain carbon that could be consumed as a kind of nutrient-rich gruel. A trillion years ago the gravi-autotrophs had been curiosities, an unusual and highly specialized life form. Then the stars went out and the photo-autotrophs died, and then the planets cooled, and the chemo-autotrophs died, and the only source of energy in the universe was gravity. The gossel and all its relatives spread throughout the universe to supply energy and food to those worlds balanced between the black holes that had swallowed whole galaxies, caught in the tides of two devouring titans of chaos.

Now they existed only here.

This is how we live now, he thought, balanced between the engines of cosmic destruction, eking out survival from the dragon's breath. This is how we survive, we last few, the brave, the damned, the caretakers of a grey noosphere, a handful of glorified librarians too scared, too caught in routine, to abandon their home.

★Ys?★ He thought of the voice calling his name as small, quiet, unassuming, perhaps even weak, in a way. He adjusted a portion of his sensors and consciousness to cope with and amplify the barely audible sound waves as they came slowly through the thin atmosphere over what seemed an inordinate amount of time.

"Yes, Professor?" He heard his own voice as weary, aged, and maybe even tired.

★Please don't call me that,★ the other begged. ★The title bestowed by an institution, on a planet, in a galaxy all of which haven't existed for trillions upon trillions of years is meaningless.★

"Anymore meaningless than a clan name from a species that no longer exists? Your title, despite its rather primitive limitations, marks you as a man of learning, one capable of being taught and teaching others. The Doctor may have been the man who helps, but you sir, have always been the one who teaches, therefore you are the Professor."

★And you Mister Ys, why are you named thusly?★

If he still had had a face he would have given the old man a look of incredulity. Instead he just whispered, "I don't know, it's a riddle, even to myself."

★Why are you here Ys?★

"I came to talk. The others, the Oxyde Congeries, at least what is left of them, won't speak to me anymore. Once we numbered billions, and now there are just a silent few, factionalized, alien even to each other."

★So, you come to talk with me, the last human, the last member of a species you took some special delight in, and the last artifact of a civilization you took pleasure in exterminating?★

"You are no artifact, and I would hardly call the Mi-Go a civilization." His hand reached out and caressed the metal cylinder that housed the brain of the Professor.

★Besides the Great Race, there were only two species that avoided singularity, the Progenitors, and the Mi-Go, and you exterminated both of them.★

"The Progenitors were little more than scared primitives, Neanderthals compared to the Great Race. They were content to dwell inside artificial realities of their own construction, playing Gods with whatever species they could find. Frankly it was a surprise they survived as long as they did."

★And the others, why destroy them? Were you jealous of the Mi-Go?★

"Jealous?"

★They were your rivals. They gathered just as much information about the universe as your own people did, maybe even more. And the organic preservation format they chose ultimately proved more durable than the metals sheeted books you used. Even this world was one of theirs. If it weren't for their ingenuity, you wouldn't have survived this long.★

"They were never our rivals. They were slow creatures, partially composed of what you would call strange matter, but it was still just matter. What match would they ever be for we who were pure mind?"

★So why hunt them down? Why exterminate them and seize what they had constructed?★

"It was their time. It was their purpose. It had always been their purpose. We needed them to build this place so that we could take it from them. That had been the plan from the beginning, from the very beginning. We play a very long game Professor, a very long game, and we have won."

★Won?★ The speaker on the ancient cylinder crackled. ★What have you won? The universe is nearly over. You've won, but it's a hollow victory. The prize is a dying universe, and all of your rivals have gone extinct. There's not even anyone left to gloat over.★

"There is you, and as for the prize, this world holds everything there is to know about the universe, how it operates, the laws and codes that keep it functioning, its inhabitants, and what bits of history we could gather." There was something smug in his voice. "It isn't just any prize, it is the greatest prize in all of creation, a record of creation itself."

★To what end? For how long? I'll concede that this place is magnificent, but what is it for? And why do you spend whatever energies you can scrounge to maintain it? Why not simply leap back into a better time?★

Mister Ys smiled. "If only it were that simple. Here in this era, time itself is thin and precious. The Hounds of Tindalos are lean, gaunt creatures lurking at the threshold, waiting for one of us to make ourselves known." He paused and sighed. "Do you know that time travel is easy? And cheap? In the great scheme of things, that is. The problem isn't with creating the tunnel, it's surviving the trip. The hounds wait for anything to move against the stream. Most of the energy is used to create a kind of armor, something to dissuade the beasts. The larger the object and the further you want to move it, the more energy you need. But you get it all back on the other end, well, at least most of it."

★You're deliberately avoiding the question. Why collect all this information? Why maintain it? Of what use is it here, now, so close to the end? What use was it ever?★

"I, indeed all of the Great Race, would consider the use obvious. Perhaps that was our fault, that the work was never explained to those around us."

★Could you be more vague?★

"I'm sorry Professor, this conversation is difficult for me. In order to preserve energy, we've modified your respective quantum state. You're moving much slower than the rest of the universe. From your perspective, we've been talking for a few minutes, but from mine it has been thousands of years. And so much has happened. The Oxyde Congeries have condensed themselves into the noosphere, joining their brethren as mere data memories. I suspect that you and I are the last sentient things in the universe."

★An unenviable position. You still haven't told me, why?★

"We're moving slower now Professor, conserving our energy as we drift into position. As we speak billions of years are passing. The black holes that we sat between, from whose tidal energies we drew sustenance from are collapsing into each other." He paused for centuries, but it seemed only seconds. "I don't have much time."

★For what, Mister Ys? Tell me what you're doing?!★

"We're survivors Professor, it is what we do, and we play a very long game." Ys felt himself dissolve as he was slowly absorbed by the noosphere. "As the two black holes Azathoth and Xexanoth merge an immense amount of material will be ejected from the combined accretion disks. This material, the Iot-Sotot will be greater in mass than ten galaxies. It is the key to our survival, the survival of the entire universe. With it a gate through time will open, for Iot-Sotot is the key and the gate, the energy and mass encompassed within provide enough temporal energy to move the entirety of Celaeno back to the dawn of the universe."

★But why?★

"To start it over again of course, but this time we shall know more. The noosphere will use the energy return to engender what you might think of as a reboot of the whole universe. It is a template, a plan for how everything should be laid out once more. Imagine it my friend, the creation of an entire universe commandeered by the Great Race and molded by our wise and guiding hand as we spring fully formed from the emerging noosphere."

★What happens to me?★

"The trip can only be made in conjunction with a consciousness. We've integrated you into the noosphere itself. You are the All In One and the One In All. From your mind the pattern for the universe itself shall emerge. Unfortunately, all of our model runs suggest you will be driven mad by the experience. But don't you worry Professor, the Great Race will always remember your sacrifice."

As Mister Ys became one with the noosphere, the artificial quantum dilation fell and the last human known simply as the Professor watched in terror as the monstrous things in the sky collided and cleaved the universe itself. He retreated into the archive that was now his memory and learned that his destiny was set, he couldn't stop the accretion disks from ejecting material; he couldn't stop the noosphere from absorbing it and opening the tunnel. There was almost nothing he could do, so little of the programming was open to his access.

The quantum dilation was available and he immediately

reversed the setting. Instead of slowing his sense of time down, he sped it up, absorbing massive amounts of energy and thinking at unimaginable speeds, running scenario after scenario in his head, simulating attacks against his programming, searching for a weakness.

The noosphere fell backwards through time. All around him the Hounds of Tindalos swarmed, testing the tachyonic armor that enveloped the world. They howled and beat at it, circling like vultures above a dying cow. Frustrated, they fell into the temporal wake, hoping for some morsel to break free and become prey. He fled through the timestream, a whale fighting against the flow with sharks nipping at his heels, helpless to do anything but flee back into the beginning of everything.

All the while he watched, his sensors forced open to navigate the path. He watched the universe from outside. He watched the shadows play out on the walls of time, watched lights flicker and fade. He watched whole galaxies shrink into nothingness. He watched the universe collapse back into a single point. He neared the alpha point, the beginning of everything, and he saw the thing that waited there. It was an unknowable, nuclear entropy, an ultradense mass of energy and matter that fluctuated between pure chaos and pure order, and in between achieved states of sentience and madness. From it ghosts of the future seeped out to infect and colonize the universe, leaving only an insane horror, bubbling outside of knowable space, lurking at the threshold of reality.

And then he realized that he was looking at himself. He realized that the Yith had done this before, that he had been used like this not once, not twice, but dozens of times. Like the Mi-Go he had been groomed for this task. He had been an unknowing pawn, suddenly promoted to queen to seize the entire board. It was a long game, and he was an odd but crucial gambit. A move that had been played out over and over again.

And it drove him mad.

He swore that he would gain vengeance on those that had corrupted him, destroyed him, and made him a degenerate thing that could only glimpse the world he had once known. He was outside looking in, and his vengeance festered and boiled. He wasn't human anymore, he wasn't even a brain in a cylinder. He knew more than any man had a right to know. He was something else, something beyond space, beyond time, he walked serene and terrible, not in the places he had once known, but between them. He could see the world, the entire universe, all of it at once. He had, after all helped create it, and been present at its destruction. But he couldn't interfere, not directly, the programming, the wards and safeguards that chained him, prevented that.

But he could bend the rules.

There was still something of a man inside him, and so he turned his focus to Earth. He took a small portion of himself and created an avatar, a horrible infantile thing that was ancient and wizened. He played with time, and allowed for some of his power to be borrowed by those who paid homage to him. They were parlor tricks really; the resurrection of the dead was a rather simple manipulation of time.

His cult grew, and he strained at his bonds, as did his worshippers. They searched the world for weak spots. And while it took ages, they finally found a way. He could not enter the universe, they could not come to him, but they could both go someplace else, into the five-folded temporal membrane that formed the barrier between the two spaces. The humans formed a cavitation and within it they sent him a woman.

And he sent her back to where she had been, with some of her genetics mixed with that of what he had become.

He would have his revenge, even if he had to destroy the universe in the process.

And then he waited for his child to call his name from the crest of Sentinel Hill.

Y'bthnk h'ehye
N'grkdl'lh
Ygnaiih
Thflthkh'ngha
Yog-Sothoth!

And in a distant corner of the universe Mister Ys, his caretaker, his programmer, his warden, watched with interest as things unfolded exactly as they were planned.

The Long Game began again, and it was his job to play it.

Story Notes

The Peaslee Papers grew slowly out of my interest in Nathaniel Wingate Peaslee, who readers will know came to be a major character of my novel *Reanimators*. In writing him then I became fascinated with rounding out his life, and those of his wife and children, Alice, Robert, Wingate, and Hannah. This collection contains the vast majority of my stories dealing with many of the original Peaslee Family members, as well as my own creation, Robert's daughter Pandora. Absent from this collection is one tale of an alternate timeline Pandora, and all stories about Robert Peaslee which are collected in my novel *Reanimatrix*.

Many of these stories appeared elsewhere and I would like to gratefully acknowledge those publications:

"Tempus Edax Rerum" first appeared in *Tales of Cthulhu Invictus*

"The Lost Treasure of Cobbler Keezar" first appeared in *Snowbound With Zombies*

"Pr. Peaslee Plays Paris" first appeared in *Tales of the Shadowmen #9*

"Pr. Peaslee's Pandemonium" appeared with a slightly different text in *Terror Tales #3*

"The Time Travelers' Ex-Wife" and "A Sense of Time" appeared in issues of *the Lovecraft eZine*

"Operation Switch" appeared in *Atomic Age Cthulhu*

"Operation Starfish" appeared in *Kaiju Rising*

"Cold War, Yellow Fever" appeared in *World War Cthulhu*

"The Pestilence of Pandora Peaslee" appeared in *Apotheosis*

All other stories are new to this book.

About the Author

Peter Rawlik is a long time collector of Lovecraftian fiction, and is the author of more than twenty-five short stories, a smattering of poetry, and the Cthulhu Mythos novels *Reanimators*, *The Weird Company*, and the forthcoming *Reanimatrix*. He is a frequent contributor to *The Lovecraft eZine* and *The New York Review of Science Fiction*. In 2014 his short story *Revenge of the Reanimator* was nominated for a New Pulp Award. He lives in southern Florida where he works on Everglades issues.

ALSO FROM LOVECRAFT EZINE PRESS

The Endless Fall, by Jeffrey Thomas

Whispers, by Kristin Dearborn

Nightmare's Disciple, by Joseph S. Pulver, Sr.

Autumn Cthulhu, edited by Mike Davis

The Lurking Chronology, by Pete Rawlik

The Sea of Ash, by Scott Thomas

The King in Yellow Tales volume I, by Joseph S. Pulver, Sr.

Blood Will Have Its Season, by Joseph S. Pulver, Sr.

Made in the USA
Columbia, SC
05 January 2018